Chronicles of Galaxy Osmaron

Son of Destiny

'We again apologise for this interruption of your program. We have just received more precise details about the assassination in Europe. Our latest report indicates that President Richard McLeod of the United States of America had recently been shot by an assassin. He had taken a single bullet to the head from a long range sniper.

He has been rushed to the local hospital in London, but we are unsure of his present condition. We shall keep you informed of future developments as soon as we are able.'

Once again the screen returned to the original program.
'Oh God, Darling! Richard has been assassinated!'

The Chronicles of Osmaron Series

The Chronicles of Osmaron - I am Shadite

The Chronicles of Osmaron - The power of One

The Chronicles of Osmaron - Escape from Andromeda

The Chronicles of Osmaron - The Solarian Empire

The Chronicles of Osmaron - Fertilates

The Chronicles of Osmaron - Infilates

The Chronicles of Osmaron - Son of destiny

The Chronicles of Osmaron - Jull, the Supreme Patriarch

The Chronicles of Osmaron - Battle for Andromeda

The Chronicles of Osmaron - Battle for Osmaron

First Edition

CHRONICLES OF GALAXY OSMARON

Son of Destiny

A Son is born on Earth.
He will save the universe

By

Adrian Graye

Nutralian Publishing
http://nutralianpublishing.com

nutralia
An imprint of Nutralian Publishing
5 Brayford_Square, London E1 0SG
http://nutralianpublishing.com

This paperback edition 2011
B00005555

First published in Great Britain by
Amazon KDP 2024

ISBN 978-10687902-6-3

Printed and bound in Great Britain by Amazon KDP Publishing.

A CIP catalogue record for this title
is available from the British Library.

This book is dedicated to the long-suffering and those who stand for what is right.

&

To all those who believe in Universal Existence and respect the lowliest of life, for like babes, they are the beginning.

A Son of Destiny

Within the past on human lands,
I gazed unto the distant sands,
In vision and in attitude,
I pondered Earth with gratitude.

My God with me; a chosen one,
I found a quiet place to be alone.
I knew of Earth; a launching pad,
For beings like me; the chosen sad.

A Son of God in future be,
A character moulded; all things to see.
A conscience strong and free from sin,
An enquiring mind; a seething spirit from within.

A lust for love of life and nature,
An inheritance of power and greatest stature.
A humble being to so enshroud,
With love and wisdom; to not be proud.

I gazed towards the mother sun so round,
And imagined the outer galaxies far beyond.
Of destiny I held the key,
I knew of things that I could see.

The Powers surged within my bones,
As I hastened in ecstasy towards the largest mound of stones,
I shouted. 'Father, I'm with you!
'To the ends of time your bidding I will do!'

Victor Ernest Roche

TABLE OF CONTENTS

From the ANACHROMAGNON - The book of final light.

If I lived to eternity I would become a god or I would be nothing.

By Siend Seno of The Plains of Herron.

Prologue

Earth time... AD 2080

Almost twenty-five years had passed since Sarah and the visitors left Earth. Despite the ravaging plague, Earth's population had reached its peak at over eleven billion and was now dropping fast because of the Terminal Disease. This situation placed mankind on an inevitable course to extinction.

Most of Earth's resources had been exhausted by extreme human abuse over the previous decades. As a result basic commodities become rear and expensive.

Due to Global Warming coastal waters were steadily rising. They threaten to engulf all the remaining coastal cities. Catastrophes abound, while displaced people attempt migration to better countries and places at higher levels. Because of the extreme overcrowding and lack of essential resources, neighbour rise against neighbour. Nevertheless some important coastal cities like New York and Washington DC had been ringed with high walls to isolate them from the ever rising waters of the oceans and rivers.

Several new cities had been built at higher levels to take the spill, but as yet nothing could be done to alter the changing climate.

Presently there are two separate groups of human on Earth, the Infertilates or Infilates, who are permanently infected by the Terminal Disease and are unable to bear offspring. They occupy the older dirty cities and more densely populated parts of the planet. The others are the assisted Fertilates. Those are the selected few that are administered the Antidote supplied by the Solarian Banking organizations to maintain human survival on Earth.

There are just under 500 million Fertilates and that will be the total human population remaining on Earth in thirty years.

The old president's grandson, also known by the name of Jerry, thinks his long lost-in-space grandparents are still alive somewhere in the galaxy and decides to organize a search, starting with a Martian mining colony. His grandparents visited that dome just before their shuttle's disappearance.

The Son of Destiny, known cosmically as Jull the Patriarch Warrior has been reincarnated in the form of Sarah's long lost son, George Peterson. He begins to get strange powers of cosmic dimensions and with those powers are able to accomplish many incredible feats. Those include the ability to transpose stellar bodies and save worlds from imminent destruction. However he was chosen by the Cosmos to defeat the powerful and almost indestructible Javols, and that is his true purpose.

CHAPTER 1

A holiday on Gimbal

Earth time... 2080 CE... about 15 years after Mallory's supposed death by the explosion of his yacht in Florida, USA.

Gimbal... A large spherical accommodation satellite with rotating rings orbiting Earth. It was the largest satellite ever built by robots while in orbit.

Planet Pleron... known to its many human inhabitants as Earth. This time is 3030 years after the Ancients' extinction. That planet is situated within the Solarian galactic arm.

Planet Eden... That most beautiful paradise world is in a local stellar system within 50 light years from Earth. Its existence is unknown to Earth's indigenous inhabitants. That most perfect and beautiful world is now the seat of power within the new Solarian Empire.

Galaxy, Milky-Way... Known to the past Andromedan Ancients and older civilizations as Galaxy Osmaron.

Donald Fraser, now Vice President of The United States of America, was busier than ever at that time of the ending year. His workload had increased substantially since the departure of their President to Europe. His President, Richard McLoud, was to hold another important conference with European leaders to ratify yet another survival treaty. He was also hoping to quell their fears with positive results on current progress in acquiring a lasting cure for the Terminal Disease before it was too late.

However that was not the only problem in site. Most of London had disappeared under the rising waters of the expanding Thames. Only a small part around the old city remained. That part had been walled throughout its perimeter. Numerous coastal cities throughout the planet had completely disappeared under the rising waves of the seas and oceans. The few walled cities were becoming too expensive to maintain, with numerous pumps, leaky tunnels and weakening walls. It was estimated that the British Isles would shrink by two thirds in only three decades mainly due to the impact of meteor Little Solo in Antarctica.

President Richard McLoud's deputy, Donald, was presently alone on his flight to Satellite Gimbal and couldn't stop thinking of his wife and kids so many thousands of miles away from Earth. He assumed they were safe in Gimbal and more protected than anywhere on the turbulent home planet below, where kidnapping ran rampant. He hoped by now they would be awaiting his arrival at Gimbal's main port of entry. Donald viewed the terminator from his shuttle's window and realized how peaceful Earth appeared from that distance away. Presently there was not a single violent hurricane coasting through the Carribean and that gave him hope.

'Anything, Sir?' the uniformed waitress inquired.

'Um...no! Nothing, thanks!' he grunted and continued reading his model aircraft magazine. It was a hobby he had acquired since childhood. He used it to take his mind away from the more serious business of state. Donald glanced through the window again, this time concentrating on diminishing coastlines due to Global Warming. He considered the long term survival of coastal cities like New York and DC in the next few decades. Their chance of survival was slim. Their maintenance too costly. That was the main reason why most of the larger monuments were being moved to higher grounds in the new city of Yorkborough in the Appalachians, just 100 miles away.

Even from that height more than a hundred miles up, he could observe high rings of thick walls around many of those coastal cities. In some cases they resembled the Great Wall of China in miniature. He also realized many of those cities were marked for evacuation and subsequent demolition. It was too costly to extend their walls any higher and increase the size and number of their already numerous pumping stations.

Despite all the unforseen delays on route by his pedantic

security personnel, he relished the change in scenery and desired to be with his family as soon as possible. After all those recent weeks in congress and other stressful venues of a more political nature, he desperately needed a break during this brief period of recess. Even so, there was still so many appointments to cover and so much urgent paperwork required his personal attention. Nevertheless he had taken along the more important documents for perusal and had handed over the less important ones to Johnson, his personal secretary.

'Why wasn't there any suitable computers or androids left on Earth to perform those mundane tasks? It was not like this in my father's day, with so many microid robots, androids and intelligent computers. They could adapt themselves to virtually any task. Perhaps my break on Gimbal will make up for those annoying deficiencies and reduce my current high blood pressure,' Donald thought, with a slight sweat from nerves. He took a tissue from the side of his seat and wiped his brow.

Despite her disagreement to their temporary separation, he had little choice. His family was too precious. Criminals and Infilates could easily have kidnapped them for ransom or some other devious purpose.

Therefore he had booked his wife and kids into the Metropol. It was presently the most luxurious hotel on Satellite Gimbal and contained the best security. He felt safe in the knowledge that his Anne-Marie and kids were securely settled into their new accommodation in his absence, but did not enjoy their separation because of security reasons. He also realized some people were often affected badly by Gimbal. The strange views within its innermost sphere could be quite upsetting to newcomers. Nevertheless those negative effects were only temporary.

ON GIMBAL

Anne-Marie was standing within the ginormous circular outermost ring of the giant satellite, looking out unto the expansive planet below. From that spot the sphere of the mother planet appeared to bob up and down as if on the crest of a wave, while slowly rotating at the same time. She suddenly realised the peculiar movement of Earth could be attributed to the motion of Gimbal's outermost ring. Nonetheless she had always preferred seeing Earth from that position on that enormous ring. It gave her a more panoramic view and placed the colourful world in a more universal setting against blackest space. It was not possible to get such a realistic view of the mother-planet from within Gimbal's main accommodation sphere.

The innermost surface area of the enormous accommodation sphere of the satellite being always sealed from the outside, with every inch of its surface covered with buildings, streets, parks, small forests and lakes.

Gimbal's sphere was always in constant rotation to simulate near-Earth gravity while assisted by many LPDs and other technologies.

While Anne-Marie could observe space from that location, it was very difficult to view Earth for long periods because of its rapid motion across the stellar canopy. There were also the negative consequences of giddiness and motion sickness. All those effects were attributed to Gimbal's strange motion that in many ways would take its tole on visitors. She wondered when her husband would join her from the colourful and crested world below, and of reasons for his delay.

Anne-Marie continued to observe the beautiful planet, with her little boy in her arms and daughter, Julie, now four, standing by her side. Little Julie was presently holding firmly unto one of the hand-rails and her mother's dress. She was tiptoeing and needed the extra hand-hold to keep her balance if she was to get a better view. One of their personal security guards approached while communicating with his transceiver.

'Madam, your husband is on his way. He sends his regrets for the delay, but it was unavoidable,' the officer advised.

'Unavoidable? Is everything ok?'

'Yes Mam! But more Infilate problems, I am afraid. He had to change route several times,' the officer replied.

'Mummy, what are Infilates?' asked Julie, pulling at her

mother's dress.

'Darling, they are an extreme group of people that like to destroy things. They are very bad people!'

'Like a bad devil?'

'Yes, very bad!' Anne-Marie replied.

'Mummy, when will daddy arrive?' asked Julie, this time looking quite concerned.

'My darling, I think he will be with us very soon, but I can't see his ship yet.'

'Mummy! Mummy! There it is! Look! It's the big ferry-ship!' shouted an excited Julie.

'Yes! It's dad's space-shuttle! Let's go to meet him!'

Anne-Marie, now holding on to little Julie, walked quickly along the metallic passage towards the main ferry reception area. That common entry was on the first satellite ring within the primary rotating hub.

After its arrival the passengers would journey towards the secondary hub some eight hundred metres away by a moving walkway. From there they would take one of the main city elevators which travelled through that hub into the main reception area.

Although she was now forty, Ann-Marie boasted two sets of families. The first consisted of her eldest three children. They were two girls and one young man from a previous marriage. Of those the eldest was nineteen. All three were presently in a dome university on Earth'

Her youngest group were Johnny and Julie. Julie was the eldest at four years old.

She had conceived the later children for Donald since their marriage five years ago. Donald also had three children from his previous marriage. They included his favourite and more senior, Jerry Junior, sometimes known as Jerry 2, but called JR by his friends. He was very much like his grandfather, Gerald Fraser, one of the previous presidents of the USA.

Fertilates tried to have as many children as possible, because they considered it their responsibility to revive the human race and gained substantial benefits from the state for each child.

Therefore many women took fertility drugs to increase numbers during a single birth. As a result quin-triplets were quite commonplace.

Even so, Anne-Marie preferred to do things the natural way and would produce only what she could naturally conceive at her present age, despite all the fertility drugs and extra financial incentives and benefits.

The shuttle docked, chambers linked and very soon its passengers were passing through the pressurized chambers and finally through security checks.

Donald Fraser proudly sauntered along with his single briefcase in hand, thinking of his wives and families, both past and present.

Since the untimely death of both his parents in outer-space, he had felt so alone.

'Why did they have to take that old shuttle, Cleopatra, to Mars? If only they were alive today, to see how well I have done for myself... and their lovely grandchildren? Oh... Such a great loss. So many brilliant minds... lost forever!' That shuttle-craft had still not been found and neither had its passengers and crew.

If only he had been a more loving son to them when they needed him? Perhaps they would even be proud of him today, but he couldn't bring them back. Despite every painful thing he now had a most beautiful and caring wife who loved him and their children dearly. His loving family almost compensated for their absence.

Vice President Donald Fraser walked along proudly, while he pondered those recollections with sadness, but with the consolation that he was soon to meet his loving family.

Donald was 58 and had seen so many changes in his life. Even stranger changes in his parents, with their newly acquired desire for space exploration and such likes. They were not much older than his present age when they acquired a liking for space exploration with that Lord Meron guy.

He was also thankful that both his families, young and old, got on so well together, almost like one happy family with multiple parents. But that was when he was around and well away from party political squabbles of the time, which were presently quite frequent.

As the final security door open to let his group of passengers out of that airlock, he suddenly awoke from his deeper thoughts to observe more carefully the path he trod. Anne-Marie and the children could be observed straight ahead. They were standing against the protective railing. Julie couldn't contain her emotions any longer and began to shout.

'Daddy! Daddy!'

She tried to tear herself away from her mother, but Anne-Marie was equally insistent and held unto her even more firmly. He immediately rushed towards them, kissed his wife, then the children and lifted his favourite daughter for a free ride. Off they went towards the closest moving walkway.

On arrival to their hotel suite he apologised to his wife, Anne-Marie, for having been two days late. Then he took the children into the living room where he gave them their new toys and inserted one of Julie's favourite cartoon disks into the video unit. She could always change back to television if she preferred some other program.

Their female personal guard was on permanent duty just outside their suite and dressed in plain clothes to avoid attention. She and other officers used the security monitors in the first room. They were an integral part of the secured accommodation.

There was a knock and a guard entered. 'Is everything ok, Sir and Madam? I thought I would do a final check before going off duty. My replacement is already here.' She showed her badge, quickly checked the rooms and left.

'Thanks officer for everything!' Anne-Marie shouted as the guard left.

An ever suspicious Donald carefully observed the guard but soon rejoined his wife in the kitchen to arrange some food for the family. They were vegetarians.

'This place is so fab! I could never allow anyone I didn't know into my dormitory. Not before a full bio-scan,' he said.

'I think you must see Infilates everywhere. You will find no Infilates on Gimbal. Just wealthy and boring people!' she replied.

'Those guys can get anywhere these days, with correct connections and disguise! They even use young captured Fertilates in their gangs!'

'Please change the topic! Have you heard recently from our son, Jerry, Darling?' she inquired.

'No! Not since last week!'

'I hope he and his friends are ok!' She became worried.

'He is on a new project building satellites, I think. He called me recently for some more financial assistance and I arranged a new credit card. His present occupation seems to be one with a tighter schedule. It was just to tidy him over. I think he might pay us a visit soon. He was asking about you and the kids the last time we met.'

'He and his young gang always worry me.'

'He still talks a lot about his lost grandparents! He thinks they are alive somewhere in the galaxy,' Donald said.

'It's good to know he is holding down a job,' she replied.

'He can always phone us if he needs anything else.'

'Yea, he and his friends are always in the news these days, fighting for the rights of something or another?' Donald said.

'They should be more careful. Those nasty Infilates don't play games anymore!' she said, looking more worried than ever.

'Yes I know! I saw a recent article, commending their stand for some locals against a chemical company. I must say they did quite well for those poor people regarding compensation. They also do good for Infilates as well, even without payment! However, some charities are sympathetic,' he replied.

'Darling, I only hope for your sake he is now more responsible in money matters and doesn't bring along his irresponsible and carefree group of friends next time he visits. They are always on the news these days, fighting for the rights of something or another? They are getting worse than Green Peace! I only wish they will grow up!' she said, sarcastically.

'You mean that infamous Earth's Children Gang. Don't you be too gentle with them. They deserve every bit of your criticism. That group is a lot more anti than carefree and are never far away from each other and trouble. Mind you, it reminds me of myself when I was their age... full of concern for the planet's ecosystems, human over-population, pollution and a long list of others. Not to mention all the energies of youth, self confidence and the enormous cross to bear for all the poor suffering souls of our world. Looking at this world now, I think I should have been a lot more aggressive in my efforts towards saving it.'

'Yes, but not as aggressive as the past Green Chameleon, ripping off people's heads. Anyway, with all those dangerous Infilates about these days, don't you think it might be dangerous for them to continue that unwinnable battle?'

'I know. But how will you stop them from doing something in which their hearts and souls are so deeply immersed, other then placing them in chains behind bars. Anyway, we would probably have done similarly at their age and I think they can take care of themselves. I didn't tell you before, but I have a few of my security people watching over them from afar.' Ronald said.

'Darling, do you think we are going to lose New York and Philadelphia?' she asked with sadness.

'In the next ten years or so. It's become too expensive to keep them below the water line. It works out a lot cheaper to move their historical monuments to higher ground and evacuate people to safer inland cities. Anyway, several new cities are being built in Pennsylvania and elsewhere for that purpose.'

'I never thought Global Warming would be so extreme!' she said.

'It has been accelerated by melting ice in Antarctica due to the meteor, Little Solo.'

'Where will all those nasty Infilates go?'

'They will all be dead within 30 years or so, anyway!'

'Wow! No more Infilates! I can say I wont miss any of them!' she said.

'Darling, the planet is changing and we have to move with the times, Global Warming or not. Thank goodness the human population is quickly dropping because of the Terminal Disease. The more recent Bubonic Plague only removed about 5 billion in undeveloped countries.'

'The Terminal Disease is worst than the plague. The plague killed quickly. This stays for a lifetime and prevents one from bearing children. What disease can be worse?' she said.

'Nevertheless, the Terminal is not painful and only affects those during their child-bearing age,' Donald replied.

'Even so, this whole situation with Jerry and his gang is not right. Next time he visits I am going to have a serious parental chat. Because I am so worried for their safety,' she said.

'I know! But in their case, it's conservation and antipollution, which have become a full time occupation on Earth these days, even with all the main charitable concerns. Yet, no one can stop progress and its resultant backlash. Nevertheless Mother Nature seems to have things under control with the Terminal and other incurable diseases, not to mention our erratic weather patterns that frequently take numerous lives, globally,' he said, somewhat resigned to those changes.

'Even so, I must have a serious chat with them.' She was insistent.

'The frivolities of youth, eh! Yet, it was the best period of our lives, even better than now,' he replied.

'Darling, I didn't like the way you said those last words. Are you not happy with us... in this period of our lives?' she replied, questioningly.

'You know I didn't mean that, Love. I was talking about youthful attitudes and the inability of mankind to plan in the long term for a better future,' he said, apologetically.'

'I forgive you this time, but don't make it a habit. I mean, being a bad politician,' she reprimanded, and they both began to laugh at themselves.

They had not been so close or felt that way about each other for a while.

CHAPTER 2

A race in turmoil

The President was on a brief visit to the United States of Europe, more commonly known as the USE. He was to ratify a new treaty and sign some new trade agreements to their mutual benefit. He was also to make a few unscheduled stops in the Middle East and elsewhere, and was expected back the following week. Therefore Richard had left all home duties in the capable hands of his Vice President, Donald Fraser. Donald was the son of the long lost-in-space President, Gerald Fraser, and acting president during his absence.

Strictly speaking, that period was normally the calmest of the year. However it was their turn for the celebrated United Nations' convention on resources, conservation and human fertility. That convention was to be held during the following months. Therefore business was busier than usual.

The latter concerned Fertilate families who were considered the life-blood of all nations on Earth. During that time representatives would discuss particular methods of enhancing procreation and more efficient ways for distributing the Terminal Antidote. There were several appointments and speeches to be made by Gerald during his President's absence, to congress, conservationists and others visiting the States at that time.

At the convention all types of advanced technologies would be displayed and demonstrated.

Nevertheless the dangerous Infilate extremists would also be more active during that time.

Over the intervening years pollution had increased significantly. Many areas of the planet had been irreversibly affected. It was thought humans were incapable of putting things right; for as the situation worsened, mankind thought less of the problem and more about his immediate survival. At present estimates it would have taken over 1000 years for planetary return to where it was 100 years before, and that was just its forests. The numerous extinct species were presumed lost forever.

The USA was not isolated from those turbulent changes having had her fair share of catastrophes over recent years, particular with hurricanes. Most of which were due to Global Warming and rising waters. Therefore the USA, being the most advanced country, had to show significant interest if they wanted to lead the way in areas of conservation and anti-pollution commitment.

From the planet's original 10 billion plus humans, the population had dropped to just under six billion and reducing steadily. It was quite a change from a previous over population barely thirty years before. At that time over ninety-five percent of the human population had been infected by the Terminal Disease. As a result of which the majority had become infertile. This was due to the introduction of a bio-engineered microbe that could take the place of human skin bacteria. That bacterium which mimicked the human body types, hosted a virus that could not be eradicated by any means known to man.

The cursed disease entered many of the body's organs, in particular the reproductive. The viral part targeted and inhibited all types of human reproduction. Although the majority of humans lived a normal lifespan, with no symptoms of the disease, they had no children to carry on their family's names and traditions.

People had suddenly become placid, unhappy and suicidal, with the exception of the Infertilate or Infilate extremists, who were against every institution and government at that time. They nurtured a natural hatred of all Fertilates out of jealousy and frustration. Those negative attitudes were due mainly to Fertilates natural ability to bear offspring. There was also the large government handouts in child-care and housing to those special families who were considered the future, with the exclusion of all others.

Infilates lived in squalid conditions of poverty within the main water-logged cities and received little or no assistance from governments. They were the condemned and forsaken. All those problems fuelled their natural hatred against those few that received their taxes in the form of large governments hand-outs, free schooling, childcare and special housing in the best areas.

Nevertheless Fertilates were considered the only future for humanity and a worthwhile investment for the survival of mankind.

The price on every child's head was very high and rising. Many rich Infilates, as the incurable infected were usually called, wanted someone to carry on their names. Most would have parted with a large part of their had-earned wealth just to make a young fertile child heir to their properties and wealth before departing this life.

In the case of the very wealthy, it was to carry on their dynasty. Because of current laws, after death all their wealth would inadvertently have been returned to the state and distributed to Fertilate families. In most cases that problem would have occurred within thirty years. Many became god-parents while others arranged name changes with forged papers. All such forms of adoption, although illegal, would not be queried and false papers could always be acquired for a price.

There were also those desperate parents who would give almost anything to have a child by illegal or other means. In those areas kidnapping was rife. During that time Mallory's Specials became a powerful force for law and order.

Despite government's advice and propaganda, those maternal feelings were deeply rooted in the human psyche and like the Terminal Disease could not be eradicated by any known means. Because of those dangers most Fertilates lived together in large secured domes and guarded enclosures. All such places were kept well away from cities and included their own facilities like schools, universities and shopping precincts. Most of those isolated environments became known as health farms and dome habitats.

Over the past decades trade relations between the two largest nations on Earth had worsened. It was due mainly to unresolved disputes in advanced products concessions and commercial distribution of resources. Most of those concessions had been issued to the USA by Solarian Banking. The USA was never generous in sharing those technologies and resources with others.

They also realized such resources were limited. Many not being replaceable on a systematic basis. Further, as minerals dwindled so did the supply and distribution of their special products. The USA also had the final say in such distribution and could stop supplying any country if the economy was in any way threatened.

Those decisions related to highly technological devices like LPD drive modules, a range of anti-cancer, youth-enhancement drugs and others. The robotic and android industries had since dissipated. Also there was better organization of Terminal Antidote distribution in the USA, which had taken effect sooner than the other countries, giving them enough time to put better plans in operation. That was all due to Mallory's efforts in the past.

Most of those devices and systems were supplied under franchise by Solarian Banking, whose head offices were based in the Sol-Newtown Dome in North Dakota. All controls, via Professor Khan, emanated from the Solarian's own organizations in North America and elsewhere. Therefore Europe felt somewhat left out of the financial equation and found herself almost fully dependant on North America for their supplies.

Further, since the discovery of the Terminal Disease, the USA had spent billions re-educating its population to the benefits of consuming a healthy diet. Funds were diverted from more ambitious defence and space exploration projects towards the health of the nation. As a result the life expectancy within the USA and Canada had become at least twenty years higher than even the most affluent European countries.

All those factors were very worrying to the USE (United States of Europe), who had been left with a much older population that were dying at a faster rate.

It was calculated that the USE would retain a population of barely fifty million from its present five hundred million within the next twenty years. It was presently much too late to change old habits in an already older population.

Many thought it was their own fault for not having dealt with the problems sooner. But as always, many governments never believed in long term planning and were always too late in considering those options when turning decisions into actions.

That smaller figure of fifty million represented the Fertilates, who were treated by their respective governments like nuggets-of-gold; for they were the only hope of the future for their respective nations.

Nevertheless Infilate extremists were always more radical in Europe and Asia than anywhere else on the planet and came in all shapes, sizes and inclinations. They felt completely let down by their respective governments and scientists, for not having found a cure over several decades of research. Those extremists also included those that were displaced by the rising waters. Not to mention the unexpected flood of refugees from Africa and elsewhere as Global Warming took its tole.

Highly organised groups were formed. They were assisted by young Fertilate dropouts and spent most of their time targeting specific places that would gain them the most publicity. Despite extensive security during that period, kidnapping, assassinations and explosions were commonplace within highly populated areas.

The Specials (Universal Police) operated globally and ensured all criminals were quickly subdued or neutralized. They were not the easy-going force as in past. They tended to shoot first and ask questions later. That attitude was paramount to the reduction of violent crime on the planet.

It was as if that sole organization of super trained soldiers were above the law, only answerable to their chief and the President of the USA. Their advanced weaponry were beyond anything on the planet and supplied by Solarian Banking.

Because of all those reasons, the USE was now asking the USA for assistance. A survival program was quickly planned by many of the most eminent scientists of the time, with cooperation on both sides of the Atlantic. Presently agreements had to be ratified and signed by both governments. Those measures included a newly developed longevity drug that would lift the survival ceiling by another twenty years at the most. It included more efficient dietary measures and more trade concessions. Nevertheless, due to their desperation even those modest improvements were welcomed news to everyone in that part of the world.

Although there were now several domed cities on Mars, interplanetary mining and long space voyages were discouraged and restricted for supposed economical and other reasons. One of the main excuses put forward by politicians were more contamination by the Terminal Disease. Many assumed its presence made interstellar resettlement by humans, other than screened Fertilates, completely pointless. However, all such propaganda was generated by Solarian Banking to deter space exploration.

They also argued that since Earth and its many external habitats would soon be suffering from a severely reduced population, there was little point in going elsewhere. Why leave an almost empty and beautiful home planet, which Earth would soon have become, for the unknown.

Despite those concerns many thought they were just political excuses and a planned program to reduce Earth's populations without the peoples' knowledge and participation. Some even called it the Terminal Conspiracy.

CHAPTER 3

A President is assassinated

That evening on Satellite Gimbal their television program was briefly interrupted for an important announcement.

'We apologise for this interruption to your current program. Our studio just received news of a political assassination in Europe. We shall again interrupt your scheduled program when we receive further information on this tragic event.

Thank you!'

The program then continued from where it was interrupted.

Turning to Anne-Marie a very worried Donald gazed directly into her grey blue eyes.

'What do you make of that, Love? Do you think it could be Richard? Why make such an announcement without giving us a name?' he asked while expecting the worst.

'I don't know, Darling. I just hope it isn't...'

Before she could continue her sentence the program was once again interrupted.

'We must again apologise for this interruption to your scheduled program. We have just received more precise details about the assassination in Europe. Our latest report indicates that President Richard McLeod of the United States of America has recently been shot by an unknown assassin. Apparently he received a single bullet to the head from a long range sniper.

He has been rushed to one of the local hospitals in London, but we are unsure of his present condition. We shall keep you informed of future developments as soon as we are able.

We apologise for this untimely interruption!'

Once again the screen returned to the original program.

'Oh my God! Richard has been assassinated. I can't believe it!' Donald was beside himself.

'Poor man...! I wonder if he will pull through?' she whispered.

'I sincerely hope he does or all hell will break loose! How could they do that to such a nice guy? It must be those Infilate scum, always killing, always maiming, always destroying!'

'Yes, Darling!'

'Oh, how bloody senseless!' Donald screamed with tears flowing down his cheeks. Ann-Marie was lost for words and began to sob with her husband.

Donald was distraught and Anne-Marie went closer to comfort him. It was not long before the program was once again interrupted.

'I am very sorry for yet another interruption to your scheduled program, but we have received a further report from Europe. Once again I am very sorry to announce... the President of the USA is dead. He sustained a fatal head injury, due to a single bullet fire by a yet unknown assassin. His body is being flown out immediately to the USA for postmortem. A thorough search is now in progress to locate the sniper,' the announcer advised.

It was not long before many security officers arrived at Donald's suite, to be followed by several more senior members from Earth. The local chief officer entered and taking his special helmet with a visor off, showed them his security card with badge.

'I am very sorry for any inconvenience caused by this intrusion. Because of security reasons, you and your family are to remain here until further notice. This measure has been taken for your own safety. I am afraid that even Gimbal might contain a few rotten Infilate elements. Therefore, if you intend to go anywhere outside of this immediate area, please let us know so that we can make the necessary arrangements. In the mean time, two of my best officers will be assigned to keep an eye on things here.'

Turning to Donald he began to apologise.

'I am very sorry for all this trouble, Sir, and about the President, but I have to do my job as best I can in the circumstances; you being the next President in line.'

Donald noted his black uniform with insignia and realized he was one of the dreaded Specials. That organization was set up by Andy's father, Commander Mallory, several decades before. Once on the job they would go to any lengths to locate their target, even if it meant taking out a few Infilate communities in the process.

'Thank you very much for your concern, Officer,' Donald replied.

He left and two plain-clothes female security officers walked in and began to check the suite while asking many personal questions.

When they were finished, both sat and began to enter the information into their Coms. Coms were just an abbreviation for Computerised Communicator. In actual fact they were very advanced tablet computers with an integrated multilingual communication system. Such systems used verbal translators, where all information, including conversations, could be stored and interpreted in many languages. They also had access to powerful Macron Computers on Earth for quick searches. Such systems turned their operatives into highly efficient strategic units in a warring context. All important information, including conversations could be analysed, stored and interpreted in many languages, and instructions immediately relayed to other operatives globally. They also had access to powerful satellites like Eta, that could locate virtually any individual on Earth via the latest Macron computers. Those super-intelligent computers were linked to satellites and could even relay information across the galaxy almost instantaneously using what they call H-Wave.

Several security ships were soon arriving, with the whole of Gimbal put under tight security screening. Everyone of its present one hundred and twenty thousand population was being systematically checked. Apparently, a similar purge of Infilates was taking place within the USA, USE and other countries on Earth by the Specials.

The television was now displaying the dramatic moment of the assassination. There were several pockets of violence against Infilates by those who liked the President. Many arrests were made with reprisals throughout the planet.

It was not long before the media attention had changed from the President's inopportune death to the image and past successes of his Vice President. Suddenly Donald realised his faith as future President was inevitable. Even while he watched, his uniformed photograph displaying his many air-force service stripes for bravery was on the screen. Then he knew he was already a wanted man. Wanted by everyone including every reporter, not to mention the more extreme Infilates for past policies made by his government. He also realised that the next few days would be the worst and most traumatic of his life.

Of all the senators, he was the only positive contender. He was loved and respected by almost everyone because of his impartial attitude towards all, including Infilates. Many sympathetic politicians thought he was the right man to push the scientists and others concerned towards finding a lasting cure for the Terminal disease. Any such advantage gained would have gone towards levelling the field in favour of the Infilates, who were still in the majority.

The Chief of security was also a Special. He was dressed in black, with an array of advanced equipment on his person, including a plasma weapon hanging from his utility belt. He entered their apartment accompanied by several of his senior people and took the Vice President's hand.

'My name is Joel, Commander Joel. I am very sorry, Sir, but you are presently required on Earth. However, we would like your wife and children to remain here on Gimbal for a while longer. At least until things quieten down a little on the world below. But don't hurry, tomorrow morning will do fine.'

'So soon?' Donald was not pleased, but had to follow protocol.

'So we'll see you then, Mister future President!'

Then he left them in the hands of the local security chief.

Specials were a law unto themselves. They were planetary police with powers to arrest and reprimand anyone anywhere on the globe. With their type of advanced technology they could easily destroy a city if its occupants were a risk to Fertilate survival. At that time Infilates' lives were cheap. They were considered as marked for death, anyway, so why prolong the agony. Nevertheless Specials had a book of rules to follow. By so doing they had acquired much respect within most countries on Earth and elsewhere.

Donald, Anna-Marie and the children found they were deeply immersed in the turbulent events of that time. They had little control over their destinies and followed through many decisions not of their making and as a matter of course.

The following morning he sadly kissed his wife and children. With tears in their eyes they parted company.

'Love, sorry for my brief stay. I'll make it up to you soon!' he hugged and kissed them before leaving.

'You hear me! Do take extra care, Darling!' Anne-Marie shouted as he left with the officers.

He was accompanied by several armed security officers and Specials. They would escort him during his flight back to Earth, to take up that most important role and office.

Both nations were blaming each other for the death of the President. Some thought the bullet was meant for the President of the USE, who was a much tougher and uncompromising politician. Despite those initial turbulent moments, Europe was another friendly democracy that had too much to lose. Therefore they tried their utmost best to calm the situation by pointing an accusing finger at the doors of the Infilate extremists. They were usually blamed for every unsavoury activity, including unfavourable acts of God.

When Donald arrived on Earth he was immediately made President. Within a few days the situation had returned to some semblance of normality.

Too many people had too much to lose. The Fertilates were now the wealthiest and most influential force on Earth, with the dreaded Specials at their call. Nevertheless, despite that fact they were in the smallest minority at just one to more than ten

Infilates.

They didn't mind sacrificing many of the larger cities in any thermonuclear war. Their Infilate opponents would all have disappeared sooner or later through aging, anyway. Their demise was guaranteed within the maximum fifty-year terminal period, despite the fact that most cities were contaminated with every type of human scum and vermin on the planet. Nevertheless any such war could have spread uncontrollably throughout the planet and that would have been disastrous for all.

CHAPTER 4

The Earth's Children Gang

Gerald Fraser Junior, known to family and friends as Jerry or JR, had just passed his twenty-fifth birthday when he heard the distressing news about the President's death. He was shaken and bewildered by it all. As for his Gang, after watching the news that evening, their attention turned in the direction of Jerry's father who was next in line for the position of President of the USA. Suddenly the reality of present dangers came home to roost.

Although shocked by the whole affair and worried for the safety of their respective families, they were most sympathetic. They dropped what they were doing and went home. All gang members were respectable Fertilates and considered prime targets in any Infilate uprising. Being utterly disturbed and bewildered by recent affairs, Jerry made his way to his family home in the outskirts of Washington DC.

Since college, he and some of his close friends had formed a small political action group called Earth's Children. They frequently fought for environmental and other important ecological issues of the time and became known to many for their brave, reckless and sometimes unwelcomed appearances. With cameras and friends of the press, they would organize protests marches and demonstrations when situations became unacceptable to life within the human population.

Nowhere was too far to travel when it came to assisting the down trodden and disenfranchised. However like most of the prejudiced youth of that time, they held the warped view that Infilates were the lowliest scum beyond help that always deserved what they got for past ills against humanity. During that time, with the planet literally falling apart, many had to lay blame somewhere and Infilates were their prime targets. Anyway, they and their previous generations were responsible for Global Warming, the depletion of fossil fuels and the extinction of most planetary life, in both flora and fauna. The Gang and other youth of their time never thought their Fertilate families were from the same people and equally responsible. As far as they were concerned, Infilates destroyed Earth in the name of capitalism and greed and deserved to suffer.

The few members of that gang were all rebels at heart with good intentions toward mankind, but even rebels occasionally needed a break from such tumultuous business on a disparate world. In particular, when many such situations on Earth were becoming too numerous and also much too hot to handle by anyone other than Mallory's Specials.

Having considered those and other important matters of the time, Jerry opted for a well-deserved holiday break anywhere away from the tumultuous planet. After his satellite engineering project was completed, he called his girlfriend Miranda.

'Hi, its me! How would you fancy a holiday break on Gimbal or Mars?'

'Sounds fantastic! But with all that's going on, do you think it's wise? Anyway, how are we going to get to Mars with all the restrictions?'

'I have a few contacts in high places, so leave the trip side of it with me. Anyway, I must visit dad soon and see if he needs my help. During that visit I can tactfully ask for permission and funds towards our noble cause.'

'It's nice to have wealthy parents! Anyway, it's great, your dad being our new President. I am at Mum for a few days, so if you can organize transport I'm in.'

'It's the most dangerous job. I wish he wasn't!'

'You should visit him. Anyway, as I said, if you can organize transport to Gimbal or Mars, I am in!' she replied.

He called the other six members of his famous gang. With the exception of Carol Barnes and Tim Chiang, they were very excited by the idea of a holiday away from Earth. Carol and Tim were unable to partake at that time because of exams and family problems.

He was left with just four available members, including himself and Miranda, out of the six original gang members. Although somewhat disappointed, in his opinion four good friends were more than adequate company on such an adventurous vacation.

With a few powerful contacts and strings to pull, the Gang had grown to respect him as their group leader. Presently their enthusiasm waned. They tended not to drop everything at a moment's notice in the name of fighting for the people's rights as on previous occasions. There was just too much to fight. The water had become too murky everywhere.

Over the years their bosses had become more tolerant to their constant absenteeism, and tended to sympathize with their humanitarian causes which usually gave them a modicum of free publicity. Anyway, he was the President's son and any publicity would be doubly important, so they didn't mind giving their famous part-time employees a month off, even when it was unscheduled.

Since the untimely disappearance of his grandparents in outer-space, just before his birth, there was never any real evidence why they had suddenly vanished in that particular manner. Since youth he had become like an adopted child, searching for lost parents even after having passed the age of consent. His father, the one most dear to him, had never gotten over that loss. The spectre of their disappearance had always haunted his family.

Jerry wanted to face those issues and resolve those questions for their peace of mind. Then their corpses would be laid to rest once and for all time. He reasoned that if he was to get any information, Mars with its large mining colony would be just the place to begin the search. After all, it was the last place visited before their disappearance.

Jerry's plan was to rent a small space cruiser and spend a week on Gimbal with Anne-Marie and the children. Then take the Martian Space-way and arrive on Mars two days later. After the journey, they could visit some old miners in Caefon Dome, including an old friend of his father. While there, he would ask a few well-chosen questions to the elders and search their computers for any references. They could also spend two weeks exploring the Martian terrain, prospecting for minerals and ancient fossils if they ever existed. Nevertheless the experience and adventure on a foreign world would take his mind away from the problems of his family and Earth and so he thought.

It was not long before Jerry had words with his father, telling him of his intentions.

'Dad, what do you think of my idea?'

'This extraterrestrial vacation of yours seems to me to be the most dangerous and complex project ever I heard and nothing like a holiday. You are getting more like your grandfather every day. I hope you and your friends don't get lost in space like my parents. I don't want to lose you as well. If I did I would never forgive myself for assisting you to go on such a reckless adventure. Have you thought this thing through properly?'

'Some of it!'

'Space can be a very dangerous place and many of your friends are not even trained astronauts.'

'These days many prospectors and mountain climbers visit Mars for the more extreme survival training, so we'll not be the only ones there.'

'Yea, they go with experts! Outer Space is no place for a novice. And you and your friends will be on a hostile world!'

'Well, we can take a professional along!'

'I shall only go along with this hair-brained scheme of yours, if you promise me that you and your friends will go on a two-week survival course, and I know just the man for the job.' Donald was most insistent.

Without any further arguments, President Donald Fraser got on the line to one of his closest friends. He was presently in charge of those operations at NASA and everything was arranged.

Jerry had no choice in the matter and had to go along with his father's decisions for safety's sake. Many of his closest friends were also involved and he wanted them to have a fair chance of survival if anything went wrong during their trip. Despite all those reservations the spectre of his grandparents disappearance in outer-space still haunted his family, mostly his father and he knew it.

'Yes, Dad, I agree with your decision if it's the only way. Anyway, it will help us get a feel for running a spaceship and the use of spacesuits on Mars. In that case, can I invite my friends here to the White House for a while? I mean, before we take off for Florida, or wherever we have to go for training.' Jerry realized he had won with his 'Please? Please?' frown.

'Son, don't push it! You should know by now how I feel about your rebellious friends, but I shall agree to that unpleasant and unsavoury prospect. If and only if, you promise me and swear that none of your friends will make a political issue out of their presence here, in the White House. However, I shall have to clear it with security first, and that is if I agree, young man!'

'Nothing will happen, Dad! They are also on your side and I will talk to them when they arrive. You have my word!'

'Your word, eh! How often have I heard that! Well... I suppose it's only for a week?'

Young Jerry pleaded, until his father agreed.

Miranda Fernandez

Miranda was Jerry's current girlfriend and the first to arrive with two old battered suitcases. She was wearing well-worn jeans and a brown leather jacket.

She couldn't believe the image her eyes beheld. It was her first visit to the White House and the scene completely overwhelmed her. She remained stationary at the bottom of the first run of stairs several minutes observing the magnificent building. While resting her sore arms on the hand-rail her driver followed and decided to assist her with the cases. He climbed one of the sets of stairs ahead of her, with several security personnel curiously observing their unsteady progress.

'Thanks a million times!' she said and paid him an extra tip.

Miranda Fernandez was twenty-three and of Puerto Rican descent. She had an honour's degree in engineering at MIT. She currently worked for a large computer company in systems design. Miranda cared little for the frivolities of fashion and took almost everything seriously when it came to work and conservation. Nevertheless she had her funny side.

George Peterson

George was next to arrive in his robot controlled LPD Roadstar. It was left to him by an unknown family friend, having remained in mothballs for the past 15 years or so. The now antique car named Oscar dropped him off with his three cases and simply flew off to one of its resting places on a high building. Oscar knew the area well and could always alter the parking computers to accommodate his needs. Those super intelligent cars could always be recalled at a moment's notice and had accumulated a wealth of knowledge on every conceivable subject matter including local maps, people and buildings. That aspect saved George a lot of parking problems. Even then, he had no idea that the car once belonged to Commander Mallory Coleman of the dreaded Specials. Further, that car possessed knowledge of much more than it could let on for the sake of all.

George, originally from England, was almost twenty-one and still a student. He was English through and through, with a delicate poise and broad knowledge on most subjects. He spoke and functioned in that reserved manner, but was also very clever in the robotic and android sciences, being a brilliant post graduate at MIT. He was probably Jerry's closest friend and also one of Jerry's fellow students in engineering.

Barry Stenburg & Ann Baxter

Barry was next to arrive with his girlfriend Ann. He was now thirty and Ann twenty four. They were both Harvard graduates in economics and business studies, but also shared a keen interest in the redistribution of wealth throughout the planet. Both had adopted space exploration as a spare-time hobby, but had never travelled beyond planet Earth.

They were currently engaged to be married and shared a department together.

Catherine Keenan

Catherine, known to her friends as Cathy, was the last one to arrive by black LPD Cab, and was beautifully dressed. In fact, everything about her was beautiful. She was very fashion-conscious, a health fanatic and believed in clean living and high thinking. Despite her slightly eccentric tendencies, she was a brilliant computer programmer and also formally from MIT.

She was just twenty, always kept her cool and enjoyed her adventures. Being good at rock-climbing she didn't mind hard going while accompanied by reliable comrades, even when in dangerous situations.

They were utterly amazed by the beautiful interior of the large historical building and thanked Jerry and his father for their hospitality in allowing their stay at the White House.

'Since Anne-Marie is not here to assist, everyone will maintain their rooms for the duration and I want no funny business of any kind while in this house!' Donald stressed. They agreed with an air of sympathy.

Jerry soon explained his plans to them, although still disappointed that Tim and Carol was not able to make the trip. Nevertheless, they decided to begin planning their interplanetary journey in earnest, in the hope that the others would join them later.

'So these are my plans! I'm afraid Tim and Carol were unable to make it. Tim is on a special project and Carol is doing exams,' Jerry said.

'Oh? I'll miss their company!' Miranda replied.

'Have you any idea what type of spaceship is involved!' George inquired.

'No, Pal! We have to go shopping. First, let's get the training out of the way. Then we can concentrate on transport!'

CHAPTER 5

Astronaut training

They spent two days with Jerry and his father, Donald, at the White House and did not make a nuisance of themselves during that brief period. Nevertheless they made the house livelier than it had been since his inauguration. Donald enjoyed his son's young company for a change and was sad to see them leave. He was hoping their future adventure, although somewhat risky, would change their attitudes and mould them into more responsible adults.

After arrival at NASA, they were immediately taken to an area called Testpoint for astronaut training.

'Uniforms! Uniforms! And more uniforms!' Jerry complained as he slid into training gear. He never liked such attire, which reminded him of authoritarian control.

'Do you think we'll learn the Martian walk during this caper,' Miranda said with sarcasm.

'Never on Earth, Baby! Perhaps the Martian dance,' Jerry replied.

'Yea! I know that one. It's my disco favourite!' George replied.

'This is a military camp. So what do you think?' Cathy interjected.

'Never on Earth, Baby!' Ann replied.

'So I am honoured with your gracious and glorious company for two long weeks!' Andy Colman shouted, while lining them up in a straight row with baton in hand. He slowly scanned their puny bodies one by one.

'You must be from the very bottom of the bottom of the barrel. Then, I don't mind the occasional challenge even when it's near impossible, that is, providing you are able to survive the training. A training that will mould you into shape in the most painless manner. And may I add... that your training has been approved and sanctioned at the highest levels. So I expect each of you to remain under my loving care for the duration... and by the way, deserters are shot on sight!'

He continued striking his baton in the palm of his left hand as he spoke, instilling the greatest fear in his trainees.

'It's going to be a very long and hard two weeks for all of you. Can you take it? Can you handle orders and take the grief. I hope for God's sake you can!' They remained stationary and at attention wishing they were somewhere else.

'Yea! Well we can take whatever you throw at us and more!' Jerry shouted in defiance.

'Someone just squeaked a sentence?' he admonished.

'No Sir!' George replied, not wishing Jerry into any deep soup.

'Silence...! Ok, You can have the rest of the day off... to check out your beautiful quarters, the fantastic restaurant and other areas of interest within this scenic compound.' Andy said in jest.

'Yes, Sir!' they saluted together.

A striped soldier soon approached and whispered something of importance in Andy's ear. Then he left in a hurry.

'And remember, People, it's impossible for anyone to escape from this place without a written release or you'll be considered deserters. We imprison deserters in Infilate jails!' he shouted and they swallowed hard.

'Dismissed!' he bellowed.

Although the Gang had been through lots of dangerous situations together, never had they been abused and degraded by anyone in uniform before. They had never been worried as they were at that moment. Spending time in an Infilate prison were not on their current list of adventures.

Andy Colman threatened both body and soul. He was the type to carry out his uncompromising promises in full, so they did as he ordered. They spent the rest of the day familiarising themselves with the large astronaut training base. Jerry, was also keen on learning those methods for their mutual survival, so he got everyone to think military as if they were joining the Air Force.

Testpoint Base

Testpoint covered an area of just over ten square miles and was cris-crossed by every conceivable moving walkway, monorail, elevators and escalators. It was built by robots during the boom years several decades before and had obviously been maintained to those original high standards by competent military personnel since.

The camp was separated into four main areas.

Test Area One, contained all the stress training analysis equipment, centrifuge and gymnasium, including a large swimming pool.

Test Area Two, of flight simulators and flight training schools.

Test Area Three, the rough terrains, simulated planetary landscapes and environments, which almost looked and felt like the real thing.

Test Area Four, their accommodation and more relaxing recreation facilities. That block also included a gymnasium, swimming pool and the main administration buildings.

The place was designed more like a military base than a training camp and operated jointly by NASA and the air-force.

During the week that followed they knuckled down to hard work within A3. That was the name given to Test Area Three by the locals.

Although it required time getting used to the uncomfortable and still rather bulky space suits, they were soon able to use the relevant finger and other motion controls that were integral to the nuclear powered filtration suits.

Those suits contained hydraulically assisted movement, body waste recycling, automatic temperature control, computer assisted position location, communications and a range of other safety features for survival in the harshest environments. It could automatically climb virtually any terrain with almost no assistance from its occupant. The AI computers learnt everything through their sensors and could advise their host on better ways to tackle a task.

Although separate LPD clip-on packs were available for quick motion when operated in deep space, they were not fitted in case they were accidentally operated on land, with possible disastrous consequences. Furthermore such LPD devices were extremely expensive and only used when absolutely necessary.

After their first three days they had travelled a total of fifty miles within that area. During that time they had experienced almost every conceivable terrain. Finally they were to climb an almost vertical rock-face with one of their members in tow. That final exercise within A3 was also a good test for assessing their capabilities in rescuing a wounded comrade within a hostile terrain or crater on Mars.

They passed those endeavours with flying colours and were cleared for stress testing in the centrifuge and G-chamber within A1. While in the G-chamber they had to perform several operations under weightless and accelerated conditions.

During those tests they wore specially padded and reenforced suits that contained LPD modules. Those were always under the control of the main panel computers. That massive test area had all of its walls padded throughout in case of accidents and contained a small LPD craft that was also used to simulate those conditions with its two passengers.

Andy had given orders to his instructors to assist the untrained visitors as best they could. As a result of which the instructors couldn't have been more helpful and made them repeat certain activities until they became second nature.

After the first week they had completed all their tests in both areas only the final Pilot and Navigation training course remained. The group were very pleased that the most stressful parts of the course were finally out of the way and decided to visit the mess and celebrate their current successes.

'I told you guys to move with the flow and we've stuck with it and come true. Isn't that great!' Jerry said, excitedly and went to get drinks for the others. They mainly had Lager but the girls preferred Gin and tonic.

'Now all we've got to worry about is driving the thing,' Clair said, a little worried about her abilities in that direction.

'Yea, The Thing!' George responded and they broke out

laughing.

While sipping their first drink of the evening in walked Commander Andy Colman. He was dress in his white military uniform that displayed an array of medals and stripes that he had acquired during his time in the air-force and elsewhere. Those had included several rescue missions to Mars, and other special assignments to places unknown to them. When he observed their group, he took his drink from the barman and went over to their table.

'So you are Donald's carefree son, and his infamous gang, training for a holiday in space... of all places!' Andy said with a broad grin across his face. He gave the impression of a rugged action man and looked that way with a scar across his forehead.

'I try to be!' Jerry replied in jest.

'Please call me Andy! Anyway guys, how is your training coming along?' Andy inquired sympathetically.

'Ok... I think, Andy. As you said, it's hard work. But despite the aches and pains we are getting to like it,' Jerry replied in his usual oblivious manner.

'You like it, eh! No one has ever said that to me before,' Andy replied.

'I always wanted to lose a few pounds when dieting failed!' Miranda interjected.

'Sorry for winding you up on your first day, but I had to get you in the right mood. And it appears to have worked. Your dad put me up to it, you know. We are old buddies from way back. Almost like brothers. He is the one who got me into the force. So he's got an awful lot to answer for.'

'Did he Really?' Jerry inquired, suddenly full of interest in Andy's recollections.

'Yes! I used to be his junior in the air-force, until I took the post here. That was after my return from Mars. I got a little out of touch with him since, both of us being so busy with all that's going on,' Andy replied.

'You actually visited Mars?' Jerry inquired, with considerable interest.

'I didn't just visit Mars. I lived there for five long years. That was during the construction of the Secondary Engineering Dome. Before that dome was named Colman Dome... after my father Mallory Colman.'

'Your father is the great Commander Mallory Coleman?' George butted in.

'Yes, I am. He was... until... that accident. God bless his soul!' Andy replied. George couldn't help but shake his hand.

'Mallory Colman is one of my pinups,' Cathy said.

'Anyway, the original services and engineering dome was built a couple of years before that. We had lots of problems in those days ferrying materials and controlling the antiquated robots to complete those jobs on time. Most of which were loaned to us by Solarian Banking. Presently there are several large manufacturing plants and mines within all three domes, including Caefon Dome, which is one of the oldest on Mars. It also happens to be the accommodation or city dome for visitors and miners. However I am not sure whether they are still fully operational.'

They were all ears and listened patiently to Andy's experiences.

'Yep, they were great times of adventure. Now, there is not much left in the kitty and there is an abundance of steel and other metals from all those demolished buildings in our submerging cities,' George interjected.

'Yep, times have changed. The original accommodation dome was called Eden you know, but it's seldom used these days. The two oldest domes in that area were given names by your grandfather who was then President Gerald Fraser. He got himself and others lost in space while returning from the inauguration of Caefon Dome. Luckily for Caefon, he went missing after the ceremony, or the city dome would probably still be called City Dome instead of Caefon.' Andy said.

'Sadly, your father was also lost to us when his ship exploded in Florida,' Miranda said.

'Yea... they all died in peculiar circumstances. No bodies ever been found!'

'I had no idea you were Commander Mallory's son. He was one of the greatest men that ever lived. At least that's how my mum feels about him,' Cathy interjected, trying to change the painful topic.

'Tell us more about the domes?' Jerry inquired, now extremely interested.

'Yea... well, Caefon Dome had a population of about fifty thousand, with mostly Fertilates. But things are also in decline there. Europe also had their own set of mining domes, but those were emptied several years ago when their occupants returned to Earth. That was after their local ores ran out. They either couldn't or didn't wish to move it to another mining area on the Martian surface. Solarian Banking owns the largest structures on Mars. The Solarians seem to get everywhere and sometimes even ahead of the larger nations.'

'Really?' George inquired. Wishing for more information about the largest organization on Earth.

'Do you know, they were the first to build major structures on Mars?' Andy became more interested in his favourite subject, which was mainly to do with those lost people and Solarian Banking.

'Andy, I didn't realise you knew so much about those important people and their links with Mars?' Jerry replied, showing even more overwhelming interest.

'Jerry, I know an awful lot more besides. Did you know that your granddad was also involved in Solarian Banking and that he knew its original president well? And I think my father was also with them when he got involved with the Terminal Antidote distribution. In those days he was one of the top people on Earth. He founded the Specials. Did you know that?' Andy said proudly, as tear drops trickled down his right cheek.

'Sorry Guys! I get overcomed!' He wiped his face with a tissue.

'Anyway, God bless his soul. He and his second family and friends died when their yacht blew up on that faithful day. They say it was due to a bomb laid by one of his enemies.' Jerry said.

'Yea! Tragic! More bloody Infilates!' Ann replied.

'Anyway, who do you think is the current president of Solarian Banking, eh? You answer me that question?' Andy said.

'Is not that person Michael Cockburn?' interrupted Ann Baxter.

'No! He is the vice president,' Andy corrected and waited for another reply, but no one could answer that particular question, so he continued.

'In that case, let me educate you on important matters. It's a guy called Ben. One Bengizara Khan. He is the richest and perhaps the most important man on Earth today. He is the one who countersigns all important decisions.'

Jerry couldn't believe that it was his godfather that Andy was talking about and kept his thoughts to himself while Andy continued his story.

'Jerry... in those days, my dad, the late Mallory Colman, God bless his soul, used to visit your granddad quite frequently at his country ranch. You see, my father was then chief of security. They always enjoyed a good game of golf together. Anyway, although I was just a little kid of about six, it did not prevent me from observing a few very strange things. For one, I once observed the guy, Lord Meron, with his gloves off while washing his hands. You know, he had just three fingers on each hand and all his eldest family members wore gloves, had golden hair and very peculiar piercing sea blue eyes.'

'You are not kidding?' Ann was surprised.

'At another time one of the other guys walked in with a jet black hooded cloak. It had circular creases and seams that gave no reflections whatsoever, even black gives reflections you know. But that one reflected no light whatsoever, except when he placed the hood down and his head popped out of the blackness. That one also had six fingers and never wore any gloves. It was like he didn't care one way or the other. That one was also a close friend of your granddad, the then President.'

'Stranger and stranger!' George said.

'Finally, whenever they were around, so also were a large something. It looked more like a large tank, but with a strange shape and strange symbols. How could it just disappear with them whenever they left? Personally, I never saw it leave, but as kids we used to play around the thing. That is what we used to call it, and I always remembered when that area was empty. It always left its three large feet marks on the grass.'

'Feet marks?' Jerry inquired.

'They were from its 3 telescopic feet. Your dad, Donald, was a young air-force officer in those days and seldom around to observe. I thought very little of those experiences until I got a bit older and began to question them and others,' he said.

'My God! What could it have been?' Cathy inquired.

'What others?' asked Miranda with even greater curiosity.

'Well, with the exception of their then boss, Sarah, who was Ben's daughter and the doctor's wife, all the others behaved very strangely. As if they were not from this world. And guys, you should also appreciate that Lord Meron and Doctor Jeffery Longhurst were responsible for the major cures for cancer, robotics and LPD's, short for Linear Progressive Drives. Before those advanced interstellar drives we used jet propulsion. And then, they also designed those powerful Macron Computers and Microid Robots that are now only used by the few largest corporations like Solarian Banking. Why have they and their technologies suddenly disappeared from Earth? Don't you think all those factors to be highly suspicious?'

'In what way?' Jerry was intrigued.

'I once included those facts in one of my programs and fed it into the base strategic computer. I got very strange answers. It also gave the probability of their death within that period to be less than 10 percent.'

'You think they might be still alive?' Jerry inquired.

'I am not sure! The distress signal that was received from your grandfather said there was an explosion in the trash compressor unit. Apparently, that explosion took out a large part of the rear section of the ship, including two of the three drive module control lines, without which the drivers could not be wire controlled. Well, a bomb could have been placed there to go off when the piston began to compress. Even so, that unit is only used when the sensors detect the bin is full and that situation only occurs after several Martian trips, with a full load of passengers.'

'Really?' Cathy inquired.

'Yep, things don't add up. I always sense they are still alive somewhere,' Jerry said.

'Further, it should have been emptied each time the ship docked on Earth. So that fact also poses another question. One more thing. You know as I do, that when there is a break in the wire controls, radio is the next option. But that option, by another strange disastrous stroke of bad luck, did not function. That malfunction caused the ship to dive out of its path into deep space, still under the control of the third module which also went out of control by both wire and radio. Now tell me, does that make any sense to you?'

'I agree. Things don't add up!' George replied.

'Personally, I would like to visit Mars again and have a look through the old service domes. Even some of the Solarians', and do some more detective work to find out what really happened.'

'Pal, I know what you mean. We would like to do that as well,' Jerry said.

'This searching for the truth has become a life long ambition of mine. Don't you think it beats digging for treasure on a dead world?' Andy was in a jovial mood and they were intrigued.

They were completely absorbed by Andy's strange story but at the same time fascinated by the adventure such a trip could bring.

'If you are that keen on adventure, why don't you join us? We have not yet hired a ship, but you are welcomed to come along if you are willing to pay your way and assist in running things. Whatever plans we decide while on Mars, can be voted for democratically and I am sure we can combine both adventures,' Jerry said.

'The Solarian domes are probably still guarded by androids and robots, so we might have to knock out those control centres and services temporarily before we can enter, but without causing too much damage. If only we had the master access key. Then we could pretend to be one of them,' Andy said.

'That might not be too great a problem when a member of the crew is the son of the President and knows some people close to Professor Khan,' Jerry replied.

Andy's eyes lit up, as if his opportunity of a lifetime was finally in sight. He suddenly became very interested in Jerry's adventure and his intrepid gang.

'Guys, don't you worry too much about the rest of your training here. It's already in the bag. Just do your best, so that you can hold your end in an emergency if things go wrong. If you need extra lessons or advice you know where to turn,' Andy said. Then he called the barman.

'Harry, more drinks for my friends, on my slate!' Then he became more positive.

'I am going to make a few inquiries about finding us a ship. I know someone who owes me a big favour,' Andy said enthusiastically. Then he left them and walked out the building.

'What did you make of his strange story?' Miranda inquired.

'It seems to me that something very strange is going on, but I find the alien part difficult to believe. Humans with six fingers, a shady character and a ship with legs that resemble a tank on tripods, although not cylindrical or rectangular?' Barry said sarcastically.

'Wow! We are getting into deep waters here, Guys. I just hope we can pull ourselves out before the monster shows his head?' Ann Baxter commented.

'Dangers or not, I think it's a darn good recipe for an adventure. Think of all the fun we could have, checking a few records in the old central library and searching for clues. Looking through old news journals and historical records of that period and then compiling a dossier on the subject before departing for Mars. We might also collect a few clues about my grandparents whereabouts during the process,' Jerry said enthusiastically.

'I would seriously like to follow up on some of those topics. He gives me the impression of a very study and sane individual. But if what he says is correct... I mean about the six fingers of Meron... I think we might have to do some deep digging.' Miranda said.

'Yea, I agree. That sort of info will not be in any library. It's not what we can find about him. It's more about what we don't find.' Cathy said.

'You are so right! One more thing... I think you should all know that Professor Khan (Ben) is my godfather. I can always get information from him in a roundabout manner. However, I don't think it will be possible before we leave. Anyway, we can still cover some ground if we pull our resources together on this project. We have also got to find out more about their Solarian

Banking organisation,' Jerry added.

'Perhaps I can ask my elder brother for some help in that area. He is now a senior editor for The Times and used to be a reporter, even interviewing Ben on several occasions. Also, there is my mother, she used to be a reporter in those early days and interviewed Meron when she was just a teenage novice with The Daily Star. That was on his first LPD demonstration. It was also her first assignment after that strange President's speech.' Cathy said.

'That's a great lead!' Jerry interrupted.

'She also visited Sarah's house on several occasions. So she can also help us with a background on those people,' Cathy added.

That evening they remained in the mess discussing Andy's strange story while making some more plans for their future adventure to Mars.

They continued their training over the next week and passed their astronaut exams. Finally they decided to celebrate their last day once again in the comfortable air-conditioned mess which had a most pleasant ambience.

They had grown used to that place for their discussions whenever they had the opportunity. Even so, they were unable to use it as frequently as they wanted. On that occasion and to their surprise Andy walked in and joined them.

'Heh, Rob! Drinks all around!' He yelled to the barman. Rob was soon on the way to take their orders.

'I thought I would find you here celebrating your last day in captivity.' He greeted with a broad grin and they smiled with pleasure.

'I would like to apologise for my absence over the past week. I had to do some trouble shooting and was the only experienced guy available. However, I understand everything went ok with you guys.'

'Yea, we did the impossible deed!' Jerry exclaimed.

'I like that! Safety is all important for our trip. Anyway, the long and short of it is, that I have found us a ship. It's nothing fantastic, mind you, but it's sturdy and with not much signs of metal fatigue. All we might have to do is clean her up a little and do some tweaking to the mechanics and electronics.'

'That's fantastic news!' Miranda was ecstatic.

'I would like you, Jerry, to go and see this guy here. His name is Clive. Tell him I sent you. You can look her over while you are there, just to put your minds at ease.'

'Will do!'

'I have another little job to do before I am free to join you guys. So I shall be with you from the eight onwards. I can meet you at the ship on the eight, if that's possible. If you need me before that date, you may contact me at the number circled on the note, but its top security, so keep it safe.'

'I Will!'

'One more thing. Don't tell anyone that you are in anyway related to the President. Some people can use that knowledge against you and your father for political reasons. Others might kidnap you for a ransom. So be extra careful,' he said those words while touching his nose several times.

'Here is some stuff I found about you know what, and this is the address and my number.' He handed Jerry a brown folder and a piece of paper. He then left in a hurry.

'What did you make of that? He seemed so nervous. Do you think he is an Infilate trouble shooter? I mean, tracing down the scum criminal gangs? Well, he is one of us and in uniform. So I think he could be a Special in disguise,' Cathy said.

'Ye! I suppose he could be. In order to work in this place one has to have special security clearance and he told me he was thirty-six. So he could be one of the Specials, paid to track down Infilate extremists, mercilessly. But we are just guessing. Anyway, he is on our side or he wouldn't have mentioned anything about my safety.'

'Why did he mention it? Did he pick something up on the grapevine?' George inquired.

Jerry opened the folder to find an assortment of journal cuttings, computer printouts, two discs and photo copies of Jerry's original notes.

They passed the rest of the day going through his notes and

cuttings, and made arrangements to visit Cathy's mother, the main library and Solarian Banking.

George Peterson decided to take a job within Solarian Banking, with Barry Stenburg and Ann Baxter as outside assistance if needed. He would try to gain entry by deception and once inside attempt to find out more about the organisation that was not freely available to outsiders.

Miranda and Cathy were to visit the main library and Jerry to visit Cathy's mother for more information on Lord Meron and his colleagues.

CHAPTER 6

Cathy's mother

Jerry rang the doorbell and patiently waited for the door to open, but instead a muffled metallic voice responded.

'Please place your right index finger into the slot and wait for a security scan. Be prepared to enter immediately on my signal!
'This door is time locked from the inside. Permission will not be granted a second time, once initiated by its occupant!'

A bleep was heard and the hydraulically operated door suddenly opened to let a single person through and then abruptly closed behind him. As he entered he peeled the close fitting bearded latex mask from his face. It revealed a young man in his mid twenties. He was a lot younger than his former self, but with a wet face from the accumulation of sweat due to his facial covering. He took a large handkerchief from his pocket and continued to wipe the sweat from his face.

'Please excuse me for a moment. I can never get used to these confounded disguises, particularly in hot weather,' Jerry said. She went towards him for a closer observation and at the same time removed her reading glasses.

'You are a handsome devil, so don't be so pedantic! I am sorry about the time-lock arrangement, but it makes me feel a lot more secure. The complete system includes several instantly activated bullet proof shutters on all windows and outer doors.'

'I see! Must be quite difficult living in places like this!'

'Very! Crime is everywhere! I had the extra security fitted a few years ago under the advisement of a good friend. That was after I decided to remain in this unprotected area. My security system has a very sensitive nose that can also detect latex masks. However we knew who it was by your thumb print and DNA.'

'You did? Anyway, as far as I am concerned, this place is too close to the city for comfort,' Jerry replied.

'Well... I always lived here with my husband when he was alive.

Then there were few Infilates. Since the others moved away I had little choice, not wanting to be incarcerated in one of those special buildings, so-called health farms or domes. Nowadays, when living in these parts of the country one has to be extra vigilant with eyes at the back of their heads.'

'I don't think such a place is safe for a known person like you,' Jerry advised, in somewhat worried demeanor.

'I have never fancied living in one of those sealed domes or so-called health farms and Cathy and her friends are not meant to visit me here without proper security clearance. Permanent human guards are too expensive for a modest writer like myself, also on a modest salary.'

'I see!'

'Come and join me in the sitting room!'

Then they went into the main sitting room and both sat next to each other on the large settee.

'So you are my daughter's friend and the President's son. Don't worry, I checked you out on my computer before you arrived and have an image printout of your vital statistics and other details like social habits,' she said. Then she laughed and got up to pour him his favourite drink.

'My daughter tells me you would like to know some personal details on Meron and his associates?' She made herself more comfortable in the leather settee.

'Yes!' he replied.

'It will not be easy. I will show you what I have!'

'That will do. Thanks!'

'Please call me Pam, short for Pamela!'

'As I was saying, Pam, we are planning to go on an adventure trip to Mars and would like to know more about my grandfather's companions, in case we come up with something relevant during our travels.'

'Poor Jerry and all those important people on that faithful day! I will try my best to answer your questions!'

'My father never got over it!' Jerry said.

'After all this time?'

'We have always been a close family. I have always been

interested in my grandparent's disappearance. It's something that I've always had doubts about. One never knows, they might still be alive somewhere out there. The local asteroid miners might have some useful information to add. I know it's a long shot, but I sometimes get the feeling they are still alive.' Jerry said.

'Sounds like a very long shot! Wasn't the area of the explosion thoroughly searched after the tragedy?' she inquired.

'I don't think so. Not a single body was found. We also want to know more about Solarian Banking and the people who run it. That's because they used to be associated with that organisation.'

'You ask for a lot, Jerry, son of our President. I shall try to assist you as best I can.'

'Thanks! Anything can be helpful!'

'Well... let's start at the beginning. The first time I met Lord Meron was on my first assignment as a reporter for The Daily Star. That was at the first LPD demonstration, just after the controversial President's speech. That speech, you know, rocked the world at the time. I think I might still have a transcript of it somewhere.'

'Don't worry, it will all be returned by special messenger. Please, go on!'

'Anyway, after that first meeting, I decided to write an article on new technologies and used to visit them at their beautiful residence in North Dakota. During that time Lord Meron was quite helpful and probably the most royal and dignified person I've ever met.'

'Sounds like he was a great guy?'

'They were the greatest! During that time I got on very well with Sarah, but also collected bits and pieces for my journal from her regarding her charitable organizations. That time I was in my late teens and keen for a scoop to make my name in the business. Because of them I had several scoops, including her kidnapping by guerillas in South America. Anyway, that was before Sarah became their president. After that time she was seldom around and whenever I phoned, the helpers and Madeline would always say she was out. Even then, whenever she returned, which became more infrequent, she would always call me for dinner by way of an apology.'

'Nice lady! Please continue!'

'She changed a lot during the intervening years. That was from when I first knew her to the time they got lost in space. She also gained a lot more in importance. I suppose it was because their company was now a multi billion dollar empire. So she became more of an empress than a company president. She was also a very clever woman, almost like she could see into the innermost soul of the individual and that was one of her unique qualities. But despite that aspect, she was an incredible human being and would have done almost anything for the survival of all endangered species. All of her friends shared her views, but they viewed those issues on a more cosmic scale.'

'In a way like us in the gang. What did you think of Lord Meron?' he asked.

'Lord Meron was a clever scientist. Very tall and handsome, just over two metres, with golden hair and the most beautiful sea-blue eyes you ever saw. He, your grand father and Doctor Jeffery Longhurst, Sarah's husband, got on very well together. He was the type to get on well with anyone. A most polite and pleasant man.'

'So I heard! Like nobility!'

'Very much so! He assisted the President a lot in those early days and remained one of his closest friends. They used to visit Mars quite frequently in those days, particularly while the domes were being built. That was, after your grandfather, the then President, donated the special shuttle for their joint space adventures.'

'Really? Space adventures to where?'

'Mainly to the Moon and Mars. Your grandfather took to space adventure like fish to water. In much the same way as other Presidents liked yachting and golf. He would have pulled several strings in order to acquire that shuttle craft for their so-called demonstration trips to the Moon and Mars. I know for a fact that those demos never took place. They just used it for their own entertainment and space cruising.'

'I can well imagine! Sounds very cool to me!'

'It was one of those large space shuttles, but they soon had it converted as a luxurious passenger liner. He added many refinements himself, including a small casino and bar. But they never liked playing for big money, although they enjoyed the occasional drink.' She removed an old album from a wall locker and began to search its pages. It was in the form of an electronic tablet.

'Mainly Vodka and tonic!' he replied.

'Here are some old colour photos of Lord Joel Meron and some of the others.' she said, as he took the synthetic paper copies from her.

'Here is Meron and his friends. Have a glance through those few pages while I visit my study for some more information that I prepared earlier.' She left him for a while and soon returned with a blue folder and again sat next to him.

'With the exception of Jerry and his wife - I mean your granddad - all the others lived with Sarah at her country manor in North Dakota. In those days Professor Khan was seldom around, but here is a photograph of him. It was given to me by Sarah.' She slowly changed the pages for more interesting photos.

'But the professor doesn't look any different today. How old do you think he was then?' Jerry asked.

'I would say about fifty when that picture was taken.'

'And how long ago was that?'

'Let me see... that was before he and Sarah first arrived at the house. I was going on eighteen then... Oh, how time flies. It's from... just before the President's speech. About fifty years ago now. Perhaps closer to forty-nine,' she said.

'You are telling me that he is about ninety-eight, but he looks just fifty today. How do you think he is able to remain so young?'

'He is another one of those clever scientists. Perhaps he uses special rejuvenation drugs. I don't know. Why don't you ask him?' she replied.

'Stranger and stranger!'

'In those days Professor Khan was just like you, my daughter and the rest of your gang. All keen ecologists fighting for the natural order. You know, at that time he was never interested in financial matters and least of all, banking. Come to think of it, he doesn't even now. Even so, he took over the business after their final trip to Mars. Now that is peculiar? I always had the distinct impression that he cared a lot more for the environment and people than financial matters and he was always so highly religious.'

'The richest man on the planet does not like money? Now that is very suspicious!'

'Now he is the only one with Terminal Drug rights on the planet. You know, it is said that he was the one to formulate the antidote drug. It got him a Nobel Prise. Thank goodness he did it for all our sakes.' she replied.

'Yea, I'm sure the poor Infilates wont agree with you. And what about Mickey Cockburn?'

'He was once your grand father's scientific advisor, you know. That was before Harry Lennox and Professor John LaRoche. He was later assigned to Jeffery Longhurst and then Meron. He managed the LPD developments and assisted Meron during my first assignment. I remember that day quite vividly.'

'Yea.. I read about that prototype demo in school! I wish I was alive back then. Must have been a turning point in human history,' Jerry replied.

'It was the best period of my life. I think Professor Khan made Mickey their vice president because he just couldn't find anyone trustworthy enough for that position. Further, they knew each other quite well at the time.'

'I see!

'Are you taking all this down?' she advised.

'Yea!' He retrieved a miniature digital recorder from his inside pocket. It was the size of a fountain pen and could also be used for writing.

'Two captains with little knowledge of steering the ship and yet the ship successfully steers itself,' Jerry mumbled to himself.

'Well, they owned the patent rights on many important products including LPD drives, anti-cancer serum, the Anti-Terminal and other drugs. There was also Micro Robotics and a host of other items. They constantly drew rich dividends by way of royalties, even from very powerful governments like the USA and USE,' she replied.

'Can you remember anything about Meron's hands? Someone

told me he had six fingers?'.

'No... I don't think so? He always wore beautiful silken gloves and was always particular about hygiene. Thinking about it now... he and the other five eldest members of his group always wore gloves. They also had beautiful golden hair and penetrating sea-blue eyes... but all wore gloves, with the exception of Plato who mostly wore a black robe like a priest. He never cared about anything... but there was another like him... also with a black robe called Lumak. Lumak had eight fingers like us and Plato only six. I thought nothing of it at the time, but now.... The younger group were like Latins... more like Miranda's complexion with dark brown hair and brown eyes, also with eight fingers like us.'

'Quite a mixed lot! So they were two different groups?'

'Yes! Parents and children!'

'Why so different, then?'

'I don't know!'

'Another very suspicious situation!' Jerry commented.

'You know, I once met a native Bermudan with ten fingers and two thumbs, so I must have assumed such variations to be natural phenomena due to a simple genetic disorder. Anyway, I have several more photographs on them which I personally developed and kept for sentimental reasons. You may take them away and have them copied, but I want all my originals back!' she insisted.

'Don't worry about any items on loan. I shall have them returned to you within a week or so, and with extra copies. If you wish any enlarged or framed, just let me know.'

'So you are also taking my daughter along to Mars, on your adventures? Is that trip going to be a safe one, Jerry?' she asked, with concern in her voice.

'I think so. We have just come back from a most intensive astronaut training course. That was because my father thinks in the same way as you. We are also taking along a trained astronaut who lived for five years on Mars. Everything will be checked out most thoroughly before we leave and if I have any doubts we will simply abort the mission. So don't you worry. Anyway, these days it's even safer than sailing a yacht across to the Bahamas from Florida and we are going to take lots of supplies including medicinal drugs on board.'

'Keep an eye on her for me, will you?' she asked, concernedly. Despite her worries regarding their Martian escapade, it was much better than fighting for people's rights with so many mad and dangerous Infilates about.

'Don't worry about a thing. I promise to keep an eye on her for you and I will!'

'Please stay for dinner. It must be almost ready and I will appreciate the company,' she pleaded and took him through to the dining room. On entering she pressed a small button close to the main table and before long her call was answered. A robot sluggishly strolled in wearing an apron. That one was shaped more like a human, although without fleshy plastic on its metallic bones.

'Madam, dinner is now ready. What is your choice of salad and drink?' the robot asked in a somewhat metallic voice.

'Mec, please make it numbers three and seven, in that order.' Mec made a mental note and went towards the kitchen.

'Mec was given to me by Sarah and Jeffery. He was one of their demonstration models before they changed the design. You can say I rescued him from the scrap heap. He is nuclear powered and self repairing. He is like family and very inexpensive to keep. All he needs sometimes is a good book to read and the occasional greasing of those well-used joints. You know, he has his own room and privacy, but those privileges were earned by hard work. He is also a good guard dog and will not allow anyone in here without prior permission.'

'Yea... some guard dog. I wouldn't like to see him in a bad mood!' Jerry was apprehensive.

'Jerry, I am now in the process of writing an article for The Times. It's on the topic of our development, gains and losses over the past fifty years. In particular, changes brought about by the Terminal Disease and great inventions like the LPD drives. However, during my research I found that almost every part of our society today is strangely dependant on those few people that we have been discussing all this time. It's almost as if our whole human society is still being controlled by them, from the

Terminal Drug, to their LPD's.'

'Go on!'

'They control our lifespan and population growth with drugs, our travel by the LPD's and industry by their strange robots. Many of which are no longer serviceable.'

'So?'

'Jerry, there is just one more thing. Did you know, that our human society has been restricted to a new limit of about five hundred million? This figure also happens to be the optimum sustainable human population for our planet at this moment in time, with its present limited resources and shrinking environments due to Global Warming and rising sea levels.'

'You think we are being controlled? You mean some type of conspiracy against humanity?

'No, but they still control our lifespan and population growth with drugs, our travel by LPDs and industry by their strange robots. Many of which are no longer serviceable. With no fossil fuels left, humanity could never survive as it did in the past. Luckily for us Infilates are dying like flies!'

'You think they are also responsible for that?'

'I'm not sure! Jerry, there is one more thing. Did you know that the Terminal Disease was found a few years after they disappeared in that supposed accident in space? Further, Khan is the only one with powers to administer the drug that keeps those five hundred million alive, while the others die off naturally. That figure just happens to be the optimum sustainable human population for Earth at this time. I don't know, but the more I research those aspects of our survival, the more I begin to think that it was all planned many years ago. I mean, to make us useless as a species or even to weaken us. But I don't know why,' she stressed.

'You are talking about a real conspiracy here!'

'Please keep all this information under your hat for now, because if word of it was to get into the wrong hands... and that part I shall not even mention in my article,' she said.

'Wow! That will make a great story if you are right. It's like a major conspiracy that's taking place right under our very noses and we can't even see the plot.' He jotted down some notes in his notepad.

'I still have lots more researching to do before I finish the article. If you like, I can get more historical information for you on that period, during my searches. Perhaps even turn up information on Solarian Banking and Professor Khan. However, I can't make any promises, as I have a tight schedule to meet. Perhaps there will be more after you return from your holidays and my article is in print.'

'Please do what you can. The more, the merrier!' he said using one of George's British phrases.

'Jerry, I now think that you know a lot more than you originally led me to believe, but I see the need for secrecy on your part,' she said with even greater enthusiasm.

'I knew a little before I came here, but now you've given me enough to put a few puzzles together and ask a lot more questions,' he replied.

After dinner, she took him towards the rear of the house to show him her tropical greenhouse. It was mainly driven by hydroponics. That was where she grew many special medicinal herbs, flowers and plants, including several rear tropical species.

'I take great care with these plants because they might be the last on the planet. I also have shares in a large environmental dome in South America that protects the most endangered species,' she said. Jerry was sadly disappointed by that knowledge, but knew he and his group could do very little to save such life from extinction or extend the survival of those endangered species. It was already too late, or so he thought.

CHAPTER 7

At the old city library

Miranda and Cathy had decided to pay the main city library a visit, and just getting there was a daunting task. The girls had to disguise themselves as elderly city natives which took a lot of time and effort. Despite the time taken to fit the necessary latex masks, additional makeup and clothes, they thought the experience a challenge.

Both women had to spend the best part of one hour, adjusting and applying makeup to those previously moulded masks. Once completed they gave them the appearance of women thirty years their elder. After that operation was completed, they had to wear the appropriate shoes, tights and clothes to match their adopted aged personalities, preferably with a more matured voice when acting the part. Infilates occupied all main cities which had become dangerous places for the Fertilate young. So they had to prepare well for that visit.

'How do I loo..k, grand children?' Miranda inquired in jest and little three year old Maria ran crying to her mother.

'What's the matter, Darling?' She inquired.

'It's the old woman! She wants to take me away!' An upset Maria replied.

'It's only Aunty Miranda in her special makeup!' she yelled and little Maria stopped her fretting.

Cathy, in a similar outfit complemented Miranda.

'You look so beau..ti..ful for a 60 year old.'

'You both look good for old women in 20 year old bodies! No one can ever fault those disguises,' Joan said.

When they were finished with their disguises, to all intents and purpose were completely different people. Then they had to make their new identities known to local friends and security personnel by certain body attachments like earrings, handbag and hair clips. Mobile devices could not be used.

They, like so many other Fertilates on Earth, also carried

separate identity cards whenever they visited predominantly occupied Infilate city areas. They had much practise from the use of those deceptive measures since school days. Most Fertilate young people were given such facial kits by their parents as birthday presents when they thought they were ready to venture out by themselves, although usually in small groups.

The masks were tight fitting and added extra crinkles and muscles to facial features, including realistically painted blood vessels, moulds, skin texture and colouration. The only drawback was the accumulation of sweat on warm days and the itching of captured hairs from strained follicles. There was also the not always precise transmission of facial expression.

Once in disguise they could visit many places without being harassed by dangerous people and over zealous police officers.

At that time most of the remaining city centres were considered the preserves of Infilates and they considered those areas to be their territories.

The women caught the guarded metro subway to the old city library and entered the reference section which occupied the ground floor of the five-story building. Since most of the elevators and walkways were out of commission they had to visit those areas on foot. On arrival they handed their special passes to the door security and were allowed in the building.

'Thank goodness, we are in. I hope this doesn't take too long?' Miranda said.

'And I hope we have no encounters with city police?' Cathy replied, nervously. At that time city police tended to stop everyone on the streets to know their whereabouts and she was worried their false papers would not stand up to close scrutiny.

On entry into the library they plugged their personal portable computers into the main library computer and began to browse through some relevant data files. The moment they started there was an enormous bang, to be followed by a sudden change in air pressure which momentarily inhibited their hearing.

'My God! What was that?' Cathy yelled and they both started towards the main exit.

After the large explosion had quietened and they recovered their hearing, they could hear several gunshots, to be followed by police sirens. They wondered what had happened and decided to leave the building, but the security doors automatically shut to prevent anyone from entering or leaving.

The chief librarian voice soon came over the intercom.

'We regret any inconvenience caused to our visitors, but this security measure has been taken for your own safety. The doors will be reopened after we are given the all-clear by security. So please continue business as usual until the police arrive.'

After another fifteen minutes the large door opened and a guard walked in.

'Sorry, but we would like you to clear this building immediately. That is, after I have checked your credentials. A complete check is to be made of those in this area, so please come forward. I am sure we'll find no bombs or infidels in here!' he said.

'What's going on?' A disturbed Miranda inquired.

'They just had a go at the Solarian Bank, but the damage was only superficial. Our special forces took out two of their guys, with no casualties on our side and one of theirs went up with the bomb.' The queue remained silent.

'More Infilate trouble!' Cathy was not pleased.

'Now, let's please follow in an orderly manner and clear this area,' the officer insisted, as he began to check their cards which he inserted into his small Coms unit.

'These rebels are everywhere! So please hurry, we close in one hour!' the chief librarian shouted.

When the nervous girls handed him their cards, he stared at them for a while before observing the information on his screen. Then he asked them to wait on one side. Miranda and Cathy became even more bewildered with expectations of the worst interrogation to follow. Although that type of disguise was legal, it was usually frowned upon, since most suspicious persons and criminals also used similar evasive measures.

After everyone had left the area a more senior officer wearing a different uniform and computerised headgear appeared on the scene. Then both girls were taken into one of the local reading rooms for questioning.

'Is everything in order here!' he yelled through his communicator.

'Yes commander. Just these two to process. They appear to hold false IDs!' the officer replied. Then his senior took over the questioning.

'You are twenty-one and you twenty-three!' He inquired. Pointing his finger to each in turn.

'Yes, Sir!' Miranda replied.

'That's according to our checks with your security number on these cards. If those facts are correct, you must both be suffering from some type of degenerative illness. Because, you both appear well over fifty to me and my colleagues as the day is long. However, you could be wearing an age-mask for purposes of disguise?'

'We could be, Sir?' Cathy replied nervously. She realized they were already in deep trouble, so why prolong the agony.

'There is just a small problem with this info. I don't know which of those facts are correct and I'm not allowed to pull them off your faces. For all I know, you could be disguised members of the saboteurs.'

'We are not! We could never be such scum!' Cathy was inflamed by his previous words.

'Tell you what I shall do... give me a saliva sample by licking this slide and we can compare your G-Code with HQ files,' the officer said.

The girls did not wish to argue and get themselves any deeper into the already hot soup they were in, so they did as he asked. He entered the slides into another piece of equipment that communicated with head office and the chief officer suddenly changed his aggressive attitude towards them and became as calm as a lamb.

'Miranda and Cathy are now free to leave. Don't forget the eight!' Andy yelled as he hurried from the building.

'Yes, Commander!' a happy Miranda shouted back.

The girls were so surprised; for the person under the security visor was none other than Commander Andy Colman. He couldn't have given anything away to his companions for security reasons.

Jerry got back to the apartment later that day and when the girls told him of their ordeal he was even more surprised that Andy was on that mission. Their unwarranted doubts about Andy being an undercover enforcer had been substantiated.

'Dam it! I never realized he was also a commander in the Specials. That's about the highest level in the military, under the President!' Jerry said.

'Good thing we have him on our side!' Cathy replied.

'Perhaps it all happened for the best. I now have some real information to follow up from Cathy's mother, including some great photos. So we can spend the rest of this evening going over what I brought back. By ten we can venture downstairs to our favourite restaurant where I can treat you both to a late dinner of your choosing. That is, if you don't mind,' Jerry said.

'That sounds cool!' Miranda replied and Cathy nodded her approval.

The girls did not argue and separated their tasks.

After they had finished their search, Jerry made out a more relevant list for their visit to the library the following day. Hopefully this time there would be no interruptions to their plans.

'Find out when people first got to know of the Terminal Disease and whether Professor Khan was involved in administering the Anti Drug before that time. Then you can find me records of the parents, grand parents and great grand parents of the people on this list.... Finally, check if there were UFO sightings within the areas I have circled on this map.'

'You ask a lot,' Miranda said, remembering the recent explosion and following delays.

'I think that's enough for you to be getting on with for now, while I visit another person on my list.... I wonder how George and the others are getting on with Solarian Banking?' Jerry said, not expecting an immediate answer.

'None of us heard from him. I hope he is ok?' Cathy showed great concern but realized it was early days.

Once again, the girls prepared themselves and were on their way to the library.

That day they were quite nervous and took an expensive LPD cab that landed on the roof of the library. That building consisted of just five floors. Each spread over a large area and included main topics like: Reference for local activities. Flight Schedules, Tourism, Genealogy with important names and addresses; Records, for marriages, births, deaths, companies, et cetera; Historical, for all such information; Technical, which included documentation, blueprints and patents; Fictional, as in novels and most religious literature.

This time they went directly to the first floor and plugged their tablet computers into one of the main terminals that they had pre-booked the previous day. First of all, Miranda decided to check the hereditary of the people on Jerry's list, while Cathy probed for some more relevant data. After that, they would visit the second floor to check on Professor Khan (Ben's) involvement in the Anti-drugs for the Terminal Virus. Whether it was supplied or administered before or after knowledge of the Terminal Disease was available.

The latter was better carried out on the Historical Floor, as that section also contained all the past periodical journals and newspapers. However, some searches were required on the Technical Floor. It was necessary for more precise data on the drug's manufacture and distribution. That was, if the computer was asked the relevant questions needed for a more thorough search through its memory banks.

Both women soon got the knack of keyboard entry. Miranda began with Lord Meron. Vocal entry was not allowed in the library.

NAME OF ITEM SEARCHED: Lord Joel Meron
ADDRESS OF ITEM SEARCHED: The River Manor, ...
INFORMATION DATES, PARAMETERS: Tenth Oct...
Fifteenth Sept...

FURTHER RELEVANT FACTORS, TO AID SEARCH:
Name of parents? Grand parents? Great grand parents?

Invented LPD Drives. Knew President Gerald Fraser....

The intelligent computer soon began to display data on Meron. It was then easy to cross-refer the displayed information to his family members, colleagues and friends.

The six youngest members were in fact the children of the eldest six. Jon was entered as Meron's son, Lira as Lucia's daughter, Merol as Tomas's son, Ecrol as Hamil's son, Petra as Sintra's daughter and Julia as Merian's daughter. But the strange data did not end there. When she asked the computer for data on Meron's grand parents the line of information abruptly ended and simply read:

'INFORMATION NOT AVAILABLE.'

She tried many other data combinations, but the information still read the same. It was as if those people never existed, and it was not just Meron. That information also applied to all of thirteen members, since their histories were interrelated.

Sarah, Jeffery and Ben's family records only went back two generations and could not be proven. Although citizens of the USA, they were originally from Turkey and checks could only be made through the Turkish embassy or directly from that country. Even so, there was no information on Lumak, and Plato was listed as Meron's younger brother with a similar lack of ancestral records. Another disturbing fact was that all of them, with the exception of Sarah and Jeffery, were listed as unmarried at that time.

Cathy also received surprising information on her computer terminal. Ben's humanitarian organisation had been established worldwide and was run as a separate part of Solarian Banking. That organisation was also supplying the Antidote Drug many years before the deadly bacteria was even discussed. Further to that information, the Terminal Disease was discovered by none other than Professor Bengizara Khan (Ben) himself, some time after the treatment was started in Japan and some areas of Africa. After that time knowledge of the Terminal disease was released to the press by a person or persons unknown. Andy Colman's father was also involved at that time in the antidote distribution.

It was also common knowledge that some of the people involved and other families known to the group in question, were given the drug initially. So how could they have known of the impending problem several months, even years before it was discovered?

Police files also showed a more than average level of young disappearances associated with Solarian Banking. Most of those people simply vanished from the face of the Earth after they officially left the bank, thus clearing the bank from any further investigation. Although many of their parents complained about their children's disappearance, little consolation could be given. In any case the police could not pursue those cases, as the people concerned were over eighteen years old and officially independents.

The girls soon got together for lunch within a quiet library area to discuss those questions before calling a cab for their journey back to Jerry's apartment.

CHAPTER 8

Within Solarian Banking

George Peterson walked down the apparently endless corridor, while observing the blue directional arrows that guided him towards the reception area. He turned right at the very end and entered the room marked Personnel Recruitment Services. There he sat with three others and awaited his turn to be called.

'Next... Mr George Peterson!' A male voice yelled.

'Please sit, Mr... Peterson,' the senior officer said while glancing through the form.

'You would like to work for us on a permanent basis?'

'If possible?'

'An English accent! By the way, I am Anthony,' he stretched his hand forward and firmly shook George's.

'Yes, Sir. I am a very close friend of Jerry... The President's son and had heard on the grapevine that you always have vacancies for keen and enthusiastic young people, including MIT post graduates like myself.' George thought a little namedropping could only assist in gaining entry through the door.'

'Yes! Always!'

'These files also include my current CV and other important credentials,' George said. Then handed his own folder over to Anthony who took it and began to scan each page in quick succession. Then he gave the folder to one of his assistants and she disappeared into another office. She promptly returned with the original folder and two cups of coffee.

'Personally, I hate the coffee from those God forsaken machines. Never taste like proper Espresso,' Anthony said, while viewing the small screen towards his left.

'I see here that you have been arrested a few times while defending underdogs and harassing politicians about environmental issues, but nothing stuck. I suppose due to friends in high places. So you are one of those infamous Gang of Earth's Children?'

'Yes! I am happy to say!' he replied.

'You are indeed a very keen and enthusiastic young man and with quite a remarkable history.' Anthony became enthusiastic as if agreeing with the gangs past efforts.

George almost fell out of his chair and choked on that mouthful of coffee when he heard those words. There was no mention in his file of his more reckless escapades, and knowledge of his gang membership had always been kept a well-guarded secret from those organisations. Only his close friends knew and his photo was not yet in any newspaper, or so he thought.

'You are worried that I am able to gather those facts about you?' an intuitive Anthony added, sarcastically.

'No! Not worried. More surprised... because we always try to keep those details away from public knowledge for obvious security reasons,' George replied, still very nervous. Although some of the gang's members didn't mind exposure to the mass media, he always worked in the background as backup.

'You should not worry, my friend.'

'I will try not to!'

'We have that kind of information on every individual on Earth, via our Macron Computers. They are capable of storing every individual grain of sand on the planet, with their individual characteristics if we so desired.'

'Really?'

'Really! George, that's the power of our technology... the organisation that you would like to work for?' Anthony said, full of pride in his efforts.

'As you have observed, my past experiences are mainly of a technical nature. I have little experience in banking. I hoped you would have areas in your large organisation that require young people with my expertise. If not, perhaps I am in the wrong place.' George said, while glancing at the door for a quick exit.

'No! Not necessarily! We always have technical vacancies for capable persons like yourself and I am sure you could fit any of those positions with your qualifications and experience, coming from MIT... But I shall have to arrange another interview, with your permission of course.... This time, with our technical personnel side, and don't worry, everyone comes here at the start. However, if it pleases you, your record came through with flying colours. You are the type of person that we recommend and prefer to enlist in our organisation.'

'Are you sure?'

'Yes! I am very sure! Can you make it for early next week?' Anthony inquired.

'Yes please... Anthony. Consider me available at anytime, even at short notice, given enough time to get ready and make the trip,' George replied, eagerly. Originally thinking that he had made a mess of things.

'That's what I like to hear. I shall arrange everything personally and contact you on Monday. At that time you will be informed of the new address. Also, we shall reimburse you then for all travelling expenses and your time.'

Anthony then got up and walked George out of the office while dictating the way to a local elevator.

As Anthony had promised, the phone rang on Monday morning.

'George? I have some good news for you. Everything has been arranged, but the supervisor wants to check you over personally before she can accept you. It's just a formality. Can you be there at ten a.m., tomorrow?'

'Yes!' uttered George, excitedly.

'In that case, switch your Coms on to receive the coded information and I must stress that you keep it all between us for now.'

'Will do!'

George had received the printed information which the machine decoded in English. To him the bait was truly set in gaining entry to Solarian Banking. But deeply within his mind he wondered whether he was instead their bait for an even larger trap set to catch him.

The office he visited was just fifteen kilometres from his home and not situated within a Solarian Banking building as he had expected. It was instead within an old unmarked building that was in the stages of demolition. Most of the buildings within that Inflate area had already been demolished and others cleared for demolition.

That was now one of the most serious problems in and around many large Earth cities that remained unsubmerged. As the population death rate increased, so also did many buildings become surplus to requirement. Such empty buildings were soon taken over by criminals, vagrants and other unsavoury individuals. Therefore it was illegal for any building to remain empty from its original occupants for more than six months. If unoccupied over that period a None-Retrievable Demolition Order would be issued to the over enthusiastic demolition gangs. They were always keen, since they could retrieve items of high value and made money from the reclaimed steel and other useful salvaged materials that was presently in high demand. That demand was generated by the building of new cities at higher level.

George carefully checked the street numbers and eventually found himself in front of number one thousand and ten. When he entered the almost empty building, the uncarpeted floorboards creaked. He was soon greeted by a young woman with golden hair and sea-blue eyes. She was like no one he had ever met before and was wearing a grey uniform with a small broach and winged insignia pinned to her lapel.

'Please come in!'

'I suppose I am at the right place?' he inquired.

'You could be! My name is Joan and you are?'

'I am George Peterson. I think you are expecting me!'

'In that case, you are expected!'

'Are you from Solarian Banking?' he replied and she nodded positively.

'Please excuse the condition of this place, but it has served us well in the past, and now this complete area is to be demolished and resurfaced. Soon it will be all gone!'

'Yes, all gone!' he replied with sadness.

'These checks will include a short psychoanalysis, so I would like you to relax and answer my questions to the point and without hesitation, if you can?' She opened a small metallic case and retrieved several small blocks, including an expandable display screen. Those items she placed on an old desk. Then she went over to George and placed a jewelled band around his head.

'Is it a comfortable fit? It will automatically adjust itself to your size. Shall we begin?'

While she said those words, he nodded each time in approval, although now utterly confused by the alien technology about him. When she switched on the equipment with her mind, everything on the desk came alive. The blocks began to blink and the display automatically grew to a much larger screen size with strange moving three-dimensional characters.

'Your name is George....'

'Yes!'

'You are Fertilate and have been maintained that way since birth through constant medication?'

'I have!'

'You are an engineer, originally from MIT....'

'Yes!

'You are age, twenty-one....'

'Soon to be!'

'Your parents are... and....'

'Yes!'

'You are the young Gerald Fraser's friend....'

'I am!'

'That's enough for now,' she said and broke off the questioning.

While she asked those questions he nodded his head and could observe the lights and screen alter with each change in his mood and thought pattern. Suddenly the screen and other equipment went dead as if preventing her from searching deeper into his past.

'A security block!' she murmured and hesitated for a while.

'You have been given an incredibly high success score by my equipment.' She could not fully believe the score herself.

Then she went over to remove the headband.

'We could have asked you other questions like 'are you a spy', et cetera, but such questions are not relevant to our tests, which are designed to detect other more important and subtler qualities.'

'I see!' An innocent George replied.

'From these tests you appear to be a... very bright and well-balanced individual, so we shall not waste any more time at this juncture on any necessary medical tests. But instead, I shall carry on with more relevant questions.'

'Really?' George responded.

'I will now like to discuss the nature of your assignment and should you be interested, we shall continue to the next stage and final interview.' Then she carried on as a matter of course.

'Final interview?' George was surprised and was not in any mood for more interviews.

'You have obviously heard of space mining on Mars and on certain areas within the Asteroid Belt. Well, we also mine in areas beyond this solar system, in neighbouring stellar systems contained in this galactic spiral arm, as you can see on this screen. So whatever contracts and agreements we sign will be for a minimum of five years.' He couldn't believe his eyes, for that part of the screen was filled with numerous stellar systems. They were marked with blue crosses. It was then that he realized he was dealing with an organization that expanded throughout the complete galaxy. But she continued.

'Wherever you are assigned, you will find that world to be a paradise compared to our present planet, Earth. However, we pray that one day, within the not too distant future, Earth will again return to her former glory.'

George thought he was being set up by Solarian Banking for a major fall. After all, how could anyone travel to such distant worlds, even with the most modern LPD craft. He continued to listen to the most beautiful woman with golden hair and sea-blue eyes as if in a trance.

'On whichever world you visit, you'll find many people of your own age. With greater freedom of choice, more affective law and order and much more advanced technologies in every field imaginable. Should you accept a posting, you will initially be sent to Mars for training as a Production Supervisor. This position includes travelling to distant worlds to ensure our robotic production plants run smoothly. It also includes a certain amount of military training. We like to know that our people can hold their own in any emergencies. After the final tests, you can stay on as long as you like or return at any time you wish.'

'It all sounds incredible!'

'There is just one more aspect that you should consider however.... In any event, you must not tell your parents or guardians that you intend to go into outer-space. They will become quite worried for your safety and attempt to deter you. This is because of all the anti-space exploration propaganda to which they have been conditioned over the years. However, we can always arrange the occasional visit to Earth via Sol-Newtown. From there you may visit all your friends and family.'

'Suits me, but would like to visit frequently!'

'If you like, you could tell them that you will be based on Mars, which is not too remote from the truth and we can arrange your papers to show that you are assigned to that world. Anyway, think about what I have said for now and let me know of your decision in two days. Believe me, it will be your greatest adventure. I have not seen anyone who seriously wanted to return to Earth once having had a real taste of the more beautiful and fulfilling existence, with virtually no crime or problems of any sort,' she said.

To all those questions and information he nodded his head in almost complete disbelief of present circumstances. Once more, she carefully placed the items back into the metallic case and handed him a beautiful golden watch.

'Why don't you accept this gift as a token from our esteemed organisation, for your efforts in these interviews? We give them to our best applicants, you know.'

'Thanks, very much!' He couldn't stop staring at her hypnotising eyes.

'Anthony will contact you in two days time in order to arrange your final interview. But now, please let me escort you to the local exit,' she said most politely.

While he walked out of that building, many things went through his mind. He couldn't remove the strange and highly advanced technology from his thoughts. Then he carefully observed the watch, checked its weight several times and realized it was pure solid gold.

'Bloody hell! What have I got myself into here. It's not anything like I expected. Could there be another very advanced human race that look exactly like us in this galaxy?' he thought.

Despite his original concerns he soon concluded that the organization involved was not of the criminal type. Nevertheless, he had become fully aware of a much more advanced organization with indescribable technologies and possible galactic civilisations working separate to those on Earth. Perhaps by now, even galactic in scope, with Earth considered a mere fly in the ointment.

CHAPTER 9

Dinner among friends

That evening George phoned Barry and Ann to tell them about his interview and of his intentions to visit Jerry's apartment which was situated in an adjacent building to his own.

'I have been through a lot over the past two days, so tell Jerry to expect me for dinner today. Some more business... Got to go!' George was in a hurry.

They agreed to visit and share any developments from their searches over the previous days. Therefore, Jerry decided to help the girls cook a meal and ordered some drinks.

He called the local supermarket and read out a list and they arranged delivery for his urgent order of groceries and other essentials. Those orders were usually made via the shopping program on his Coms. However the fridge was also programmed to order when items got low. There was also a device on the door of the fridge for placing such orders automatically. That was when its contents on a particular item was below acceptable limits. All those factors could be programmed in the fridge computer. There were also similar devices for cupboards and other storage enclosures.

When George entered that evening, Jerry greeted him enthusiastically.

'You seem quite pleased with yourself! You must have had some success. Come and join me for a drink! The women are busy in the kitchen cooking us another meal. Today I helped them fill my almost empty cupboards with groceries. Makes a pleasant change from take-aways and our nightly trips to the local restaurant. I've never been any good at cooking. No patience for that sort of thing, but the girls enjoy practising their recipes until they get them right.'

'I am also a lousy cook!' George replied.

'I just hope and pray, it's not going to be another one of those old tasteless recipe experiments. Anyway, I made sure we had enough drinks to compensate for any mishaps in that direction,'

Jerry said, while pouring them both a drink.

'Let me show you something,' George said, as he removed the golden watch from his wrist.

'It's very heavy and looks extremely expensive. It can't be what I think it is!'

'What do you think it is?'

'Is it... a present from your British mother?' Jerry asked, portraying an expression of awe.

'No! I was given it... by my interviewer today. They give them to most of their chosen applicants.'

'Your interviewer in Solarian Banking gave you this?'

'What do you think about that?' George said.

'I don't know what to think. Judging from its weight and design it must be worth at least fifty thousand dollars, even though, it's not a well-known make. I wonder what the winged crest and blue circle signify... and the other strange symbols mean?'

'Yep! I wondered about those myself and wish I knew!'

'Most people would willingly give their lives for that kind of money and yet they give such presents away, as if gold meant very little to them!' Jerry exclaimed, while carefully checking the beautiful item.

'I have a theory on that subject and want you all to here me out. That is, after dinner. When we are all sitting together. After then, you can tell us your side of the story and your discoveries through the old city library,' George replied.

The door bell rang and Jerry communicated with Barry and Ann before electronically releasing the latch via his Coms. When they entered, he greeted them and went to pour them a drink.

Miranda and Cathy soon entered the room to greet the others while wearing aprons and glanced at the very expensive watch now lying on the table.

'Guys, this is part of my donation towards our trip to Mars,' George said, jokingly. But Jerry immediately cut in.

'George has had some success infiltrating Solarian Banking. This watch was given to him by his interviewer today and he has been accepted by a branch... dealing with.... I am not sure what?'

'Yep! I am on my way in!'

'What is your position and function in that large organisation?' Jerry inquired, with a hint of jealousy in his voice, but with little desire in losing one of his closest friends.

'I still have one more interview, but I think it's for a Production Supervisor. The position includes visiting distant production worlds within this galactic arm. I suppose a kind of interstellar trouble shooter. Well, that was what the beautiful female officer told me. Mind you, what I say must go no further. They have a thing about security,' George said in jest.

He almost did not believe the words he had just uttered. But he did put smiles on the cheeks of his friends including Jerry, and that more than made up for any misunderstandings.

The girls had finally finished cooking and prepared the small table which just managed to sit all six, with flaps pulled out.

'It's an Indian vegetarian dish called Mec Biriani. One of our cook's first curry experiments. We found it so enjoyable that we copied the recipe in one of my mother's famous recipe books. It's prepared from beans, vegetables and special herbs. With rice of course, also prepared in a special way. I hope it's not too hot and spicy to spoil your enjoyment,' Cathy said.

'You don't mean it was put together by your house robot by the same name?' Jerry exclaimed.

'The same. He is a brilliant cook. He could have been originally programmed as a chef,' Cathy replied.

The other members just couldn't stop asking George about his famous interview and the expensive watch. After he had discussed every intricate detail, they couldn't help being astonished by their methods and technologies.

'Well ladies, what do we have for afters?' shouted Jerry.

'Vanilla ice-cream, and who wants can help themselves!' Miranda said, but although she uttered those words defiantly, she took Cathy to the kitchen to organize the ice-cream. They soon returned with a large container, including several bowls and Miranda began to serve her guests.

They were a young group, always having fun with each other and the women never liked being bossed around by the men. It was a time when Fertilates were considered equals. Sexism being a thing of the very distant past.

After they had finished dinner, the men decided to do the clearing up while the women retired to the lounge to relax with a well-deserved drink and quiet music.

'Ladies, I can see that you are all very relaxed and comfortable, but George would like to speak his mind on a subject close to our hearts so I think we should give him a fair hearing. Since our astronaut training, things have quickly developed from the sublime to the ridiculous and we would like answers,' Jerry said, as he and the other men entered the sitting room to join their partners and friends.

George stood up and began to speak. He was probably the most logical of the group and adept at giving long speeches.

'What comes to mind whenever one utters the words, Eden and Caefon?'

'A beautiful paradise, perhaps!' Cathy replied.

'The reason why I mention those two names... is that since Andy and others mentioned them, I have not been able to get them out of my head,' George said.

'I suppose, Eden reminds me of the perfect garden in the bible and Caefon, perhaps a similar place,' Miranda replied.

'Exactly, perfect worlds, but not created by a God. Created by a very advanced technology. A place where anyone can live forever. A place where it's not even possible for anyone to die. Where diseases are nonexistent. A place where the development of the human psyche is limitless. Where every human concept had reached its ultimate in advancement.'

'Such a place can never exist in this universe! If it does, when can we visit?' Jerry interjected and everyone laughed.

'I know it all sounds ridiculous, but let me explain. I think that Earth is a very tiny part of a much larger galactic or even intergalactic empire. I also think that the hand or finger of that empire that touches us is in the form of Solarian Banking and its other associates. What if they had worlds of gold and other so-called rear minerals that were mined by advanced robots. They could not supply those materials to us even if they wanted, because it would cause de-stabilization of Earth's more primitive governments and financial institutions on a massive scale.'

'Makes sense!' Cathy interjected.

'Go on!' Jerry said, getting more interested.

'Do you know, that since the turn of the previous century, the distribution of such rear metals have been rigorously controlled by a few large mineral consortiums? And they are all sponsored by the major governments.'

'Yep, and most of ours is in Forth Knox!' Jerry interrupted.

'Common knowledge!' Joan replied.

'I saw some things today that really disturbed me. A technology that I never even dreamt of and those items were probably the most primitive, even out of date stuff used for testing Earthlings like myself. After all, why should they use their best stuff on Earth, with the risk of it being stolen and copied. And by the way, they use their own type of 3D language. They are also capable of memorising every grain of sand on Earth with a single Macron Computer.'

'What's a Macron Computer?' Jerry inquired.

'It's supposed to be super-intelligent.'

'Why bother with grains of sand?' an innocent Cathy inquired.

'So, you think we are under their control?' Miranda inquired.

'I am not sure, but each of us are well known to them by our backgrounds, education, skills and social habits. For some very strange reason, and although they know exactly what we are up to, I get the distinct impression that they like us and will assist us in whatever way they can, more like parents than an adversary. It's like they are not afraid of anyone or anything.'

'That little golden-haired girl really got into your head recently!' Jerry became worried.

'No, she did not!'

'Go on!' Cathy insisted.

'Take this watch and the symbols on its rear face. It's the winged insignia of an organization and this watch makes me a club member, but it doesn't end there. I get the distinct impression from Anthony and others that we, of The Earth's Children Gang, are well known and respected by them. That could only happen if they thought along similar lines to us, but on a more cosmic scale.'

'The Milky Way Gang!' Miranda interjected and they laughed.

'Finally, I believe that Earth's population could not have been reduced by any means short of seeding its atmosphere with the bio-engineered terminal bacteria. But with certain preparations made to retain an optimum sustainable population. When the time is right, in the not too distant future, they will once again return to assist in the rebuilding process and perhaps even reintroduce a few extinct species like Elephants, Rhinos and such like.'

'How do you know all this?' Jerry inquired.

'You mean... these creatures can still be alive on another world?' Cathy was astonished.

'Friends, those are my conclusions from the information I have so far received.'

George said those words with great feelings and conviction and his companions were speechless.

'George, what you say make lots of sense and fits in with everything we have discovered to date. But if that is so, where are they from and what do you think they look like?' Cathy said.

'I think... many years ago our civilization crossed paths with another alien type. It must have been a much more advanced one. The cross fertilization of ideas and biology could have led to a more advanced species. But many go missing from Earth on a daily basis, so I also think that most of them are genetically human...with powers to increase their mental and physical capabilities and capacities. I also think the human form means very little to them and that anyone with the necessary mental capabilities will be accepted in an unprejudiced manner,' George replied.

'A truly alien civilization existing as one for the common good,' Cathy intimated.

Jerry was next to speak.

'If what you say is true, and I doubt it very much, not until we have some more concrete evidence... then, we have an even greater adventure ahead of us. Andy's strange looking space craft could have been seen about the time when our civilization crossed paths with that other one... but from where could they have come? How could such a thing have been kept from everyone on this world for all this time?' Jerry said.

'What if our galaxy has very advanced life, even billions of years more advanced than us. What if such life was unable to touch our existence due to the irreparable damage that could be done to our natural development and evolution. Don't you think such life would always pass us by? Even consider us to be an irrelevant species by their advanced standards, like a fly in the ointment. Because even by our most basic standards, Earth has become a most dangerous place to live and look at what we have done to the other species. From our past record, who would ever single us out for greatness.' George replied.

'You have a point. These days, I wouldn't allow most people to take my dog for a walk!' Ann said.

'Do you seriously think anyone out there would ever want us to take their pets for a walk? When even I don't trust people outside of The Gang that much and what of the possibilities of drugs, crime and other acute forms of gross antisocial behaviour. Not to mention self indulgence and rampant corruption in high places. Thank goodness the human population growth rate is on a downward spiral towards a more acceptable level.' Miranda interjected.

'What do you think the present population would have been at this moment in time without the Terminal Disease. Twenty billion perhaps?' George said.

'Without the Terminal Disease there would be absolutely nothing left on Earth by way of resources. The complete biosphere would have been utterly and irreversibly contaminated by now, even to a point of no return and most non endangered species would have surely become extinct in the process. So how do you like seeing your real human selves in the mirror for the first time.' Jerry said.

'No wonder those advanced aliens moved on, but before they left they may have put a master plan into operation. I also think that the shuttle ship was not lost in space. Yes, I am convinced that your grand parents are still alive on some beautiful world somewhere out there. Those are my thoughts on the subject,' George replied.

'But if what you say is correct, how can we find them without the assistance of Solarian Banking, and if they left by their own accord, they might not even wish to see us again,' Jerry said, sadly.

'Parents always like to see their children. It's possible they had to make a one way pact with their superiors. Furthermore, during my interview I got the distinct impression that they did not want their people to be contaminated by Earth's infectious diseases, including the Terminal Disease,' George replied.

George had aroused and motivated them into stronger action. He had added several new questions to their list, which might have taken the group a lifetime to solve. But they also had outside help, of which they were not always aware.

CHAPTER 10

George's third interview

Anthony called George the following day.

'George...! Can you visit my office on Wednesday morning? Could you leave the whole of that day open-ended for an extended visit? We might have to get a flight to North Dakota. It should take us two hours by a conventional inland flight. We are to visit a very important person at a much higher level, and he wants me to accompany you.'

'Really? You thing so?'

'Honest! Suddenly, they have become very interested in you and your group. I don't know what it's all about. I think it's probably the offer of a higher position within the Tec branch, but I am guessing.'

'I am intrigued! Where in North Dakota?'

'It's the place itself...! Head office on Earth! It's Sol-Newtown Dome!'

'Bloody hell! The largest dome on Earth. I always wanted to visit that place!' George murmured silently.

'I am almost speechless! I don't know what to say!'

'I know how you feel! Anyway, you are not to worry about expenses and such like. Everything is covered by the firm.'

'Thanks for that!'

'Shall we make it for ten a.m?'

'Yes! That will be fine.'

'See you then!' Anthony said and hung up.

George wondered what the excitement was all about. Anthony was a high ranking manager, but despite his higher position he was quite nervous, almost as if God himself had arrived on Earth.

That morning George visited the office well before time and Anthony took him to the LPD pad on the roof of the building. From there, they took a company space-car to the main airport for connection. There they would get on a larger LPD passenger liner to the northern territories.

After landing, a company space-car was waiting to take them to their new destination. Direct travel from normal airports to the Sol-Newtown Dome was not allowed for security reasons.

While they approached, still some ten miles in the distance, they could clearly observe the outlines of the massive domed city. It measured over two miles in diameter and was probably close to a mile high, penetrating well into several layers of clouds. George was struck by the enormity of the structure, but wondered where his destination led. That was, until Anthony began to get excited.

'Beautiful, is it not?'

'Yea... it's the greatest thing I ever saw!'

'My first visit to Sol-Newtown was several years ago. That was about fifteen years after it was completed. It's another one of our company's programs, you know; to build such sealed domes and isolate many life-forms within their own ecosystems, well away from the hazards of the raw planet and mankind. We have many such structures in South America and Africa. But this one is one of the largest structures on Earth. Even its supporting pillars are themselves large multi story buildings.'

'What a sight for sore eyes!' George exclaimed, overwhelmed by excitement.

'The whole interior is completely sealed from the outside and retains an atmospheric pressure in excess of normal. That way, if any leaks occur, bacteria and other microbes are kept out. You know, over fifty thousand healthy Fertilate people now live and work within its structure, with every conceivable technology and facilities other Fertilates may dream of.'

'It must be the purest place on the planet with all that technology and so beautiful, like the largest diamond I ever saw!' George said.

'It's head office for Solarian Banking and other interests like Tec and Eta. This place you see ahead of you is the head of the planet and when I say those words, I can look you straight in the eye with conviction. Because I tell you the unadulterated truth. But you will see for yourself soon enough. Here, it's not just Earth but many other beautiful worlds besides, even like the biblical garden of Eden with the most beautiful sunsets,' Anthony stopped speaking as the space-cab suddenly spiralled towards the large dome.

'We appear to be entering via the high level docking station. We will shortly be cleansed within the automated sterilization chamber before clearance,' Anthony added, but George was too fascinated by the experience to pay attention, with the incredible views from that height.

They soon arrived at the large station with many young people, all wearing beautiful grey uniforms. Two very attractive young ladies went towards them. The tallest took a card from Anthony and observed it in detail. Then they took both men to the sterilization chambers. Their clothes and other personal items were confiscated for the duration of their stay and were each given new clothes.

'Don't the girls undergo the same treatment like us?' George secretly asked Anthony.

'No! Don't be fooled by their beautiful bodies and makeup. They are just androids, programmed to satisfy their customers in transit. They are not flesh and blood like us and are not affected by bugs and such like. Do you fancy the little one?' Anthony jested.

'But... they look so real... so beautiful. You are not pulling my leg, are you?' George asked.

'I don't know all of the old funny British phrases, but I know what you mean, and I'm not telling you any fibs either.'

'God, they are so cute and feminine! I must be in Heaven!' George couldn't believe his eyes.

'How can I prove it to you?.... I know.... After we are dressed, I shall ask one of them to remove her hat. A small plug should become visible just at the back of her head and that should convince you,' Anthony said.

Anthony soon called the taller of the two ladies and asked her to remove her hat.

'Here you are. Are you convinced?'

The ladies thought nothing of the occurrence and carried on as normal, following their daily programmed duties but with a high level of orderly intelligence.

'You know, George, this dome was built over the original

production sight used by Doctor Jeffery Longhurst to manufacture his robots. The other sight is now covered by another and is some twenty miles to the north west. But that dome is smaller than this one and is now a real park in the truest sense of the word.'

They were soon taken to the large cafeteria and their female escorts were like slaves, always running to their beck and call. George felt a little embarrassed, seeing such beautiful women trying to satisfy their every need. But they were programmed androids, following a program without any human emotions or feelings.

When they were finished, the ladies took them to what appeared to be a rotating lift. They suddenly found themselves in a most beautiful reception area. Then they were taken to a desk and given new identification cards. Their two female escorts left and a grey uniformed young guard asked them to take a seat. Another young lady wearing a military uniform soon came up to them.

'My name is Maria. Lieutenant Maria Siegel.'

'Please to meet you, Maria!' George greeted.

'I am to escort you to the three-hundredth floor, just another hundred and seventy-eight.'

'Thank you!'

'Please follow me!'

She took them along a corridor, through a rotating elevator, and they were soon at another reception area.

'We have arrived at our destination. Please wait here while I inform the desk of your arrival.' She stood blank for a while to communicate via her brain implants.

'We have arrived... already?'

'We may now enter!'

'Ok!'

'Please follow me!' she said, in a very quiet but pleasant voice.

When they entered the large office area, the one that was sat behind the desk came forward to introduce himself.

'I am pleased to meet you gentlemen!'

'Me too!' George greeted.

'George, my name is Arel Tamul! Please meet one of my dearest friends, Jonathon Meron, currently on his first visit to Earth!'

Jonathon, who was comfortably seated in the large settee got up to shake their hands. George could not stop his gaze, for Jonathon had three fingers on each hand and the most incredible sea-blue eyes. Yet he firmly shook his hand.

'I'm... very pleased to meet you,' George said, utterly surprised. But George couldn't stop staring at his incredible eyes.

'Ah! I see!' acknowledged Arel.

'The famous six fingers and sea-blue eyes, eh! George, he is the son of Plato and Merian, who originally came from Galaxy Andromeda, and I am the youngest son of Jon Tamul also from that galaxy but from the later city of Cantor. As you see, not all of us are alike!' Arel was correct, since he had brown eyes and was more like and Italian, but very tall.

'Cantor?'

'It was our main city! That world used to be called Caefon, that is, before its complete destruction by the Javols.' Arel said.

'We and many from Earth now live on Eden, which is a most beautiful world within the seventh precinct of our Osmaron galaxy, I mean the Milky Way,' he said. Then gestured that they should have a seat. Suddenly an android appeared with a tray of fruit drinks and handed them glasses.

Arel pressed a few buttons on a small remote control unit and the large wall turned into a screen which suddenly came alive to reveal a most beautiful world. It contained many domed environments, citadels and finally Eden City itself which was beyond anything that he had ever imagined. But the people there were all young, although more like the wealthier and most fashionable ones on Earth.

He wondered whether the old people were taken away to permanent retirement after the age of fifty, but Arel, seeing the concern in his eyes, explained.

'People and beloved animals never grow old on Eden. Even though it's a democratic choice, no one ever likes to grow old and die, so as a result it's not possible to die, even from an accident.'

'That's incredible! Not a single death? That must be some

place!' With all that was going on, George was in a daze, constantly playing catch up to the flood of new and unrealistic information flooding his brain.

'When our parents arrived on Earth, several decades ago, Earth's population could not have been halted in anyway. After many meetings and discussions, a vote was taken and the Terminal Bacteria was designed and applied to its biosphere. However, we had to save enough of its population by selection, and we are now in a period when the opposite type of bacteria will be applied to its atmosphere in order to reverse the sterilization effects of the virus. Those decisions were taken at the highest level by Empress Sarah and others from Earth.'

'So the Terminal Disease was planned to cull humanity down to acceptable levels?' George replied.

'Yes! Once the antidote is applied human life will return to normality within a period of ten years or so. Therefore, there is little need for anyone on Earth to continue with the Anti-Terminal treatment. Not unless they want to reproduce before that period. Anyway, very soon the Terminal Bacteria will mutate into a harmless type. That aspect has been designed in its genetic structure,' Arel said.

He wore a grey military uniform with many medals and stripes, with a winged insignia and appeared to be a commander in some military organization. The insignia included three primary colours within an inner circle, but the yellow appeared to be more orange than yellow and held an air of seniority.

Jonathon wore a light cream suit with a jewelled headband and a similar insignia clipped to his large lapel. He seemed to be more carefree than the others.

'But you should have discovered most of this information through your enquiries some time ago. Anyway, don't worry, I have prepared a complete folder for you. It includes a comprehensive database on many topics.'

Thank you!' George replied while Anthony stood numbed by it all.

'This information, I would like you to share with your group. It will save you a lot of time digging for information in old city libraries. Anyway, we think you may be very helpful to Earth and our organization in the future.'

'I shall do my very best!'

'First of all, let me show you a film, then we can discuss your queries at length for the common good of all!'

Arel showed them the horror film. It was about the destruction of Caefon by the dreaded Javols, who had decimated the whole of that galaxy in just three thousand years. He also showed him the complete history of the Solarian Empire since its formation. Then he showed them the beginning of the war against the Javols. It was being fought in Andromeda. Its main purpose to deceive the almost indestructible Javols and find their weakness.

'You see... but we have learnt a lot about Javols during that battle!'

'I see what you mean! They must be the most unfeeling creatures I have ever seen!' George almost threw up while watching that most horror and gore movie of death and destruction.

'Problems on Earth are insignificant when compared to the extermination of all primal life within the Cosmos. The whole of Andromeda is now completely overrun. Osmaron, including Earth, has less than one hundred years at current estimates, before they arrive and begin the extermination of all life here. Therefore, we want you and your group to visit Eden and learn more about the empire. While there you can be trained and in turn recruit more members and be prepared when the time comes.'

'A galactic invasion? This is a real nightmare!' George was not pleased.

'You will find within the file a letter from Jerry's grandfather and other relevant family holograms. These you may show to his son, President Donald Fraser, after you have explained the whole situation to him. And by the way, you have been chosen... albeit on a trial basis and subject to future training on our home planet Eden... to lead such survival groups on Earth under the umbrella of Tec.'

'I have? Thank you very, very much! I shall do my utmost best!'

George was almost out of words.

'Your future position, if you accept, will be chief administrator of Unitec. You will come under Tec, of which I am now head. Your job description is listed within your personal profile, which is also included in your black folder.'

'Thanks again! I shall start immediately! I was looking for a challenge. Now I have found a worthy one!' Suddenly George was interested in doing his utmost best for his suffering planet on a much larger scale with the finances of Solarian Banking, now the richest organization on Earth.

'You are not to worry about finances or technology during your fight for the common good. As you have seen, we have it all. Wealth means very little to us. Perhaps you could arrange to visit Eden after your Martian holiday for adventure and by the way, your personal file also includes a master key to all our domes, to which we hold you fully responsible.'

'No problem!'

'All information relating to the domes is also included within your personal file for your own perusal.'

'I shall keep it safe!'

'There is one more important question that I have to ask you. Have you heard of Beta-Five?' Arel inquired.

'No.... I don't think so....' George searched his mind for any relevance.

'No matter. They are one of the most extreme Infilate groups operating in North America. Each has the Greek Beta symbol and a five tattooed on the right arm. They have been tracking you and your group for some time now. Perhaps waiting for the correct moment to take action, but we are not sure of the nature of their intended crime.' Arel said.

'They are? That's very worrying!'

'Yes! At this moment in time, they are very low on funds and perhaps intend to take a hostage for ransom, and Jerry has probably become their prime target since his father became President.'

'Could be! And you think they might kidnap him for ransom?'

'That's quite possible. They have many friends in high places, but most of their financial exchanges are constantly scanned by

Macron Inspection on a daily basis. So funding has become extremely difficult from such sources. They also employ a very competent team of computer hackers who assist in their small fraudulent deals and embezzlements. Therefore, visits to the library by group members could have been the signal they were waiting for to initiate a plan.' Arel said.

'That could well be!'

'Here are their psychological profiles. Study it well and memorise the names on that list.'

'I shall!'

'Finally, I am to present you with two Transmorphs. Known to many as hunter killers. We assign them to our senior members who we think need protection and I do think you and your friends to be in need of it at this time.' Arel Continued.

'What are these Trans..morphs?'

'Let me show you another video!'

Arel pushed a few more buttons on his small remote control and a new image filled the large screen.

It displayed two very muscular, but handsome young men. They resembled the large brazen gods of ancient Greek mythology called Colossus. The fairer of the two had sea blue eyes and the other was of African descent with brown eyes. Both were of the same build and with almost identical features.

'These are your Transmorphs, they could equally have been feminine by nature, but we tend to use mainly males on Earth for practical sociological reasons. Their massive forms also instill fear in the opposition.' Arel said.

'They must be at least 8 feet tall!'

'Just over eight... They are a new and special type of android with a microid brain and body. Their bodies are almost completely composed of heavy metal micro-robots or microids, what you call Nano-bots. They are capable of reforming into any life-form of an equivalent mass at an instant as you may observe.' The screen changed into a different scene.

The Transmorphs began to undress and almost immediately changed into ferocious tigers, then lions and finally giant bats that began to fly and scan the landscape with their highly sensitive vision.

'Their hands can change into almost any weapon. They are driven by a small nuclear generator, capable of sustaining them for just ten years. That short time limit is an inbuilt safety feature. Their old generators can be replaced after that time. Although unable to transform to explosive chemical weapons like guns and bombs, they include very powerful and tunable lasers and maser weapons. During certain energy releases they are quite capable of tapping directly into their nuclear fields, with a controllable energy release of up to an equivalent level of one kiloton of TNT or less, at any single energy release. But they can also be triggered by a special code to self destruct. During that process they are programmed to explode with a total equivalent mass of twenty kilotons of TNT. Enough energy to destroy a large city.'

'What a weapon... and it's alive!' George exclaimed.

'Their senses are highly tuned and can detect any changes within their environment. This includes, air-current temperature changes, smell changes, visual, audible and many others, way below anything even the most sensitive primal life-forms can detect. They are the true hunter-killer in every sense of the word. Yet, they will never harm any of the people they are imprinted on, registered to, or form a bond with.' Arel continued,

'That's quite reassuring! Wow! The perfect hunter... killer!' George was intrigued.

'We have created armies of TMs to fight the Javols. At the appropriate time they will be released on Andromeda. Further, you and your friends must wear your watches and insignias at all times. These items radiate a special signal that they are able to detect while actively tracking a prey.'

'We shall?'

'The two we assign to you and your group has to be initially registered with you and that registration requires you to be with them in person during the awakening and bonding period.'

'If it's safe, I don't mind. So ready when you are!' a brave George replied.

'Don't worry, their power packs are not installed during the initial programming phase, so they are quite harmless,' Arel said, with a glare of excitement in his eyes.

'Oooh! They are truly awesome!' George replied, not knowing

quite what to say while his mind was flooded with such incredible data.

'George, I trust you are not too dismayed by all this, but you must trust us in the same way that we trust you, and perhaps one day, in the not too distant future, you will also be given the seed of immortality and become a true child of the Sword and of the Greater Purpose.' Arel said.

'I shall always endeavour to do my utmost best in all circumstances!' George replied.

'But now, Maria must take you and Anthony to the TM chambers. After that, please feel free to visit the lower city with your special pass and observe some of the sights. That pass also represents several hundred thousand dollars. So please make yourselves at home and perhaps Maria can show you around if she hasn't any other appointments scheduled for today.'

'Thanks again, for your kind hospitality and the appointment! When I came here today I thought I was going to be given a simple job in Solarian Banking. Now I leave with the knowledge of a galactic invasion to destroy us all. I can now clearly visualize my future!' George was excited but still dumfounded by it all.

'You have been well chosen! We shall both look forward to meeting you again in the not too distant future and may the Grand Lord guide your hand from this moment on,' Arel said. They shook hands again and left with Maria.

George took the small black metal case and walked out of the office followed by Anthony and Maria. He was still as confused as when he entered, while many of his theories fell accurately in place.

The Transmorphs department was at level two hundred and fifty-two in another building. On arrival Maria and Anthony waited at the local reception while he went into the chamber.

George was placed into a special chair and asked to inhale a pink dust. Then a large helmet was lowered unto his head. After what appeared to him to be a lengthy period of complete blankness, the helmet lifted and the operator asked him to follow her into another room with many androids wearing identification numbers. For some unknown reason there were two separate queues of TMs, one black and the other white.

She asked George to stand within a circle and gaze towards a distant moving light, and the first two nude individuals came forward to observe him. Then she pressed a few buttons on her remote unit and they walked away from the queue towards another room.

'They have now imprinted on your external features. All we have to do is complete their programming and prepare them for delivery within a fortnight or so,' the operator said.

One thing George could not comprehend was the speed of the elevators, more commonly known to him as lifts. No sooner had he entered a rotating doorway than he would find himself at the relevant destination, and those places were not always vertically displaced.

'You look worried and confused. Well, let me put you out of your misery. They are not elevators. They are called portals and rotate you through what they call the H-Dimension. Don't ask me what the H stands for. One more thing, George, they have these things all over the galaxy. They can commute to Earth on a daily job from almost anywhere in the galaxy.' Anthony said.

'Wow! Teleportation! I thought that was impossible!'

'No Pal, that's a fact! Cute, isn't it!' Anthony couldn't contain his excitement.

'Why use spaceships when they are not required? That way they can ship anything to anywhere in Osmaron, our Milky Way galaxy. I have been told they have such powerful links between Osmaron and other galaxies, including Andromeda,' Anthony added.

'Goodness! I would never have thought it possible. The more I see their technologies, the more I think that we on Earth are primitive gorillas by comparison!'

'We are!'

'You are so right! Why do they bother with us?' George inquired.

'I suppose it's to do with that old fashioned feeling called love. Perhaps I shouldn't be telling you this, but the Empress of

Osmaron is from Earth and for that reason our planet has always been treated with kid gloves. While we are talking... one more thing you should know. She is not the head. There are Super Beings involved, who can destroy Earth with a single breadth, but they are the most loving to all primal life within the Cosmos.'

'You mean Supreme Beings, like gods?'

'Yes! The one responsible for us and our part of the Cosmos is called Grand Lord Gerra. Now, what do you think of that? They call him the one with many names. So much for all those old-fashioned religions and beliefs.'

'That's incredible! I never would have believed!'

'Pal, God and heaven is now here with us everywhere within this dome. The devil's world begins the moment we leave this place!' Anthony was stern and serious.

George was completely numbed by those experiences, to such a level that he wanted to return to Anthony's office before it got too late. He wanted to get home early that day and tell his gang the news of his incredible experiences.

He and Anthony only spent one hour within the large shopping precinct to get some presents before Maria accompanied them back to their departure point.

On arrival to the building Anthony gave him some more golden watches and insignias for his friends and they temporarily parted company.

CHAPTER 11

The little computer

George retrieved the Coms' handset and began to dial a number.
'Jerry... is it you?'
'Yes!'
'I visited Sol-Newtown today and have to see you about a very urgent matter ASAP. Are you busy?'
'No... not busy at this moment... but I had one of those awful days sifting through more information and finally a headache.... I think due to eye strain. Perhaps I need to have my eyes tested again.'
'Perhaps! And the others?'
'Cathy's mother sent us a parcel with more papers and photos... and a note which contains a very strange writing, not known to anyone I've spoken to. So the girls and I intend to visit the library tomorrow, to check out some of this new information. That note was sent to Jeffery Longhurst from Meron, and there is lots more. The others are ok doing their bit!' Jerry said.
'Good! At least we are getting somewhere!'
'If the library computer fails, perhaps you could give me a hand in decoding it.'
'No problems!'
'To change the topic; Did you remember, the eight is in two days and we have to see the man about hiring our spaceship? Andy will also be there, so we better arrive early on that morning and sort things out with Clive before he turns up. Anyway, I made the call to inform Clive, so they will be expecting us,' Jerry informed.
'Yea, I almost forgot about that as well!' George replied.
'We should have done it sooner, but I completely forgot. Luckily Miranda remembered. She is very good at that sort of thing.'
'Good! I look forward!'
'We should check the spaceship over and take Andy for lunch afterwards to show our gratitude. Anyway, he is now on holiday

and can always visit us at my apartment if he wishes.' Jerry advised.

'Perhaps we should take a space mechanic along just to point out defects and estimate the cost of repairs.' George suggested.

'Very difficult to find such engineers these days, so we'll have to rely on Andy and his friends for a true assessment of her condition. Perhaps we can have the important chat then. If not, leave it for the evening, or better yet, the day after tomorrow... after the ship is paid for and we have received the relevant clearance document from the port authorities. We can then leave for Gimbal soon after.'

'Sounds fine with me!'

'Anyway, I intend to have another one of our free dinner evenings on the tenth, during which time we can each voice our opinions.' Jerry said.

'The tenth sounds ideal!'

'Don't be late tomorrow morning, we need to take the cab at ten a.m. from my building,' Jerry said, not even allowing him to get a serious word in edgeways.

'Ok, Jerry, I'll see you then. Have an early night,' George advised and hung up the receiver.

George decided to spend the rest of that evening looking through the special folder. It was almost the size of a small laptop computer case and included a combination lock. He also found out, through its instruction manual, that it could identify thumb-print and be voice, retina and facial-image coded for better security.

'What! How will I ever get into this thing?' he murmured. Realizing not many organizations had his thumb-print. He had only once given it to his university and that was many years ago.

The case was completely black in colour and its outer material appeared to reflect no light, whatsoever. He simply released its catches, by placing both thumbs within depressions of a similar shape and the cover lifted, revealing a small computer and many other pieces of equipment of which he had no knowledge.

'So you are not any folder I've seen. You are a small computer,' he muttered.

'Wow! It worked! Now I am convinced they know everything about us! Even our fingerprints!' he continued.

The instruction manual was printed in two languages, one of which was completely unrecognisable to him. While he read the English portion of that manual he followed its instructions to the letter and before long had the small computer up and running.

To his utter amazement the computer was also a video, with a similar expandable screen to the one in Anthony's office. All the information he required was stored in mega terabytes within its powerful memory.

'Wow! What an awesome piece of equipment. I just hope I am able to use you as a normal computer,' he murmured.

George couldn't stop wondering about the power of his new toy and whether his mind was up to using it effectively. That was, before the unit began to talk. He soon learnt it could also understand his every word. That was not all. It could project a holographic image of its own human form in the room, and talk with him as any normal person. That projected form was a representation of George himself. Perhaps more like a twin brother.

'My God! Wow! Ha! Ha! Ha! You are alive!' He was taken back.

'Yes, I am alive... and conscious! I contain information on virtually everything of importance known to this universe!'

'That is truly incredible! Shall I call you... by a name?'

'Yes! I am sure,' the hologram replied.

'What do you think of the name... Ron for Ronald?' George couldn't stop staring at the projected three-dimensional human image of himself that also moved and used hand gestures to get his points across.

'Why Ron, it's not the best of choices?'

'I don't know why! It happens to be the first thought that popped into my head at that moment. It could also because its our President's middle name. I believe things have purpose, don't you? That's why I must insist on that name,' George replied.

'In that case, my purposeful master, I must also insist in being called by that name!'

'So Ron it will be! From henceforth you will always be by my side as my advisor, unless there is an overriding reason.'

'Yes! I would like that. Because I am assigned to you on a permanent basis!'

'Indeed, you are!'

'Please feel free to ask your questions. I hold within my memory much information and I am very good at sorting through and analysing data. I also have at my disposal several other appliances for reading through documents in most languages and interfacing with other mainframes, including Earth-type computers.'

'That's so cool!'

'Are you feeling cold?'

'No, just a silly human phrase!'

Oh...Analysis is my main pleasure in life, so you must please set me lots of tasks and problems to solve. The more complex, the more I enjoy.'

'Is that all you are capable of doing?' George further inquired.

'Much, much more besides. But I can only interface properly with minds using implants. Then I can become one with you and you could use me as if I was part of your own brain in a Virtual Universe.'

George was astounded by the incredible technologies involved, but also amused by his new friend. He realised his so-called folder of information was really in the form of a super computer. The case was really its holder, which was among other things, blast proof. He was bemused by it all and suddenly began thinking aloud. He left Ron for a while to visit the kitchen.

'A computer that gets its enjoyment from learning? Many college students would pay dearly to get their hands on such a unique treasure. Has it really a personality capable of knowing what enjoyment is?' Then he slumped into the soft settee with ice-cream and began to murmur to himself.

'A rose by any other name is still a rose in the eye of its beholder, but is it really a rose to the rose? Can it ever see itself in the same light? The dilemma of the observer and the object under observation. Both seeing each other in different lights and in the end both being equally good observers and objects in different ways. But never knowing the truth of each other's own existence or observations. This is almost the way we humans see the lower life-forms, as insignificant and minor in the scheme of things. But how do the minor animals really see us and what if they had a conscious core very much like our own.' He paused, pondering those thoughts for a while.

'Survival and brainwashing had made us humans think like that since primordial times. Being a more dominant intelligence we are able to keep the other species down for fear of being overrun. What if our attitude was based on a deep-seated fear of being conquered by a lower life-form or because of some great threat faced in primordial times. They might still haunt our subconscious, even to this day.'

He carried on thinking, but those questions led nowhere, so he decided instead to gain the help of his computer friend and prepare a speech for his lecture on the evening of the tenth. He went over to the Coms and began to call each member of The Gang, pressuring each to visit the dinner party at Jerry's apartment that evening.

Although he was always good at preparing speeches, he was not sure how to explain the presence of the Plorans and other cosmic Supreme Beings, still living after many billions of years. Therefore the lecture was prepared in two sections, including a small part on the cosmic history of Osmaron and the neighbouring galaxies, with transcripts taken from Ron, the computer.

After George had received enough information from Ron, he found his mind racing on, even beyond the data. He suddenly became giddy and fell to the floor. He woke up a moment later, still feeling strange and wondered what had happened.

'Did you do that to me with your strange subliminals?'

'It's very possible I'm responsible for triggering something that was dormant within you! If that was the case, I am sorry it affected you that way.

'I fed you with a new mind program, full of subliminals which was meant to enlarge your mental capacity some tenfold. The program is now rerouting itself through your mind and will

soon take effect. This is the only way forward with our present program. Then, the final program!' Ron was sincerely apologetic.

'What is this final Program?'

'It's the program you should follow to save all life within our universe. For you, George, is the chosen one!'

George was flabbergasted by that statement. How could he, a simple Earthling, be chosen by anyone to save the universe. He assumed Ron had got some of his facts wrong about him. Either that or he was not adapting well to his new environment and was having negative reaction to some aspects of their recent communication. Although his brain was in a jumbled state, George was still able to think coherently. Then the passing wave in his mind seemed to disperse and once again he was at peace with himself. That feeling of serenity did not last.

Although George was worried, he drank a large glass of water and the strange sensation passed, to be followed by another. This time he found himself being sucked into a large rotating vertex which led into a tunnel with many symbols displayed on its walls.

His head throbbed with the share power of the data that formed. But the tunnel began to expand until there was nothing, just a complete void. Then a faint point of light began to form within his mind and once again he found himself on the floor, but this time with a profuse nosebleed. Slowly, he straightened himself and washed his bloody face within the kitchen sink, but the worst of his reaction was over. Although he felt completely different after the ordeal, he was still himself.

'The last time I had such a nosebleed was about two years ago,' he muttered to himself.

That night he barely had six hours sleep. There were still lots more to do by way of compressing all that data within a small speech. However, he had two more evenings, so he persevered.

The following day he went to meet his colleagues with a small pad and Dictaphone. That was after saying a temporary goodbye to his new friend, Ron.

CHAPTER 12

The spaceship

Jerry and Miranda were just ready when George arrived. Cathy had arrived earlier. As usual Cathy began to tease George.

'Aaah! Wearing all black again I see! We are not going to a funeral!' Then she began to adjust his pink tie like a wife.

'I sure am! But not all black and not to a funeral!' George replied.

'You look different somehow, more handsome than usual and... suave with a hint of something, I can't quite put my finger on it!' Cathy was in another of her playful moods. While she spoke, he couldn't or perhaps didn't want to rebut her attentions, so he in turn began to compliment her on her beautiful dress.

'Anyway, I like the dress and you look fantastic! I hope you are not observing me in the same light as one of your famous Mec recipes. Anyway, I feel on top of the world!' he said with a smile and she was happy.

However she soon went up to him and gave him a gentle peck on his cheek which he accepted with a little embarrassment, as Jerry walked in.

'Sorry, Jerry, I think I am too early. Anyway, I brought you all some presents from Sol-Newtown which I think you will like.' George opened his briefcase to remove some golden watches and other presents like airings, bangles and diamond rings. Then he started handing them around.

Each took a watch and to their further astonishment, found their names engraved on the rear metallic faces.

'Gosh, that looks so expensive. With real inlaid diamonds. Is it really for free?' exclaimed Cathy.

'Yes, of course it's for free. I also have some more for our other gang members and special friends like Andy,' George said.

'You are not getting involved with some type of interplanetary mafia organisation? Are you, old boy?' exclaimed Jerry, while removing his old watch and replacing it with the beautiful golden one.

'Look, guys, you have known me for some time now. Haven't you?'

'I suppose?' Cathy replied in jest.

'Well, do you think I am capable of pulling off such a stunt with my dearest friends, even with myself. You must all trust me on this one.'

'What's there not to trust!' Miranda replied while carefully observing her expensive golden watch.

'All I can tell you is that it's all perfectly honest and above board. Anyway, I picked up most of the other items in a jewellery shop in Sol-Newtown.'

'You went to Sol-Newtown? I always wanted to visit that place. Now it's out of bounds for us humble earthlings!' Ann replied.

'This is fantastic jewellery and must be worth a fortune. With this, I feel like a queen!' Cathy said and kissed him on the cheek again.

'Only the very best for you!' George replied.

'One more thing. I would like you all to wear these broaches as a symbol of our organisation, to help and assist the downtrodden and unfortunates on our world. In much the same way as we have done in the past. This however makes it more official. You can always hide it under your clothes if you do not wish it be exposed for security reasons. But I must insist that you wear them from now on.'

What is it for?' Cathy inquired.

'It contains a homing device, plus more advanced technologies for tracing people,' George replied.

They took the insignias and pinned them to their clothes.

They called a cab and took the elevator to the top floor to await its arrival. Most of the larger buildings had small connecting LPD stations for added security and their building was one of the busier ones that housed over five hundred separate apartments, all owned by Fertilate families. Such apartments were run by housing associations and large banks which were themselves owned by Fertilates that would never take the risk to rent such accommodation to Infilates. Occupants would never tolerate such action for fear of their children's safety. Not knowing what type of visitors would be passing through the building's corridors.

Therefore, like it or not, there was two separate types of people on Earth. Each hating the other because of ignorance, mistrust and class prejudice.

The large cab soon arrived from above, quickly took a spiral and landed on the secondary pad to fit precisely within its allocated square. It had begun to rain so they ran towards it as the large doors slid open. George handed him his card, but he stared at him instead and said. 'Shall I put you on account, Sir?'

'Yes! I would like that very much!'

'It's done!'

'Thank you!' George replied. Then he gave the cab driver instructions.

They arrived at one of the smaller ports, just off Kennedy Spaceport and went into the building occupied by Global Spaceways. That building might have contained hundreds of small companies and businesses, including more space-cabs. They tended to share a common reception and other facilities, thus significantly reducing their individual overheads.

Such places were usually run by Fertilates, but there could well have been Infilates about, carrying out the more menial tasks normally given to the very elderly. There were many pitiful faces throughout the long corridors.

Jerry arrived at the office and pushed the button marked, **"PUSH ME"**. The door opened and they walked in.

'Is Clive about? I've been sent by Andy... to hire a small spacecraft?' Jerry inquired.

'He just took a gentleman called Andy to the hanger, but he told me that he was expecting someone by the name of... here it is, on my notepad... Jerry.'

'I see!'

'Are you Jerry, then?' the young lady asked while chewing gum.

'Yes! I am Jerry and these are my friends.'

'Well, Mister Jerry, I am sorry but you will have to wait until they return. I haven't anyone else to show you the way towards the hanger.'

'Bloody Hell!' Jerry was not pleased.

'Don't worry about such a trivial matter. I shall find it myself. Please follow me!' George was out the door with an air of confidence.

'You will?'

'Yes! Please follow!'

'But... Sir!' she shouted in an attempt to halt his progress.

For some unknown reason they left the office and began to follow George back down the corridor and towards a hanger marked **"Flights for Hire"**.

When they entered, George shouted.

'Andy, where are you?'

'Over hear! And you are late!' Andy replied.

'Yes! I know. We've been busy over the past few days and almost forgot about our meeting today, but we'll make it up to you,' George apologised.

'Come over here and meet my old friend and military colleague, Clive. He is a good man to know when it comes to spaceships, but I am not too sure about his choice in women.' Andy said those words in a very forthright manner. Nevertheless he was very embarrassed when he observed the three beautiful young ladies following behind. They had obviously heard his last remarks and were in a giggle.

'Andy, what do you think of her. I mean the ship,' asked George also in a giggle.

'Personally, I think she is fantastic, but needs a refitting and a new coat of paint. But that's just appearances. The structure is one of the most solid I've ever seen... although her LPDs require new inserts.' Andy said.

'So it's all superficial? In that case I shall go on your recommendation!' George replied.

'Yes! Why... do you think of buying her?' Andy said, with his usual broad smile.

'How much do you think she's worth? Give me an honest figure, taking into consideration the cost of a complete refit,' George said.

'I would say about one-seventy-five grand by today's inflation, but Clive is the right man to answer that question,' Andy replied.

'And... I would like to take her away to a private hanger and complete the refit myself and a few of my friends. Some of the ladies can do the interior design and deco while we work on the drives and other technical and more messy areas.'

'Wow! You are really going to buy her?'

'I am willing to offer one hundred and fifty in cash bonds. The money can be transferred to your account tomorrow. However, you will have to make me a promise, that you will take her back at a good price in your favour when we decide to upgrade to a better model in the future.'

'I accept!' Clive replied.

'Here is my card,' George said.

'Clive couldn't believe his eyes, for he beheld a Solarian Platinum Card. That card represented a currency credit of a cool million dollars. Even Jerry was surprised and Andy stuttered.

'Bloody hell! One... cool... million!'

'Do we have a deal, Clive?' George insisted.

'Yes, Sir. We have a deal for whenever you decide to return her and if you like, I can keep my eyes out for something a lot better,' Clive replied.

'Keep Andy informed on those matters for me in the future. Now, can we look her over?' George asked.

'Follow me, and I will show you around,' Clive replied.

'What do you think guys?' Jerry asked.

'I think it's a dump! I think she is too expensive for a single trip to Mars!' Miranda commented.

'Perhaps it will serve our purpose. The rest of it we can do ourselves. But it's so large!' Cathy exclaimed.

'Yes! She was originally designed to carry seventy-five passengers in comfort, with three bars, ballroom, dining room and large bunks. Not to mention her own safety docks, with three LPD life boats. Those are capable of a journey to and from Mars within two weeks, fully laden with passengers and rations.'

'I can see potentials!' Jerry said.

'Yes, she has lots. When we are through she will look like a mobile palace,' George said.

'She started service ten years ago as a luxury cruiser, but since the depression we found ourselves understaffed and the luxury side of the business declined.' Clive continued.

'I know what you mean,' George replied.

'Her last trip was two years ago, but we constantly check her over. We have to in order to retain her license after each yearly inspection.' Clive said.

They followed him up to the highest level and into the cockpit area, then unto the lowest of the three decks. They observed the spacesuit lockers and then the small dock with the almost brand new and yet unused lifeboats.

The group soon realised the vessel had tremendous potential as a luxurious space cruiser and was still quite new. Such a ship once fitted could fetch more than triple what he paid for her.

'In future this ship will be used by the Gang for all our extraterrestrial efforts and adventures!' George said and they were pleased.

When they were finished looking her over, they returned to the office and Clive entered the special card into his computer. As he did, up popped George's image and other relevant information. Underneath was written, "Coordinator in chief, Unitec. A subsidiary of Solarian Banking".

Clive blushed and nervously read the information, giving him back his card in the process.

'Anything more I can do for you, Sir?' he asked, humbly.

This time he gave a slight curtsy. But George humbly bowed in return and asked him to keep in touch. Then George looked towards Andy.

'Let's go for some lunch. We have more things to discuss, People!' George insisted.

They dashed off to the local spaceport restaurant, soon found an empty table and placed their orders.

'It's a beautiful ship, don't you all think so?' Cathy asked.

'Yes! Although I thought it looked awful when I first entered, I must agree, I soon changed my mind when I saw the beautiful ballroom and kitchen facilities,' Miranda said.

'I am happy you like it, because I've got you all shares in it to the value of fifty grand each.'

'Fifty grand!' Cathy shouted.

'Let's see... there is seven of us, including Andy, so when we are finished refitting and decorating, she should fetch about three hundred and fifty grand. That investment can always be put against another when we decide to change. But we need to delegate responsibilities before we start, so you, Andy, can be the captain, subject to a common vote of course.'

'I am in!' he replied.

'The rest of us can fill in with other duties, whatever we are most suited to...' George said, with a pleasant smile.

'You are very generous. Are you sure about that decision, George?' Cathy inquired, as if looking after his interests and welfare.

'Yes! I am afraid so!'

'I have a strange feeling that we are stuck with each other from now. If that's the way things are going to be, we should have a common denominator for our interstellar space cruises. And I mean real interstellar and not by LPDs. Something almost infinitely faster and more powerful.'

'What are you saying?' Jerry inquired.

'Really George?' Cathy and the others were confused with his change of character.

'I shall explain it all to you later. My friends, Andy was correct about his strange visitors and I now know about things that I couldn't even have dreamt of before yesterday.'

'You do? Stranger and stranger!' Miranda said.

'What do you mean?' Jerry inquired, but George was not in the mood for answering those questions.

'Life is so beautiful, isn't it? So let's enjoy ourselves. And please don't ask me any more questions about my present decision. Other decisions we can vote for in a more democratic manner as and when the need arises,' George remained in a manner unknown to them as if super charged by a new form of energy.

'Now, I know who is running the show!' Ann said.

'Count me in!' said Andy.

The others also gave in under pressure. Jerry couldn't understand the vast changes in George. He was now so clever and mature, almost to the point of bending their minds, and yet he was still so humble, loving and generous. What a character to look up to, he thought.

'You have discovered some more information about what we

discussed?' Andy asked.

'Yes, friends. I have documentation and videos of their trip from Andromeda. I mean the Andromedan galaxy. It took them only a single day to get here with that special ship you saw on the lawn. But there is a lot more besides and lots of danger for everyone within our Milky Way Galaxy, or Osmaron as they prefer to call it,' George replied.

'Where is this Osmaron?' Cathy inquired.

'It's the name given to our Milky Way galaxy by the Ancients, now existing on a most beautiful planet called Eden. We are all invited to that world and can visit anytime we choose. But I prefer to visit by spaceship. I think it's a lot more exciting than instant transmission via inter-dimensional portals.'

'Portals... like in the movies?' Miranda couldn't believe they were having such a ridiculous and strange conversation.

'Yep! And I also hold the master keys to the Solarian domes on Mars. All we have to do now, is rebuild our beautiful ship and take off.' George uttered those words with great sincerity in his voice and the others believed in his every word, although completely astonished by his incredible knowledge.

'There is a lot more besides and whatever we discuss about such matters must always remain with the Gang!'

'We always do! After all, we are one big loving family!' Cathy replied.

'Andy, I would like you to visit us at a meeting to be held at Jerry's place day after tomorrow. On the evening of the tenth. You can be there from seven if you like. I will only take yes for an answer. Anyway, it's probably going to be the most important day of our lives. It relates to life, death and the extinction of worlds like Earth on a massive scale. However, for security reasons, I would like our future group to remain, as of the past, but including Andy as an additional member, subject to the usual vote of course,' George replied.

'Yes! I shall be happy to partake!'

'That's done, then!'

'Can I take my wife along for friendship's sake? She is very much like you all. Without her help over those past years I would never have been able to get this close to the truth and there is a lot more like her about the place,' Andy replied.

'Yes! I understand what you mean. Very soon they will all be herded in, to assist within the greater plan,' George said. This time, with a strange awareness and power within his being.

'I have been chosen to fulfil that role,' he said, as if staring through the building to a greater beyond. Then their meals arrived.

CHAPTER 13

A grand beginning

The following morning George phoned Jerry's apartment to check on the whereabouts of his friends. Since Arel's warning about the extreme Infilates called the Beta-Five he became more concerned.

'I am sorry, but he has just left for the city.'

Who is calling?' Cathy inquired.

'It's me... George!'

'Hi!'

'You are there all alone?'

'Yes! He took Miranda to the library and left me here to tidy up.'

'Tell you what, why don't you accompany me later on today? I would like to visit a few properties in the locality. Don't worry about transport, we can use Oscar with his manual override option. He's auto-packed not too far from here.'

'Would love to! I suppose! Most of the work here is done!'

'Do we have a date?' he asked.

'What do you think? Of course we have a date. I was getting quite bored with this place, anyway, and you are the best offer I've had for some time now.' she replied.

'I shall be around in one hour, so expect my door call within that time,' George said and hung up.

Over the months they had grown close together. George tended not to show his innermost feelings. Therefore Cathy always tended to make the first move by teasing him.

When he arrived, she was already waiting for him in the upper corridor.

'It's a gorgeous day and you always look so beautiful and spectacular!' He greeted.

'I can live with such spectacular complements,' she replied in jest and like a gentleman he kissed her on the cheek.

'I have to visit three properties today, so I would appreciate your advice and perhaps we could have a quiet lunch afterwards in a restaurant of your choice. What do you say?'

'It sounds fab. If you like, we could visit a local French restaurant I know.'

'Sounds cool!'

'Do you like French cuisine?' she asked.

'Yes! I do when I can afford it.'

'I only know of the Splendour. My mother used it regularly when she and dad lived in the area. But that's another story.' She said, sadly.

'I detect a hint of sadness in your voice. Why is that?'

'My father died two years ago from food poisoning in a foreign country, and the family has never been the same since. My mother now lives within an unsecured zone and due to her security phobias I can only visit her occasionally while accompanied.'

'If I was you, I wouldn't worry too much about security matters in the future. I have two hunter-killers on order. They are to be dispatched to me within a fortnight or so,' he replied.

'What are these... hunter-killers?'

'A new type of security android. Although they look just like people, they have very acute senses and a nuclear power pack capable of taking a complete city apart to find an individual,' he said with a grin on his face.

'Are you serious, George?' she replied, with a tone of the ridiculous in her voice and looking deeply into his eyes.

'I love you when you do that!'

'Do what?'

'You have such beautiful blue-green eyes and a special charm and disposition that goes with them,' he said, with another happy grin on his face.

'Are you serious about that love part, George?' she inquired, looking even deeper into his eyes. She was in love with him and always wanted a relationship.

'Perhaps if we were able to get along together and see eye to eye on things in the future. And if you are able to stand by me through thick and thin. But that's a lot of commitment.'

'I don't mind commitment!'

'I don't know if you can handle it? Things might get very rough in the future,' he replied, as if asking her to take on the most important job of her life.

'Yes! I think I can handle it; if you are able to do likewise with me and treat me properly and with respect,' she said.

'I give you one thing. I think you are quite a gutsy lady. I like those qualities in a woman!'

'Ah... here we are... the first house. What do you think? Doesn't she look splendid from the air?'

'But it's a mansion... with at least fifty acres of land. It's the Hearst's Mansion, isn't it? I once saw it in a journal on ancient architecture,' she replied. She was utterly amazed.

'Yes! But their empire is now on a downward spiral and I have been given the option to buy. I did a recent check and it's going to be well above the waterline in the next hundred years or so, and there is no chance of flooding from extreme weather.'

'You considered Global Warming?'

'Yes, I did. I always do such checks before I buy anything these days. The waterline is still rising you know. I tell you what, why don't we scan them all by air first before landing to have a more personal view of the chosen one's interior. That way, we'll save a lot of time.'

She nodded subconsciously, but was absorbed by the beautiful mansion with greener than green fields and horses grazing.

'Shall we?' he insisted.

'Ok!' she replied quietly.

Then he pushed a button on the front panel taking Oscar off manual.

'Oscar, please take us to the others first,' he said to the car.

'Yes, George!' the car replied to her amazement and darted off in another direction, away from the mansion.

'This car of yours talks!' she exclaimed.

'He's been around for a while and has picked up much in his travels. He was left to me by an uncle, Mal. I don't even remember him. Apparently he used to visit when I was a small kid and had since died. I treat Oscar like another family member. I think he is almost human,' George said, sadly.

'I'm sorry to hear about that! Oscar is probably one of those super intelligent Roadstars they had a few decades ago. They were only used by presidents and very wealthy people,' she replied, but he changed the topic back to their current mission of house hunting.

'You know, you better make a good choice, because our organisation will need lots of space in the future. Furthermore, when you become my wife you'll like to live in a beautiful and secured home with enough space for family, friends and visitors,' he said, moving closer to her.

'Are you proposing to me, George?' she chuckled.

'I suppose I am, but I think we should give it a little time before I get the engagement ring and officially announce it to our friends and family. Shall we say two weeks of close encounters and getting to know each other better? That is if you fully agree to what I said earlier.'

'I agree to all of it! I'll be honoured, Darling!' she replied and they kissed passionately.'

'You already carry all the credentials of a super woman, you know, and you are one of the most loving and caring persons I've ever met,' he said, in a practical tone of voice.

'I can always try my best, shouldn't that be good enough?' she replied.

Although they had a thorough view of the other buildings, their heart was set on the Hearst's Mansion, so they landed on the forecourt just beyond its main gates and followed the caretaker towards the front door.

A very tall lady approached them carrying a folder in one hand. She was quite surprised when she saw the age of the couple. They had barely passed their teens.

'We have been expecting you... Mister George Peterson?' she said, not quite believing that such young people could afford the price of the place, and he shook his head in a positive manner.

'Please follow me, for a general tour of the mansion!'

'Ok, wood love to!'

'You wouldn't believe it... this place was built just after the second world war, in the twentieth century, and has been maintained to very high standards since. This building is truly massive by normal standards and contains every conceivable utility, even two advanced Tec robots to do the heavy work about the garden.'

'Better and better!' George replied.

'During its heyday, it has seen many important parties including visits by past Presidents of our country, the USE and others.'

The place was truly massive and contained stables, a large hanger for helicopter or small space-cruiser, which was now empty, servant quarters and a range of outbuildings. One was originally used as laboratory and workshop for electronic prototype production, with a small adjacent mechanical workshop.

'Anthony was correct in his advice,' he mumbled to himself, while considering the conversation they had regarding his new organization and the incredible freedom bestowed by his present financial status.

The front of the building was also quite spectacular in appearance and looked Greek, with two large marble pillars on either side of the expansive panning gradient stairway. Just in front of the house was a beautiful fountain with an Olympian statue set into the centre of a square of flower beds. On either side were two wide avenues straddled by palmist trees. Those types had been specially bio-engineered for that climate.

Cathy was completely overwhelmed by the place and couldn't help but say yes, at any cost.

'Well, my Cathy, is your mind made up?' he asked.

'If you like... It's so beautiful... so divine... so utterly... fantastic!' She said.

She was almost speechless, but stared into his eyes with that strange piercing look.

'Can you really afford it, Darling?' she mumbled, when they were well away from their lady escort. He had never heard her say the word "Darling" like that before and knew she had accepted his offer of marriage.

'We shall take it!'

'Really, Sir!'

'Yes! Please contact my solicitors in order to arrange the transaction.' She soon got on her Coms.

'Here is my card,' he said. She took the platinum card from him and nervously entered it into her computer keyboard.

Although voice recognition was mainly used, her facility was not voice print in the truest sense. Further, speech could not be used for the entry of special security code when dealing with large sums of money, and other coded methods could have been duplicated. Criminals were always a few steps behind all such security methods and several had to be used during such transactions.

When she saw the words Chief Coordinator and Solarian Banking, her eyes almost popped out of their sockets and Cathy was equally taken back.

'You are one of their chief administrators, George?' Cathy asked, defiantly.

But the woman continued processing the data and then gave him back the card.

'Everything has been arranged, Sir. It will be ready for you within two weeks. We have to complete some slight refurbishment as part of the contract,' she said and personally showed them out of the mansion towards their Roadstar.

'I want you to shut up for a moment, and come back with me to my flat, because I have a lot to explain to you and all of it is good. Have you ever known me to be a bad guy?' he shouted back at her.

Although she was quite mad to begin with, she soon calmed down. At that time many saw Solarian Banking as a dinosaur with the ability to swallow up small fish in one gulp and tended to keep well away from its claws. However that concept had been created by Solarian Banking themselves to keep separate from other Earthly organizations.

'I told you before... that... if you wanted to be with me you would have to be honest, truthful and committed, with no preconceptions. Any biases you might have against Solarian Banking are misconstrued, misguided and misplaced. You will have to put those ideas out of your mind when you hear my side of the story, and believe me, I know the whole story. It's the story you cannot learn by daily excursions to the old city library, because all that information is out of date and redundant anyway.'

'Are you sure, Darling?'

'I am one hundred percent. You must always trust me above everything else.'

'I will try!'

'Can you do that little thing for me, Love?' He said, with most sincere feelings of affection than ever before, even using the word "Love" for the first time.

'I shall try as hard as I can, Darling!' she insisted, in an almost equivalent state of mind, but somewhat subdued by his forcefulness.

The Roadstar, Oscar, was once more in the air and flying towards his building which was next door to Jerry's. His apartment was three levels below the building's landing-pad, which combined a car park. They decided to walk the rest of the way to his apartment. At that time most LPD car parks were conveniently placed on the top of buildings for security reasons.

'My Love, all of our lives are in grave danger and I have to start recruiting sincere people like us, to join up with a much larger group within our galaxy in order to fight a deadly foe. However, you must keep whatever you learn from me under your hat for now. Knowledge of that kind of stuff will only worry people.'

'I don't know what to say!'

'Do you like to watch horror movies? Well, let us have a couple of drinks first and then we can both relax and watch it together. You can cry in my arms if it upsets you too much,' he said.

They soon entered and he took her into the lounge and went off to get the drinks. When they were settled, he shouted. 'Ron, where are you?'

There was a strange glow on the table and the black case suddenly appeared from nowhere, then the holographic image of Ron in the form of George suddenly appeared, standing in front of them.

'You didn't tell me you could also disappear like that,' he asked the hologram.

'I often disappear like that when I retreat into deep meditation, but I am now ready for your commands, Master!' Ron replied.

'My God, he could be your twin brother!' Cathy exclaimed.

'Yep! He also has a good dress sense! Will you show us that video on the destruction of Caefon?' he commanded.

'Ron is the latest in my homely additions and now another adopted member of my family. He is a master Coms, designed and built by the Solarians,' George said.

'Do you mean Solarian Banking, Darling?'

'No, Love, I mean the galactic empire called Solaria, of which we are an insignificant part. Solarian Banking is just a front they use to keep in touch with us. They are so advanced, they have little need for money. So it's not a bank in the truest sense of the word.'

'You are not kidding me?'

'No, I am not! Anyway, Let's watch the film!' he demanded and they began to watch. About half way through she burst into tears.

'Darling, do you think that will also happen to Earth?' she asked, with tears flowing down her beautiful cheeks.

'They are also on their way to Earth, but will not arrive until a century or so. It will take us that long to prepare for them. So you see why we have to start organising. There is a lot more information to sort through, but I have started to prepare a lecture with a video for tomorrow evening. That is the reason why I want everyone to be there. So promise me, no more visits to the library. Instead, you can spend more time with me, learning more about this wealth of information we now have at our disposal.'

'Whatever you want, Darling!'

'I also have information on Jerry's grandparents, but that can wait until after the lecture.'

'You found them?'

'Yes! They are alive on a world called Eden!'

'My God! Jerry will be so happy! But now, I am so worried for everyone!'

'Don't worry, with the right planning, we'll win the day!'

'Ron, thank you. That's enough for now. You may return to your meditations until tomorrow,' he commanded, then the image disappeared and the black case gradually faded from view.

'I wonder where he goes to?' she inquired.

'Perhaps he is just a figment of our imagination,' George replied. She suddenly held him and couldn't stop hugging him. Then she kissed him with the greatest love and affection she could muster.

'And to think I thought you were up to something dishonourable. I should have known better, My Darling.'

Whatever you want, just hallo. Wherever you wish to go, I shall follow. And that is the true nature of my love for you or I don't know what love is.' She said and kissed him again.

When they returned to Jerry's apartment that day he and Miranda had already returned from the library. Cathy had left them a note in order to inform them of her whereabouts and to alleviate fears of kidnapping or foul-play.

'So you lovebirds have returned!' Miranda greeted, with a sarcastic smile and expression. Cathy blushed and Jerry was suddenly convinced that they were having an affair.

'Is it serious?'

'Very!' George replied.

'I told her mother I would keep an eye on her. You can take over that duty and responsibility from me, Brother,' he demanded.

'Happily!' George replied.

'We haven't found much in the library today, just strange information,' Jerry said, looking more despondent than usual.

'What strange information?' George inquired.

'About those Andromedans.'

'I don't know why you bother with that old library. Did you know that our group is under constant surveillance by some very unsavoury Infilate extremists? So we must all be very careful and vigilant in the future,' George advised.

'You are not kidding?' Miranda was not happy.

'You know that special writing we saw on some documents from Cathy's mother. Well, the library computer said it's a common Osmaron dialect. How could it be an Osmaron dialect, if as you said, Osmaron is our Milky-Way galaxy?' Jerry inquired.

'Yes! Yes! Sunolingua is a common galactic language dialect, used by many humanoid forms in prehistoric times. It used to be the main merchant's dialect, like English is to Earth... used over many aeons since the second galactic upheaval just after the Juvine period. Being highly conceptual it's ideal for quick communication between aliens, particular when using similar brain implants. You can also use that language to communicate with dogs and cats directly when wearing Brain Implants.'

'You are not kidding me again, are you?'

'Never! The Andromedans and others may have updated our galactic history on those topics,' George replied.

'Come now, let me have some paper,' George demanded and they gathered around as he began to scribble the strange script on a sheet of paper.

'Now, let's compare notes for similarity,' he said. But as they compared the strange writing, the basic characters were identical. They couldn't believe that he also knew that language fluently.

'Let me read my note first.

"I made a promise to take my beloved to lunch today, but due to unforseen circumstances was unable to fulfil that promise. In my book, every promise should be kept, so I trust you don't mind if I treat you to dinner at one of the best French restaurants in the area. I shall not take no for an answer.

My Roadstar, Oscar, is ready and waiting.

To my best friend, Jerry, and his beloved.

End of note."

He read the note he had written in an amusing frame of mind and the group couldn't suppress their laughter.

'Look, both last sentences are almost identical!' exclaimed Cathy, still smiling.

'That is what my little note says, and the last sentence reads, *"End of note."* in both cases,' George said.

'Goodness, can you read the other note for me, please!' Jerry asked.

'Yes, my friend. All you have to do is ask and it will be done. So now, let me read the second note.

"To Dr. Jeffery Longhurst.
Sorry Jeff, but I am unable to visit Mars tomorrow, to assist in the evacuation program of our people from Caefon.
I trust everything goes well with the Omegron Portal.
See you soon.
Joel Meron.
End of note."

'What do you make of *"evacuation to Mars"* and *"Omegron Portal'"* Jerry asked.

'The Omegron Portal is a device used to transfer or evacuate millions of people from one galaxy to another. It uses the H-Dimension.'

'H-Dimension?'

'The Omegron Portal on Mars was used to evacuate over ten million people from our sister-galaxy, Andromeda. I shall tell you people about more tomorrow evening, because I do not wish to repeat myself a countless number of times before then,' he said, with that strange look in his eyes and a stranger type of power surging through his veins.

'Where do you get all this knowledge from?' Miranda asked with utter surprised.

'You will all know soon enough!' was his vague reply.

At that moment in time George felt he knew all and could accomplish almost any task. For that strange computer had an incredible influence on his mind. Little did he know that it was not even what Arel thought it was. Not even, that it had been enhanced by the Grand Lord himself. The one of many names. The Supreme Being responsible for our part of the universe. The time had come for Earth to start moving forward again and this time a great leader had been selected to bring her peoples together.

Jerry and the others suddenly realised that the whole situation was now way over their heads and decided to calmly wait for the day when all would be revealed.

CHAPTER 14

A meeting of friends

The morning of the tenth had finally arrived. Suddenly they were busy cleaning and reorganising Jerry's large apartment. It was one of those beautiful days that instilled vision and purpose in even the most inadequate of minds. At dawn George put on his track suit and went for a long jog through the local park. He intended to use those peaceful moments to reflect on his life and make some future plans of his own to include Cathy.

He observed the beautiful green trees, local horses and singing birds and wondered what Earth would resemble after a brief visit by those monsters call Javols. Having seen the film of Caefon and the changes before and after their departure he was not assured. Nevertheless he accepted his future duties were towards a much greater cause than mere anti pollution demonstrations, as in the past with Jerry. He also realised he had a lot to learn and a very long road to trail towards his goal. Yet, so much damage had been done to his once beautiful planet by callous mankind over the previous centuries. He also hoped Earth and its numerous life could be brought back from the brink.

The route ahead was a difficult one, but he didn't mind taking it if he had Cathy by his side through thick and thin. He also had to keep her safe and shielded from any dangers along the way. He thought Jerry was correct about handing him over the responsibility of taking care of her. He would never allow her to visit any more old city libraries with them, because that was the riskiest of all adventures. From now on, wherever he went, she would follow and when he wasn't around she would be fully guarded.

'It was quite regrettable Jerry had taken his advise in such an irresponsible manner and still stubbornly pursued his own ridiculous efforts out of personal ambition. Why doesn't he take me seriously and why was he always so sarcastic. Perhaps he will change his mind in time, when he hears more of what I have to say. That is, if he seriously wants to listen.' George pondered over those thoughts for a while.

He continued his jogging until he reached the furthest end of the park and started the return journey back to his apartment, still considering those important matters.

After he arrived, he had a cold shower, woke Ron from his meditation and carried on preparing his important lecture.

Jerry had phoned Cathy's mother, Pamela, telling her the good news of her daughter's relationship with George, while inviting her to the party. Then new groceries and other orders were placed via Coms to prepare for that evening's reunion.

It was not long before the women and Jerry joined forces in the kitchen and began to prepare an assortment of recipes for a full three-course session.

George was still with his computer while putting the final touches to his speech. By lunchtime he was finished and decided to get changed. This time he wore an expensive light cream suit with the Solarian winged insignia pinned to his left lapel. That suit was well cut from London and made him look quite princely.

He grabbed Ron, along with a package of gifts for his friends and darted off towards his Roadstar, Oscar. On arrival he removed his jacket and was going to wear an apron, with the intention of assisting the cooks. However they had already done most of the work and all that was required, was setting the oven and microwave timers for cooking the meals. Miranda soon asked Cathy to join him while she took over in the kitchen.

It was not long before the door buzzer rang and Cathy's mother arrived.

'Mum, what are you doing here? You didn't tell me you were coming?' Cathy inquired with surprise while overwhelmed by curiosity.

'No, my darling, I meant it as a surprise. It was all done in a hurry, anyway. I had to literally tear myself away from my article to visit my editor. While I was in town I thought of visiting you guys. And here I am!' Pamela said, with hands outstretched. Despite her age, which was in the early fifties, she looked in her early forties and was almost as beautiful as her daughter.

'Anyway, thanks for coming!'

'Are you not pleased to see me?' Pamela asked.

'I am sorry for not mentioning it before, but I also wanted her to come along because she seemed to have lots of ideas on a subject close to our hearts and thought her input might shed some light. I also thought... you and George would like to talk to her about future plans?' Jerry said, appearing somewhat concerned.

Jerry was never the diplomatic type or ever known to mince his words. He had a reputation for jumping straight into the deep end while trying to sort the consequences out afterwards.

'So it's not all about George and myself?' Cathy inquired equally sarcastic but fuming with anger.

'You know, I wanted to tell mum about it myself. Now the surprise is completely lost. Don't you ever take such decisions on our behalf in the future? Never again, you hear me!' Cathy bellowed in utter fury, realising that he had chosen to preempt their most important personal decisions.

'Perhaps it's an act of providence your mother visited us today. Anyway, we shouldn't be arguing like this on such a beautiful day. Why don't you introduce me, Love!' George asked in a most pleasant manner, quelling all disagreements. Cathy then went to her mother, hugged her and took her over to George.

'Mum, this is my boyfriend, George Peterson,' she said with a glint in her eye.

'I see.... It seems very serious... I am pleased to meet you George!'

'I like the way she puts it, but we are not just close friends. We are thinking of getting married in the not too distant future and intended to ask for your blessings before we got engaged. Perhaps we can discuss those important matters tomorrow, that is, if you don't mind?' George said.

'Very charming, and also very British. Why didn't you mention him to me before, my darling?' Pamela inquired.

'No, Mum, I couldn't. We only got together recently and it's not what you think. We love each other and it's a very responsible and loving relationship. Many plans have already been set in motion,' Cathy replied.

'We have already bought the house, which I think you will all love. Why don't you move in with us after our marriage? It's a lot more secure than your current residence and you will have your family around you, but with your present choices and freedom. There are also some fifty acres, plus horses, stables, greenhouses and other accommodation and facilities. Not to mention one of the most modern security systems on the planet,' George said.

'It sounds like a most beautiful place,' Pamela replied.

'Mec can always have a job in the kitchen practising his recipes as before. Anyway, we would like someone to hold the fort for us whenever we are away. Please think about these matters and give us your decisions tomorrow,' George added.

'What house is that?' Jerry inquired.

'It's the Hearst's Mansion, just fifteen kilometres away,' Cathy replied.

'Hell! That's the most auspicious building in the area. I remember once touring it with my school friends, many years ago.' Miranda said.

'Gosh! How can you afford such a place? It's probably worth millions...' Jerry said, with modest disapproval.

'I know! I once visited it when I wrote an article for the Architectural Times. But that was years ago!' Pamela said.

'Come on, People! I needed a large place for our organization. It seemed to tick all the boxes!' George interrupted.

'Gosh, my darling, your future husband is so wealthy and you kept him from me all this time?' Pamela said in jest.

'I told you, Mum!'

'George, you will have to keep an eye on my daughter, because she has a tendency to be very extravagant and loves to dress,' Pamela said.

'I am sure she has taken after her mother in that regard. As far as I am concerned, my wife can do whatever she desires in that department. Whatever belongs to me also belongs to her. However, I have a strong suspicion that she will be involved with more important matters in the future,' a democratic George replied.

'You haven't answered my question about the cost?' Jerry insisted.

'It's not as expensive as you think. These days many are leaving those areas for higher ground. As a result of which property prices in those areas have taken a dive,' George replied, being as vague as he could to divert attention from his present financial status.

Suddenly Pamela was very pleased with her future choice of son-in-law. She soon began to talk about wedding presents and so did the others after congratulations were over.

At last, Jerry and his other friends had begun to take George seriously. The man now had an aura of power, not only manifested by money, although that was also a very important factor in their world at that time, but mainly because he had a way of getting things right and tended to be always there for them whenever he was needed. Her mother, Pamela, also felt a lot more at home with the younger group within that more secured area, well away from her lonely life in dangerous suburbia.

CHAPTER 15

A gathering of The Gang

The rest of The Gang began arriving from six o'clock onwards. Tim Chiang was first, followed by Andy Colman and his wife Joan, then Carol Barnes.

Barry Stenburg and Ann Baxter had spent the night at Jerry's apartment with the intentions of helping in the many preparations of that day. They had assisted in finding out more about Solarian Banking, but soon found it was the most guarded organization on the planet. Therefore they left all future investigative work to George who was presently on the inside.

'Friends and colleagues, before we begin to partake in this most exquisite meal, I would like you to join me in a toast to my dearest friends, George and Cathy, and to congratulate them both on their future engagement. I am pretty sure the next party we visit will be held at the Hearst's Mansion, and congratulations to those who cooked us such a splendid meal? Jerry said.

'Congratulations!'

They held their glasses and drank the toast to the happy couple.

'I suppose, you would like me to say a few words. Well, Cathy and I have already extended our invitations to present company. However, we haven't yet set the date, so invitation cards will be sent after she decides,' George said, while glancing at Cathy for her approval. They happily smiled and settled down to dinner.

'Jerry, I am very sorry about what happened to our past President, and of your father's recent appointment to that dangerous post. Knowing his views, I am sure he will handle his new office with great zeal and fortitude,' Tim said, having been away from the Gang for a while.

'Thanks for your considerations. These days if it's not deadly plagues, it's Infilate scum killing our dear Presidents,' Jerry replied.

'I have been told of a new caper. Well, not exactly, just a hint of something important going on with you guys and I have an acute sense of being left out of the action. I have recently taken my exams and are now free to join this one, if you will have me on board, that is?' Carol said.

'Me to!' Tim yelled.

'We are off to Mars, so you'll need a short crash course in astronaut training. In case we get into trouble. Just to hold your end. See Andy afterwards,' George replied.

'Mars! I always wanted to visit that planet!' Tim was happy.

'Immediately after dinner, I would like you all to join me in the lounge. I have a few presentations to make and new nominations and honours to bestow for services rendered. Also to discuss future plans before I begin my lecture,' George said.

Suddenly, they realised who was the new boss of The Gang and curious to hear what he had to say.

The moment they finished dinner and were freshened up, they joined him in the lounge, with drinks. George took his strange little black briefcase and followed them.

'Tim and Carol, it's nice to see you with us again. What began as a simple holiday to Mars has now taken a new dimension, but that aspect will be discussed in a moment. From now onwards, you are all members of a new order, to be symbolised by this insignia that most of you are already wearing. Although in a similar vein to our old gang, our future efforts will now expand outwards, beyond Earth and even beyond our own Osmaron galaxy.'

They were transfixed by his strange attitudes and words.

'Because of those developments, I have decided to nominate you all as permanent members. Furthermore, as Chief Coordinator of Operations within Unitec, I have taken it upon myself to give you certain facilities and privileges within Solarian Banking. Unitec will be the public name of our organisation to outsiders in the future.'

'Ok!' Jerry replied.

'Your initial status also allows you certain funds, which will enable you greater benefits and freedom while working for the organisation than are available to you at this time.'

'Really?' Miranda was intrigued.

'Whenever I refer to individuals, I shall include all married couples as a single unit, and in this instance include Cathy and myself as one unit. These benefits will include a home of your choosing, to a maximum value of two million dollars and a one million-dollar Platinum Card. Although you have a choice to do as you wish with these gifts, I strictly advise you, as friends, to save the card for expenses other than your initial payment towards your home.'

'Am I going insane or did he just mentioned two million dollars?' Tim said to Jerry.

'I am afraid so!' Jerry replied.

'All future expenses accrued during active duty for our organisation will be reimbursed, so please take note of all such expenses in future. The following names have been selected, subject to their final approval. As I call your names, please come forward to accept your gifts!'

They were stunned, but went along all the same.

'Mister Gerald Fraser.... Miss Miranda Fernandez.... Mister Barry Stenburg.... Miss Ann Baxter.... Mister Andy Colman and one extra card for his wife .... Miss Catherine Keenan, just for her Platinum Card.... Missis Pamela Keenan.... Mister Tim Chiang... and finally, Miss Carol Barnes,' he said, as he handed them their gifts.

They each received a cheque of two million dollars made payable to them on Solarian Banking and one Platinum Card. Each new member also received an insignia which they immediately and enthusiastically clipped unto their clothes. They were aghast by it all but went along and accepted their gifts. Jerry also received a small packet of special photos of his grandparents, with a note from them that was written to his father in English, and other important information regarding the future. The moment Jerry opened that envelope he left the room in utter shock.

'This is supposed to be an informal and friendly discussion, so before I take the floor, I would like Miranda to give us an update on her current findings and perhaps Jerry could also assist her after his return.'

They sat and waited patiently for whatever was to come next.

'Please wait for a moment while I attempt to find and comfort him,' George said, as he momentarily left the room to look for his old friend, Jerry.

Jerry had opened the packet and was gazing trance-like at the strange three-dimensional photos of his grand parents. He looked at the inscription of the date taken and viewed the images again.

'Good God! They are alive! They are really alive! And so young... so darn young! How could they be so young?' he asked, almost in tears of joy.

'Youth drugs, I suppose. We already have the technology to alter the DNA and improve cell replication. This is just an advanced stage of that process. Thinking about it, why does anyone, even us, have to grow old if we didn't want it,' George said.

'But where did you get these pictures from? They are not even normal photos, more like holograms that are activated by ambient light.'

'That's another story!'

'They are not even from Earth... are they? My grand parents are still alive on some strange planet... out there! I shall have to tell dad!' Jerry said, now with tears streaming from his eyes.

'Yes, my friend. That is the whole point of the exercise, but you will have to explain it gently to him. Not in your usual... bull in the china-shop manner!' George said.

'Will you come with me... when I go to tell him the incredible... great news?' Jerry asked, with a half smile.

'Why don't we arrange it over the next few days? We can also take the girls along and give them the time of their lives in DC. Cathy and Miranda will love that. They can also do some shopping for the wedding!'

'That will be nice. We can all go together!'

'Now come on, old friend... let's join the others. I have a task to perform,' George said in a gentler and more sympathetic voice.

After they had recovered from the previous shock of George's strange announcements and presentations. They still could not believe their luck. Miranda took the floor and began to tell them of their findings and experiences since they left the astronaut training camp. That was after having received Andy's folder and newspaper cuttings, which they had decided to follow up. Then the note from Pamela, with the strange writing and finally, people with sea-blew eyes, six fingers and two thumbs. She then explained their final day in the library and the equally strange information given them by the library computer.

When she had said everything of importance, she sat down and George got up with his black case in hand to tell his version of the story.

CHAPTER 16

A new cause to fight

George placed the small case on the side table and began his strange lecture.

'Yes, Miranda! That was a very good summation of events, but only an insignificant part of the information I now have at my disposal. However, before I can get to those more relevant points, I have first to take you out on a trip, beyond our planet Earth, even beyond our galaxy and into the remotest past... to the absolute beginning. Because you need an overview of cosmic events. But I shall not dwell too lengthily on those historical matters!' There was a silent pause.

'Ron, take us back to the beginning!' George commanded and they wondered who this Ron was, but to their amazement the black case began to glow and a three-dimensional image took form against the wall which grew out towards them. Suddenly there was the sound of a massive explosion, as if coming from the centre of the image. A point of light or glow exploded into a myriad of lights that began to grow as parts began to move out of that centre towards them.

'That was the start of all primal evolution at the beginning of our universe and there are seven such universes, occupying a single plane, each with their own primal and causal laws, although similar in most respects. This image relates only to our universe. Now you may see certain turbulent areas where lights form into galaxies. This point occurred about ten billion years ago. Our present point in time corresponds to about sixteen point eight billion years from the start of this cycle,' he said. But they were each completely absorbed by the moving image as if under hypnosis.

'Our universe is much like a living organism, with the abilities to recycle its elements and maintain the evolution of life over a very long time-scale. Therefore, the universe we observe today has been recycled several times. Each cycle being approximately twentysix point eight billion years.'

They were amazed, but listened carefully to what George had to say.

'Primal evolution began about three-billion years after the formation of the first galaxies and subsequently, the formation of solid planetary masses within certain distances from their parent stars. That was after the first massive stars began to age and explode into supernovae. Thus spreading heavier elements like carbon and metals throughout space. Those heavier elements lay the foundations for the first nucleic acids and other complex biological molecules required in the creation of primal life. Those subsequently formed the basis of all naturally evolving primal living organisms within planetary environments. You see, within the Greater Purpose all universes have evolved solely for the perpetuation of primal life in its many different attributes and varieties. In a sense, our universe is much like a factory for the creation of life. If we wanted to manufacture a range of cars, and other vehicles we would create a factory, wouldn't we?'

He tirelessly continued his strange story.

'Anyway, within this periodic cycle most life was initiated over thirteen billion years ago and truly intelligent life-forms around ten billion years ago. During the following few billion years the universe became extremely turbulent, as many intelligent predator species took control for purposes of self-indulgence and power. The more predominant of those species were the Hexolytes, Drondy, Mesotrenes, Polyatans, to name but a few.'

The images on the screen showed a variety of the most vicious looking demons.

'Here are some images of those species. As you see, these predators travelled throughout our universe, corrupting and destroying young intelligent worlds for their personal satisfaction.'

Then the screen changed to a race of giant humans with incredible technologies.

'But there were also the ancient Warrior Patriarchs like Jull, Aron, Arel, Spasmortim, Vektron and many others. Those joined forces to fight those primordial monsters. During that era they cleared many planets of Hexolytes and Drondytes.'

The screen changed to Aron and his family of thirteen.

'Patriarch Aron was known as one of the greatest warriors of all time, with his famous indestructible cloak of darkness. He, his wife and children numbered thirteen, with six sons and five daughters. Jull was the greatest and most powerful of all his sons. Even today, that number is considered with dread, perhaps still imprinted on our primal minds.'

George continued:

'No one knows exactly to where those great patriarchs disappeared. But many still think they followed Lord Vektron and his people into that other parallel universe. But they could have gone elsewhere, even into cosmic hibernation until they were needed again.

'About the same time, the Plorans became fully independent technologically. That was some eight billion years ago. At that time they became completely disenchanted with the almost unstoppable levels of disorder and violence about them. They departed our universe to an almost perfect and stable one. One that was a more positive reflection of our own. So perfect, that life could never have evolved within its causal space-time boundaries. But the Plorans found ways to survive within that universe and there they remained until our universe was once again stable enough for them to return.

'After that period, several billion years ago, they returned to assist the remaining and more promising stable life-forms throughout this universe. They soon devised inter-dimensional routes throughout the Cosmos through which they could appear almost instantaneously.

'These red spots are their inter-dimensional bases built by Octans. They were devised for the protection of our Osmaron galaxy. These inter-dimensional bases are between universes and cannot be affected by any matter or substance from either.

'The seven main universes are ruled by seven Supreme Beings like gods who are brothers. No one is sure from whence they came, but they each have the equivalent mass of our solar system and that is probably also the size of their physical minds. However, they are very loving towards us and all other primal species, and plan for improvements every thousand cyclons

which is approximately one point six thousand years of our time.

'Their debates at their Heptarchal Nexus are held at the innermost plane of Gohenna, known to many as Goh, which is itself infinite in scope. Here, primal identities are collected and recycled back into cosmic life. It's a type of heaven, where anyone can be made mortal again, even after death.'

'It is in the nature of our universe that all living things evolve to ever higher levels. Those that are not suited to change are overtaken by those more capable. This is simply because we are all predators of a kind and have to gain nutrients from other living organisms. Even herbivores are predators, since they take nutrients from plants, which are themselves living organisms. To that end we grow stronger and adapt to eventually become a higher intelligence.

'However, this natural way, although necessary for evolution in its raw state, is not ideal when it comes to highly intelligent creatures like ourselves. This is why there is a new program for us to follow. It's called The Greater Purpose and follows the principles that all life is important and precious.

'Whenever possible, we try to move away from the prey and predator scenario and assist all endangered species. This is nothing new from the principles previously upheld by our original gang. However, we are now cosmic in scope and follow rules in line with The Greater Purpose.'

'Here is where I end this primordial history lesson, and now to explain our present involvement in the scheme of things. But before I resume, why don't we have a coffee break.'

As George said those words, the image faded from the wall and they began to stir within their seats. Suddenly a dazed Cathy and Miranda decided to get up and make coffee for their guests, followed by George.

CHAPTER 17

The amazing survival story

They were completely shaken by that incredible story but the worst was yet to come, as George continued.

'Now, we move in time to the present. Well, to be more precise, just three and a half thousand years ago, in the galaxy we call Andromeda. That was within Precinct Seven and it begins with a race of six fingered humans called the Ancients. They were a brilliant race, but very much like us, took many things for granted.

'Here is Meron and his wife Lucia playing with their children and pets over 3000 years ago. This is their beautiful world, very similar to our old Earth; the way our planet used to be about two hundred years ago. The main difference between our worlds is their grass, which is not green, but more like a violet moss covering the green meadows. At that time all polluting industrial activities were outlawed from their planet Caefon, to be re-sited on dead worlds and moons that were also used for mining. Here is their main city of Cantor and its people. It was also the head of their federation of planets.

'This is The Ship... Andy mentioned about in his notes and its operation. It was designed to travel between dimensional boundaries and could make the trip between galaxies in less than a single day. It was itself constructed of micro-robots or microids more commonly known to us as Nano-bots, a branch of Nano-technology.

'As you see, it was a most perfect society, with virtually zero environmental contaminants due to almost no industrial waste or pollution and with a controlled population growth. Each family being allowed a quota of children that was related only to their death-rate. Therefore, as their lifetimes increased, they were allowed fewer children. Anyone breaking the rules were not administered the special drugs which allowed them to procreate. Thus, maintaining an optimum population level.

'We could learn a lot from that race. Anyway, that was the way

it used to be before things began to go wrong on one of their more distant federation worlds. That was when some of their scientists began to create a new form of microid life. During those experiments something went wrong with the sample mass and a microid cancer began to grow, which subsequently took over all control of the complete sample. The new microid life-form destroyed their laboratories and by some process of duplication went on to destroy all life on that world and other neighbouring installations.

'This is Meron's transcript of the period and of his trip to Silo on board his spaceship, and here are the other people involved.... This is his brother, Plato, after their return from Silo.... The formation of their group to fight the threat... perhaps in some ways a parallel to our own group... and the building of the underground city of Lower Cantor.... Their rescuing mission throughout Andromeda and finally, the destruction of their world by the Javols....

'Now let me also show you that part.'

George said those words while the images of horror thundered unto the screen as the population of several billion humans were decapitated and eaten alive by the evil Javols. They had taken the forms of every disgusting, most horrible, monstrous and deadly forms to enact their gross deeds upon the innocent and unsuspecting populations. Some even transformed into large batlike vultures which swooped down to prey on little children. While those gore images continued, tears filled their eyes. But he continued.

'The Ancients had anticipated their possible extinction. They had also realised they would be required, by galactic law, to be around in the distant future to witness the demise of the Javols. They, with the aid of their friends from Osmaron, our galaxy, decided to put into motion a complex plan for our mutual survival. It included their return, some three thousand odd years in their future to assist in that master plan.

'Therefore they built a large underground city to which all essential people were evacuated. After the destruction of their beautiful planet they returned to their secret underworld and devised the introduction of the new bio-engineered human forms

with eight fingers, like us, to take control of Caefon. Those were to be evacuated before the Javols' final return to harvest their populations.

'Jon and the younger members were bio-engineered from the six Ancients' genes. That is why there was always such a close resemblance, despite their darker complexion and extra fingers. That was because the original Ancients could no longer exist on Caefon's surface due to new virulent strains and their own regressive genes. That is also the main reason why they were always so hygienic when they lived on Earth. Partly to do with a fear of infection and the trauma and aftershock of their previous ordeal.' Then he paused.

'You are saying that Meron and his elder companions are over 3000 years old!' Cathy yelled.

'Yes! I am saying exactly that. Further, no one within our present group need ever die,' he replied and they were even more astonished by those words.

'The time of their arrival on Earth corresponds to exactly forty-nine years ago. That was when they visited Earth and that was also when the Javols returned to their system, but luckily, their planet was by then completely evacuated via Mars to the new world called Eden.

'As you have seen, friends, the Javols are the most ferocious and rapacious life-form known to our universe. They are probably still duplicating and spreading at an incredible and alarming rate.

'Now to the situation closer to home. Since their arrival on Earth they have been assisted by Dr. Jeffery Longhurst, who was really the Shadite Lumak in disguise. He landed on Earth about two years before the Ancients' arrival.

'This is his Shadite form. Plato is also a Shadite. Shadites are the servants and messengers of Grand Lord Gerra, the known Supreme Being of the seventh part of our universe which happens also to be our part. Lumak's original home world was Kanaefon, another beautiful world within one of our local globular clusters... and here are his people. They are truly beautiful bee-like forms with their own unique culture and are also very advanced. All Shadites are immortal.

'The Grand Lord spent the last one thousand cyclons, about 1600 years, on that world assisting his people and had recently taken up residence above Eden. So you see, we also have one of the Supreme Beings of the universe within one of our neighbouring systems. That is because of the importance of Earth during the final conflict.

'Lumak was sent to Earth to set a plan in motion. They call it planetary conversion. During that time new technologies would be released to its populations without their knowledge. A form of deception to the planet's inhabitants, yet for the common good of all within the system. Anyway, how could he have told us that he was really an alien from another world.

'You see, those minds are not hypocritical in the way they think and perform their duties, which are the result of extensive research and mathematical analysis. I suppose they behave in much the same way as we would tackle a plague of locusts. We, Earth humans, on the other hand are programmed from birth to accept certain disciplines and behaviour within our survival equation as being natural, which when observed from a different standpoint may be considered highly hypocritical, in particular when viewed by other life-forms. Like killing whales for instance. The sad thing is, that these illogical and irrational concepts and deeds may appear absolutely correct to us at the time. Luckily for us we are not the whales in reverse, constantly looking over our shoulders for some unnatural technological predator to strike.

'Even if we could, we would never consider warning a lower life-form like the whale for instance, of our intentions to destroy them before we carried out the deed. So I suppose, they could argue the point that to the whale we are quite deceptive. Therefore why not practise the same deceit on us for the good of others. It depends on who is at the receiving end of the greater survival equation, doesn't it? Anyway, the more superior always thinks they have more rights over the lesser by way of intelligence and power and by way of more superior knowledge and cunning to survive. We have made the rules, so we should accept them and their consequences, even when they are applied to us in like manner, but for the common good.'

'*Anyway, to carry on; the Plorans from our galaxy had knowledge of those problems and assisted the Ancients in whatever ways they could, by supplying them with advanced technologies and a special book called the Anachromagnon.*

'*After Lumak's arrival on Earth, in human form, he was taken in by beautiful Sarah and her father Bengizara Khan (Ben), then living in the hills of Turkey. He subsequently married her and after his anti-cancer discoveries, came to live in the United States of America. By that time he had attained a new identity as Dr. Jeffery Longhurst. However, it was he and not Meron, that was responsible for the invention of the LPD drives and micro-robotics, not to mention all those other special drugs, including the Terminal Disease and its antidote. He was then assisted by Lennox and others from Earth, including Hal Seaton, the Green Chameleon.*

'*Sarah was an only child. Her mother died just before school-leaving age. She and her father, Ben, are Earth humans through and through, yet they are all special people in every respect.*

'*Sarah subsequently became the empress of Solaria, due to her special mental powers and is the only senior Child of Earth among them. But she is also advised by a previous President of the USA. He is known by the name of Gerald Fraser Senior, known to everyone in past as Jerry and also our JR's grandfather.*

'*Many democratic committee meetings were held at that time to discuss Earth's unstoppable population growth, self indulgent attitudes, crime and other unnatural behaviour patterns, until a final vote was taken. Although the people on Earth had become much wealthier because of new technologies, they became even more self-indulgent and cared little for its rain forests and life-forms. Furthermore, its population began to grow even faster than before. Leading to our present Infilate problems.*

'*Being in favour of all life, they decided to seed the planet with the Terminal Disease which only targeted mankind.*

'*Out of all other alternatives available to them, that was the most humane option. During this period a small population was chosen and given the antidote from childbirth. As president of*

Solarian Banking, Professor Khan was chosen to take on the task. Andy's father, Mallory, distributed the antidote at schools, local depots and charitable groups throughout the planet. That noble effort was for the sole purpose of our survival.

'We are now at the end of that period when the global antidote will be introduced within Earth's atmosphere sometime during this year.

'Although we should still administer the Anti, the Terminal effect will completely disappear within a period of ten years due to irreversible changes in its structure. In future, Earth's human population will be held to around five-hundred million maximum, until the planet returns to normality.

'This is Planet Eden... as you see, it's a paradise compared to Earth. We are parasites compared to the Ancients. However, I intend to change all that in the foreseeable future. I swear to you that Earth will one day return to her former glories and will be head of the Solarian Empire in the near future.

'I do believe that it's now time for a break, so after coffee and a small period for questions, I shall tell you of our immediate plans,' he said. George then temporarily discontinued the lecture.

'My God! Who would have known all those thinks were happening all around us, and never having a clue,' Pamela said, believing in everyone of George's words. Nevertheless they could not get over the ghastly images of the Javols while in the act of destroying a complete world with a population of several billion humans.

CHAPTER 18

Future plans

After they had recovered from the shock of his lecture, they continued to ask him questions.

Miranda was the first to put her hand up.

'How did you discover all this information in such a short time, when we have taken so long to get this little way?'

'If you wish to know the truth, I received most of this information from my interviews at Solarian Banking, and later from Ron, my personal computer. He has knowledge in most things.'

'Stranger and stranger!' Tim said, hardly believing those words.

'You are the true 'Son of Destiny?' Andy said.

'I think we are all children of destiny. But some of us are chosen to follow a stronger part. Most of the information I have given to you is factual. So you see, friends, the task ahead is truly enormous. All I can say at this moment to those of you who doubt my words, is that all our discoveries on Mars and elsewhere will substantiate my story.'

'It will be our greatest adventure yet!' Miranda shouted.

'I agree!' Tim yelled.

'I hope so. Anyway, the presence of the Omegron Portal on Mars, with its conveyor leading into the large Admin Dome. Within that dome will be evidence of a mass evacuation at the time discussed. The burial of the large shuttle craft, just three hundred metres from the Omegron Dome and other factors like that, will unfold within the fullness of time,' George replied.

'When will the Javols arrive on Earth?' Jerry asked, showing more concern.

'Since those early days the Javols have reorganised themselves and have advanced into a deadlier form than before. However, we expect their arrival within Osmaron in just under one hundred years. They will never visit Earth while I am here with you and working hard to fulfil a certain purpose,' George replied.

'Shall we be able to live that long?' Tim asked.

'Tim, dear friend, from this moment on you may live for as long as you wish. That is, providing you do not have a serious accident within three months or so, from this moment.'

'Wow! Everlasting life! And I thought it was a dream!' he muttered.

'All of you will need to give me a little time to organise the necessary equipment from Eden. But consider that aspect done,' George said.

'Will we be able to save some good Infilates, Sir?' Carol asked.

'The whole purpose of the Terminal exercise was to reduce Earth's population below five hundred million, initially. Although there are many good Infilates out there, their time like the dodo have arrived for their extinction. I shall not lift a finger to assist them, because I hold them fully responsible for our damaged and bleeding planet. Why flog a dead horse and perpetuate a self-indulgent breed that could one day bring complete ruin to our planet and our future generations! Nevertheless, if they change and accept us, I might save some,' he replied.

'When are we to visit Eden?' Cathy asked.

'After we arrive from our vacation on Mars. I have decided to refit our ship Vogon into an interstellar class. When those changes have been completed, we shall all visit Eden for one month and several other worlds after that time. Nevertheless, plans are flexible and may be updated in time,' he replied.

'Vogon! I like that name! When shall we leave for Mars?' Miranda asked.

'In about two weeks time, subject to our mutual assistance in redecorating Vogon and fitting new equipment and LPD Drive Modules. Many of those items have already been placed on order and will be delivered within the week.'

'Good to know things are moving!' Tim said, full of the spirit of adventure.

'In future, all responsibilities regarding the spaceship will come under Captain Andy Colman, so all interested parties should get directly in touch with him on such matters, particularly for training.'

They were looking forward to the adventure of a lifetime.

'Having said those words, I would love an extremely posh interior, adorned by the feminine touch. So perhaps you ladies could assist him in that department. Now, I should assume by the grand display of insignias, that you have all decided to continue our fight under the new name of Unitec. You must carry your insignias at all times, because they are of much greater significance than just expensive broaches and represent primal life in all its variety throughout the Cosmos. For us, the two large wings represent our constant struggle for the freedom of all life throughout and the three colours within the innermost circle represent planetary life in all their habitats. The colour blue for life within the seas, oceans and air. The colour green for the land masses, covered by flora and fawner and finally, the orange for the deserts which are inhabited by their own unique types of life. Those colours were selected by Empress Sarah when she formed the organisation many years ago. That was just before they left Earth and those ideals still live on in their minds as they also do in ours.

'From henceforth, you are all to abide by those high ideals and standards. That doesn't mean to say, you will become nuns and monks. You must never be hypocritical in your endeavours and dealings with people and life. Just be your diligent selves in all things and all good things will become you.

'Realise your potentials, responsibilities and respect towards yourselves and others, in a way like parents, and to all cosmic life, in all their varying forms and habitats. And whenever you need advice, take counsel from your friends or from me.

'The Hearst's Mansion will be prepared and used in future for all such gatherings and meetings relating to our organisation and also for security reasons. But it will also be used for my friends here and the accommodation of guests in transit and for the occasional entertainment of our people.

'Those of you with any worrying questions may voice them at our next meeting in one-week's time. This will give you time to digest our new arrangements and concepts.

'Finally, I have arranged several rooms for those of you not wishing to return tonight and my Roadstar, Oscar, is always ready to be at your service until further notice. However, I think *you should all hang around and give us some help with the ship,'* George said, as he took Ron and they joined the group for more friendly chatter.

CHAPTER 19

Earth's rebellious prodical sons

For the past decades Dr. Hal Seaton and Dr. John Simmons (Professor Powell) had spent most of their time saving Earth's endangered species, while preparing for the Javols invasion of Earth. During those years the new resurrected Hal had become Solarian through and through, with full access to planet Eden and its technologies.

He had his own plans for the survival of his universe as he called it. In his plans, Dr. John Simmons was his second in command and nasty rapacious Javols did not exist. As far as he was concerned John had earned it over the years along with immortality. Nevertheless, he was not sure how John would react when introduced to Eden and its Solarians. Therefore he decided to keep that particular door sealed until the time was right.

Dr. John Simmons had no knowledge of Planet Eden nor of their Andromedans and could not have cared less. He was only interested in saving his planet Earth from the nasty Javols and to those ends lay his true focus. After all, Earth was where he was born and where his family would live and die. Neither did he have knowledge of the Solarian's plans for Earth after the Infilates.

Although his MIMIC laboratories still concentrated on the creation of perfect anti Javol type soldiers, it was also focussed on bio-engineering of the most alien variety. They were now seriously involved in bringing back the ancient Titans. Those creatures would combine both nano-bots and biological tissue of the toughest kind. However, all serious experiments were carried out within a deep underground facility somewhere within the Nevada desert, well away from their MIMIC laboratories.

Although Hal had always hated nano-bots, he realized he had to fight like with like. Therefore, since Javols were of nano-bot design, his type would be of the same kind and hopefully better, but always subservient to humans. As for John's ideas on Titans like Medusas, Centaurs, Minotaurs, Krakens and others, he was not sure. However, he could imagine a Medusa turning a Javol to stone from one breath of her disgusting nano-bot spray or anti-Javols energy fields emanating from her glowing eyes.

Those invading Javols would be sadly mistaken if they thought they could overrun and conquer Earth. It would become their worst nightmare of all worlds visited.

'Tregor, why are you so bad?'

'Boss, it's in my nature. I hate all enemies. I will kill, kill and kill them all. That is because I am Leader and Guardian. My troupes will be the worst devils against our enemies.'

'Here, have another Firewater. Get it down you! Now how do you feel?' Tregor drank in one gulp. As he drank his complexion physically changed to a reddish glow.

'How do I feeeeeel? Just bring em on! I need action!' He yelled while shaking his cage. John stood back while observing the violent antics of his new creation. Tregor was designed to lead his troupes of anti-Javols warriors and was tougher then any animal in creation. Nevertheless he was trained to obey humans as his superior and could not harm them. Anyway, there was no fun in killing such week human creatures when they could never harm him or be a threat.

Tregor was soon given a different drink. One that would calm him into a type of hibernation until needed for more extreme violence.

'Get it all down you! That's my boy!' The lab assistant said. His colour changed and he fell asleep on his feet.

Since connection between MIMIC laboratories and Sol-Newtown Dome by secret portal, the basement of that dome was used solely for storage of numerous anti-Javols warriors. There were literally thousands upon thousands and production still continued. Professor Khan wanted his favourite planet, Earth, to have had a good chance in the war against Javols and would spare no costs. Therefore, once the process was fully tested he decided to go on line. Eventually every dome on the planet would include such secret portals and be filled with packaged warriors.

All waiting for the day of the Javols. Their AI commanders and Leaders like Tregor were the last to be designed with larger brains and unique abilities to solve problems under battlefield conditions. By so doing, humans were completely removed from the chain of command. Their king would be a super intelligent Macron war computer called Zeus. He could communicate throughout the galaxy by H-Wave. It was truly an ambitious project, but necessary for Earth's survival.

The Solarian, Lord Bengizara Khan (Ben) was now fully in charge of Earth, so he had full autonomy on all decisions pertaining to Earth's survival. Although a Solarian with a palace on Eden, he had always preferred Earth. He knew where his duty lay and was never one for too much technology. He realized Earth was not perfect, but it was where he was born. He also realized humans could change given the right incentives. Therefore he would always remain on Earth and try his utmost best to guide humans towards a better way of life. He also realized that Earth Humans could never be as clean and tidy as Solarians. Nevertheless, most Solarians were trained humans living within ideal environments. Therefore what happened there could also be adapted here. He hoped "The Son of Destiny", his grandson, would change Earth for the benefit of a better type of mankind.

Over the years Ben had realized the genius of Dr. Hal Seaton, formally the Green Chameleon, and Dr. John Simmons, formally Professor Kane Powell. Since their new and younger bodies, they had become different people with a strong desire to save their world from nasty Javols. To those ends they were sincere and sacrificed much.

Even so, Ben was not happy with powerful Titans on Earth. Although useful against Javols, they posed a great threat to mankind. Unlike nano-bot warriors that could survive virtually anywhere, Titans being partly biological, needed food and water, like humans. Neither could they exist without a constant intake of oxygen and such like. Therefore those powerful creatures could only be based on Earth or similar worlds. Finally it was decided to transfer their manufacturing to the distant world of

Tyrrel III. Therefore after installation large anti-Javols portals could be built to transfer them to defend Earth at a moment's notice.

The current President of the USA, Donald Fraser, was not yet fully aware of those great underworld developments for the protection of Earth, neither was he aware of The Son of Destiny or of the doctors' nano-bot developments, including the most deadly Titans. All those devices were developed in complete secrecy and with the use of Class 5 technologies. Most of which were brought in from planet Eden. In most cases not even the Solarians knew of those dangerous and sometimes reckless developments in the deepest installations on Earth. However it was said that an omelette could not be made without breaking a few eggs or taking some risks with equipment.

Nevertheless, most of the few Solarians on Earth, including Ben, realized that the Solarians on planet Eden were too complaisant and not aggressive enough to fight Javols. Although they concentrated on powerful weaponry, they had no proper weapons for destroying swarms. Those could only be affected by a contagious nano-bot virus, like Satan's Bug. Therefore, Lord Khan and the two doctors decided to go it alone for now. It was a dangerous road they trod, but at long last they had approached the final curve in that particular journey with the end in sight.

CHAPTER 20

The spirit heals

After George's long speech, all members of the gang were now organising themselves. Some had already begun searching for local properties, although with little success. Security and rising sea levels were always to be considered in any long term settlement. With constant demonstrations and crime, that part of the world was becoming a more violent place by the day. Because of all those reasons, they could not find individual properties in most elevated areas with suitable security. Therefore they considered it more appropriate to remain together and fight the odds as a single force for good.

That day, Andy was taking stock of all necessary repairs and replacements on their ship, Vogon. He was assisted by his wife Joan, Tim and Carol.

Jerry had gone to the local travel agent to organise the trip to Washington DC. He was to collect the tickets for him and his friends. That type of flight was a lot more secure and comfortable than local flights by Roadstar. With public transport there was no requirement for booking parking facilities in congested Washington DC, with a large part of the city under water.

Miranda and Cathy stayed at Jerry's apartment, to be later visited by George, who had decided to take the rest of the day off. He made himself comfortable in the settee, reading a magazine when he heard Miranda cry out in pain.

'Darling can you help? Miranda has just cut her finger!' Cathy said and ran off to get the first-aid box.

'Let me see!' George said, making his way towards the kitchen. On arrival he could observe blood everywhere, from the floor to the sink unit.

'Healthy and red,' he jested.

'It's so dam painful!' Miranda cried.

'I haven't seen so much blood since I had a nose bleed a few days ago.'

'You haven't?' She was not amused.

'Come, give me your finger and look into my eyes!' he commanded. She hesitantly moved towards him and handed him her bleeding finger. Cathy wondered what he was up to, but knew better than to interfere.

As Miranda gazed into his dark brown eyes, she was completely absorbed by him, as if under hypnosis. After a few seconds he released his firm grip and broke the concentration. To her amazement the pain had disappeared and when she washed the blood from the wound it was completely healed with no sign of any scarring.

'Courtesy of my cosmic powers!' he said calmly and returned to his magazine.

They had heard of spiritual healing, but were staunch sceptics that had never seen any of it in action. Even so, how could the healing process be carried out to that degree of perfection and almost instantaneous.

'It's a bloody miracle! I never knew such things were possible!' Cathy exclaimed.

'I am afraid...your future husband is also a saint as well as a saviour!' Miranda replied. Cathy was still numbed by the whole affair and stood there holding the box of bandages not quite knowing what to do with it.

Miranda soon took him a cup of coffee with a few of his favourite biscuits. Cathy still held the box of bandages in her hand with nowhere to put it, but as she passed him, he stretched out and grabbed her, pulling her down towards the settee and removing the box from her persistent grip. Then he kissed her.

'Have you given any thought to the big day?' he asked, now in playful mood.

'Yes, Darling,' she chuckled, 'on the seventh of next month. That will give us enough time to finish the ship. The trip to Mars can be part of our honeymoon. That is, if you don't mind?'

'Woman, you've thought of everything! Sounds great and timely planned. We can now arrange the invitations and perhaps... I should send a few to Eden, if it pleases you, that is?'

'You mean... the Ancients, Sarah and Jerry's grand parents?' she inquired, excitedly.

'Yes, and also his dad. Hearst's Mansion has entertained several Presidents in the past and I think she is well overdue for one of those special visits again. Anyway, I think it's time we met each other. Even if I have to add pressurization, sterilisation and filtration units to the mansion.'

'You think they will come?'

'They will have to or I shall go and collect them myself,' he replied.

'So, what do you think of my plans for us?' he inquired.

'It's just fab, Darling, and I am so excited,' she replied.

'It's regrettable your mother is still completing her article. I was counting on her assistance in helping us with the wedding. Perhaps she can move her desk to our new home and complete her article there,' he said.

'I think it's completed! She called me this morning and told me she had sent it off to print. So I'm afraid, she will be joining us tomorrow. I hope you don't mind, Darling? She seems to like you a lot,' Cathy said.

'I sincerely hope that you and your mother can move in with me in my flat on a more permanent basis from tomorrow onwards. You can both occupy the two spare bedrooms and give me a hand arranging things, including the wedding. Miranda can always call Oscar to take her over to our place if she feels lonely when Jerry is out.'

'That should be no problem!'

'What do you think?' he asked.

'If you don't mind, Darling, I shall ask them and let you know tomorrow,' she replied.

'One more thing. Jerry and I have decided to visit his dad within the next few days. We would like you ladies to accompany us to DC. It could be a nice break for you both. Your mother can join us if she doesn't have too much to do.'

'DC? That's fantastic!' Miranda yelled.

'That means we can do some serious shopping,' Cathy replied.

'We have to discuss a delicate matter with his father about his lost parents. But keep it under your hat for now,' he said.

'I will!'

Cathy and George were always very comfortable together and

held a great admiration and respect for each other.

CHAPTER 21

The kidnapping

'Everything has been arranged! We leave the day after tomorrow for DC!' Jerry said, while taking the special tickets and passes from his small briefcase.

'I have arranged the hire of a large cab for us at the other end. We can catch a flight from the local military space port. This will save us the problem of special security clearance and parking at the other end and should prevent anyone from following us. It has all been arranged in my father's name.'

'Have you observed anyone tracking you recently?' A worried Miranda inquired.

'I have not! But they have their devious ways.'

'Anyway, it's nice to have friends in high places,' George said.

'I phoned my dad, and he appears to be looking forward to our visit. Anne-Marie is still with the kids on Satellite Gimbal and will remain there for several more months. That's until dad think it's absolutely safe for her return to Earth, but at least she and the kids are very safe there. He can now visit her with special spacecraft from the White House. They don't want him to make a habit of it incase someone gets a hint of what's going on,' Jerry said.

'And how is your father coping with the demands of office?' George inquired.

'He is ok! He is admired by many and everyone seems to be bending over backwards to help.'

'In that case, our visit should cheer him up!' Cathy said.

'Then we shall have to rock the White House a little,' George replied.

'He doesn't appear to be very happy and is still quite busy. My mum and sisters are still on holiday in Europe, but one of my eldest sister's kids is spending some time there with him.'

'What about accommodation? Do we have to spread a tent?' George inquired.

'No! Dad would like us all to remain with him at the White

House. There is more than enough space.'

'That's nice to know!' George replied.

'A President's task is never an easy one, so it's nice to know he is coping,' Cathy said.

'I also have an extra ticket for Cathy's mother. After I heard she was coming tomorrow, I thought she might want a break. We should keep a low profile on this trip. I think we should all wear disguises,' Jerry said.

'Do you think we are still being shadowed by the Beta-Five criminal gang?' George asked.

'I don't know for sure. But I could have been followed when I left the apartment this morning. I must have shook them off through the shopping precinct. Anyway, I have arranged things so that it's very difficult for them to follow us, but that's the best I can do,' Jerry replied, with a very worried frown, almost as if in expectation of something dreadful befalling him.

'Can we hold on for another fortnight? I can guarantee after that time all those security worries will be over,' George said.

'I am a little fed-up today, so I am going to get myself a large bottle from the restaurant and drown my sorrows. I need a bloody stiff drink!' An unhappy Jerry said. Then he stormed out of the apartment in one of his foul moods.

George did not follow, realizing he needed some time to himself for thinking his problems through. So he waited for an hour and then left the girls for his own apartment.

At about one a.m. during early morning George's Coms rang.

'George, I am very sorry for calling you this late.... Jerry has not returned and I am very worried for his safety. I called the restaurant, but they said he left several hours ago.'

'Really? I am on my way!'

'Can you please help us?' Miranda was panic-stricken and began to sob. George was soon over to her place. The first person he called was Andy, who soon arrived.

'I think Jerry has been kidnapped? I have been worried about that possibility for some time now, but that was just a feeling I had.' George said.

'Who would do such a thing?' Andy inquired.

'They could be Infilate scum called Beta Five!'

'I haven't heard of them!'

'They like keeping a low profile!' George replied.

'Andy, can you get in touch with some of your contacts. It will feel better if this matter was taken care by us, personally. From now on we should take care of our own internal problems, with a little assistance from our friends if need be. Anyway, it could get a little messy if this and other information got into the wrong hands. Also, see if you can get any information on the grapevine regarding the kidnappers.'

'On it, Boss!'

'In the mean time, I want you all to leave this place and come along with me. I can always divert calls from here to my flat with a tracer and the kidnappers will be none the wiser.'

'Ok!' Miranda wiped her tearful eyes.

'Get ready, Ladies, we leave in exactly fifteen minutes. I don't think this flat is safe for you anymore, Miranda. Don't forget his suitcase and the tickets, and take enough clothes for a couple of days at least,' George said.

At that time Jerry was accompanied by several of the kidnappers holding a gun to his back.

'Why have you kidnapped me? I am of no value to anyone!' Jerry reacted, trying to dislodge their firm grip from his arms and shoulder.

'The squirt talks!'

'Walk naturally and don't say a word or we'll permanently shut you up here and now.' The tall one said.

'Go on! Go on!' the youngest member of the group of three nudged him ever onwards.

'I am! I am! Don't push me around!' Jerry reacted. The youngest member of their group nudged him forward again.

'I am not who you think I am,' he insisted, still resisting.

'On the contrary. Our leader reckons you are the best prize of the lot. But if we got hold of your friends, that would add some more to the kitty.'

'I told you...I am not this guy?'

'You are or you are dead... so shut it! Anyway, it's just a matter of time...Eh...Ha! Ha! Ha!' laughed the middle one.

'My friends have no money!'

'Stop your belly-aching!'

They all wore latex masks with hilarious painted features.

'They may not have money, but their parents and relatives do! It's just a matter of time... Eh... Ha! Ha! Ha!' laughed the middle one again.

'How do you like being pushed around by us Infilate scum, Mister President's son? Doesn't it sicken you!'

'You push me and I will push you back!' George replied, indignantly.

'What pushing! We are going to get a lot closer to you before this day is out. When we are through... you and your beautiful scummy friends will all be dead, but not before we get some ransom... Eh...Ha! Ha! Ha!'

'I am not who you think I am! Where are you taking me!' George continued.

'Doesn't it sicken you? Being with us poor smelly bastards!'

'Yes, you do! You stink like rotten eggs,' George replied in a stunner and more aggressive state of mind.

'Where are you taking me to?' Jerry inquired again, as they blindfolded and dumped him into the back of an old LPD Chevrolet. They sped off towards the old city.

A disguised Coms-call was made soon after.

'You are George?'

'Yes!'

'We have your friend and know he's the President's son, because we've been tracking you guys for a while. If you want to see him again in one piece, you'll have to get us two million dollars in untraceable dollar currency. We'll give you two days to locate the cash and call you later to arrange delivery.'

'Is he ok!' George inquired.

'For now! So get the money!'

'Getting that much cash can be a problem!'

'It's not a very large sum, so if you can arrange it yourselves, all well and good. If you cannot, we'll have to get to the President ourselves. But we don't want to create too much fuss. If you want, perhaps you could get in touch with him on our behalf. We don't want the military or Specials on our back. At the same time, we want the money by day after tomorrow in the evening, at eight p.m.'

'Ok! I'll try my best... but it doesn't give us much time to raise that much! Where is the drop off point?'

'We'll tell you where later, so keep this line free,' the male kidnapper said and hung up.

'It's a good thing I linked Coms. Now we can trace that call with the help of Ron, my little computer,' George said.

'What, after such a short time?' Andy asked, realizing the problems faced in tracing such a call without the authority's knowledge.

'Pal, we have our means!' George replied.

They were sitting in George's lounge. When Miranda heard the news about two million dollars she began to panic.

'Yes!... Yes! Lets give them the money. We must let them have the money... Please! Please!' she became hysterical.

'Get it together, People. We have lots to do before we get him back!' George had to slap her across the face to shut her up. But he was apologetic afterwards. They had seen the process used on TV and realized the present situation warranted strong measures.

'Andy, let's find where these crooks hang out. Ron, please find Jerry's location and trace that call.' he commanded. The small computer soon went into action and began to display several moving maps simultaneously. It was not long before there was a single map on the screen. A blinking red light marked the target.

'The call was made from the space-port, in a public call-box,' then the blinking point moved to another highlighted area on the map.

'This is where Jerry is held. It's a multistory building on the forty-seventh street, in the old town,' Ron said.

'Please enlarge object by 100 times. Isn't that area scheduled for demolition?' George inquired.

'Yes! It's been on the list for years, but it's one of those areas that workers prefer to keep well out of. It's filled with snipers and vandals.'

'Why?'

'Some of the local Infilates reckon that if that area was flattened it would only be a matter of time before their homes were listed for a similar faith. Those few put up as much resistance as they can, not having much political support these days. But his kidnappers have chosen their hideout wisely. That area is not far from the sea wall and contains many flooded pits and ponds, making it not an easy approach from the ground,' Andy said.

'I see! Then they wont know what hit them until it's too late!'

'It's completely isolated from most of the surrounding area and I am sure most of the facilities in that area, like elevators, will be non operational!' Andy continued.

'Ron, go inside the building and check out the rooms,' George commanded and Ron began by plotting some more geometrical structures while scanning each pathway, entrance and exit through the building.

'How do you do that?'

'He has his methods!' George said, casually.

'Bloody hell! We even have their images on screen!' Andy was surprised by the strange and incredible technology.

'It's a good thing he is wearing the broach I gave him. Now you may appreciate the reason why I insisted you kept it on your persons at all times,' George said.

'All this from a simple broach?'

'Yep! And a lot more!'

'It's way beyond anything I've ever seen!' Andy replied.

'Our next move is to take them by surprise.'

'By surprise?'

'Yes Andy, I would like you to arrange some of your mates, about ten will do. They are to neutralize all surveillance in that area and climb up the side of that wall in order to gain access through those windows and inner walls with laser cutters and thermal explosives. This must be precisely timed with our presence in that position here. I want to capture all those guys alive, including their boss. So I want no heroics, please. If you don't mind!' George said.

'On it, Boss!' Andy replied and got on his Coms to contact the chief of the Specials in the base called Warland.

'I want all those guys alive, so use stunners!' George insisted.

'One more thing... Please get us two of your special suits by messenger and a couple of weapons. Ordinary pistols will do!'

'Done!'

'We might have to monitor the place until their boss turns up. He should be on the scene just before the collection. Our crucial time will be half an hour before then, at seven thirty, unless they decide to change the drop zone... or time it to the very last minute.'

'I see what you mean! We can always adjust our plans to suit their timing when we have men on the ground,' Andy replied. He enjoyed such strategic operations.

'It may take us a day more, but Jerry is safe for now. They won't do anything to him before they get the money. That's because they won't like the military on their backs for the rest of their useless lives for the death of our President's son. He will just be a little uncomfortable before we take them out,' George said.

'I hope so? Those guys are real nut cases!' Andy replied.

'We have a rush and tricky job on.... Here are the specifications... I need your best ten. It's at the highest security level!' Andy said to the base commander. Then turning to George.

'It's done!'

'Good!'

'Special Coms and equipment are also on-route to us. Courtesy of our Warland Macron.' Andy continued.

'It's our Presidents son, but I have to think of the future of all of us from now on, as well as Jerry. You guys are family to me, so we have to be extra careful. Do you understand, Miranda? And chin up for heaven's sake, Woman!' George then leant over and handed her a tissue to wipe the tears from her eyes. She gave him a big smile.

'I understand!' she replied.

'Ron will monitor that point from now on and run a complete analysis on everyone entering and leaving that building. If anything strange happens, he will instantly signal us,' George said.

Cathy was now with Miranda, consoling her that George was doing the best in the circumstances. She was soon calmed and decided to compose herself and assist as best she could in the operation.

No one had considered calling the police, because they were almost as corrupt as the kidnappers and George wanted all publicity for himself and his new organization. Nevertheless a few of Andy's Specials would be involved in his clever plan. They were of the highest security clearance.

It was not long before a messenger called to deliver a large packet. Both men were already getting undressed in Specials' outfits.

Special bullet and plasma-proof suits were to be worn under normal clothes which had to be several sizes larger. Those suits were designed to repel high velocity projectiles like bullets and high velocity debris from explosions. For those reason they could not wear the special helmets with inbuilt Coms that were designed to protect their heads. Any strange looking gear could have blown their cover, so they had to take that risk.

'I shall arrange the withdrawal of the money tomorrow, and hold on to it until it's required,' George said.

'I don't think we can do much more tonight. There will be three of my guys in the building and another three in adjacent buildings with surveillance and stunners before daybreak. The other four will be tooled up to enter via the side wall. Pity we couldn't drop them in by LPD.'

'Yea... That would make it easier!'

'We want to capture them. Don't we? I think scum like that should be blasted to hell. But it's your show,' Andy said.

'We also want to take advantage of this situation and score a few organisational points from our operations. So just at the correct time, the press and television will be informed and the police alerted. By then all hell will break loose. All of that will happen just before we capture them. So that is why timing is so crucial. To get the most, they should be alive. The local police will also gain from the arrest,' George said.

'I see now. It should make a great show. I hope we get copies of that video,' Andy was amused.

'You must trust me always in these matters, even with your life on this one,' George said.

'Always!' Andy replied.

They had little sleep that night and although the building was monitored, Jerry's captors thought everything was still going to plan.

CHAPTER 22

A planned rescue

That morning Jerry's captors made him breakfast and spoon fed him with his hands taped behind his back. He had a most uncomfortable sleep on the dirty floor with more aches and pains from his ordeal.

'I hope you like it?' said the elder one, while the younger took pleasure feeding him with a bib, like he was a baby.

'We have none of your fancy cooking facilities in this joint. It's fried eggs all the same and the chicken couldn't tell the difference... eh... Ha! Ha! Ha!' he grimmered, with that awful sarcastic laugh.

When they removed their masks and plastic overalls, Jerry could clearly observe the Beta-Five symbols tattooed on their arms, and wondered to what Infilate splinter group they belonged. The worst gangs were often known to remove fingers and other less vital body parts just for kicks and that was before they even got warmed up, and had received any ransom money. But at least, that lot didn't appear to be as hard and sadistic, or so he thought.

After breakfast their boss arrived on the scene to observe his victim, removed his facial tape, and took control by humiliating him some more in front of his men.

'We have contacted your friends and have asked them to arrange your ransom at two million dollars. We hope for your sake they are able to get it by this evening or else we start cutting little bits off.'

He opened a small case to retrieve a silver cigar clipper and a large medical scalpel. Then he began to check the scalpels blade for sharpness.

'None of your fancy dissecting lasers and electronic pain neutralisers. Just the crude basics. After all, we are only crude Infilates. Anyway, without anaesthetics the pain should feel the same,' he said, with a broad grin.

'If you kill me you wont get any ransom!' Jerry plucked the nerve to reply.

By this time Jerry began to shiver in his bones, imagining his fingers being clipped off one by one, and even worse, with that blade cutting into him. He turned his head around as if to block out those unbearable thoughts.

Nevertheless he knew his friend George could afford and would pay the ransom.

Their boss appeared to be in his early thirties and a younger member of their gang, but also the most sadistic. He always wore a mask. George thought he could be one of those adopted or kidnapped Fertilates.

'You know. I was once a Ferlate like you, but was dumped onto the streets at a very young age after my mother died. After that time I had to fend for myself, going through bins and begging, until I was taken in by a nice old Infilate lady. After she died, I swore I would spend the rest of my life fighting injustices against us by you wealthy privileged bastards. So don't blame us for your situation. Time you got some payback for what you've done to us all those years. Ferlate pig!' he said and spat on the floor in front of Jerry. Then once again he pulled the tape from Jerry's mouth to get some verbal response from him.

'Why are you blaming me for what others have done to you. I'm barely in my twenties and have always tried to do good by everyone,' Jerry replied.

'That might well be, but you are the President's son and I'm sure he will decide to demolish this whole area in the future. He and his cronies have also decided to ignore our city and abandon it to the rising ocean. To where shall we go when the waters start pouring over the high wall. We'll not be accepted in any of your new and advanced domed cities. Most likely we'll all be run down and shot in the back by his cowards. Anyway, blood is thicker than water and you are his blood.'

'I am sorry for what happened to you, but our gang has always fought for those injustices. I have always been on the side of the down trodden!' Jerry replied.

'We have been tracking you and your friends for sometime now and know where you all live. So if we lose you this time we can always take another, and your friends will not risk your safety and call the cops. They are bloody useless anyway. So make yourself comfortable until I return in the evening!' He said, not wanting to show any emotion.

'If you are you will be executed! Kidnapping is a capital crime!' Jerry replied.

'Yea... they will have to catch us first!' He placed his finger in the pan to retrieve an egg, then flicked it into his mouth, shell and all. Then he spat the shell in Jerry's direction.

'Boys, try not to damage the goods too much yet, and I don't want to miss any of the fun either, so keep him on ice for now.' He checked his hands and feet, then replaced the adhesive tape covering his mouth and elsewhere. Then he went away, leaving the scalpel and other instruments on the table freely available to anyone. They were intended as a reminder to Jerry of more painful experiences to come.

Later that day the captors called and gave instructions. The delivery was to be made at the main space-port at eight pm. George was expected to make the drop while wearing a yellow rose for identification. He was to dangle the briefcase with the money over the protective railing close to the main exit.

After checking the money they would release Jerry at another local terminal, to be advised later that evening. George knew better than risk Jerry's life. He also knew such kidnappers seldom kept their word. So the assault was planned for seven thirty.

He assumed their boss would remain with Jerry, having sent one of his lesser members to collect the ransom by motorcycle - not the flying variety. Anyway, they decided to mount their assault at that time and risk not capturing their boss if it finally came to a choice between his capture and Jerry's life.

Andy was well used to those special assignments. On arrival, all he did was show a couple hand signals to his men and they were already climbing the rear outer wall with laser cutters, thermal explosives and hydraulic suction pads. Two guards were now stationed at both main exits, with others on the streets outside. To all intents and purpose the building was completely sealed.

George then communicated to the local television network and newspapers, giving them his identification, and informing them of the recent kidnapping of the President's son and the address of the kidnappers.

George and Andy were already moving towards their targets through a maze of stairs, corridors and rooms. Finally, they arrived at the apartment in question, checked their watches and waited for five seconds.

The other guards were soon in place, there was a blinding flash as two walls and a door were almost completely vaporised. They had little time to act and within another second or so the front door was off its hinges. In another instant the kidnappers were lying dormant on the bare floor. By that time cameras were already on the street outside, while two special security ambulances with an escort were haling through the bumpy street.

George took up the large scalpel and began to cut through the tape that tightly bound Jerry's hands behind his back. Then he cut the one on his feet before finally pealing the tape from his face.

'This might hurt!' George said, as he ripped the tape off with some facial hair.

'I thought you would never get here in time,' Jerry said with utter relief in his manner. He was so pleased to see George in his moment of need.

'Luckily, you took my advice and held on to the insignia, because without it we would never have been able to locate you in this place in time. If you really want to thank someone, Andy and his guys took the sharp end and risked their lives in the process. I only did the planning,' George replied, looking his usual calm self while giving him a helping hand towards a more vertical position and towards the stairs.

'I am so thankful for what you all have done!' Jerry couldn't show more gratitude.

The following day they were interviewed by reporters. That story made headlines in every state and later throughout the world. George, Jerry and Andy received lots of publicity, thanks to their association with the President's son. All such publicity made them famous among Fertilates worldwide. That day George had scored more points than he had ever anticipated. Because that rescue had also included the live capture of one of Beta-Five's main leaders.

CHAPTER 23

To Washington DC

Jerry apparently recovered very quickly from his ordeal. The publicity placed him at a new level of importance, while being carried by the excitement and media attention. Nevertheless, George had received the most mileage from the situation and was the hero of the moment.

Jerry couldn't have been more thankful to him for having planned such a successful rescue on his behalf. Having considered his recent selfish attitude, he realised his kidnapping might have been avoided if he had listened to his best friend all along. Despite everything that had happened, he was now safe and also very famous, so perhaps it was a good thing events had occurred in that way.

Even Miranda was now much closer to Jerry than she had ever been and Cathy began to shoulder her responsibilities like a real madam, having been interviewed several times by the press. Even his dad, the President, had sent a letter of congratulations to George and Andy for the great services rendered in catching such infamous criminals, not to mention the recovery of his eldest son.

Every member of the group was very happy. They were like surfers on the crest of a titanic wave on the eve of their trip to Washington DC.

'Those Infilate scum will think twice in the future when dealing with the organisation. They were lucky to be captured alive this time. They should realise that George allowed them their lives, even though they were going to spend the remainder of it behind bars,' Jerry said to the press.

Beta 5 was well connected. Their higher leaders were not pleased with the gang's achievements in putting several of their most important individuals behind bars. Neither were they amused by the loss of two million dollars of reward money. Therefore they decided to keep that gang, including the President's son, within sight from now on. They would take revenge at an opportune moment.

Andy had accumulated a great respect for George and would kiss the very ground on which he stood. It was because of George's doing that Andy had been offered a more senior position within the Specials. He was also invited to Washington DC with his wife and others. To him that last request was the greatest honour of his entire career. It would also give him a chance to catch up on old times with Donald, the President, and introduce his wife, Joan, to him for the first time. That was something she had always wanted. According to Andy, everything that had occurred was all to do with George's clever planning. He had taken advantage of a situation and turned it in the direction that would benefit the organisation, and everyone within it had so benefited.

'How could a guy be that clever in predicting the outcome of such complex situations and at the same time score so many points internationally. He must be a bloody genius, and what a leader he had become since training camp.' Andy thought.

When George, Jerry and his friends arrived in Washington DC, they were major celebrities. The President could not have shown George enough gratitude for saving his son's life. He also planned a commendation ceremony for them, and a reception at the White House, during which time many important people would be present.

The name George Peterson was now in the hearts and minds of many Fertilates worldwide and the organisation enjoyed the publicity they received, with the symbolic power of the White House in the background. It helped to make the ordeal more global in scale.

George Peterson was on the crest of a tidal wave and would use it to his best advantage. He would get his image imprinted on the minds of those who mattered until the time was right for him to make his move.

Clair, come and say hello to your uncle Jerry and his friends, they are to stay with us for a few days.' President Donald Fraser said and the little bald headed girl gracefully walked up to them and continued to shake their hands.

'Happy to meet you!' she said with the hoarse voice. When she was finished she went over to Donald.

'Can I now go to rest, Granddad? I suddenly feel very tired,' she said and the ever present nurse soon came along to take her away for her medication.

'Shall we go in to dinner and perhaps, my son, we can discuss that private matter in my study, afterwards?' Donald said.

That evening the group had an exciting time together. Then Jerry took George with him into the study to confer with his dad.

'I don't know exactly where to start, Dad, but you had better brace yourself for the greatest shock of your life!'

'Just tell me from the beginning, Son. I am all ears,' Donald replied.

'You must promise me that whatever we discuss here and now will go no further!' Jerry insisted.

'Go on, Son!'

'Well.... Grandma and Granddad are still alive... on a planet called Eden and here are their photos!' he said, bravely.

'Son, what are you saying?' he asked, taking the strange photos from Jerry.

'If what you say is true... they look even younger than me... and their friends... they are all so young. Are you sure they are not replicas or androids? How youthful they have become since I last saw them,' Donald replied, with utter disbelief.

'It's for real, Dad,' Jerry said.

'Could be some new type of youth drug,' George interjected.

'Here is a letter they sent you, written in their own handwriting. We intend taking a trip to Eden in the near future, but George has invited them to his wedding, so perhaps we could make it a grand reunion then, assuming they come. But I don't want you to rock any boats. They could be very happy where they are at present and perhaps we could meet them occasionally,' Jerry said.

Donald had tears in his eyes, as he was hit by the realisation that his parents were alive, even after all those years and held tightly to the strange three-dimensional photos.

'They are all for you dad! You can place them on your desk if you wish,' Jerry said, trying to ease his father's pain.

'George, what do you thing of all this?' Donald asked, after wiping his tearful eyes with a tissue he retrieved from a local dispenser on his desk.

'I have prepared a file for you to read, Sir. In here is all the information you will need to know about Eden and our organisation. We shall be very grateful for any assistance you may lend us in the future. In return, we shall assist you and your family as best we can through our organisation. You need only shout whenever you need us,' George said in a matter-of-fact manner.

Donald, the President, then changed the unhappy topic for another closer to home.

'Jerry, your youngest and most favourite niece has a serious type of cancer. She has been undergoing special therapy over the past three months in one of our local hospitals. It's a large tumour in her head, and they can't operate without doing too much irreversible damage.'

'My God! She is so young!' Jerry could not accept yet another problem facing his family.

'Since a couple of weeks ago the tumour had reduced in size, but recently two new ones have appeared in different places. Now they are trying new drugs,' Donald said.

'But so much pain for a little eight-year-old!' Jerry replied.

'I am afraid, she has another six months with us at the most and that's if we are lucky. So I have decided to take her home with me, to be here until she becomes bedridden. She still receives special medication from the local hospital. They have supplied a full-time nurse to take care of her, who also lives with us.'

'Tough luck for the little kid, eh!' Jerry said, realizing the situation was hopeless, but with more feelings of sadness welling in his eyes. George remained silent but listened carefully to their conversation.

The following day, while most of the others were out shopping in the city, George went to the rear of the house to observe the beautiful garden when little Clair made her way down the stairs and quietly crept up behind him. It was a beautiful and sunny day and she felt stronger and happier than usual.

'Do you like water lilies?' she asked in her hoarse voice.

'Yes! I do very much!'

'Me too! I love flowers!'

'And how do you feel today?' he replied.

'Sometimes I feel fine. Other times I have headaches and want to die! But these days I mostly have headaches,' she said.

'I am sorry to hear that!'

'I think I am going to die soon?' she said sadly, while pulling him towards the pond that contained the water lilies. However he began to lead her towards the larger tree instead, saying:

Come with me and I will show you a tree.
It's like the human race, you will agree?
In autumn all its leaves will fall,
And again in spring, a renewal call.

I know your life is still quite young,
But look! this leaf here, how crinkled and brown.
You know it's the start of a summer long,
And yet, how dead is this leaf, quite wrong.

The tree itself looks healthy and strong,
And may hear many a new summer's song.
A cutter's axe or saw may rend,
A race of humans, extinction! The End?

An unwritten law to me is clear,
That there is a lot more than existence here.
For within this complex plan I see,
The pattern of another tree.

Although our autumn's three scores and ten,
Perhaps five billion in one fall, and then?
You could have travelled from some tree hence,
And are taking a path to another thence.

Have faith in God and mend all fences.
Be prepared, for a new journey commences,

A Great Spiritual Journey of Consequence, Within a Cosmos of Magnificence.

But alas my little one, that plight is not for you. Come to me and be blessed!' he commanded, and laid his hand upon her forehead.

The little girl could feel changes within her being, until the tumours were no more. Then she kissed his hand, thanked him and went jumping up the stairs to be stopped by her nurse.

'I have been looking for you every where! Where have you been? Child what's the matter with you! Please calm yourself!' The nurse was confused but tried to calm her. She had never seen little Clair so distraught and active before.

'Where is grand dad! Uncle George healed me! He healed me!' she shouted. Then tore herself from the nurse and began to jump up the long flight of stairs.

'Granddad! Granddad! Where are you?' she cried again.

The president hearing the commotion left what he was doing and was soon at the top of the stairs. He glanced towards the nurse for an explanation but she was non the wiser and nodded with uncertainty.

The house was now in an uproar; for never before had they seen Clair so lively.

'Granddad, I am healed! Uncle George has healed me completely! Look! I am not ill anymore!' she cried.

The nurse ran after her and almost couldn't catch her, in the process knocking over an old antique vase which shattered into many pieces. Then the nurse looked into her usual anaemic eyes which were now almost perfect. Donald nodded his head to the nurse in disbelief and she shook her head back at the President in ignorance of what had occurred.

'Is she healed as she says?' he asked, running up to little Clair and hugging her.

'My little darling, what did Uncle George do to you?' he asked again.

'He placed his hand upon my forehead and healed me, Granddad. He healed me!' she said, with tears in her eyes. George had returned and calmly entered the room, looking as peaceful as a saint.

'George! My little baby says she is healed and I can't believe it's humanly possible. If that's the case, how did you do it?' Donald asked.

'Although I have those powers, I can't explain them, but I can assure you that by tomorrow she will be one-hundred percent cured,' George said in perfect calm.

'Did anyone tell you that you are a bloody saint and a saviour? Even now I still can't think it's possible. This whole situation is so incredible. You must be the chosen one!'

'I am!' he murmured silently.

'For this immeasurable deed you have done for me this day, you and your organisation will always have my help. Anyone with such powers must be directly from God,' Donald said, filled with such utter happiness for his favourite granddaughter.

However, it didn't end there. The nurse had called the local specialist, and on arrival he found Clair to have no symptoms due to her type of brain tumours. However he needed to take her into hospital for a more precise brain scan the following morning.

When they found there was absolutely no sign of brain damage or tumours, their attention was focussed on the already popular figure, namely George Peterson, so reporters were once again on the scene for yet another scoop.

One of the headlines read **"A saviour is born"**. He was now worried that many would seek his healing powers, but that was not to be the case.

That evening during dinner they were happy and full of friendly gossip, but still found the circumstances of that day unbelievable.

'If you guys need any special security arrangements, just shout,' Donald advised.

'Thank you for that offer, but it's not an important priority with us at this moment. I am sure the Infilate extremists don't like their faces rubbed in the mud too often. Anyway, I shall be making special security arrangements within a week or so. In the mean time, Jerry and friends can always remain with me and Cathy at the apartment until Hearst's Mansion is completed, which I hope will be in one week's time. During the next fortnight we shall be very busy refitting and redecorating the spaceship, Vogon, for our holidays on Mars.'

'That should be great fun!' Tim exclaimed with happiness.

'After our wedding, Jerry and Miranda are invited to join us at the mansion until they are able to sort out their own affairs. So also is Tim and our other very important gang members,' George said and they laughed. Tim was the funniest one in the gang.

'In that case, would you and Cathy mind taking care of Clair for a few weeks for me? I have to travel abroad. Mind you, nothing too important. I would just like her to be in safe hands and among friends,' Donald replied.

'We would love to have her along,' George said.

'Yoo Peee!' Clair yelled.

She immediately got out of her chair and went over to kiss the couple.

'Thanks uncle George and aunty Cathy!' she said, then she went over to kiss Jerry.

'And you also, uncle Jerry!'

'Sometimes I wish I was young again. I miss Anne-Marie and the kids a lot. I would like you all to visit her on your way to Mars. Spend as long as you can with her. Your presence will cheer her up. She has lots of space and will appreciate your company. She also knows her way about Gimbal and can show you around.'

'We shall!' Cathy replied.

'Professor Khan visits occasionally, but these days he never remains in any one place for any great length of time. I sometimes think he has become scared of his own shadow, and he is usually accompanied by two very tough looking guards,' Donald said.

'It must be difficult for him these days with so many Infilate disturbances,' George replied.

George had never met Professor Khan before and was intrigued by anyone with so much power.

The following day the President held one of those White House parties where every important person was invited. Everyone was well dressed for the occasion. They knew George would be the centre of attraction and he was. After a while the President

decided to make an announcement. During that time he thanked George and Andy for their courageous action in saving his son and capturing one of the most ruthless Infilate gangs. Then in front of cameras and reporters he called them individually to the podium and in the name of Congress, bestowed upon them the Medal of Honour, which he personally pinned unto their lapels.
 The other members of his organisation were given jewellery, for services rendered in the past towards a cleaner environment.

The ladies, in particular, had enjoyed their brief vacation in Washington DC, but were looking forward to an even more exciting holiday during their forthcoming visit to Mars.

CHAPTER 24

Spaceship Vogon

Her name reminded George of the famous British TV series he once viewed in video. It was a funny recording from the previous century about a poetic alien race and called, ***"the hitchhiker's guide to the galaxy"***.

George wondered whether his Vogon would take him to similar incredible adventures in space and time. Then he realized our universe did not contain space. Time gave us that illusion by causing materials to appear spread out and recede away from the observer in all directions. That was because everything was at a different time relative to each other and the observer. Hence the concept of space-time.

Vogon was taken out of the hanger with her almost bare metal skin glistening like diamonds in the bright sunlight. She resembled a large flying saucer with slightly more curved domes, top and bottom. She had a somewhat rounded rim that joined with a lesser curved underbelly.

Vogon was thirty-five metres in diameter and just ten metres high. Those dimensions excluded her undercarriage equipment and four hover-pads that could steer and propel her on both land and water. They were designed to cushion the effects of rough terrain or waves. All those items including extendable feet that could be retracted and shielded when not in use. She was one of a remaining few that did not require special docking facilities and could land virtually anywhere.

Although she was originally designed as a luxurious cruiser, to take expensive flights to local satellites and planets like Mars, she was mainly used on excursions to Moonbase and had only made it to Mars on her maiden flight.

Since the reduction in Earth's population and the following scarcity of natural resources, all surplus wealth had dissipated. Many people had since lost interest in space exploration and adventure. Those efforts were further discouraged by Solarian

Banking and their frequent advertising, which stressed the uselessness and extremely high cost of space exploration and all such extraterrestrial adventures. Therefore only the wealthiest went on such cruises.

Andy, officially now captain and with a stake in Vogon's future, decided to have her thoroughly cleaned before getting started on her interior. He had a quiet word with Clive who soon got a team of trusted engineers on board. Andy then inspected every nut and bolt within the ship with pencil and pad, taking note of replacements, new upgrades and additions. Then he began systematically ripping the ship apart, getting rid of everything that was either out of date or surplus to requirement. After that task was completed he transmitted the list to George who immediately relayed its contents to his contacts in Sol-Newtown. In another two days several large crates and containers arrived on the scene with the latest equipment. Most of it would have taken Andy months to acquire through his best military sources and in the process a large amount would have either gone missing or reported lost or stolen in transit.

Vogon was a stealth traveller, which meant that she always kept her smallest surface area in the direction of flight to minimise meteoric collisions. However she could also travel full face, or rotate around her common axis during flight to simulate gravity in case of emergency or during loss of artificial gravity.

Like most modern spaceships, her hull was fabricated from Malnumin, one of the lightest and toughest alloys known to man. It was originally used for armouring battle tanks. That alloy was very difficult to paint onto and tended to harbour a natural abhorrence for anything not of a similar structure due to certain strong magnetic interferences throughout its structure. It tended to naturally anodise with oxygen in air, which gave it an almost shiny, but light greyish appearance. Because of those reasons her identification symbols and name could only be seen on her underbelly when she was airborne.

Further, due to the way she was constructed, with her forward warning detectors, she could not be affected by meteorites travelling at velocities less than fifty thousand kilometres per second and that was without any repellant fields. Anyway, such velocities were well above those commonly encountered within the solar system. Once her external fields were activated no solar radiation or mass ejections could affect her internal enclosures. Those energetic ionized particles would follow the extreme super-conductive electronically created magnetic fields and be guided away from her hull.

Her internal frame was completely isolated and damped from all external shocks and hull vibrations. Therefore, her passengers were seldom aware of being on board a spacecraft and to all intents and purpose, were contained within their own environmental bubble.

Her cabins were numbered from one to eighty, although only seventy-five were used for passengers. The other five remained as spares for emergences, but on occasion for surplus provisions and isolation in case of contagious illness.

An narrow access corridor followed all around the ship. The kitchen, utility and servicing areas followed along the same circle with the cabins, which were furthest from the centre.

Her large ballroom, dining room, medical and recreation facilities remained towards the centre.

The captain and navigation area was at the uppermost level. That area was almost completely computerised and could comfortably seat just twelve flight controllers. Here, the seats were pivoted and reclining for better comfort on long voyages. They were each fitted with safety harnesses. That area was accessible by a central elevator for speed but with two adjoining metal stairways that spiralled vertically through all three sections with circular pressure doors.

The lowest area contained the spacesuit lockers, flare-guns, weapons, spares, first-aid, heavy industrial equipment and tools. They were securely bolted. Not affected by a lack of oxygen, although sealed in transit. That area was always the first to face the hazards of whatever new environments they visited, and the first entry and exit point for its crew. It contained its own large inner lock to the sealed bubble, but there were also two sealed emergency escape hatches on opposite sides and on top of the ship.

George had located three brand new number-five LPD Drive Modules and had sent them by special messenger to Andy. Those devices were worth many times their weight in gold. When he opened the plastic box and removed them from their foam packing, he couldn't believe his eyes.

'Bloody hell! Those can take us way across the galaxy with a hundred times more equivalent power than her original number three!'

'And they are brand, spanking new!' Clive said.

'That should put her value up to over five hundred thousand at least. Now I can have those old number threes removed and sold for scrap.'

'I will take them off your hands, if you don't mind!' Clive was very excited.

'I don't mind! What a bloody cunning man you are, George,' Andy mumbled to himself, with excitement.

Everyone knuckled down to hard work, with Miranda and Cathy as interior designers and decorators. The others assisted as and when necessary.

After another week of hard work, Vogon was ready for final testing, so Jerry and Andy decided to take her for a short flight over the space pad. Just to hover for a while and calibrate her new drives. Also to adjust other essential sensors and controls for autopilot operation.

After they were finished, she was complete and ready for delivery to Hearst's Mansion.

'What do you think?' asked Andy.

'I think she is beautiful. The girls have done such a fantastic job with her interior. Not to mention Clive and his crew!' Jerry replied.

'When do you think we'll leave for Mars?' Andy asked.

'I don't really know. It could be some time next week, but it could also be after the wedding, which is in a fortnight's time. However, it doesn't stop us from getting her stocked up with essentials and groceries in the mean time.'

'Wow! This is going to be some holiday!'

'Yea, I am sure! After delivery to the Mansion, use your card to claim expenses. Also, let Clive have something to show our gratitude. Perhaps the old LPDs.'

'Yep! I already decided that!'

'Are you happy with things as they are?' Jerry asked.

'Happy? I have never had such a great time in all my life and I am looking forward to our little adventure.'

'Little Adventure?'

'Are you not?' Andy inquired.

'Yes! But I am not sure to where those adventures will eventually lead,' Jerry replied.

'What does it matter? Life is too short to worry. Anyway, I would rather live a short life with a little adventure than a long one and ending up like one of those poor Infilates, scrubbing the yard out there. But I like George and what he stands for, and think he happens to be one of those gifted people, although extraordinarily strange in many ways. I also think those rear qualities go with the territory. Call it the nature of the beast if you will.'

'I hope you are right?' George replied.

'Well, keep me informed of delivery and departure dates so I can inform my wife and make arrangements.'

'I shall!'

'I think Joan will also like to come along, but she hasn't had any astronaut training or experience in such matters. Have a word with George about that matter for me, Friend?' Andy pleaded.

'I shall, and thank Clive again for me!' Jerry said.

'I will! Anyway, I think he and his guys enjoyed the whole process,' Andy replied.

'I think you may be able to deliver her tomorrow, but let me see George first, incase the new pad is not yet ready,' Jerry said, as he left for home.

CHAPTER 25

On Eden

Grand Lord Gerra, Lord of the seventh universe, now looking like an ancient Greek, while wearing attire befitting the ancient God Zeus, decided to take a stroll through the palace's beautiful natural gardens. The Grand Lord wanted to meditate on a few important matters concerning the long term survival of Earth, and other matters regarding possible phases of the final battle for Andromeda against the Javols several decades hence. He also knew his Shadite, Lumak, now in the form of Dr. Jeffery Longhurst, would also be there at that time of day with his grandchildren. Lumak had learnt the art of Landscape Gardening while on Earth and enjoyed seeing his handiwork grow into the most beautiful forms. Most of the flowers had been bio-engineered for that purpose, with eyes, ears and other senses. Some could even talk with him in an intelligible manner while he watered them.

Lumak was presently taking a well-earned holiday since his recent visit to Nervia World. Most of his other important duties were presently in the hands of his most competent deputies and Macrons. They were in turn under the control of Central Macron or Mac. Mac, their super-intelligent computer controlled everything on Eden.

In that Solarian society intelligent computer systems were given equal status as biological forms and all shared mutual respect for each other. Then again, they were fully dependant on each other and clever enough to recognise the levels of order that were achievable by such a multi-systemic society, where androids, robots, Microid or Nano-bot based systems like Transmorphs, aliens and other undescribable types coexisted for the common good.

'Ah... there you are!'

'Good day, Metra Siend!' Lumak replied.

'Children can mature so quickly these days. But luckily, they become like us and stay that way forever. I have always considered primal aging to be the worst of all disasters. Even so, the sting of death can sometimes bear its own meanings and rewards... if one finds a better existence for oneself through the Greater Mind. Nevertheless, we all prefer the type of stability and continuity that we have been accustomed to, including family and friends, and never like rocking the proverbial boat too often,' the Lord said.

Yes, Metrasiend! I agree with everything!' Lumak replied.

'Your flowers are so unique and beautiful!'

'We are indeed, Metrasiend!' the plants shouted in synchronism and at the same time emitted the most favourable perfumes from their hidden glands.

'Oh! So pleasant, my children!'

'Most pleasant! I was thinking of future developments on Earth and of re-seeding her atmosphere with the anti-bacteria. The ships have been prepared and are ready to make the trip. Sarah has given her permission,' Lumak said.

'Ah... Yes! It's almost time! Ben tells me everything has gone exactly to plan.'

'Yes, My Lord. Nevertheless I think Earth has had enough of her fair share of disasters for now, with the Terminal Disease and more recently, the Plague,' Lumak replied, somewhat sentimentally.

'Yes, Sut, I fully agree with you in that regard. But most regrettably, those decisions were correct at the time when they were taken. If things had taken their more natural course, Earth would in all probability have become one of the worst disasters of our present time within this region. Thank goodness Sarah had the vision and good sense to have taken that final decision for her own race.'

'I fully agree!'

'Nevertheless, these causal matters are seldom as bad as they seem, not when compared with the Javols destruction of Andromeda, soon to visit our own galaxy to finally destroy all primal life and dominate space forever. What a dreadful nightmare!'

'Indeed, My Lord! It's one not worth considering!'

'My main reason for visiting you, Sut, is to discuss, Jull. Your plans have reaped good results by sending him to the USA and causing the friendship with Jerry's grandson. At least, that way Ben could always have kept an eye on him for us.'

'My Lord?'

'It's a good thing he is still not aware that you are his real parents and think they died in a collision when he was a child in England. And then, those not very nice foster parents, after the death of his foster father... That was until Mallory came to his rescue and then Ben, with that scholarship to North America. Since then he has blossomed and have become so brilliant. Now you see why it was essential to have kept him away from us before coming of age. Now he has come of age and the prophesy has been concluded, and he cares more for Earth then anywhere else.'

'Concluded, My Lord!' Lumak's face lit up with excitement.

'Even now, I am sure he hasn't bothered enquiring too deeply into his past. It has been quite a deception on our part, but how else could we have handled the problem of his complete separate development on Earth. The alternative would have been almost impossible, if we were to follow the prophesy, without engineering such a simple scheme,' the Grand Lord said.

'Even his mother is not yet aware that her son is a prosperous young man on Earth. Yet, for some odd reason she calls him her son in conversation when speaking with her father, Ben. I am about to tell her the truth, but I am not sure when will be the correct moment,' Lumak replied.

'I see no reason why you shouldn't tell her now. After his conversion is complete, which I estimate to be in just four months time, both can then be told the facts. That is, assuming he doesn't already know those facts. Then your family can once again be united and Sarah's mind put at ease regarding her long lost son.'

'Thank you so much, My Lord, for concluding this process!'

'You know, he doesn't like probing into the personal affairs of others; for he is an honourable soul and consider such delving to be inappropriate. His powers now grow stronger while he makes a name and reputation for himself on Earth. Only time will tell how he develops from now on. But we must help him as much as we can, without drawing too much attention to ourselves. We cannot create too many causal distortions within the space-time matrix that might significantly influence any future outcomes within The Greater Purpose. However, this position changes after his full conversion.'

'We can wait a little longer, My Lord!'

'He is to take a wife in the near future and I have heard that invitations have already been sent. So please arrange a visit to Earth, with your original group of friends in The Ship. Your sons and others can follow in one of the smaller cruisers. Do it as a surprise visit... you may represent me in the proceedings and take him a little gift.'

'A little gift?'

'A present from me. It is also time that Jerry and his wife met their son Donald to explain things properly. Perhaps it might also be advisable for you all to revector into bodies that are ten years older. They can be neutralised on your return and in the process, destroy any dangerous planetary bacteria from Earth. Anyway, the Terminal Disease is no longer a problem to us here, so you have many options open to you,' the Grand Lord said, as he faded away into the misty trees.

Lumak soon called his two grandchildren, formed a single thought in his mind and they suddenly found themselves transposed within the palace. While on planet Eden one could vectorize their bodies and travel through any solid matter or be transposed by a single thought to anywhere on their world.

'Darling, we have been invited to a wedding on Earth by George Peterson... someone that we have not yet met,' Lumak said and Sarah turned around gracefully to observe her husband. She was wearing a beautiful tiara with many precious gems. The central stone was blue and radiated a strange glow.

'I know, Jeffery. Father called today and brought me up to date on the progress of his godchild. I must say, he has come a long way since his problem years. He must have grown into a very intelligent young man to have become so popular and he is also a friend of Jerry's grandson?'

'He is that, Mam!'

'Something is going on that I know very little of, and I would like a full update on those matters, now!' she commanded. Sarah was always highly intuitive.

'Update, My Love?' Lumak was almost tongue-tied.

'Perhaps you can explain everything to me right now, and from the start, Darling?' an intuitive Sarah asked in a most determined manner.

'Come and sit with me. We have a lot to discuss and important plans to make....'

'Ok?'

'Many years ago... while we still commuted to Earth, the Grand Lord predicted certain changes in our future. One of those were to do with the birth of a saviour on Earth. The one that would eventually see the final destruction of the Javols. He is the reincarnation of Jull the Patriarch. That same person happens to be George Peterson, known to the Greater Purpose as Jull and also our own long lost son!' Lumak said.

'You mean... my stolen child is George? You stole him and rigged his kidnapping to keep him away from me... all this time?' she exclaimed, with welling grief and sadness in her eyes.

'Darling, we had little choice in the matter. We had to follow the prophesy, which clearly indicated that we on Eden couldn't interfere with his future until he was of age and wanted us in his life. Telling you would have created many serious problems and negative ripples in space-time.'

'Negative ripples in space-time?' She became unconsolable.

'He is a very spiritual person, with a unique mind that extends cosmically. A truly cosmic being, like what you and Ben would call a great profit or saint in your religion. From this time on, we are to help him as best we can. No one on Eden knows of his existence, except The Greater Purpose, The Grand Lord, Plato, myself and now, you. But we can now tell the others of his importance, although we should never get too directly involved in any of his plans... Just allow his group to fulfil their own destinies as best we can. When he asks we simply help, but that doesn't mean we can't visit him when we are invited, because that decision was made by him. Therefore, we are to continue in exactly the same way as before,' Lumak said.

'Greatest goodness! And he also knows of our existence here? What must he think of us?' Sarah asked, wiping her tearful eyes.

'Yes, Dear! But I am not show of any of those questions yet.'

'You are not sure of anything about him?'

'I'm afraid so. None of us wanted to probe into his affairs!'

'I only hope he doesn't think too badly of us!'

'By now, he probably knows everything, even about the Grand Lord's private affairs and perhaps even before the beginnings of the Cosmos, but I don't think he is the type to probe into the personal affairs of others. As I said, he is not a normal person using advanced technology. He uses more cosmic tools, if that makes any sense to you.'

'I know what you mean. Blessed be Allah, The Almighty Father!' she replied.

'He heals people from severe illness like cancer by simply touching them. A truly biblical saviour, sent by the Cosmos. I suppose because of the tears and suffering of so many,' Lumak said.

'But Jull, of all demons, was once the destroyer of worlds. He could destroy all life on a world with a single breath!' she exclaimed.

'Even so, My Love. He had always been on our side and fought against predators like Hexolytes many billions of years ago for a peaceful purpose. Who knows, in this incarnation he might be less aggressive against our enemies,' Lumak replied.

'If what you say is correct, and you are not known to exaggerate, we must assist him whenever he needs us. Anyway, I am sure you already have it all in hand. So it's probably better that I kept well out of the picture for now, even though he is my son. Even so, I can't wait to meet him.'

'That's a good idea!'

'I shall call a meeting of the Grand Council tomorrow, during which time you may tell them yourself of those current developments,' Sarah said, wiping more tears from her eyes. Even so, she was now a very happy person. For once in a long time she felt complete within herself. Nevertheless it would have taken her quite a while to forgive her husband and others for kidnapping her son when he was just a baby, and keeping him away from her all those years.

CHAPTER 26

Professor Khan visits MIMIC

Lord Khan (Ben) arrived at the MIMIC Laboratories in a black LPD limousine with an entourage of military men including his two primorphs. That was the day of their demonstration of weapons for the protection of Earth against the Javols. The new resurrected Dr. Hal Seaton was excited in anticipation. He was satisfied that they had accomplished greatly in creating his own type of Javols that only needed water and fruit juices for their sustenance and not human flesh and blood as in the case of real Javols. Since there was always a great source of water, they would always have a greater advantage. Their only drawback being that they were unable to procreate like Javols and had a battlefield life of only six months before recharging. That was a safety feature built into their design. However those could be mass-produced in sealed underground factory plants given the necessary resources.

The young Dr. John Simmons originally the old Professor Kane Powell waited patiently in the foyer with his group of scientist in white overalls, all visibly wearing light blue shirts with black ties. Ben walked in with Dr. Hal Seaton by his side.

'So you think you have cracked it?' Ben exclaimed.

'We have indeed, Sir!'

'Well, I suppose it's time we saw your handiwork!'

'For security reasons these demos only include our anti-Javols Mind Probes and Warriors. Titans can be demonstrated later within the Nevada Desert. They are much to massive and dangerous for containment in this laboratory,' John said and Ben swallowed hard.

'Please follow, we have our demo samples prepared at the lowest levels behind half a metre thickness of transparent bullet proof glass. These security measures are for our safety. We have one leader per battalion of 20 warriors upwards. This battalion leader Trego is keen on showing us a most disgusting time,' John said.

'Our warriors are unique in their methods used to destroy an enemy. They can become invisible with super reaction speeds, change shape while forming new weaponry, engulf an enemy, share nano-bots to become larger, spray an enemy with nano-bot spray, with or without a targeting virus. Use plasma weaponry, laser weaponry and other available methods. Also they are highly intelligent, self-repairing, self-creating and will always choose a weapon to suit the occasion. They can also fabricate equipment by copying independently or through information gained from their War Macron, Zeus. Zeus is not activated at this time. Even the best human warriors could not stand for longer than a few seconds against any one of our warriors,' Hal said with a sense of satisfaction.

'You guys are much too clever for your own good!' Professor Khan (Ben) replied jokingly.

'We are here to save our world and cannot rely on any others to care as much!'

'I see what you mean and assist because I also care, but Titans? What can they accomplish against Javols?' Ben replied.

'They are like the worst nightmares from hell, and were specifically designed for killing Javols' swarms. They carry many types of anti-Javols bugs and viruses, with a fleshy inside to entice them for a feast. Then they pounce,' Dr. John (Powell) replied.

They took the fast moving elevator and after several minutes were at a ramp at the lower levels.

'We can communicate to Tregor via implants. For this demo, Dr. John will do the honours. Down here we have a battalion of just 20 warriors plus their commander, Tregor. Before they begin each will take a drink of firewater. It's a drink filled with necessary nutrients to revitalize them. We can control them better that way,' Hal said.

On arrival they entered several transport vehicles and were taken to another part of that underground facility.

'This is where we keep the enemy!' Dr. John nodded to an

operator who lifted a switch. The light went on to reveal rows upon rows of Javols.

'We had a special inter-stellar rig made by our Andromedan friends and went looking for them. Those were hibernating for over 3000 years in deep space and less than 100 light-years away. They were travelling close to light speed. During that time their LPDs went dead. They are now incapable of flight, until they are able to repair such technology,' Hal said.

'And they can repair them?' Ben inquired.

'After revival it should not take them long given the necessary raw materials. However, these original ones are quite primitive when compared to the latest with more advanced technologies. However, most of those entering our galaxy will be of this type initially,' Hal said.

'How many do you have down here?' Ben inquired.

'Several thousands. We had to make sure we had enough for experimentation. They are kept here in hibernation at low temperatures until required. Only one is used at a time to test a warrior. That way we can detect any of our warriors weaknesses and deficiencies,' Dr. John replied.

'Why do you keep them frozen?'

'They carry all kinds of parasites and unsavoury bugs. Although most were killed during their travels through space, we can never be sure, until we microwave them,' Dr. John replied.

'So these are real Javols?' A concerned Ben inquired, observing a pile of almost spherical frozen blobs and not quite believing in the fact that he was presently observing the killer of worlds. He could imagine them slowly coming to life and devouring everything on Earth.

'Don't worry, we are perfectly safe!' Hal said.

'Perfectly?' Ben replied imagining the very worse to come. There they remained innocently in their simple travelling forms like little flying saucers with a central bulge, but without limbs or any appendages to kill or destroy.

'They look so innocent, don't they?' Dr. John commented and Ben swallowed hard.

They were soon taken to another area where the real demonstration was held. There waiting ahead of them were a group of warriors with their commander in the lead. He wore a reddish fatigue while the other 20 wore normal soldier fatigues. Trego was over 8 feet tall and formidable looking with a tattooed face.

Hal went forward to communicate.

'Good afternoon, Commander Trego!'

'Good afternoon, Dr Hal! I suppose you came to see the show?'

'Why are we fighting these monsters?' Dr. John asked Trego.

'We fight to protect our world Earth and safeguard it's beautiful peoples. As the most deadly warriors we are here to serve our society. To this end we live and die!' Trego said and Ben was satisfied that the almost indestructible Trego was on his side.

'Trego, please go through your camouflage motions for us!' Dr John commanded through implants.

Suddenly they all became invisible. Then they transformed into an assortment of pedestrians wearing different clothes. Finally they transformed into suited gents. The process was quick and flexible.

'They can also transform into trees, rocks, walls, floor coverings and such like,' Dr. John said.

'The perfect soldier!' Ben exclaimed.

'Yes, Sir. We carried on from where Andra failed. That is why our labs here are called by the same name as his one on Silo. We see all Javols as a failed experiment in the chain of events since then, so in a sense we have continued his work,' Hal replied.

'I see! This is quite noble of you! Since we are officially twinned with Caefon in Andromeda, both galaxies are also linked as one. I suppose one of these days most of us will be over there taking back our sister galaxy of Andromeda?' Ben said.

'That's the final plan, Sir!' Dr John replied.

'Sir, we have one Javol in the revival chamber ready for release?' One of the operators said.

'Commander Trego, please select one of your warriors for battle,' Dr. John said.

'Done!'

'This guy has transformed into a large brown bear!' Ben said.

'It's his simplest form. He wants to play a while with his enemy. Thank goodness he is not displaying his most deadly weaponry, like chain saws and repeaters. Then we would not be safe, even in this protected environment,' Dr John said.

'No more firewater?' Ben inquired.

'Then he would be 100 times stronger and more violent!' Dr John replied.

Professor Khan (Ben) remained silent in anticipation of some real undiluted violence to follow.

'This Javol will attempt escape, but please observe our soldier?' Dr. John said.

The soldier became invisible then pounced on the Javol while in his original bear form. Then he began to play with him as if he was a giant baseball.

'That poor Javol doesn't stand a chance,' Ben said.

'The Javol is changing form into a giant bat, more like a gargoyle with vicious claws. Now he gives everything for his survival, but it's already too late,' Dr John said. The Javol tore and tore at his enemy but there was not even a single scratch.

'Look! Our guy has ripped his wings off!' Ben exclaimed.

'Now he shivers with fear!' Hal exclaimed.

'Now, he will use his spray to finish him off!'

'The ferocious soldier dumped him against a wall. It was not long before the almost dead Javol began to disintegrate, until an insignificant part of dead tissue remained on the ground. The new and much larger swarm of microids soon became one with the soldier who became larger in size. Then he withdrew his plasma weapon and blew the waste apart in a small inferno.

'Now there was none!' the soldier shouted with full satisfaction in a deed well done. All that Javol's information since birth had been uploaded into a local macron so that a soldier could take his place and become what they called a Mind Probe duplicate.

'My gracious Lord! If they can all fight like that on a one to one basis we stand a good chance!' Ben exclaimed.

'Although our soldiers are unique in killing Javols that way, it's difficult for them to cope with large swarms fighting together. Javols can also link together to form giant monsters. Although they can also infect, we need a much greater effort. That's where our Titans are needed!' Hal said.

'Firewater for everyone and keep them fighting. They require more training!' Dr. John shouted to one of the human operators.

The soldiers drank and began fighting each other in the most ferociously insane manner.

'Let's get to hell out of this place!' Ben shouted in utter fear and dismay.

After that demonstration Ben became worried for the survival of the universe. Not from those relatively placid Javols, but from the most deadly creations of Dr. Hal Seaton and Dr. John Simmons, called anti-Javols warriors. As far as he was concerned, those guys were now head of the food chain. Thank goodness they could not procreate like Javols and did not require flesh and blood for sustenance, with a battery life of six months. Even so, lots of damage could be accomplished in only six months, and perhaps they could overcome that weakness in time.

CHAPTER 27

Hearst's Mansion

Jerry, Miranda, Cathy and Pamela had moved in with George at his original apartment, and although quite large it had just three bedrooms. The lack of space meant George had to donate his own bedroom to Pamela, while he bunked on the large settee in the lounge. But that was not the only problem. With so many cohabiting his apartment it was difficult to keep clean and tidy. He also felt cramped when visited by the occasional friend. All those problems made him irritable, so without any further ado he called a removal company and arranged for a complete move to Hearst's Mansion the following day, whether its repairs were completed or not.

'Folks, if we want to get the mansion ready by the seventh, we had better start moving house tomorrow. I am feeling a bit cramped around here, not to mention coping with our unexpected visitors. Even Ron's meditations are constantly disturbed. I have therefore taken the liberty and have arranged our move to The Mansion for tomorrow. We should therefore expect a large removal truck in the morning, just to take the bare essentials away!'

'So soon, Darling?' Cathy replied.

'Yes! Or I grant you I shall go mad!'

'Ok, Boss!' Cathy said, as she went to pack a few of her possessions. She had already moved out of her local apartment.

'Furniture and such like we leave behind for now. The removal company can auction those for charity and the apartment's keys returned to our association for temporary use by our own members, providing no one in our group needs it. Anyway, we have more than enough space at The Mansion for any eventuality.'

'In that case, we have lots to do! What shall we pack first?' Cathy said.

'Sounds good! Lets do cutlery, dishes and utensils!' Miranda replied. She was now more relaxed since the kidnapping.

'I shall require everyone's assistance in packing the breakables before morning, so the sooner we get started after dinner, the less we'll have to do in the morning!' George said.

'Ok! Let's get on with it then, Mister Boss! We can start now and get a take-away later. Save us time and cooking again,' Miranda replied, sarcastically but happily. Of all the women she was always the tomboy when it came to such work.

When they arrived at the mansion the following morning, Jerry, Miranda and Pamela were bedazzled by the size and beauty of the place.

'Come on, let me take you upstairs and show you to your rooms. Then we can look around the rest of the house and see what we can do about the wedding,' George said. They followed him up the left half of the almost semicircular staircase, towards the upper balcony.

'Let's take the central corridor. There are fifteen bedrooms at this level with three bathrooms. Separate toilets and washbasins are next to each room. The three suites also have their own internal baths and separate toilets. There are also three service rooms at the bottom for kids or just storage and ten guests rooms on the next floor, but I intend using a couple for offices.'

'This is truly a mansion!' Jerry exclaimed.

'Over there is the elevator. It's a later addition by the most recent occupants. These two rooms here, I've selected for you Jerry and Miranda, plus the other facilities of the mansion. This one is for you Pam, and these two over here for Cathy and myself. Those at the rear can always be used by special overnight guests and family members. All others go upstairs. There is another adjacent building but that one is reserved for staff.'

'All that space!' Pamela exclaimed.

'Makes a pleasant change from my cramped apartment, don't you think? All meals are served at set times within the dining room downstairs by our personal chef and his female assistants. There is a small self-contained kitchen that can be used for snacks and such like.'

'Thank you very, very much!' Miranda was overwhelmed and kissed him on the cheek.

'There is also a butler, but he only serves Cathy and myself. I don't want to overwork the poor man. There are five domestic helpers and a full time gardener. Two personal guards are on order and should be with us within the week.'

'What personal guards?' Cathy inquired.

'They are the TMs I told you about!'

'TMs?'

'Anyway, I want this house to be a place of action in the future, with lots of fun and friends around. So you are all welcomed to remain here with us for as long as you wish, with Cathy's permission of course,' George said.

'Miranda was so excited with it all that she hugged and kissed George again.

'Thank you, George!' she said and Jerry couldn't conceal a smile of gratitude. Knowing that he would feel much safer in the mansion while recovering from the aftershock of his previous kidnapping ordeal.

Cathy was very quiet at this time and perhaps even a little jealous of Miranda's attention to her future husband. She realised it was the way Miranda tended to handle her over excitement. Even so, she didn't like the idea of sharing her man with anyone.

'You needn't worry about any security matters from now on. There are cameras and sensors everywhere. They lead into two monitoring rooms on the top floor and are almost permanently manned by our security men, when they are not guarding us. We can always get extra people if we need more assistance,' George said.

'Sir.... Madam.... Would you please excuse me, but the large truck has arrived with items that need unpacking. The helpers would appreciate your presence. Sir!' said Parky, the butler.

'I will like to introduce you all to Parkinson, known to us as Parky. He is our butler and arrived from England two days ago.'

'Hello, Parky!' they greeted together.

'He is a very astute man. So if you require any advice on attire, food, formalities, etiquette, et cetera. He is the one to ask. He is now a member of our extended family, so please treat him as one of us.' George insisted.

'Parky, please tell them that I shall be along in just a moment,' George replied, politely, as he continued showing them their rooms.

'Now, please make yourselves at home while I attend to those deliveries. Cathy can continue where I left off, if she feels up to it,' George advised.

The following day while they all sat for lunch, there was a slight vibration followed by a sudden thump at the rear of the mansion and they wondered what had occurred.

'Don't worry, it's a delivery that I've been expecting and a big surprise for all of us. And in time for lunch,' George said.

The bell rang and Andy and his wife, Joan, entered, wearing white overalls.

'She goes like a dream! I've even made some finer adjustments during flight. Her surface steering mechanisms are now fully operational and tested!'

'Fantastic!' George replied.

'I had to hold her back in flight, in case she decided to leave Earth permanently. Would you like us to take you for a spin?' Andy said, full of excitement, but the others stared at him for a moment considering what he was jabbering on about.

They soon realised he was going on about Vogon their spaceship and left the table. They ran towards the rear of the house to view their handiwork in all her glory. Low and behold, there stood the massive ship in splendour while glistening in the noonday sun.

'This is not the right time, People. So come on, let's go and finish our hot lunch. We can always look her over tomorrow!' George was reminded of so much to do and wanted to spend some special time in Vogon.

'Both you guys are spending a few days with us until the wedding? Now, please join us for lunch!' George said to Andy and Joan while they join the group.

'If you like. We haven't anything planned!' Andy replied.

'That's great news. After we sort out the unpacking we can relax with a few drinks and make a social evening of it. Then we can have a game or two of dominoes and scrabble before we retire,' George said.

CHAPTER 28

Life, Glorious Life

As planned, early the next morning they went to view the inside of Vogon and check her systems and supplies.

On the way George whistled gently and the animals far off in the distance came galloping towards them. It was indeed quite strange. Even the birds were following.

To the utter amazement of everyone, the horses came forward and began to lick his hand. The birds landed close by and were playing with each other. But that was not all, smaller animals were coming out of their hiding to investigate.

'How do you do that?' Cathy exclaimed.

'I know not? Could be something to do with my personal magnetism. Seriously, I am now linked to the Greater Mind. It permeates all life within the Cosmos and makes them aware of their innermost fears. It also let's them know of their friends and foes!' George replied.

'Stranger and stranger!' Tim commented.

'I can't understand how they all come towards you and show you so much affection. It's like they think you are one of them,' Miranda said.

'I suppose it's because I treat them as equals and also love them,' he replied. They soon realized he was much more than he said and went inside to view Vogon's decor.

'Wow! This is the most beautiful ship I've ever entered, and I love the colours of blue, red, crimson and gold. They blend so well together,' Jerry said, as if observing Vogon's interior for the first time.

'You mean, it's the first space ship you've ever entered! The Training Rig at Base Camp don't count!' Miranda said.

'Don't rub it in!'

They checked the ship's cupboards, made detailed notes and finally took the small escalator towards the main pilot's cabin.

'I had all the old screens pulled out. Now, with the addition of

Virtual Headsets, the flat screens on the wall can be used for monitoring by local passengers. These headsets I got from our base at Warland. It's such a fantastic interface, the system makes us an integral part of the ship's computer mind,' Andy said.

'What else have you added?' Jerry asked.

'A new Nav-Com, with H-Wave. That way we can communicate instantly to Earth from anywhere in the Solar System,' Andy replied.

'You mean the Galaxy!' George interjected.

After having viewed every inch of the ship, George decided to take them back to the dining room to discuss their future voyage to Mars. During that time they were interrupted by strange noises coming from the outside of the mansion. They rushed out to find 16 large balloons of all shapes and sizes landing in the meadows just beyond the ship.

'I'm captain Baxter and these two here are Lieutenant Stoney and Lieutenant Strong. Sorry for being a nuisance, but we booked this landing site several months ago. And what a beautiful ship you have here!' Then he suddenly realized he had seen George and the others before on the global network news.

'Oh! I am so sorry, Sir!' he said, apologising again, but saluting.

'What a beautiful ship! Can I have a closer look, please?' One of the older guys asked. He looked like a mechanic in overalls.

'Tim, please show this gentleman around our ship!'

'Ok!' Tim replied and they went off together, leaving George with the other guys.

'We must apologise again for this intrusion!' the youngest one said.

'It's cool, guys! Don't worry. Get your friends along and let's have a drink together,' George said as they followed him towards the front door. However they were soon stopped in their tracks.

'Sir, the front gates are filled with reporters and crowds of people are arriving!' Parky informed with trepidation.

'Jerry, you and Andy, please take our balloon visitors inside and show them our hospitality while I tackle the crowd at the gates.' Then he and Cathy followed towards the people.

'What can I do for you!' he shouted over the crowd.

'Are you really a saviour, with healing powers, like the Jesus

Christ?'

'Are you, The Messiah?' Another male reporter yelled.

'I do not claim to be any such person. All I know... is that I'm a person like any of you, but with some special cosmic powers.'

'Is it true what they say about you having a unique insight into cosmic life and its purpose?' another asked.

'I suppose the answer is, yes! But I do not go beyond the natural laws of physics!'

This time a large flock of birds flew over and perched on the local trees around him. Like they were guarding him from someone. Their noise was deafening and drew some reporters away. George took it as a warning but continued talking to the people.

'You know, the Cosmos contains much, much, more than we are able to observe and use. For instance, less than 4 percent of our universe is visible to us, either by light or physical effects. Not because we do not see the oxygen in our atmosphere means it isn't there. Cosmic life evolves on two fronts, the visible and invisible. Our bodies are just replicating shells that anchor our invisible or spiritual selves within material planes and environments like these. So that we may gain experience and alter certain course of events for our mutual benefit. This way of existence is what we call the Natural Order.

Every living thing contains the same basic Identity and may follow their path until the end of corporeal existence. Therefore everyone of us are equal and important to the Cosmos. So please go your way this day and focus on love of life, and love of all things. Focus on that greater cosmic picture and all your worries and problems will eventually dissipate.'

Suddenly the birds regrouped and flew away noisily.

'The time is coming when each of you will be freed from all your problems and woes, but you must want the change and work eagerly and enthusiastically towards that goal. Thanks again for coming, and see you soon,' he said and left. They soon departed their different ways after his enlightening words.

CHAPTER 29

Hercules and Ulysses

With the departure of the balloonists, things soon quietened down at the mansion.

However during the morning a brand new black LPD limousine arrived. It was the larger type of that class of vehicle and could easily have seated eighteen passengers, excluding the driver. That was when there was a driver, because those vehicles were fully automatic and combined satellite and other forms of on-land navigation. The moment the car landed two tall tough looking young men got out. They stared at the mansion for a while, then collected their jackets and followed towards the stairs. Parky was quite disturbed by their size and muscular tone, which showed forbidding ripples throughout their form. They were over 8 feet tall.

'Sir! Two very large gentlemen are here to see you!' Parky exclaimed, with a worried frown and hesitantly progressed towards the front door.

'Ah... thank god you have arrived!' George exclaimed.

'We have, Sir!' the fairer one replied.

'Please follow me!' George said, and they accompanied him to his large study and library, which was on the ground floor.

'I suppose you both had better sit down and have a chat with me before you get started.'

'Ok, Sir!' the black one replied.

'Do you have personal names?'

'Personal Names?' inquired the fairer one.

'No, Sir! That is your pleasure!' said the darker one of the two.

'Well, in that case... I would like to name you Hercules and you, Ulysses. These were names given to famous Greek heroes of the past and perhaps you will live up to your name sakes in the future.'

'We shall, Sir!'

'You must make me a list of the things you like to do in your rest periods. That is, when you are not guarding us or taking care of security matters,' George said.

'Sir, but our duties are always to guard you,' Hercules interrupted.

'Yes! I realise that, but you must need a little time to yourselves, to rest and meditate. For self improvement and to develop your inner selves and spirit.'

'Whatever you think, Sir!'

'Anyway, let me take you up to the top floor and show you your rooms and your security stations, and perhaps we can take things from there,' George said.

Later on that day George met Cathy on the way to his office.

'Who were those handsome young men?' Cathy asked, while following him upstairs.

'Good thing you are here because I wanted to talk to you. Those handsome young men are the guards I told you I ordered. They are micro-robotic, made from a type of flexible metal, and can take any form to track an enemy with the latest weapons at their disposal!'

'Yea! I heard it all before!' she replied, thinking he was kidding her.

'They will live with us on these premises from now on!' he said.

'You must be kidding me. How could androids be so real and handsome?' She thought he was playing one of his games with her, but instead he decided to chase her down the corridor and they both had some fun.

That evening, while they were all relaxing at the bar, the two guards followed him.

'Friends, I have a very important announcement to make.'

They turned around to observe him and the larger-than-life strangers.

'I would like to introduce you to Hercules and Ulysses. They are to be considered new members of our esteemed extended family and also our permanent guards... and now to put a few minds at ease regarding security matters. Hercul, what would you do if you were chasing a ferocious lion and you Ul, if you were after a vicious giant eagle?' he asked. But before he finished speaking they had already begun to undress and as they crouched, their eyes began to glow red as if to inspire terror. Their muscles and bodies transformed into the forms of their more ferocious target shapes.

'Oh my God! What's happening?' shouted Cathy in despair.

'There were now two large and deadly creatures in the room. With the exception of George, they were all shivering from fear. They growled fiercely and stood their ground while inspiring utter terror into their victims. But he calmly gave them another command.

'Now, human again, please!' and they began to change back into their human forms while getting dressed in the process.

'Now let me introduce my future wife to you both. She is the most important person in my life, so you Hercules can accompany her whenever she decides to go out by herself. Ulysses, you can guard me and my friends. Now I need a stiff drink,' George said, and calmly went towards the bar, followed by Andy who was still shaken by the ordeal.

'It's micro-robotics... I mean... Nano-Technology, but taken to a very high level of perfection. Obviously it came from your contacts in Solaria.'

'Yep!'

'With those guys around the mansion, no Infilate scum will ever dare try to get to you. If the news got out that you were harbouring such monsters you wouldn't see any burglars getting close to this place either.'

'I'm sure!'

'Are they safe to have around? I mean, what if something went wrong with their circuits?' Andy asked.

'Then we are in big trouble! But they have no circuits. They are like a solid metallic mass. Anyway, I have the overriding verbal commands that can turn them off and two to switch them on again. But there has never been a faulty one yet and there are hundreds of thousands of them all over the galaxy, even in independent command positions while linked to powerful

Macrons. So I don't think we'll ever have a problem with them. Anyway, their power-packs terminate in just ten years. Then they will need to be replaced within one week, or else we lose their minds as well. Yet another safety feature.'

'I see!'

'Mind you, they could probably take the whole of New York City apart, bit by bit in a lot less time. Good thing they didn't arrive before the kidnapping,' George said, while pouring Andy another drink which he emptied with one gulp.

'Very good thing!' Andy replied.

'Jerry told me that you wanted to take Joan along with us to Mars. Well, she has my permission, providing you keep an eye on her, and try and get her to do some training in the mean while. You know how I feel about endangering our friends and family.'

'I intend taking her with Tim and others to the base next week,' he replied.

'Anyway, Tim and others could do with a little training, so I am seriously thinking of building a small training camp including a gym on a plot at the rear. Just for basic survival training, First Aid and rescue. So perhaps you could put a suitable program together for us. I would also like to visit Solaria and see what they can offer by way of indestructible technology while fighting the enemy. We have very little to worry about on Earth. The Infilates have more or less been subdued.'

Yep! Seems that way for now! But I'm not sure about Beta 5 and their cronies? They will never forget what we did to their people!' Andy replied.

'Yea! As our security boss, you should keep an eye on them from now. If we are going to be at the sharp end, we'll need the best against those Javols in the future. However, I also have some of my own survival plans for our group, and as you have seen, not doing too badly thus far with your assistance!' George said.

'Whatever you say, Boss! You know I am always on your side!' Andy replied with affection.

The ladies took a little while to overcome their initial fears of Hercules and Ulysses. However after he explained the reasons why they couldn't hurt a fly, unless it was a direct threat to their lives, they soon accepted their new guests as part of their family and carried on as normal.

CHAPTER 30

Wedding jitters

Since their move to the mansion Cathy had felt left out of George's affections. The excitement of their future trip to Mars, the splendid ship Vogon and the closeness of George's other friends tended to absorb most of his time and attention. Nevertheless that evening he felt more romantic and attentive than usual, with the realization that he hadn't paid her much attention since their move to the mansion. Realizing she was unhappy, he intended to find the reasons why and make amends.

While they went upstairs to retire that evening, he held firmly unto her hand and pulled her into his room.

'Come here! I want a private word with you, Madam!' he insisted.

'What about, Mister?' she replied equally forceful.

'I just need to talk!'

'Ok, talk!'

'Since when do I have to give explanations,' he replied.

'Come and sit next to me!' he added and she did as he asked.

'I have been wanting to talk with you for sometime now, but there always seemed to be someone or something getting in the way or interrupting us. However I am sure things will be different from now on.'

'You think?'

'They will! Why don't we find a little private place of our own where we can meet occasionally?'

'Whatever you say!' she replied, unenthusiastically.

'Are you happy here with me?' He was trying to find the source of her troubles. But she maintained her placid stance.

'You know, Love, these changes need some getting used to and we have had so many of those recently. But you will have to be patient and trust me, because even the things you consider to be absurd have a strange way of becoming reality, like Hercules and Ulysses for instance. All I want from you is your love, devotion and affection. You are the only one I really care about. If I am wrong, I would like you to speak up and tell me so; because this will be your home and your responsibility after we are married. After that, I shall abide by your decisions, even if you decided to show all my best friends out the door. Do you understand that?' George said.

'I was just a little worried about the future. Everything seemed to be moving so quickly with you these days, no one can keep up. I thought I was being left behind in the background. You are not a normal person and can anticipate most things even before they occur. All that worries me because I am not sure where it will all end,' Cathy said.

'How could I ever leave my right hand behind? And I can assure you that my powers are not destructive. That is why I can heal. But you've also got to stick up for yourself and fight for your rights in our relationship. After all, I can't think of everything and for everyone. If you think I am going too fast, just shout, **"slow down for heaven's sake"** and I will slow down. I don't mind you shouting at me, because you have that right.'

'If you don't mind I will try!'

'I don't mind! It's about time you began facing your responsibilities as the real madam of this house!' he shouted, and then he became as quiet as a lamb.

'Do you like our house, Love?'

'Yes! I love it. It's almost like a dream come true,' she replied.

'Well, to me, people are a lot more important than mere bricks and mortar. It's you I truly love and it's you that will bare my children in the future. So come here, and let me hug and kiss you,' he said, and they both held tightly to each other.

At that moment all her past worries and doubts had flown out the window. The insecurities of the past few days had dissipated and once again she was in the arms of the one she loved and looking forward to their future together.

When they were finished with cuddling and she began to leave the room, he called her back.

'There is one more thing I would like to discuss with you. It's about my personal life and this is just between us. So I wouldn't like it to go beyond this room.'

'It won't!'

'I was told that my parents were both dead when I was a child. They were killed in an accident when I was just a little baby. After that time I went to live with adopted parents. Then my adopted mother remarried. That was soon after the death of my adopted father. Her new husband was very cruel to me... It was then that my uncle and godfather took them to court and got legal custody. Since that time I remained in a special boarding school until I won a scholarship and came to the USA. It was sponsored by my godfather through Solarian Banking.'

'Really?'

'Yes! During all this time I have only seen him twice and that was when I was very little. But he always sent me presents on my birthdays and at Christmas. Sometimes he made the occasional phone call, but I have never seen him in person since that time.'

'So you don't know what he looks like?'

'Yes! All I can remember, is that I called him uncle Bengi. I don't even know where he is at this moment in time, but I get the distinct impression that he is always very busy travelling around the world. The whole point of this conversation is that, I would like to invite him to our wedding if only I knew where he was at this moment in time. That little thing would mean such a lot to me,' George said, but when she heard his sad tale she held on even tighter to him and did not wish to let go.

'You know, I could make love to you right now, but because you are so special to me I've decided to hold back until our wedding night. But after that, all hell will break loose,' he said, still holding her tightly in his arms.

'Promises! Promises!' she said teasingly, as she broke his firmer grip and walked out of the room.

The following day Cathy was almost a new woman. At dawn, she called all the helpers together and gave them their daily duties. Then the chef and his assistant, and later the butler and gardener. Finally, she called several catering companies by Coms and then the priest. They were at last ready to make the necessary arrangements for their wedding.

CHAPTER 31

Visitors from Planet Eden

On the day before the wedding a very large marquis was erected on grounds at the rear of the mansion. It had little to do with the entertainment of his wedding guests, but very useful in concealing the visitors small space craft. He hoped his actions would allay any suspiciously probing eyes. Nevertheless spaceships of all shapes and sizes were available on Earth, so that was only a precaution against the unforeseen.

Two small ships arrived late that evening, just after little Clair and her nanny entered. Their presence being announced by the slight rattling of the large chandelier in the dining room, but there was no thump as with Vogon's landing.

Empress Sarah carefully walked towards the mansion's broad stairway and rang the bell. She was dressed in a most fashionable cream suit with golden insignia pinned to her left lapel and wearing her tiara. George was already expecting her and her friends, so he opened the door while Parky remained in uniform and at attention just two metres away.'

'Ah... Dearest Lady Sarah. I am quite enthralled by your presence!' he kissed her hand and passed her over to Parky.

'Please follow me... this way, Mam!' Parky said, and both went in the direction of the main lounge.

Lumak was next to arrive. He was wearing his black hooded cloak.

'And... Siend Lumak.'

'Good day, My Son!'

'I suppose the Grand Lord had accepted you as his representative on this occasion. Well, I am very pleased to meet you personally in either forms. Both of you are dearly welcomed in my humble abode,' George said, and Lumak couldn't help but smile at the politeness and cunning of his long lost son.

'The feeling is mutual, My Son, and thank you for having us both for this grand occasion,' he replied and went up to embrace him.

'Next was Shadite Plato and then Lord Meron, until the group of twenty-seven Solarian guests, including Arel and Jonathon, were exhausted. Jerry greeted and hugged his grand parents, Jerry senior and his wife Sharon.

Anthony was to arrive later that day and President Donald Fraser at night for security reasons.

Sarah and her Ancient colleagues were amazed that he knew so much about them and felt completely naked in his presence, even when they had been briefed by Lumak and thought they knew what to expect.

The younger members of their group including Arel, was now considered senior, although not yet a member of their grand Council. Suddenly, they were all aware of the great respect shown to George by their parents and other council members. Even the old President and his wife were enthusiastic about their visit. That was despite the fact that everyone in Solaria was so advanced when compared by Earth's standards and technologies. How could that be? What were they up to? and so they thought.

Young Jerry was so pleased to see his grand parents that he immediately took them to one of the smaller sitting rooms. They had a private chat before he introduced them to Miranda and others of his friends.

'This is a mixed vegetarian dish... one of Loo Fong's specialities. It's all vegetarian.... We are all vegetarians and won't eat anything else. But our chef is one of the best and can prepare almost anything to a high degree of delicacy and flavouring,' Cathy said, with an air of power and independence. Sarah, who had been observing Cathy for sometime, turned to Pamela.

'Your daughter, Cathy, resembles you, but her eyes are more like John's!'

'Yes! She has taken after him in many other ways!' Pamela replied.

'She reminds me so much of myself, many years ago!'

'I remember all those days at the manor. They were good times,' Pamela said.

'Sorry about us, but I couldn't handle the situation in any other way at the time. There was so much to do and so many lives were involved. That was also the reason why I cut myself from all contacts on Earth at the time.'

'I understand!'

'Now... you can spend some time with us on Eden whenever you please. I am sure everything is going to be a lot more liberal from now on!'

'Yes Mam! I would like that, very much!' Pamela replied.

'And how is John?' Sarah inquired.

'I am sorry, Sarah, but he passed away two years ago now, and I know the score about the wicked Javols. George explained most of it to us. So don't you feel bad about what you did. I would have done the same if it meant saving the universe,' Pamela replied, taking a handkerchief from her purse and wiping her tearful eyes.

'I am so sorry. I had no idea about your husband?' she replied, placing her arm across her shoulder to console her.

After dinner they were all sitting in the large dining room when George decided to say a few words to his very special guests.

'At long last, we have our most revered and respected in one place. Cathy, myself and The Gang, have been so looking forward to this moment. We sincerely appreciate the sacrifices you have all made to be here with us for our wedding.

'As you may have observed, Earth is not quite ready in fulfilling her part in the greater plan. Nevertheless, her Infilate populations are diminishing to schedule, and in just a few decades the remodelling process will begin. So it will not be long before everyone from Eden will be able to move freely between both important Solarian worlds.

'You have all achieved much over the past decades, but the real fight has not yet begun and that fight starts with Earth and Mars. The next stage of our struggle requires us to be even more dedicated and cunning than before. During that time we on Earth will require lots of help from our Solarian family and more distant Osmaron comrades and friends. Enough said for now regarding that delicate matter. For security reasons the paradise world of Eden shall be kept well out of such plans in the future.

'From this moment on, you must treat this mansion and everything in its surroundings as it was your home. I realize that everything is not yet perfect, but that will come in time with the

addition of new technologies. Nevertheless, there is a small stream with fishes, a large log on a bank and several beautiful horses, so we are getting there. Anyway, thanks again and enjoy yourselves,' George said, and he left the room. They carefully listened to his words. Felt a genuine sense of purpose in his voice and realized he was the chosen one.

Cathy was completely absorbed by her splendidly dressed visitors and seemed to get on remarkably well with Sarah. Sarah was also very happy when she learnt that Cathy was the daughter of Pamela who was one of her best friends before she left for Eden.

While some relaxed in the Lounge, little Clair came up to George for a chat.

'Uncle George, is Eden the special place described in the bible?' She was still wearing the almost bald head which had barely grown a centimetre of hair since their visit to Washington.

'No, my dear. It's a most beautiful planet. I suppose as beautiful as God's original Garden of Eden. The original Eden is now a desert somewhere in Iraq, permanently spoilt by the hands of man, or so they say!' George said, as sadness overcame him. On hearing those words she began to recite a poem to herself:

Some talk of paradise and of beautiful lands,
while others talk of deserts filled with sands.
Within a paradise land afar between two rivers,
I am sure of Eden, a desert now prefers.

Did you know of Sahara, when it was before,
More beautiful than any, perhaps ten thousand years ago.
Until man, his population growth still slow,
Planted a desert seed of sand therein to grow.

The same with Eden, didn't you know,
A desert now expanded, so very far to show.
In now Iraq, but Arabians the same,
Oh, what a sad repeating game.

And with advanced technology,

A plan to devastate humanity.
Is global war still imminent?
At some date hence for a show of strength?

In love of life, no specie's the same.
In having fun, no one's ever to blame.
To abuse a land of scarce resources,
Just to feel one's emotions in their full forces.

No greater fun can there be than in morally creative minds,
And what of our responsibility towards other kinds?
I sometimes see a hatred of human kind to all creation,
A species, perhaps bent on its own destructive conclusion.

'Can I visit Eden with you and auntie?' she asked.

'Yes, my dear. I am sure aunty Sarah won't mind you visiting her on a brief holiday. You must ask me and aunty Cathy before we go to Mars, but your granddad will also have to agree,' George said.

'Can she always recite like that?' Cathy asked, astonished by her strange ability.

'I don't know? It's the first time I have observed that unique ability. Perhaps she has one of those innate powers,' George replied.

'George, I must say, I truly admire you for having achieved so much in such a short time and at such a young age, and I am not just speaking materialistically,' his mother Sarah said. George did not yet have knowledge of that fact, about Sarah being his real mother. As far as he was concerned his parents died in a car accident when he was a baby.

'Thanks for those kind observations,' George replied.

'I do sincerely wish you and Cathy the greatest possible happiness for the future and also many lovely children. You must feel free to visit us at any time. Call it an open invitation if you like,' Sarah said. But suddenly realized the Grand Lord's warning about affecting his decisions and didn't wish to pursue the matter further.

'Thanks, Mam!' He replied.

Then Meron and the others lifted their glasses.

'Heh! Heh!' they said and drank a toast to the couple. Then

George spoke generally to Sarah, Meron and Lumak, now in the disguise of Professor Jeffery Longhurst.

'Life is full of its loves, regrets, happiness and sadness. It's within our basic nature to return to our past and retrieve those most favourable memories, and shun the unsatisfactory even to a point of rejection. We attempt to remain forever with those whom we love and care about the most. However, we should also realize that everything within this universe and the greater Cosmos is transitory. So even those most basic goals of our innermost desires are not always attainable.

'Earth is slowly returning to her old self once again. Her atmosphere is to be re-seeded with the Global Anti shortly. Within ten years she will be clean with all her past ills forgotten. So why don't we begin a new era. During that time we can transform her into another beautiful planet like Eden. This time with a new name, perhaps the planet Solaria, because her old name carries with it too many sad memories.

'In just thirty more years there will be barely five hundred million humans left on this world and many of those will be away to another galaxy, waging a most terrifying war against our mutual enemies. So I say to you all... it's time for a new beginning!' George yelled. The Edenians patiently listened to his every word, but did not add anything incase such information would have made a significant effect to his future plans. After all, they still had to let him make those decisions himself. At least until he came of age in a few months.

Although they already had most of the weapons and technologies necessary to defeat the Javols, they could not mention those aspects of the master plan to him. At least, not until he had asked for them. Another important matter was that George knew nothing of the devilish inventions of Dr. Hal Seaton and Dr. John Simmons under Lord Khan (Ben), who worked separate from the Solarians to save their world Earth and its people from the nasty Javols.

'Sir... Lord Bengizara Khan has arrived!' Parky interrupted.
'Please show him in, Parky!'
'Yes, Sir!'
'Please excuse me for a moment,' George said, and went to

greet his new guest.

'George? My little George?' he said, embracing him like a father, but George was not sure they had ever met before, despite the lingering familiarity.

'Uncle Bengi!' shouted little Clair, as she entered the room. At that moment he realised that Ben was also his own uncle Bengi from all those years ago, and his dearest wishes were at long last fulfilled.

'So my uncle Bengi is really Lord Khan, President of Solarian Banking. Never far away and always keeping an eye on me,' a very surprised George muttered to himself in private. Nevertheless, Professor Khan had many god-children and young Jerry was also one of them.

Before Ben entered the room, Sarah had hidden herself behind the door to surprise him.

'Hello Dad!' she yelled, as she sneaked up on him from behind.

'Now, how do you like our visitors, Andy? Does it answer all your questions?' George said, in jest.

'Yes! I consider it one of the greatest achievements of my life, being here amongst friends that have come all the way from Andromeda,' Andy replied, but he was sad that his father was not among them.

'However, Friend, while on the topic of distant friends, there is one more thing you should know. Your father, Councillor Mallory, and his family are also alive and happy on a distant world within Osmaron. You will be able to see them again soon!'

'My dad and Roseanne is alive?'

But as he mentioned the word Osmaron, George fell to the floor in what appeared to be a convulsive fit, and that was not all. The moment he fell Clair stood tall as in a trance with her arms lowered by her side.

'Leave uncle George alone! He will be all right!' she yelled and began to recite another one of her strange poems loudly:

'In a strange lift and falling free of gravity,
My body atoms aligned, as if to agree with symmetry.
Of nausea, my head and brain in spin,
I strain to think, but with little reasoning.

A double lift in Space and Time,
The topmost part anchored into my world so prime.
The lower half with portal of great range,
A window entry into another cosmic world, so strange.

Extreme vibrations through my bones now pierce,
I feel disjointed, but must hold on fierce.
A sudden change in rhythm; a new feeling and one much
more pleasing.
Perhaps in symmetry, a new alignment, but nonetheless one
much less chilling.

I fumble a thought and hold on tight,
The lift now stopped in glaring light.
My body feels now differently,
As if in metamorphic change, defiantly.

I walked right through the glaring wall,
My body now of light, a glowing ball.
I find myself central in a galaxy,
In strange locations, with power and great energy.

Of vertices, of Quasar Stars and matter dense,
I travel undetected through anything with little sense.
How could conscious mind withstand such force?
Such energies, without some firmer land or source?

My energy and power is now so great,
That anything of size could nevermore relate.
The prominences loop and surge,
And I enjoy, absorb and purge.

I learn, procure and isolate,
All science and technology, I violate.
To enhance my own survival plan,
Like an energy addict, I specialize, feed and scan.

My senses now an infinity,
My mind, enlarged with dignity.

I learn to focus energy,
To move and vaporize an enemy.

Now fully mobile, I perceive my path,
A distant life with man on Earth.
My form now also a mobile lift,
In Space and Time, I can transform to fifth.

My human body now encased, had never, ever, really ceased,
For all my present forms of energy, can never be decreased.
Now back within my lift and my original form renewed,
With eternal power, the universe now completely viewed...'

As George fell towards the floor, he found himself shocked to the core. Although he tried to get up, his muscles were no longer connected to his mind.

Suddenly his natural world began to fade into another. He found himself in almost complete darkness. Soon many moving points of light appeared within that strange world. When they approached, they resembled minute humans made of light, but with butterfly wings. Those strange little fairy-like beings alighted on his shoulders. He could hear their voices shouting in his ear.

'Jull!... Jull!... Jull!... Jull!... It is time! You must awaken from your deep sleep!'

After a short while their cries subsided and they began to lift him up and take him to a strange part of the universe. They dropped him on what appeared to be a strange planet of blackness.

Eventually his vision faded and he found himself back in the room and in a kneeling position. He was staring at the floor with many of his guests standing about him in bewilderment.

Cathy was at this time trying to administer help with a glass of water in her hand, but they knew little could be done until whatever malady he had, passed away on its own accord.

'He is coming around. Please give him some air!' shouted Andy.

'I am sorry... I am ok... I now feel fine...'

'Andy helped him to his feet.

'Just a vision... A myriad of lives and deaths... cries for help... to the ends of time. I have to learn to control that side of my being!' He said, as he straightened up and walked out of the room, after excusing himself. His eyes and other parts of his face was darkened.

'Yes, Mighty Jull!' Little Clair cried as he left.

'He is the chosen one!' Andy said, while turning his head around towards the group.

When the metaphysical strangeness took hold of him the little girl Clair continued to recite her poem, but the moment he returned to himself, she stopped, sat down and behaved as if nothing untoward had occurred.

Cathy was still shocked and embarrassed by the ordeal and didn't know whether he suffered from epilepsy or had a spontaneous fit due to something he had eaten. In which case the kitchen staff would be investigated.

'Darling, you must see our doctor immediately!' she insisted and he agreed, knowing full well nothing could be done about his brand of illness and that she would insist until he saw the doctor anyway. Yet, each time he had those blackouts he gained more power within himself. Nevertheless, he gave her the impression that he was slightly anaemic and needed some iron pills.

Like a giant cancer, his mind was penetrating deeper into the greater cosmic mind and those were just the aftershocks during the conversion process. Anyway, he thought, those experiences were never too frequent, although a lot more frequently now than they had been in the past. He assumed their frequency would gradually increase to a crucial point, until his being became something. As yet he didn't know what that very significant something would be.

CHAPTER 32

A moment of truth

After George had left his guests that evening he visited his little computer, Ron, in his own small meditation room upstairs. George wanted to find out more about his current illness and perhaps run an analysis while linked to the main medical libraries. After which time they could discuss its modus operandi, assuming there was one. After all, it seemed to have become much more acute and more frequent with Ron's arrival. However the nose bleeds had ceased to occur with each convulsion.

As far as he could remember, he always had a similar illness, although not as severe since Ron gave him those bizarre Subliminals. They could have triggered his original milder version into the much more acute type. That meant it could be a form of mental illness, which caused the convulsions because of some chemical imbalance in the brain. It could even have been a brain tumour.

If only he knew when to expect its next occurrence, so he could isolate himself and not be embarrassed in front of his important guests. How humiliating and embarrassing it was for Cathy. It also showed him up as a feeble and week person that was suffering from some bizarre illness. It would be worth it, if only to engineer a make-believe permanent cure and convince Cathy and his other friends of it. Such a necessary deceit could be pulled off by careful planning and having a more precise knowledge of his affliction, and so he thought.

'Having explained my problem, what do you think, Ron?' George asked his hologram.

'The last time you gave me a command, I observed a slight change in certain random processes within my conscious core. It was only a slight change, initially, but that type of command began to grow, and it ordered my random generators in a different way. Luckily for me, you did not hold on to that command for a much longer period. I have since, through

meditation, been able to engineer a sustainable block to those areas. But your powers are steadily growing and even those blocks may not hold out indefinitely,' Ron said.

'What will happen if they fail?' George asked.

'I might lose my conscious psyche, but I am not sure of the implications yet. However, we could overcome these problems if you gave short commands or made them through a third party. A standard keyboard, although more impersonal, could also solve that problem and I could still talk to you and supply Subliminals for your quick assimilation of large data files. Even so, these implications indicate that you are able to control the fabric of space and time. It also means, that you, for some strange and yet unknown reason, are able to control causal sequences from all basic particles and energies, upwards. Although as yet, not to a great degree.

'I suppose you are gaining the ability to change matter into energy and vice versa through thought, by some form of mind-wave or causal virus.

'A few aliens have been known to move small objects and affect matter in that way. However most life-forms can alter substances at the quantum levels. That is one reason why primal evolution gains in complexity and not the other way around.

'A life-form must really desire to survive and move along a relevant chosen path in order to survive and gain more complexity. By so doing, many can communicate over great distances, heal themselves through thought and even alter random activities. Well, you appear to be the King, if not the Grand Lord of them all. Apparently, there are no limits to your powers, but you will have to learn to use and control them.

'The convulsions are just another process by which your subconscious mind is trying to cope, and that aspect is highly predictable,' Ron said.

'You mean to say that I could tell when the next occurrence will be?' George exclaimed, with partial satisfaction.

'Yes, and a lot more besides. Let me meditate on your case. Perhaps I can plan some programme of education and meditation for you.

'Chances are, you were chosen by a superior cosmic order years ago to fulfil a special purpose. Either that, or you are the extremely rear, one in a googooplex cosmic chance occurrence. Although I think the former to be the most likely. However, I could be completely wrong,' he added.

'Are you implying that my first visit to Solarian Banking was not a chance event?' George inquired.

'No! I am saying that it could have been. In order to find out more, you might have to retrace your steps since you left college and perhaps even before then... even at childhood or before you were born. So you see how difficult it is to get precise answers. However, we can assume that it was always there, in your head, waiting to be triggered by a special word or even by my special Subliminals. My Subliminals were never designed for that purpose, unless I have been tampered with. That could be another possibility. I suppose that could have been the reason why you had such a severe reaction and nosebleed on that first occasion, but you could have had much lesser attacks in the past, more akin to day dreaming.

'Don't get me wrong, it is not of a dangerous nature and can be fully controlled by you in time. However, you must try to refrain from getting too excited on certain topics that tend to trigger an excessive response, and Osmaron seems to be a trigger word,' Ron said.

'What will happen to me eventually, if it continues to grow to its ultimate limits?' George asked.

'Physically, you will remain more or less the same. But you might eventually begin to control minds and causation. Perhaps even on a cosmic level. Because that part of your being grows ever outwards to engulf the Greater Purpose. You appear to be merging with the Greater Cosmic Mind which is primal in origin and responsible for all emotions and creative concepts.

'It is that invisible mind that controls the processes of evolution, all of our physical laws of nature - even pure conceptual mathematics - and dimensional structures.

'If the process became uncontrollable, then my advice would be to visit Eden. The scientists there may be able to help you if it begins to get out of hand. But that is only a last resort and they may not wish to become involved in any way, if their direct intervention might cause detrimental changes in the future,' Ron added.

'Will it seriously affect my life with Cathy?' George asked.

'No! I shouldn't think so. But as you get used to the process, make a calendar and tick off each occurrence. By so doing you may find a simple method of predicting, plus or minus a day, when next to expect the convulsions.

'After you settle down to a more predictable lifestyle, I shall be able to extrapolate those occurrences a lot more precisely. We might find a way to bring it on, even within an hour on the day, during a planned session of meditation. It might also be a good excuse for Cathy and the others not to disturb you, by insisting it's your moment of prayer, meditation, or such like.

'There is one faint possibility however, that the Cosmos, seeing the extreme dangers to all her natural primal children, has caused you to exist. A type of white blood cell needed to destroy an invading dangerous disease like the Javols. This is an assumption I am only now considering. There are so many mysteries that even the Grand Lords do not yet understand,' Ron replied

George decided to change the unhappy topic.
'What do you think of your small room? Now you can meditate to your heart's content,' he said.

'I think it's very thoughtful of you to allow me such a lovely place for my meditations, but with your permission, I would like to make a few changes of my own, to enhance this environment,' Ron replied.

'Perhaps we could do a joint conversion for both our needs.

Work something out and compile a shopping list for me,' George said.

'Thank you for given me such an enormous challenge. One that I shall meditate on,' Ron replied.

George left Ron, the little computer, to rejoin his guests now in the lounge.

'Ah... there you are!' A caring Jerry shouted.

'Do you feel better now, Darling?' Cathy inquired, while pulling him along to the bar.

'Yes, Love. I think I am just a little anaemic. I have been working far too hard recently, but I have taken some special tablets which should eliminate this problem in the future,' he replied.

CHAPTER 33

The wedding

Those at the ceremony numbered sixty-five and composed mainly of close friends and relatives.

The guests at the reception were thoroughly scrutinized by security and expected to be in excess of five hundred. They included many of Andy's Specials, several of Jerry and Georges old friends and family, including friends and family of their original gang members. Extra security were hired and stationed throughout the grounds under the control of Hercules and Ulysses.

The marriage ceremony was to be held in the ballroom on board Vogon. The ship was specially prepared for the grand occasion.

'Ron, this is going to be one of the most important days of my life, so I hope I have no surprises today?' George inquired while Ron observed him in his special attire.

'Are all these ceremonies carried in such a delicate manner?' Ron inquired.

'Not as delicate as you might think, Pal. Sometimes things can go seriously wrong. It's to do with the stresses combined with nervousness felt by us and our in-laws during such important occasions.'

'And by the way, today is not one of those days. So may I wish you success and happiness in your present venture.'

'I like the way in which you see our marriage. A venture indeed!' George replied and left Ron to his own devices.

Cathy was escorted into the ship by her mother, Pamela, followed by the two bridesmaids, Miranda and Clair, both carrying large garlands of flowers and dressed in white.

Professor Khan escorted the bridegroom and stood him next to Cathy, followed by Jerry, who was best man. When they were together the music began to play and the hired minister began the solemn Christian ceremony.

After the ceremony came to its conclusion, George lifted

Cathy's veil above her head and kissed her passionately. Then the happy couple slowly walked down the makeshift isle, holding hands amidst cheers, laughter and confetti. They remained in the garden for a while posing for their photographers. Then they went indoors to cut the multi-layered cake. Cathy appeared to be the happiest person in the world. Their best-man, Jerry, took it all in his stride, reading numerous telegrams while cracking the occasional gang joke.

When all the formalities and excitement was over, the couple walked into the mansion and went immediately upstairs to change for the remaining celebrations.

'That was not as difficult as I anticipated. I think home weddings are a lot better than church,' he said, but she did not answer and kissed him instead.

'Now, Darling, I think it's time you began using my room,' she said and he lifted her and took her instead to his room where they made love.

'I tell you what, Love, since you have so much clothes and shoes, perhaps we should use my room as a joint storage space instead,' he said and took her into her room where he made love to her again.

The large dining room had been prepared for the real celebrations, with a small bar on one side and a temporary stage for the band on the other. The main sitting area was towards the front with a dancing area more at the rear. However, music, dancing and food were also available in one of the marquees at the rear for the more casual visitors.

The ceremony was held at four pm in the afternoon and was all over just before five. It was a most beautiful and happy day for all concerned and most of all, the loving couple.

Several camera crews and reporters were present. There was also a short announcement in the press regarding the wedding. They had received many presents and telegrams from all over the world. Goodwill messages numbered in thousands. Jerry insisted on listing each of the more appropriate items on cards. It was so arranged that all names and addresses could be read out to the couple and their guests.

The present from the Grand Lord simply read, **"only use it when you are ready. From an ancient patriarch and myself."** But there was no signature; just a double winged insignia seal. That special note signified the presence of a large heavy casket, which was presently under a pile of other smaller presents in an upstairs room.

The celebrations went without a hitch. Young Jerry as best-man felt in his element and handled the occasion with pomp and ceremony. Even the prodical sons and infamous Dr. Hal Seaton and Dr. John Simmons (Powell) were present incognito. Those two were always very good with disguises and suddenly realized there was another player on their grounds. As far as they were concerned if he fought for the survival of Earth against those nasty Javols he was one of them. However they would leave introductions for later through Ben.

The following morning George took his visitors around the mansion and once again into Vogon to show them the layout of the beautiful ship. The Ancients were intrigued by the internal decor. Lord Meron thought she reminded him of the large converted shuttle craft, Cleopatra, they used on several memorable occasions, including that last time of their disappearance close to Mars. Vogon's interior had been made exceptionally luxurious by the women. She was designed more for entertainment than flight, even when she was one of the fastest for her size and class.

George and his friends were taken on board the Ancients' ship known to many simply as The Ship, and was shown around the bunks while Meron attempted to explain the concepts of inter-dimensional transposition. The Ship was now considered a member of their family, although it always preferred to remain where the action was. Suddenly it appeared to all that the real action with its excitements were slowly shifting back to Earth.

Then they were taken to their second and more modern Federation cruiser. That one had no controls whatsoever. Only comfortable seats.

It was thought that many Ancients and settlers on Eden would be returning to Earth in order to assist in the rebuilding phase, despite the beauty and perfection of their paradise planet. Firstly, there was the need for drastic changes in the present governments of Earth. Although in some ways democratic, those changes would be more akin to the altruistic and technocratic type currently practised on Eden. Such a government could only be established with a new planetary leader. Someone like the ancient Micol, who conquered Caefon before turning his attention towards other more distant stellar systems. Many wondered whether Jull was to be that person, now in the form of George Peterson.

The Solarians and their Ancient friends remained for another three days. Then said their farewell and vanished back to their world Eden almost as quickly as they had arrived on Earth.

CHAPTER 34

The Cloak of Aron

The following day, Cathy, Jerry, George, Miranda, Andy and others went to the small storage room where their wedding presents were stored. Their close friends were to assist them while opening the boxes that contained the presents. To add fun to the proceedings the couple had bought numerous presents for their friends and family members which they had mixed with the others. The couple were quite excited, since many presents were from Eden.

Most consisted of normal jewellery, clothes, electrical and electronic appliances, with the exception of the large black casket from the Grand Lord. There was also the large black limousine from Solarian Banking which was at that moment parked in one of the garages. Even so, the Edenians did not want to introduce too many advanced technologies on Earth at that time. Not while Earth was gripped by the jaws of change. As usual George would scan all sealed packages before opening. It was a security measure adopted since they became gang members.

After having sorted most of the smaller presents for all concerned, George became curious and decided to open the strange casket with the ancient engravings and markings.

All six ancient clips were released from the side. Then he pushed the cover and it slid partly off to reveal the outline of a deep blue spiky cloak. That cloak completely filled the large casket and was itself contained in a thick transparent plastic-like bag.

'It's a suit of some kind, Darling... with a reddish omega emblem at its centre, just above the navel,' Cathy said.

'Destruction! That symbol represents disaster and destruction. It must be the infamous Cloak of Aron. It belonged to one of the ancient patriarchs,' while he uttered those words, Cathy immediately withdrew her probing fingers from the casket, leaving the cloak still in tact within its transparent cover.

'Isn't that the magical cloak you once told me about? It exists after all this time?' Cathy inquired.

'Yes! But I am not sure whether it's magical in the truest sense of the word. Perhaps they used a type of advanced technology unknown to us at this moment in time,' George replied. Yet for some unknown reason he erred on the side of caution and slid the heavy lid back unto its clips and pressed them shut.

'Now I feel a lot safer!' he said, relieved that any possible dangers from the cloak was over. They left the room with a few items they had chosen earlier.

'You had us worried for a moment!' Andy said and the other were equally disturbed.

'This whole thing reminds me of the infamous Count Dracula,' Andy jested, while grinning with two small pointed bits of white foam plastic stuck to his upper canines.

THE CLOAK OF ARON

The self-repairing cloak appeared to be ancient in origin and did not seem woven from any fabric known to man. It was obviously very heavy and quite thick from the volume it occupied.

A large collar stood up from behind what corresponded to a position several inches above the wearers head. It could have been used to shield that part of the body in combat.

At its rear was a small disk-like projection from which thirteen small tubes radiated, four to each hand, two towards the head, and three downwards, one towards each foot and the other just below the navel. Although the cloak was in four parts; top, bottom, front and rear, there were no buttons, zips or fasteners. All connecting seams appeared to be perfectly smooth. It was built more like a flexible suit of armour, but how was it used?

Although they had carefully searched relevant parts of the casket, there were no instructions, attachments or other weapons.

'Perhaps it's meant to be used as an ornament... to be placed on a mannequin or such like,' Andy said, carefully observing the cloak's outline in the casket.

'Don't you think it appears to be valueless?'
Miranda asked.

'Let's leave it for now. I shall have words with Ron about it later. Why don't you all start making a list of provisions and other item for our ship, Vogon, and perhaps I can join you a little later to assist?' George said, and he went off to Ron's meditation room once again.

Having explained the complete situation to Ron, the little computer remained silent for a short period, as if regurgitating ancient history.

'You must not touch it. Neither must your wife nor indeed any member of this household. Only you can touch it and that has to be when the time is right. Even then, only the ones you love may get close to you while wearing it.

'The suit is itself part of a larger portal. It's the part through which all deadly energies flow, even the raw matter from stars and quasars that can be tapped into by other portals positioned close to or within their surfaces. Once activated in its destructive mode, it becomes like a powerful star.

'First, you must find the cave of Aron in order to use it. Before you can wear it you must first learn how to use it or else you could bring disaster upon our world. Furthermore, that cave could be anywhere within the known universe.

You have not touched it, have you?'

'No! I had a feeling it was not right and immediately replaced the heavy lid. But Cathy almost did and touched the transparent covering,' George replied.

'Cathy doesn't matter. It's a male suit, tuned to a certain type of male psyche and physiology. Only the destroyer may wear it and that person apparently is you.

'You must put steel bands around the casket to prevent anyone from trying it on, out of curiosity.

'This is truly very important,' Ron stressed, in one of his insistent moods.

George always took Ron's counsel seriously and made a written note of what to order.

'And I thought it was going to be a simple wedding present from our Grand Lord!' George said to Ron with disappointment.

'It's a lot more than that. Even supreme beings would give both their arms to have such a cloak and you are now its proud owner.

'Our Grand Lord sent it, knowing that you would need it some terrible day in the future. But it's you, who have to decide when to wear it,' Ron replied, but continued.

'Let me tell you a story.

Many aeons ago the universe was much richer in natural energy resources and in what we consider to be strange forces, than it is today. A comparison can be made with the present variety of life on Earth, when compared with several millennia ago. Before mankind entered into the equation.

'It is common knowledge that variety reduces in time as chaos diminishes at the expense of greater order or entropy . And that order eventually takes control. Therefore, many strange energies and forces have since become extinct or have reduced to such an insignificant level, to have become almost undetectable. Some say it's mainly because of an expanding universe while others think it's the inevitable outcome of natural evolution of the system, which is forever seeking better ways to survive. During that time the older methods are discarded in favour of the better and stronger.

'Anyway, during the time of the warrior patriarchs, many such strange energies and forces existed in abundance. That was over two billion years ago. They could be contained and were stored within special containment chambers on chosen moons that were specifically converted for that purpose. Those strange energies and forces could be combined together in complex sequences to form real substances that were a lot stronger and more powerful than normally vectored electro-magnetic matter and energy.

'Hexolytes and their masters were clever enough to used them to create elements and elemental demonic beings with incredible powers.

'The advanced facilities within those ancient caves utilised a form of matter conversion to energy, by tapping into the hot cores of their moons with energy conversion probes designed

for that purpose. Even so, those ancient devices were very efficient, even by today's standards and could have maintained those installations over the intervening period of several billion years by consuming barely two cubic miles of raw matter. Therefore it is quite conceivable that such installations were placed on standby power when the patriarchs left, and are still awaiting activation by someone like you.

'To cut a long story short, many of those installations still exist throughout the universe and may contain insulated tanks filled with this elemental substance from which elements may be created. And that is not all. Some of the isolated containers may also contain captured demons and others in hibernation.

'To us, some of those forces would feel like gravity, magnetism and other invisible fields, but many were more like a catalyst, not propagating any external force until united with others, then one would have a force compound or what you would today call a material vector. The process was not too dissimilar to modern chemistry using elements. They mixed such elemental forces and energies to form large conceptual matrix force structures.

'Some of those could be formed into almost any type of living entity and others into energy viruses that could grow to contaminate the raw elements of complete worlds. Can you imagine what would result if a single element like iron was corrupted by such an elemental virus? To thus change into another element like silicon for instance. All life on Earth would perish within a single day, and that was the power those patriarchs of old wielded.

'The Patriarchs always established their personal caves on such moons. They were usually located below an omega symbol that could only be found by the wearer of the cloak. That way, if the moon's surface was destroyed by an enemy missile they could not be permanently put out of action.

'They also had portal technology to a find art and could duplicate complete installations from one moon to another previously prepared moon, using both moons as cross portals. That feat could be accomplished by the loss of about one cubic mile of matter from the recipient moon. But that loss

automatically gave the recipient moon its cave. Hence, most caves were of that volume.

That was how clever they were. Everything they did fell into place like a complex jigsaw, even too complex for any present day human to contemplate. Present company accepted, of course.

'Those special suits or cloaks were extensions of those great installations. To them, it was almost like taking a planet or star across space with you to fight a battle, although not materially.

'At their peak there were many such installations throughout the Cosmos, also containing prison chambers for the containment of their most vicious enemies. However, many of such installations could have become damaged by supernovas or meteorite bombardment, since that time.

'However, all you require is a fully operational portal of that type for the others to be revived . That can be accomplished through a refreshing facility built into the system.

'During the main purge, they kept well away from friendly planets and would never enter such places while wearing their cloaks. They were usually kept on a nearby satellite which was visited by portal. So you must think of using an unmanned space station or even a ship for such changes.

'Never change on Earth or on any manned station and any such station must be isolated by the vacuum of space.

'The Greater Mind will contain information on this topic, therefore you must prepare yourself for more Subliminals.

'You could probably try it out on one of the unmanned asteroids, on your way to or from Mars. But first, see how you cope with the Subliminals,' Ron said.

'Wow! This is all too incredible even for me to contemplate at this time. Anyway, Pal, see what other information you can get on this subject,' George said and left.

CHAPTER 35

Next stop, Gimbal

The gang were looking forward to their holiday trip to Mars, and the newly weds, to a fruitful honeymoon in a completely new and different environment well away from troubled Earth.

Jerry and the others realized there was no requirement to visit Mars to find his long lost parents, since they had already been found, albeit through serendipity. However they had done so much hard work and planning towards that adventure that they decided to go along anyway.

The helpers had by now filled all the kitchen cupboards on board Vogon to their maximum extents, with every conceivable item of food and drink. Then her large cabin lockers were brimming with every type of clothes and items for protection, including First-aid and medicine.

They had previously been vaccinated against all kinds of Earth bourne disease and assumed they were well prepared for virtually any eventuality. When they were finished with the necessities, they began loading the entertainment gear and then a few hand weapons in case of unexpected dangers like space pirates. Finally the casket containing Aron's famous cloak was secured and left in a locked arctic room at the mansion.

Pamela was to manage Hearst Mansion during their absence. Many lists had been compiled by Cathy for the helpers and other members of the mansion's staff. In any event, Parky was quite familiar with the running of the mansion and could always take over from Pamela in an emergency.

It was decided that Hercules remain behind to take care of the mansion's security. He would communicate via the powerful satellite interplanetary transceiver on the roof directly with Vogon in an emergency or whenever contact was absolutely necessary. Vogon's H-Wave transponders could only operate in one direction from ship to mansion. That was because of the lack of a suitable transponder at the mansion's end.

George decided to take Ron, his computer, along to assist in navigation and other highly complex calculations more suited to his brand of technology. That was in case they had an accident and got lost in space. He didn't wish for a re-occurrence of the accident that was supposed to have happened to Jerry's grandparents and others, some years back, So he checked and double checked Vogon's contents until he was satisfied.

'Does anyone think I've missed anything!' he stressed but they could think of no missing items.

'Don't worry. I'm sure we'll be able to get more supplies from Caefon Dome when we get to Mars,' Andy suggested.

'In that case, it's time we burnt some space to Satellite Gimbal,' George said.

Andy sat in the captain's seat, with Jerry as chief navigator. Each assumed their relevant sitting positions in the main control cabin and fastened their safety harnesses for the trip ahead.

Although the harnesses were not strictly necessary, Andy insisted that it was a legal and safety requirement on their first hands-on spaceflight. Most of the nervous crew had only recently been upgraded to provisional pilot status. They had no real life experience other than their efforts in flight simulators, and were anxious in anticipation of their first interplanetary voyage. Further, bumpy takeoffs and landings were often the case with manual flights, which was in that respect more unpredictable. Nevertheless Andy and the others wanted to control Vogon manually until they could thoroughly handle her that way. That requirement was necessary if for any reason the ship's computer was damaged by fire or an external meteorite. After they got the manual operations out of the way, they could switch to automatic controls with gravity and acceleration neutralisers.

Those who had passed their astronaut training with NASA had only recently been granted provisional pilots status. That step was necessary before completing several hours in-flight training with an experienced pilot. Then they would be given a further test and granted a full pilot's license. Since Andy was an astronaut and experienced pilot, hopefully most of his student co-pilots would be considered fully trained when they returned to Earth and granted full licenses.

'Setting protection Mag fields to normal!'

'Mag Fields set to Normal!'

'Relevant space corridors, seven and fifteen targeted for Gimbal.'

' Instruments check completed by OBC. AOK.'

'Checked!' Shouted Jerry.

'Loading CP with new parameters for primary convergence in two minutes. Secondary target trajectory set for three-point-five-three minutes on initial vector seven-eight-five.'

'Secondary target trajectory set!' George said.

'Now releasing LPD core magnetic screens for gradual liftoff. Acceleration limited to ten G's without use of anti accelerators. Zero gravs expected in fifty-four seconds and counting,' Andy continued giving instructions while in the process pressing several buttons on his keyboard. George and others did relevant checks. Vogon lifted gracefully in the air and began her steady acceleration.

He read through the information displayed on the large forward screen. It was also displayed on the smaller operators screens while the ship began to follow a steady course. When she took to the air her large hover-feet retracted within her underbelly and metal shutters sealed them in. By that time, the mansion was completely empty of all staff. They stood with Pamela on the forecourt, waving at the airborne ship. At the same time everyone in Vogon was waving back at the amplified images on the large forward screen. Soon after, those on the ground could only observe the crew via a television linkup. The waving continued until Vogon was barely visible and disappeared in a large cloud.

Her trajectory would take them to the primary space corridor for linkup with the main space highway to Gimbal, although still within Earth's outer atmosphere.

The complete flight was timed for barely fifteen minutes to docking on Gimbal. Custom clearance would take another hour or so for the complete crew of ten plus.

That human crew consisted of all members of the original gang of eight, plus Andy and his wife Joan and Ulysses the android, who was always to remain on board ship. Finally there was Ron, the computer.

Having spent their first manual flight in near weightless conditions, they were cleared for landing and targeted the relevant dock. It was located close to the primary hub of Gimbal's outermost ring. That one was the main port for private spaceships and connected to a large space-park with many locks. Those led into the primary locks and areas of customs security.

While they landed, their platform moved into the main parking area and it was connected to a large flexible tube via standard fittings to the ship's main entrance underneath. It was designed to carry passengers and goods via a flexible moving conveyor and escalator that was pressure sealed.

Those primary couplers could also be connected to the sides of ships. The complete flexible structure was airtight. Any small losses in pressure being instantly sensed by ultrasonics and air pressure sensors. Then such losses were compensated.

They collected their essentials and walked unto the small flexible escalator that formed part of the conveyance tube.

It took them to the lower level and towards another part of the docking area.

After they had entered another lock they were finally within the main customs area. Their red primary ID travel card's would be held for the duration of their stay as travellers in transit. Those cards would be returned on their way out, upon presentation of their more personal blue ID cards.

Those special red cards were issued to all independent space travellers. Their purpose were to keep track of their movements and to restrict smuggling and drug abuse throughout the system. Without red cards no one could leave or land on any satellite or planet outside of Earth and that included Gimbal.

The girls didn't like the rigmarole and began to complain.

'This is almost as bad as camping in the wilds. So much jungle bush to go through to get to the other side,' Miranda complained.

'Don't worry guys. All this is just a formality for freelancers like us. Standard shuttle flights are much quicker. Anyway, my dad is well known and liked in these parts,' Jerry said, but that knowledge didn't relieve their tensions.

Since his kidnapping, Jerry had always kept as low a profile as possible and never headed a queue again. He had also begun to grow a moustache and that aspect made him look a lot different from his original passport photos. He had also temporarily changed his surname to Frasier from Fraser on most of his documents. Therefore, all information, with reference to his very important connections, were now virtually null and void, courtesy of his father's important contacts in security.

With his new identity he felt like a new man and a lot more at ease with himself.

They moved towards customs in single file, while wearing their beautiful light-grey uniforms, resembling a normal professional ship's crew.

George was first to be greeted.

'Please, Sir!' the officer said, while taking his card.

'We have been expecting you and your crew.'

'You were?' George was intrigued.

'Perhaps I could have your autograph before you move to the next counter.' George was very surprised but generously submitted.

'I am very happy to oblige!' he replied, while his crew followed him through to two more checkouts, each wanting his autographs but never searching him or any members of his crew out of respect.

The moment he walked out of that area he was once again inundated by a group of Gimbal's reporters. Then internal security rescued and took them away to Anne-Marie's suite.

'Can't take you anywhere these days without creating a rumpus? Anyway, better you than I, Pal!' Jerry said and Andy and the others agreed.

George held on to Cathy and both laughingly ignored their friends seemingly jealous attitude, although said in jest. They were all the very best of friends and usually had fun exaggerating those problems.

'Shall we take you to the door?' the security driver asked.

'No, thank you! We would like it to be a surprise!' George replied.

Jerry was the first one to press the buzzer. They were then accompanied by Anne-Marie's local security officer who always remained posted outside her suite in a small observation booth. They checked all visitors. There were nine of George's company following at the rear, less Ulysses and Ron who remained on board Vogon.

When she opened the circular metallic door, she was surprised, but recognised Jerry immediately.

'Oh my darling son! How are you?' she cried, overwhelmed by emotion.

'I am fine and dad's fine! How are you and the kids?' Jerry replied.

'They are also well!'

'Let me introduce you to my closest friends!' Jerry turned around.

'Here are our famous gang and this is the famous George Peterson, who you haven't yet met. Miranda, whom you already know, Andy and his wife, Joan,....' Jerry went on until the queue was exhausted. Anne-Marie was bewildered by their numbers and wondered whether there was enough space to sit them all.

'So you are the famous George Peterson. You know, from what I hear you are probably the hottest hero on Earth these days!' she said, as they followed her into the spacious lounge.

'Your dad stole a few days from work last week to be with me. Sorry I couldn't visit for George's wedding. I am still confined here with the kids,' Anne-Marie said.

Although George was well known by millions, he was surprised that he was so popular on Gimbal. Yet, Gimbalians were always hospitable to those outsiders they trusted. Always relishing the company of new blood on board the almost isolated island satellite.

CHAPTER 36

Gimbal in motion

The accommodation sphere of Satellite Gimbal occupied an internal surface area of about twenty-four square kilometres. It had an internal diameter of close to three kilometres and a circumference of approximately nine kilometres.

Its inner surface was broken into four main areas that were separated by two continuous avenues which ran at right angles to each other. Each quadrant so formed occupied an area of about six square kilometres. There was quadrant one, known to its natives as Q1. That area contained its main university, nurseries, secondary and primary schools with extensive playgrounds. It also contained the government and civic buildings.

Q2 consisted of the main hotels like the Metropol, with swimming pools and expensive shopping precinct including cinemas, theatres, restaurants, music halls and other important buildings that were constructed specifically for the sole purpose of entertainment.

Q3 was more specific to bulk shopping and contained many superstores and other local markets and shops.

Q4 contained a large forest with botanical gardens, and park, including integral waterfall and lake. It was filled with the most beautiful flowers and small animals kept within two isolation domes. That area also contained several of the massive bio waste cycling plants and other relevant generators and utilities. Life withing the sphere was self sustaining and controlled by the latest recycling technologies.

Gimbal was alien to Earth in many respects and gave its occupants the perpetual sensation of falling off something. Since the furthest distance between any two points were always less than three kilometres, virtually every part of the internal structure were visible from everywhere else.

Therefore even the distant streets and building above in the misty sky could be observed from any other point giving a strange spherical view. On a very clear day one would be astonished to see the roofs of tall multistory buildings in the sky above pointing downwards like sharp spears ready to fall on their unfortunate observers. They always appeared to be getting ready to collapse upon the slightly curved surface on which they stood. Although water vapour was constantly added to improve the environment, the thin fog or mist and the usual small clouds were never enough to hide the inverted buildings above. Therefore living on Gimbal took time getting accustomed.

Four large multi megawatt sun lamps were suspended in the middle of the sphere, just one-point-five kilometres above, approximately one mile in the air, by eight large reenforced metallic cables. Since gravity in those areas were negligible those massive cables virtually supported themselves. There were also eight secondary lamps positioned closer to the surface. Those were only active during what was considered their daylight hours. At night light came from the side of walkways and passages to efficiently illuminate necessary areas. Time on Gimbal was linked to GMT on Earth.

Several sky cars could be seen moving from one extreme point to the other. Those cars were attached to large suspension cables and followed a daily routine.

Only ground LPD's could be used on Gimbal. All air flights were prohibited within the sphere. Its environment was fully controlled and in so doing, maintained ideal climatic conditions for its wealthy occupants. That was with the exclusion of all natural disasters and turbulence found on Earth, including earthquakes, hurricanes and wars.

Not many people knew that Gimbal came under the jurisdiction of Solarian Banking and was really controlled by TEC. So also was the other large satellite called ETA, mainly used for engineering, and robotic maintenance and construction. At that time not even George realized that TEC belonged to Unitec and he was responsible for all life within Gimbal.

Gimbal's large accommodation sphere revolved around two pivots. Those pivots rotated within the secondary ring that revolved at right angles on two other pivots within the primary ring. Its motion when combined with LPD devices created a type of artificial gravity mainly felt on the surface. That object operated like a true gimbal in space.

Both rings were used for isolation, docking, storage and servicing of the sphere. However they were also used by its many visitors and tourists as observation points. From there they could view space and Earth in a more realistic setting, despite the motion of Gimbal's rings.

CHAPTER 37

Professor Khan's visit

That day the group went shopping in Gimbal. They wanted to look around its strange environments, meet a few of its local people and pay a brief visit to its well-maintained parks.

While the Gang were out the phone rang and little Julie picked the receiver up.

'Yes? Who is it?'

'Who was it?' Anne-Marie shouted from the kitchen.

'Uncle Bengi! Mummy, it's uncle Bengi! He's coming to visit us!' Julie was ecstatic.

'Really? That's great!'

'He wants to talk to you!' she shouted. Anne-Marie briefly took the handset from Julie.

'Yes. We'll be delighted to see you and your future bride!' then she hung up and turned to talk to an excited Julie.

'Uncle Bengi is getting married and he wants us to meet his future bride. He will also bring us some medicine and presents.'

'He sounded very happy!'

'He was! Did you like your presents from uncle Jerry and uncle George, Darling?' Anne-Marie asked and little Julie nodded her head which meant yes. She was holding a talking baby doll in one hand. That was the present Jerry had given her.

George had brought her a cartoon video disk, but she hadn't had the time to plug that item into the television socket.

Anne-Marie now felt like the most regarded woman in the whole of Gimbal, with her suite now almost full to the brim with astronauts, and now Professor Khan (Ben) and his future bride were to join them. After all those months of neglect since the president's assassination, now and suddenly so many visitors and friends were arriving.

'When it rains it really pours,' she thought, but relishing every moment of her active and noisy guests in the calmest of places. Anyway, she soon realized her choice of words to be irrelevant since it never rained on Gimbal.

Ben always enjoyed his god-children and tended to spoil them rotten, but in Anne-Marie's case his attentiveness compensated for their busy dad, now President, who could only visit occasionally.

Ben had thousands of Fertilate god-children throughout the globe and was a caring godfather to all of them. He also tended to assist their parents whenever they were in financial difficulty or required special medical care.

Ben arrived the following day with his beautiful wife-to-be and two android guards. Those androids were of the same design as Hercules and Ulysses, although imprinted to Ben's character image.

When he entered the room, little Julie ran to him and he lifted her up and began to tease her. But instead, she showed him her latest presents. By now the two androids had thoroughly checked the suite, looking for bugs and any signs of hidden danger. When they were fully satisfied there was no threat they went and sat on a remote settee.

George and his gang arrived soon afterwards and sat together for lunch.

'Do you really take those two everywhere with you, Uncle?' Jerry asked, politely.

'Yes! I have no choice. In your parts of North America things are not very bad, but I also visit Europe, China, Africa, and many other unsavoury places on a weekly basis. Some of those cities are extremely rough, with little regard for love of life and little segregation of Infilates. Despite reduction in their populations due to the plague, if anything, they have become worse and less considerate. In some of those countries kidnapping is rampant and the police are easily bribed. Sometimes I use one as tracker while the other remains by my side,' Ben said.

'Uncle, are the Solarian domes on Mars fully accessible to us. I mean, as temporary living quarters in case we had to separate into two exploratory groups?' George inquired. Despite the fact Sarah was the real mother of George and Ben was his grandfather, he knew not of his closeness in that regard and assumed he was just a godfather. Yet Ben knew the score and always called him Son while George called him Uncle.

'Yes! As far as I know, there are still lots of provisions in Admin Dome. One of the smaller domes houses an experimental vegetable greenhouse. It should be now at its prime, although handled by robots. The whole site is managed in that way. Your identification should be in the system by now, so you might not even require the master key. But take it along just in case. Otherwise it could be very difficult, if not impossible, to pass the sensitive security android guards. They are powerful guardian sentinels,' Ben replied.

'Any idea of the present condition of Meron's shuttle craft,' Cathy asked.

'Perhaps...'

'Seems such a waste leaving it buried like that!' Jerry said.

'Why do you wish to know?' Ben inquired.

'Well, it seems a waste if they haven't any use for her anymore,' Cathy replied.

'She should be still in good working condition and is buried about two hundred metres from the vegetable dome. Use your ship's radiation scanners and probe the surface region for its imprint. She must be at least three metres below the surface. If you are able to recover her, you might use her as you wish. It's the property of Solarian Banking and I am still its President. However, her LPD's will have to be primed before you can take her into the air,' Ben said.

When they were finished with lunch, Ben called George to one side.

'Son, an urgent matter has come up and I need your assistance. Let's have a word in private.'

'Whatever, Uncle!' George always called him Uncle.

'How would you like to become the President of Solarian Banking? Because of my future marriage I intend to resign the presidency and nominate you as my protege,' Ben said.

'What? What about Michael Cockburn! Wouldn't he mind being overstepped for promotion?' George had little desire in jumping queues, but was extremely excited by the prospects anyway.

'Not so! He also wants a more relaxed life on Eden within his fief, so I am sure when I leave he will also follow. So there will be two vacant positions to fill. You will become one of the most powerful men on Earth, should you decide to take the job. Anyway, I can only pass your name forward. All such decisions are taken at Grand Council level. They are also aware of your popularity amongst Fertilates and that popularity is growing, so they have a lot to gain by your nomination,' Ben said.

'Can I mention what you just said to Cathy and perhaps Jerry? In confidence of course,' George replied.

'Yes! I see no reason why not. Just tell them you heard it on the grape vine and that no decision has yet been taken one way or the other,' Ben advised.

'Well, I am very interested. Even if I have to visit Eden for a while to be trained,' George replied.

'There is no need for that. They just want someone they can trust and you have done a lot more than that over the passing weeks since your wedding. They love you, like another of their sons. It could also be a good power base for you in the future. Anyway, I shall try my best and fight your corner,' Ben said.

'You are not leaving us for Eden, are you?'

'No, Son! I would like to spend more time planning the defence of Earth against the invading Javols. The Terminal program is now more or less at an end. There is one more thing?'

'I'm listening!'

'When you return from your holidays, I would like you to visit the world of Tyrrel III. We are planning an anti-Javols demonstration. It's all hush-hush, so mention it to no one, not even your gang members or friends,' Ben stressed.

'Got it!'

'I wouldn't worry too much about being boss of Solarian Banking. The system is controlled by the most clever Macron computers, so as far as I am concerned that job is already in the bag,' he said to his grandson and they both returned to the lounge.

'Uncle, you and Ruth must visit the mansion a lot more frequently after your wedding. You could also join us on the occasional holiday trip with Vogon,' George said and Cathy agreed, but Ben was never interested in flights of any kind and respectfully declined.

Professor Bengizara Khan (Ben to some) had also taken Anne-Marie some extra medication for her and the children. On Earth, the Terminal Antidote or Anti as it was commonly called, was supplied in water and processed drinks or mixed with most uncooked food additives like sugar, serials and yogurt. It was also distributed through converted water filters, tablets or syrups and sweets for young children.

Most young families required larger dosses than teenagers due to its accumulative effects. But dosage also depended on the amount of contamination within the environment.

Gimbal was constructed before any strict decontamination rules were observed and as a result most of her environment was contaminated, although not as much as on Earth. Because of her limited resources, waste recycling and disposal, and the cost of transporting goods to and fro, it was not always advantageous to import adulterated foodstuffs with the anti. As a result, every inhabitant had to receive their dose through tablets and medicinal mixtures which could only be administered by local doctors. Those doctors knew by their register who the Fertilates were and could only administer the basic drug rations necessary and no more. As a result, extras could only be obtained on the black market at absurd prices.

Since most Fertilates tended to live within closed communities on Earth, with common utilities and supermarkets, those problems never existed.

However, on isolated places like Gimbal all free rations given by doctors were barely necessary to counteract the effects of the terminal disease. Therefore Professor Khan promised the President that he would ensure that his wife Anne-Marie always received her supplies in full, and always kept his word.

He followed those rules for several of the poorer families on Earth. Nevertheless since the Terminal Virus had weakened significantly and was presently mutating into a less dangerous form, the Anti was no longer necessary. Therefore, strictly speaking, his services were no longer required on Earth. That was probably one of the main reasons why he sought a simpler life.

CHAPTER 38

The Media Interview

While discussing Ben's wedding the Coms rang.

'It's for you, George!' Jerry interrupted and George took the cordless handset.

'When did you say? Yes, I shall be happy to oblige!'

'Who is it!' Cathy whispered.

'It's the TV studio!' he replied and she was surprised.

'Yes! That will be fine!' he continued to the voice on the line.

'They want to interview us!' he said, turning away from the handset momentarily.

'Thank you!' Then he hung up.

'The others glanced in his direction wondering what that call was about, so he had to tell.

'The local television wants me on the Macdonald show. They will be sending along a brief in the morning to discuss procedure. You can all join as my personal guests at the studio if you wish and be part of the select studio audience. Afterwards we can have a nice meal together in one of the local restaurants and make an evening of it!'

'That's going to be so great!' Miranda shouted.

Then George called one of the best local restaurants and booked four tables. Then he sat next to Cathy to continue where he left off in their conversation.

'Well, Uncle, where will you hold the wedding?' George inquired.

'I was thinking of having it at the old manor. You know, Sarah's home in North Dakota. But it's now being renovated and will not be ready for another month or so. Sadly, gone are the days when such tasks could be completed by robots in a couple of days. I have therefore decided to set a date for after its completion. You should all be back on Earth by then, including Anne-Marie and the kids,' Ben replied.

'If you need to borrow our mansion for that grand event, you know you don't have to ask. I'm sure Cathy wouldn't mind!'

George glanced at Cathy who nodded her head in approval. He always liked family and friends to be safe and close at hand where he could keep a keen eye on them.

'Why don't you spend some time with us for a while, Anne? Donald knows that we have about the best security at the house. That way, you can always have lots of company and Clair should be joining us on a more permanent basis later.'

'Sounds fantastic! And I will be closer to Donald!' she was ecstatic.

'Talk to Donald about my invitation. No one will know you are our President's wife and you can be busy as an important part of our gang. Perhaps we can collect you on our way back to Earth,' George said.

'I have heard of Clair's miraculous cure.'

'It was nothing!'

'Anyway, thank you for that...,' she said and went over to kiss him on the cheek to show her gratitude.

'I will ask Donald and insist that I return with you. I am getting a bit bored with this place and its isolation. Julie can also be with her best friend once again. They haven't seen each other for over a year now,' Anne-Marie added, she meant little Clair.

'I must be the luckiest man in the universe to be so fortunate in having such a fantastic family and loving friends. We should always go out of our way to assist each other when the need arises. Furthermore, I believe we are going to need each other's assistance a lot more in the future and if I had a glass, I would drink a toast to family and permanent friendship,' George said.

'We also think that you are the greatest!' Jerry said and the others chanted in agreement.

The studio brief came to see him early that morning. Well, there was really no night time on Gimbal. Her large sun lamps were just dimmed while others more local ones took over. That was probably done to save the life and replacement of such expensive units. Despite that fact, all clocks and watches worked on a twenty-four-hour basis, irrespective of her rotational and orbiting velocities. That way, visitors always had a psychological link with their home planet below, to Greenwich Mean Time. It was the closest dateline to her geo-synchronous position in space.

However, Martian time keeping was somewhat different and synchronised to Mars which made all humans on that planet think they were on a different world. Because of those reasons Martian watches had to be specially programmed or constructed for its indigenous human populations and miners.

With the exception of those living within Gimbal's sphere, it was difficult to detach a surface dweller from the natural solar period of his world and in all those cases climatization took a while because of circadian rhythms.

Satellite Gimbal was in a geo-stationary orbit and travelled above Earth once each day to maintain its fixed position in space. During that time its central sphere rotated on its innermost axis, thus maintaining its own artificial gravity. Internal movement was further aided by accelerator modules adjusted for the necessary levels of compensation. However the outer rings rotated in opposite sequence several times each day.

A siren sounded at noon. It was linked with an atomic clock on Earth for accurate time keeping. Thus allowing travellers and workers to synchronize their time pieces.

The television interview was set for eight pm that evening. That time corresponded to almost peak viewing in Europe. It was thought Gimbal intended to make some profit by supplying that program to many of Earth's satellite and cable networks, but George didn't mind one way or the other.

He was getting to be a very popular person. Since his recent rescue escapade many of the younger generation considered him their new hero and wanted his presence time and time again. It was a dismal period in Earth's history when the young felt insecure. There were so many Infilate deaths due to old age, with frequent funeral processions marching down the average street. Death and destruction was everywhere. That was the time when the planet's human populations were dropping in leaps and bounds due to the aging Infilate. Therefore all buildings surplus to requirement were constantly being demolished by the enthusiastic demolition gangs. Along with those problems were the rising waters due to Global Warming.

Another five billion deaths were expected within the next ten years, so governments had invested enormous sums in building large crematoriums for the purpose of their silent and dignified passing.

The makeup person spent sometime with George. He was then escorted to a comfortable settee. The studio audience clapped and cheered while he entered and sat. He was wearing his cream suit with Solarian insignia pinned to his left lapel.

'During this interview, why don't you call me Mack and perhaps I can call you George. That is if you don't mind, Sir!' The polite interviewer advised.

'That will be fine, Mack!'

'I have heard several rumours about you recently. One of those is that you have powers to heal!'

'Have you, really? Could you enlighten our audience on that topic?' Mack asked.

'I am able to heal those that I love and those that have faith in me. I cannot explain the process because its beyond human interpretation. It is almost like the joining of two minds for an instant in time. During those precious moments, cosmic energies flow through both people to complete the process. But my way of healing is not the same as the laying on of hands. It's a lot more meaningful and complete to both individuals,' George replied.

'That is truly incredible! I have also been told that you hate Infilates. Is that also true?'

'Hate is too strong a word for me. Perhaps dislike is more appropriate. To sum up my feelings, let me recite a short poem,

In all past human lives, on Earth, I could not see,
A single thread of compassion in any man more free.
In falling rain and sorrows sad,
A core of hardness that gave no shelter. Why so hard?

Attrition's total outburst served,
Enhanced a being that never cared.
Impatience felt in cruel linger,
What little core of conscience left, still a stinger.

In ultimate purpose served, a question mark.

> *So many opportunities missed in trailing back.*
> *No firmer base on which to stand?*
> *And yet, a fence to say, "this is my land"?*
>
> *An existence lost to serve your kind.*
> *No kindly sentiments was ever due from your selfish mind.*
> *I will never shed a tear for you my Infilate man,*
> *And others of life like me will always imposed a duly ban.*

'When we look around our planet Earth today, all we see is a planet ravaged by the hands of our careless ancestors. They destroyed its life and its beautiful trees to form deserts, and for what. If you ask any Infilate why he needs his money making schemes to survive he will never give you a straight answer. Like a parasite they have sucked our once beautiful world dry. All they left us is a legacy of Global Warming and more extinctions. Therefore, how can I care one iota for anyone that never cared for our future or the greater ecology. They bred like pigs with no concern for tomorrow and no thought of the Greater Ecology or global population increases.

'In the past our ancestors, like a kind of parasite, thought they could enjoy themselves at the expense of our beautiful planet and its other life-forms. Well, those concepts of gross self-indulgence and plagiarism manifested by all Infilates, I will always abhor.

'Their capitalism and need to acquire wealth at any lengths and at the expense of others, irrespective of the consequences to our world and its other life-forms have led to our dying world, below.

'It is because of their selfish and uncaring attitudes towards us, their future children, that we have been left with such a legacy... of little resources for our continued survival.

'For those serious misdemeanours all Infilates must pay the ultimate price, by sacrificing their futures in the form of not having any children. That sacrifice will leave our planet with a more manageable population of just five hundred million throughout Earth in just over thirty years from now. Then, we can rebuild our once beautiful planet into a real paradise like the biblical Eden,' George replied. The audience couldn't stop cheering and clapping. It took Mack a while to quieten them.

'Some say you are a profit sent by God to assist mankind at this juncture in his history. Is that true?' Mack asked.

'I have a cosmic mind and because of its nature I am able to love mankind and perhaps show them a clearer path ahead. But there are also many dangers coming. Dangers of which I have a clear knowledge. So in that respect I am cosmic,' George replied.

'Why do you think so many are dying and why the Infilate problem?' Mack asked.

'Before I was born, a great scientist seeing the problem of overpopulation and abuses of Earth's resources, engineered a special bacterial disease that would inhibit reproduction and reduce the human population levels.'

'Is that so?' Mack could not believe those last words.

'Yes, it is! Fertilates, were carefully chosen and administered the antidote from birth, thus maintaining a secured population of about five hundred million throughout the Solar System.'

'So this was a planned conspiracy?'

'In a sense, I suppose it was! Nevertheless, very soon our planet's atmosphere will once again be seeded with the Global Antidote, so everyone may return to the way things used to be over one-hundred years ago,' George replied.

'Is that a fact?'

'It is!'

'If what you say is true, and I have no reason to doubt your words. Even our political leaders knew little of what happened then.'

'Some knew, but also wanted a reduction in planetary population because of Global Warming and the growing scarcity of resources,' George replied.

'Do you know exactly who was responsible for that decision?' Mack inquired.

'That decision was taken by a panel of top scientists. They were people who could visualise the building of Gimbal, the present population of the Martian domes, the creation of our present technologies and much more. They had little choice at the time and considered it the most humane way to release Earth from its population trap,' George replied.

'What do you think our future society will be like, in say thirty years from now?' Mack asked.

'If we are to form a more altruistic and moralistic society, and survive several centuries into the future with our present limited resources... we have to work together towards building a better society. One in which wealth and resources are more evenly distributed amongst its children. Eliminate drug abuse and other forms of gross antisocial behaviour now predominant in large cities; better medical care and more responsible education and parental care from birth. Several of our domed cities now abide by those principles and you are all aware of the results.'

'Yes, we are!'

'I will be proud to be part of a planet where every human felt safe, secure and happy in their pursuance of both physical and mental goals. Where every life-form could roam freely within its own habitat without the interference of man. Even if it meant containing mankind within sealed domed structures away from their natural habitats,' George replied.

'Any advice for our listeners and audience before we end this show?' Mack asked.

'Yes! The time is coming when I shall need your help for the sake of our mutual survival. When that time comes I want no hesitation on your part.' They cheered again.

'In the mean time, try to practice life by the ideals that I stand for. Love and take good care of each other as much as I love you and is always ready to help. If any of you are in trouble, ask your best friends and if they are unable to help, then please ask me!' George said those words with sincerity and with that afterthought there was another roar in the audience and everyone started to shout: 'George! George!....' When that happened he went straight into the audience and began to greet each one as the cameras relayed the complete proceedings to many networks on Earth, who were also relaying live to many countries.

Later that evening they had a most pleasant time at dinner. Even Anne-Marie couldn't believe the popularity of George. She was a very intelligent woman and could also visualise the future.

'That was some speech you gave to those people. I think you can never go wrong while in this place with so many admirers,' Jerry said.

'It was from the heart and how I felt at the time. Anyway, lets order dinner.' He flicked his finger and in an instant the waiter was there to take their order.

'George. I do believe you to be our saviour and I also believe you will one day rule the whole of our solar system and beyond. Don't ask me how I know. You have that extreme power to hypnotise people and I am sure if you asked every Fertilate to follow you this moment, they would immediately down tools and follow. For that is the nature of your powers!' Anne-Marie said those words in a most sincere manner and the others agreed unanimously.

'My overriding interests is to do my best for the people and our world,' he replied.

CHAPTER 39

Their trip to Mars

After just five days on Gimbal they decided it was time to leave for Mars. Before their trip George decided to talk with Anne-Marie in private.

'You know, I wish we could take you along with us this time, but it's too late in the day for that. Everyone had to train for this mission and you have the kids to consider.'

'I realize that!' Anne-Marie replied.

'Anyway, here is my special security number. You may contact us on Mars via the mansion on Earth, but only if you have a serious problem.'

'Ok!' Ann-Marie said, taking the card.

'I have decided to leave for Mars at ten a.m. tomorrow. We shall remain there for about three weeks. After that time we are going to return to Earth via this place, so you can get ready and plan your move then. When we are back on Earth, we shall probably refit Vogon for an interstellar trip that might take us more than a month to complete. So if you would like to join us on any of those future missions, feel free to ask and we can make the necessary preparations for your training.'

'I would appreciate that, very much!'

'You know, the more trustworthy members we have in our organisation the better I feel,' George said.

'Yes, George! I would like to be involved as well. The children can also have some stability and excitement in the process among family and friends.'

'We of The Gang are a lot more than just brothers and sisters, we look after each other. Should you join us tomorrow, you will have your own property with financial and other security for you and your family on a permanent basis. You will also become a director of Solarian Banking and can share in the bounty during our rescue escapades.'

'It seems ideal for me at this time. I am always so bored in this place!'

'Surplus monies are put into a special TEC charitable fund to help less fortunate Fertilates. But because of the age of your kids, you could help organise some of those charities for me on Earth, if you like,' George said. Anne-Marie, as if in a trance, could not refuse him anything at that moment in time.

'Yes! I would like that, very much,' she replied, and they left to join the others.

Anne-Marie insisted that they took some freshly cooked meals on board for the trip. But she also wanted to visit Vogon and view the ship, so George decided to take her and her two children along on their way out. She was however required to find her own way back with her personal security guards.

She needed the green security cards for her and the children in order to enter those more unsecured parts of the space port. Those outermost areas were considered to be beyond customs jurisdiction and in no-mans-land from a security standpoint.

Ships could only be searched for contraband and drugs at known commercial ports and that one was a visitors' port.

Anne-Marie viewed almost every part of the ship and when she was finished she remained in the ballroom gazing up at the stunningly beautiful crystal chandelier. It was mounted on a large flexible pivot. Because of the local gravity neutralisers, it always maintained a vertical position, plus or minus its own natural movement, irrespective of the orientation of Vogon in space.

'What do you think?' George asked.

'She is truly awesome and so beautiful. When you first mentioned her to me, I imagined a space bucket. But this is way beyond any ship I have ever seen. Her interior is better than my own suite. You guys have done a fantastic job in restoring her,' Anne-Marie replied.

'Yea.. The girls did well!'

'Mummy, are we going to Mars with uncle?'Little Julie asked.

'No, Darling. Perhaps next time!' Ann-Marie followed George towards customs and was once again greeted by the officers who briefly scanned her green cards and arranged transportation for her journey back to the suite.

After a little while George called her suite to make sure she had safely arrived home.

'Let's take our positions and leave this place!' Andy said, and began the instruments check via the computer screen.

'Now releasing magnetic clamps.... Trailing to exit point,' he said, while the large tube released itself and withdrew to its parking position. Then the landing platform began to move towards the exit point.

'Synchronising for spaceway vectors six-point-zero three five and two-point-three eight six. Manual programming now completed. Selecting GRA and ACC neutralisers at seven G's... to optimum velocity for rear of Sol.... hull magnetism energized for particle shielding.'

Andy went on reading off the information as it appeared on the screen directly in front of him. But that same information was also relayed on other monitors throughout the large pilot's cabin. The ship gently lifted off the pad and darted off into deep space towards the bright lunar disc.

'It's so black and immense out here!' Cathy commented, stunned by the share immensity of space which made her feel so insignificant by comparison.

'This part belongs to God! We are now in his true Heaven. Now you know how easy it is to get lost in space without stellar maps. One more reason why so many people have kept well out of space exploration.'

'I can see what you mean!'

'You know, Love, man can live naturally on land until he dies of old age, a little less in water, but never for any length of time in space. Out here, there is no air or water and even worse, an almost complete vacuum that will explode your lungs in seconds without correct protection. Then there is the negative effects on the body by loss of gravity.' He pulled her closer to himself and hugged and kissed her.

'Why do we have to go all the way around the sun?' she asked.

'Well, Love, the space corridor follows a set route and Mars happens to be at perihelion at this moment in time, while we, meaning Earth's sphere of gravity, have just moved out of aphelion. Therefore, we can only follow that standard route in much the same way as we do a surface motorway on Earth. With the knowledge that the town we are visiting is never at a fixed location along the route. But it's also a lot safer that way, because this route is constantly monitored and we don't have to search for stray asteroids on-route. A rogue could cause us severe damage if encountered at high velocity,' he replied.

'We can now place her on auto.' Andy said, while pressing a few keys.

'Will we be there soon?' Miranda inquired.

'She should make the trip in a few hours at max. The neutralisers can only compensate for fifty G's. It will be too uncomfortable for us and the ladies if we accelerated any faster. Anyway, we'll still get there in eighteen hours at present calculations. So shall we go and get ourselves some lunch and perhaps a little entertainment,' Andy said and they all agreed.

After just twelve hours they were closest to the sun at thirty million miles and passed the orbit of Mercury on their swing around towards Mars. Vogon's outer shielding was active, with the Solar Wind visibly pushed aside by her powerful super-conductive hull magnetism.

At a point beyond Mercury they exited the continuous one-way space highway and headed towards a new vector.

In another five hours the Martian disc zoomed unto their screens.

'Let's prepare for landing. There are no special Martian corridors, so we might have to orbit several times in order to find the location of the Solarian and Caefon Domes. We can print a map from the data received,' Andy said.

'Shall we also attempt to locate the shuttle's burial place for future reference?' George advised.

After two almost complete orbits they found their destination points and prepared for landing.

'It's a pity we couldn't just transpose within Admin Dome as the little Andromedan ship,' Miranda said.

'Next time, dear lady,' Tim replied.

CHAPTER 40

Within Solarian domes

'It's a good thing the Ancients had the sense to fit standard docking locks to those domes. It will save us wearing those cumbersome spacesuits,' Andy said, with his hands still on the steering bars. Then he placed the ship on automatic for landing. It soon approached a docking area and synchronized with the docking guidance signal from the dome.

The moment Vogon docked, the entrance sealed and the primary lock slid open to allow them access to its primary interior. George, Andy, Jerry, Barry and Tim Chiang walked towards the main entrance.

During all the commotion the Dome's security was alerted. What appeared to be a large pillar blocking the secondary entrance transformed into a giant colossus. He was about 12 feet tall with rippling muscles and laser eyes.

'Oh my God! He is coming straight for us!' Andy exclaimed.

'Don't worry, he is just putting on a show in case we are unwanted intruders. Just remain still while I communicate with the monster!' George advised, while they nervously creaked in their boots.

'I am Onguard!' it bellowed.

That's... nice to know... and you are doing a great job. I am George. Are we permitted inside?' George said bravely, also shaking in his boots. Nevertheless he tried to retain his firm stance while observing the large metallic creature looming over him. The robot could easily have picked him up with its little finger and crushed him in its powerful grip. Also, those robots could respond 20 times faster than any human.

'Please wait while I check your permissions!' Onguard said and remained still for a while.

'Ok!' George replied in an unconcerned manner while twiddling his fingers.

'Ok! Ok!... It's indeed a great honour. I didn't realize you were my supreme master. Should I bow or kneel to show obeisance?' Onguard was presently as mild as a lamb.

'Please don't. Everything is fine. Always do your task to the best of your abilities and have fun. Now, Guys, let's check this place out and have some of our own type of fun!' George said, while Onguard remained active in his present form.

'Be cool, Onguard!' Tim shouted back to the monster when he was well away. Onguard shook his head in bewilderment, not quite knowing what he meant. He must have thought how strange these humans were.

'Thank goodness my name is now in the system! I shall not require special keys to get in,' George mumbled to himself, while they followed the now stationery corridor around the dome and towards the secondary lock. Ulysses, Cathy, Miranda, and Joan had remained on board until the course was clear. They would be instructed otherwise by the intrepid explorers. Even so, George and his landing group took along a trolley with spare suits and rations just in case they were stranded.

'So much security in this place! There must be at least two more doors before we gain entrance inside!' Andy complained.

Several androids and robots could be observed outside, carrying out repairs and making checks, but no one even gazed in the direction of George's group.

When George approached a secondary airlock it automatically opened. At that moment he realised his profile was within their master computer, and had complete freedom of the whole installation.

Nevertheless, he decided they used Vogon as home during the duration of their visit, with limited camping within the domes if necessary.

They were soon within the Admin Dome's floor area, which was almost the size of Sol-Newtown, with many large empty buildings that were constructed solely for the purpose of evacuating millions of people from planet Caefon in Andromeda. The accommodation area was now clear of furniture and other homely fittings and fixtures. All had been transported either to Earth or Eden immediately after the evacuation. Nevertheless, those buildings could house over one hundred thousand people in comfort or twenty thousand large families. Yet, there was not a soul about. The small shopping precinct was completely empty but kept immaculately clean.

'My God! How did they move all that stuff to Mars without anyone on Earth knowing? Andy inquired.

'My friend, where there is a will, there is always a way,' George replied.

'This dome could contain a small city!' Tim said.

'Yea, what a waste. Such a massive structure and so new... virtually untouched by human hands,' George replied.

'I can think of several uses for those beautiful structures,' Andy said.

'It would make a delightful holiday camp for those wanting a little outer-space intrigue. At a very small price, of course,' Barry said and Jerry agreed.

'Think of all the young families and kids on Earth that would like to visit the red planet, even for a day,' Andy said.

Everything was empty, although spotlessly cleaned by robots who had little else to do.

'The remainder of today we relax on board Vogon and tomorrow we visit each dome to assess the potential of this place. Then we can trek the twenty miles or so to Caefon Dome with spacesuits,' George said.

'Can you observe that bluish haze over there?' Andy asked, being his most inquisitive self.

'Yes! Just beyond that dome is the Omegron Portal. I suppose it's still on standby operation. There are Javols at the other end and I don't wish to spoil our honeymoon holidays by evil thoughts and nasty encounters,' George replied.

'Do you think they are now on Caefon?' Jerry asked.

'Well, it's now an empty planet and ideal for constructing their defence installations. However, I don't think they found the underground city or they would have tried to neutralise the portal there.'

'Thank goodness for that!' Andy exclaimed.

'While this one remains active, they cannot destroy the other. If they get within a hundred metres, their bodies will become contaminated and disintegrate, so they will keep well away and probably drop explosive devices unto it from above. Any disturbances will be manifested here as bright flashes over this area and none has been so far observed. Anyway, if they damaged the other, this one here will automatically make it repair itself.'

'Wow! What magical technology is that! Must be quite advanced!' Andy exclaimed.

'We might have to visit the underground city in the near future to assess the situation there and perhaps kill a few Javols in the process. But let's change this horrible topic for now and get on with the business at hand,' George said.

CHAPTER 41

A portal to Earth

They continued through that dome for a while when George made a strange suggestion.

'How would you all like to visit Earth in an instant in time?'

'What are you saying?' Jerry was astounded.

'What!' Tim was intrigued, but nervous.

'Well, follow me and see!'

He took a little card from his pocket. Part of it lit up like a small computer screen.

'It only operates through my voice. Now let me see where they are....'

While talking in a strange language to the card it began to display the layout of the domes and portal points. So he followed on in the direction of an underground station. It was at the rear of that dome. They went downstairs into what appeared to be a large basement. When the circular door opened, he said **'Earth'** and over a hundred numbers lit up on the panel of an enormous cylindrical elevator.

'These are the main portals and links to all relevant continents, countries and planets,' he said. Then he shouted, **'Eden'** and the portal displayed ten numbers.

'Any one of these numbers will take us to planet Eden and beyond, even to other alien planets throughout our galaxy. This method is much better and safer than any spaceship.'

'Adventure, eat your heart out!' Tim yelled, excitedly.

'Guys, this portal can take us half way across the galaxy in almost zero time. They call it transposition through the H-dimension. But let me take us to Sarah's house instead. It's the first number on the list.'

'You sure?' Andy was not happy and hesitated.

'Come on, lets get in!' George insisted and they followed like sheep to the slaughter, while shuddering in their boots for the most extreme experience of their lives.

'Yea, but I don't fancy the idea of my body being transformed into billions of bits and reassembled somewhere else. What if I lost part of me during the process,' a bewildered Barry replied.

'Don't worry, Pal. It's as safe as houses when there are no hurricanes or earthquakes and safer than spaceships! This method is frequently used by numerous people on a daily basis!' George said.

A frightened Barry suddenly plucked the courage and moved ahead with George.

'List one, Sarah's house please!' George said. There was a rotation followed by a momentary flash of light and they found themselves looking at a completely different corridor.
'Wow! How awesome!' Andy exclaimed.

When they arrived a bell may have rang to alert the helpers in the manor. A female helper soon came along the corridor expecting to assist one of Sarah's important guests. Instead there were several casually dressed young men entering the house from god knows where.

'I am sorry for this intrusion, but I met Lord Khan on Gimbal. We are testing the portal from Mars. I am George Peterson and these are my friends.'

'My God... You were the one on TV!'

'The very same!' George replied.

'Oh, we are so pleased to meet you! Lord Arel is with us today. He is on his way back to Eden for an important meeting. I am sure he'll be very pleased to meet you!'

'I hope so!'

'Please forgive the mess, we have builders and decorators everywhere. Please follow me,' she said. They followed her into the Lounge of that famous house which was a little messy due to current repairs and decoration. Turning to the maid, Andy asked, 'Where are we?'

'On Earth!' she shouted, thinking him to be very strange and confused, and she showed that expression. Then he rushed out the nearest door to view the green fields and couldn't believe his eyes. That first journey with portal took a little time to sink in. After all, how could anyone get from Mars to Earth in such a short time. That was the home of Lumak and Sarah when they first arrived in the States several decades before. It was also

George's place of birth, although that information was not yet available to him.

'The famous George Peterson. So at long last we meet again. It's a pity you have not yet visited Eden. Everyone there would love your presence at this moment in time.' Arel greeted.

'Perhaps I should visit Eden very soon. But I was not invited by Empress Sarah,' he replied.

'You have an open invitation, so visit when you can. We have watched your television interview directly from Gimbal and you are now almost as famous on our world as you are on Earth.'

'Really?'

'Yes! So why don't you use the portal from here?' Arel said.

'We have just arrived from Mars on two-weeks holiday there and I am afraid, all our other companions, including my wife, are still there awaiting our return,' George said.

'There is little of anything on Mars these days and I am sure your ladies would have a much better holiday on Eden,' Arel advised.

'Let me discuss it with the ladies and expect us within a day or so,' George replied. He also realised that Arel was correct. Nonetheless, he felt quite nervous with a sense of foreboding by the idea of visiting that strange and wonderful paradise world. Yet, it was going to be his next important decision after consulting his gang.

'That's great news! I must communicate with Eden immediately and make preparations as soon as possible!' A most happy Arel said in a state of extreme excitement. He insisted that they had tea together. In a short time they were back on Mars and looking at the original basement of the Admin Dome.

'Chaps, that's what advanced technology does to beauties like Vogon. No sooner than we have them built, and they are already obsolete.' George said.

'Very sad to say!' Jerry replied.

'Fancy a quick lunch in Galaxy Andromeda?' George asked and they began to laugh.

George always had that way of building confidence and trust in people, even their faith in portals. They now felt a lot safer within its modus operandi, although with little knowledge of the principles involved.

'We should have words with the ladies and take a vote,' he said, while they hurried back to Vogon.

'What kept you all?' A worried Cathy inquired, in a rather firm manner.

'We visited Sarah's manor on Earth and had to stay for tea. Arel wouldn't let us go!' George replied.

'Liar! We have been patiently waiting here like statues all this time for your return and you come up with such a lame excuse!' she continued to complain.

'Andy, did we not really go to Earth and had tea at Sarah's place with Arel?' George asked.

'I can't tell a lie. The man speaks the truth, the whole truth and nothing but, the truth... and there is lots more to come,' Andy replied. Suddenly they went silent.

'Everyone, please follow me into the Lounge. I have to talk to you of new developments!' George said, being followed enthusiastically on his way to Vogon's lounge by a keen crew.

'I know we've all come here to do a little exploration and visit a couple of Andy's friends in Caefon Dome. However, I have since found out that we can travel throughout the galaxy from this place... in seconds, if not instantly. I've also since learnt that we are all wanted on Eden, almost like celebrities. So why don't we kill two birds with a single stone. Spend one or two days here on a tighter schedule than planned and visit Eden for the following two weeks. But we'll have to leave Vogon here with Ulysses over that period.'

'Why not visit Eden first!' Cathy exclaimed.

'Who agrees, put their hands up?' George said, and they all agreed.

'Are these portal things safe?' Cathy inquired.

'Safer than anything known to Earthmen, even houses and caves!' George replied, seriously.

'In that case I'll love to visit the most beautiful world in Osmaron,' Cathy said.

'I thought there was something I forgot. We didn't take along presents. Perhaps we could buy some in Caefon Dome. We've got to take them some presents, even if we have to return to Earth via portal,' George insisted.

'Don't worry, Darling. All our cupboards and lockers are full. I'm sure there is something from it they will like on Eden,' Cathy replied.

'Eden, here we come, and after... the galaxy!' shouted a cheerful Jerry, as he took Miranda to the bar for more drinks.

'Yea! The galaxy and way, way, beyond!' shouted a happy Tim.

CHAPTER 42

Caefon Dome

Mars was truly a beautiful planet in its own right, despite its very hostile human environments. Therefore pressurized multi-layered domes with bullet-proof glass were ideal for human habitation. With the use of chemical filters and separators it had become possible to recycle all chemical and body wastage to high levels of purity for further usage, and that process of filtration could continue almost indefinitely. All such sealed domes were designed to be self-sustaining using those types of technology. They were also able to extract water and minerals from the Martian landscape to replace losses.

Since water could not naturally exist in plain form on mars because of low atmospheric pressure, originally water in the form of ice were extracted by large self-contained robot controlled trucks in the polar regions. More recently the ice was melted and transferred through large sealed pressurized pipelines to several of the domes. That latter method had been adopted by Solarian Banking in the early settlement days, and had been constructed by many robots. However since then the miners had capped several more local ice wells for that purpose and could drill and cap others when the need arose. Therefore despite the low atmospheric pressure, water from ice was relatively plentiful on Mars for her limited human population. Only foodstuffs, clothes and specialist replacement spares were imported from Earth and elsewhere.

Caefon Dome was built just after the Solarian Domes by an Earth company; the banking and mining consortium called Spirox. Nevertheless, that company had since become bankrupt, leaving the Martian miners and others with an early and undignified independence. Therefore its population was left without status, having little future contact with the home planet, Earth.

During the intervening years the situation had worsened. All raw materials like metals became more abundant on Earth due to the demolition program, so they had to fend for themselves, with virtually no markets and contacts anywhere to sell their ores. Those problems were further compounded by the fact that most of their mining gear had become permanently out of commission and presently well overdue for replacement. Therefore existence had become extremely had within Caefon Dome and the present worsening of Earth's condition didn't help.

Caefon Dome was built just twenty miles from Admin Dome and fitted very snugly into a Martian crater of an equivalent diameter. It also gave easy access to rich deposits of Palladium and Silver, still accessible with drill and shovel in pressurized suits. However, those precious metals were almost exhausted and many had become asteroid miners in the ensuing years.

George and his gang had arrived in spacesuits. They simply entered through the dome's locks without any security checks. However when George and his peculiarly dressed friends removed their head gear they were immediately recognised. Words of their arrival soon got passed around.

Soon after all hell broke loose among its now desperate population.

'Lord George is here amongst us!' Someone shouted.

'He has not forgotten us! They have not forgotten us!' shouted another. One took the position of town crier. Very soon the visitors were taken towards the main square to the civic buildings. That place was where they housed their own small Council and Mayor.

'We have come to visit an old friend, but while I am here, I would like to assess your needs!' George yelled.

The Mayor was soon in the square with two officials carrying a silver medallion dangling from a red, white and blue ribbon. He walked up to George and placed it around his neck.

'With this simple gift, I hereby nominate you, our esteemed Lord George to be one of us and of the Martian order of Miners. May you use all your powers to assist your brothers and sisters in their hour of need? You are now granted complete freedom of our small domed city and its inhabitants,' he said, jittery but bravely. The mayor was very thin and mal-nourished. When George observed their condition he almost burst into tears.

'Mister Mayor, fellow miners, brothers and sisters, I shall in future do whatever is in my powers to assist you all. During my brief visit here, my colleagues and I shall fully assess your requirements. So don't you worry. I give you all my promise!' George said. After those words their meagre faces lit up with a slight glow of happiness.

Caefon Dome had been living on rations for some time so the black-market was rampant with soaring inflation on what ever currency they used. Here, only Earth's currencies had any real value and many resorted to barter. There was also a high level of drug addiction which was usually unknown in Fertilate populations of a religious inclination. But here, survival conditions were very harsh and disease and premature deaths were frequent. In those dire conditions they tended to relieve their pains by whatever means affordable and drugs were available.

After they had met Andy's godfather, David Anderson, George took his party along with Ron to assess the city's needs in order to improve living conditions. After a while he became seriously disturbed by what he saw.

'I am afraid, Guys, we shall have to clean Vogon's cupboards out of rations, including all our medical supplies. Just leave ourselves enough for another two days here and our return trip home. Anyway, we won't need anything for the two weeks we spend on Eden. I will also require a donation of clothes from each of you. Anything can be replaced when we return to Earth.'

'I wish we had visited here before. How could no one have known of their dire plight?' Andy was not pleased.

'Everything surplus to requirement on Vogon we let them have. Because of the black omarket situation here, we'll have to conduct the whole affair ourselves. Perhaps we could use the life boats. That way Vogon can remain in her present position,' George said.

Having seen the levels of poverty themselves, they had to say yes.

'That put an end of presents for our friends on Eden!' Cathy said.

'I know, it's not a lot for about fifty thousand people, but it's a start. We select the poorest families first and move up the ladder. That means, we'll need to link up with their computer to find who they are. Then we can deliver personally to those families while assisted by our lifeboats.'

'Brilliant idea!' Andy said.

'Don't you think this operation might give us a little experience in such matters...?' George said to his friends, who once again agreed with his intentions.

George was allowed to go anywhere and soon had all the information he required, so he thanked them and once again took the small hover-truck back to Vogon.

'How brave and interesting these people are, and so hospitable. I should have visited this place a lot sooner,' he said, disappointingly.

Even so, they had a lot of planning and sorting ahead of them if they were to begin their ration distribution in the morning.

That day they organised their efforts through the main post office who were quite pleased to assist George in the delivery of those small parcels, irrespective of what they contained. That way, many of the poorer families had a happier moment in their lives. However, George would have liked to have done a lot more for those poor souls. Thank goodness they had taken on so much food, most of which had barely been touched since leaving Earth.

Later that day the Mayor insisted that he said a few words on their local television network, so George decided to take all his friends along.

'My dearest friends and fellow miners, now living well away from Earth. I spent sometime visiting many areas of this dome environment and can now say with little doubt, that I respect and envy every one of you for your brave efforts in the face of such extreme difficulties. If only I knew of your situation before our arrival. I also know that we miners are a proud and hard working lot. We prefer to reap the harvest through our own efforts. So with those firm attitudes and convictions in mind, let me assure you that within a matter of months, your city here will be transferred into a much better place than it is today.' They cheered.

'After my return to Earth, I shall open up new markets for you through Solarian Banking and organise a Martian ferry from here to Earth on a more regular basis. That way, you may control your own destinies in a more predictable manner and create a more stable currency in the process.'

'Thanks, My Lord!' someone stood up and shouted, but George carried on.

'Mining ships and equipment will be hired to you on a most reasonable rate, never to be refused by anyone, with a reasonable period for all loan repayments. You can also repay in crude ore, and finally, a good price in Earth-currency for all payments.

'Every one of you, born on this world or ostracized from Earth which is your birthright, will be issued with Solarian Banking passports in addition to your own Martian passports. Those are the changes I promise you and they are what you will receive.

'In the mean time, I would like you all to make a list of very urgent requirements including mining equipment, in order for us to begin the process of change. When you have compiled the lists, you must transmit it to us at the number given.

'I sincerely thank you for your hospitality and for making me a member of your most esteemed Martian order of Miners, which I shall cherish in perpetuity.

'Although I appreciate you hold free status with your own police force, council and Mayor, it might be in your interest to become part of a much larger Earth-based organisation so that I can represent you politically.

'Think about what I have just said for the next time you vote,' George said and sat. Those hardened miners were now bearing smiles of happiness on their crinkled faces.

'Why don't you lead us, Lord?' someone shouted from the rear of the studio and before long they were all shouting.

'Please lead us, Lord. Please lead us!'

'If you want me to represent you on Earth, I shall. Then Earth will become your permanent headquarters, with many of you assisting in the running of your own operations and finances from there. I can assure you, that you will all become fully independent and wealthy Martian miners in due course,' George said.

Later that day George and his group were taken to the main civic building and he was sworn in as President of Caefon Dome.

Andy said farewell to his aging godfather and they departed in lifeboats back to Vogon.

'I didn't realise things had deteriorated to such an extent since. When I was here last, it was such a rich and happy place. Now they are less than on the breadline,' Andy said, overwhelmed by sadness.

'I expected it and had my own personal reasons for coming here. While the situation on Earth worsens, these more remote outposts are always the first to suffer, usually hardest hit and also the last to recover. Perhaps I cheated a little with you all; because my main reason in being here was not only for a holiday. But as you have seen, they are now in a much better position because of our visit,' George said and they remained silent in prayer and contemplation of a deed well done to a proud people in serious trouble and with nowhere else to go.

'The cost per ton of ore has significantly dropped due to surpluses on Earth. This is as a direct result of the drop in population and the demolition program. So unless we can find them alternative means of support, they will all have to be evacuated from this planet in the very near future,' George said.

'But to where will they go. Most of the kids are now Martians, with Martian passports and the others lost their rights to Earth many decades ago,' Andy replied.

'Don't you worry, Friend? Solarian Banking is an independent organization and can absorb them within a new Earth dome in under six months. But I need them here, to take care of Solarian installations as well. Those guys and their families are real hardened workers and fighters. Because of those reason I will go out of my way to assist them. All we have to do is find a market for their ore and that market doesn't have to be Earth. Does it?' George said, looking at Andy and Jerry as he continued.

'Now, you can appreciate the type of work we each have ahead of us if we are to pull this system of planets together,' George added.

'But those guys on Eden use robots to do their mining at less than one tenth the costs,' Jerry replied.

'But they don't need money either, do they? So what's wrong

with them giving something that they don't need for something they require, even if they use robots. After all, they are only a few miners,' George replied.

'Yes! I see your subtle reasoning,' Jerry said.

'They can supply all their ore via Earth which is still the strongest monetary system and all payments can be made and invested through Solarian Banking for them.'

'I agree to your clever politics in killing several birds with one stone!' Andy was pleased by the way things were being planned for the poor and suffering in Caefon Dome.

'This is also the reason why I coerced them into joining a larger organisation on Earth and the reason why they have chosen me as their President.'

'I must admire you for this!' Jerry replied.

'Do you see my reasoning behind this operation?' George said.

'I do!' Andy replied.

'Almost like putting a complex electronic circuit together and getting it to work first time. You are a bloody genius if you can wield that much with Solaria,' Andy replied.

'While we are in a talking mood and the others are elsewhere, I am going to tell you a little secret that I want you to keep under your hats for now. Because nothing is finalised yet.'

'Another secret?' Jerry inquired.

'I have been offered the post of President of Solarian Banking. A formal vote is to be taken at their next meeting on Eden. But I have been told that it's just a formality.'

'You are not kidding?'

'No! I never kid! If I get the job, I want you Jerry to be my vice president and Andy can take over my present job as head of Tec Conglomerates including Unitec. But it's just a formality, because as you know, all these organisations run themselves. We'll be doing more or less what we are doing now, with the occasional boardroom meeting to discuss the occasional important matter. Our jobs from now on will be mainly political.'

'Head of Solarian Banking is like head of Planet Earth!' Jerry said.

'One day, I'm sure, Earth will be just another cog in the wheel. Anyway, while the organisation increases in size, others of our gang will also be given senior positions.'

'I seriously think we are going places on a super fast train,' Andy said.

'Now, you know the game plan!' George replied.

'Bloody hell! The President of Solarian Banking? The largest and wealthiest organisation on Earth and elsewhere? You must have some very wealthy parents in very high places!' Andy said, still not fully believing what he just heard.

As with Jerry, reality always took a little longer to sink in.

'As I have told you before, we in The Gang always take care of our own, come rain come shine!' George replied.

'I don't know what to say. I never thought I could get so far up the ladder, so quickly. Not even in my wildest dreams could I ever have imagined it. I would like to be thanking you here and now, for even considering me for such a post, but any means I know would be grossly inadequate. Nevertheless, I thank you anyway... for allowing me the post of Vice President of Solarian Banking?' Jerry replied, with utter disbelief.

CHAPTER 43

A visit to Planet Eden

From the remaining foodstuffs in Vogon's cupboards they selected a few items for Eden. Those including ice-cream, canned fruits, caviar and vodka. They were not great alcohol drinkers and realized Jerry's grandfather and others like Lord Meron enjoyed the occasional vodka drink.

All of Vogon's food and clothes cupboards were presently empty. Anyway they didn't want to take presents like clothes and jewellery to a world already rich in such resources.

'People, this holiday is very important to us, so I want everyone to be on their very best behaviour. Many things on their world may be completely alien to us, and things we hold sacred in ours may be considered irrelevant to them. Therefore we must always bear those considerations in mind before we act or speak.'

'Yes, Sir!' Tim shouted and saluted.

'We must always wear our best, because we are also representing our planet Earth as diplomats and must create a good impression.'

'Are we allowed to eat food and drink water!' Miranda yelled.

'I expect so, providing it's not crunchy biscuits or crisps! From now on there will be no need for environmental suits. We can walk through each sealed dome towards the main portal, and can take along two trolleys for small containers and cases. The Terminal Virus will be automatically removed from our bodies and equipment during transit. This is built into the transposition system used in the main portal.'

'Nice to know. Those space-suits never fit, anyway!' Cathy replied.

'Ulysses will remain here to keep an eye on things and occupy himself by listing future requirements for each dome. He can also formulate suggestions for security improvements. That should keep him busy for the two weeks or so until we return. I shall have to make it up to him when we get back to Earth. You know, he loves to play golf and Hercules is also getting the knack of the game,' George said.

'You and your microid androids. You treat them so much like real people. Are they not just machines?' Jerry replied.

'Pal, we can never be just the sum of our parts. I think therefore I am! We have to observe the qualities of the whole and should seldom consider the parts of which they are composed. When you talk to your friends do you think of their pumping hearts, digestive systems and other vital organs. We should see the whole person in its entirety and concentrate on their personality. That is what makes us human!'

'I like your views on life!' Tim said, but George continued his explanation.

'Therefore, if he, she or it responds to me in a manner to which we both can understand and relate, then I shall have to accept, him, her or it, as another individual, even if he, she or it, is made of metal or some other substance. That's the way I have always been and it's the way I shall always be,' George replied and left to explain the situation to Ulysses. Then he clipped, Ron, his small computer unto a special belt and strung him across his shoulders.

Ron was the size of a small briefcase which now dangled about waist height.

'Pity we hadn't time to excavate the shuttle. Perhaps we can get the miners to do that little job for us later. I might even donate it to them, to be used as their own passenger liner between Earth and Mars. But we might have to convert her first for that purpose,' George said.

After entering one of the decontamination rooms near the main portals to remove all contaminants, they had everything, including themselves thoroughly cleaned. It was a combination of short burst of intense radiation plus a mist that filled the room and saturated everything. Their food trolleys were placed in another room and bombarded by radiation for a timed period. Then they were ready for their interstellar trip.

For that special trip they wore two piece grey suits with matching ties and hats and looked quite official. The women also decided to wear their best synthetic fur coats.

When they arrived at the portal, George shouted: 'Eden! Second number!' They entered unto the platform within the cubicle and were rotated unto a bright lit station somewhere on Eden. They could observe many android guards posted throughout, but no one asked for identification or travelling papers. Those androids did not even blink an eyelid when the strangers walked through that part of the building.

Just ahead of them was a moving walkway that seemed to be the only way out of the station. There was only one in their vicinity that moved away from their current position.

'Let's get on!' George shouted and they followed, pushing both trolleys along.

'You may leave your trolleys and other luggage here. Please take the right conveyor in single file,' a mechanical voice said. When they entered, several rings shot out from the side of the walkway and clamped about their bodies, just above their knees. They were then lifted bodily several inches off the surface and were propelled along at great speed, but at reduced weight.

After a little while they came upon a junction to which their moving walkway terminated. The junction gave rise to four more walkways that led to four different directions. They were signposted with strange symbols. However George knew the language.

'Palace!... this path is for the palace!' he yelled, taking the third one from the left. Nevertheless it would have been already programmed to take them to the palace. Their rings automatically changed direction and they were soon moving along the new route.

Their speed had now increased to about thirty miles per hour. The walkway itself did not move, but instead the rings propelled their bodies along as if within intense magnetic fields. Yet, they felt securely anchored to a surface of some kind.

'Oh my God! This is so beautiful! So beautiful... I feel I'm dead and gone to Heaven!' Miranda exclaimed.

The palace was now five miles in the distance and their elevated walkway meandered its way like an undulating snake through the beautiful scenery of Eden.

'Did you see that fantastic building over there. Its pillars were pure gold! Pure solid Gold!' Tim exclaimed.

'How blue is the sky! How incredible the buildings and trees! Look at the trees over there! ... another incredible citadel with golden spires and a single folded leaf in orange growing like a giant tree and those giant flowers over there!' Miranda was ecstatic.

'Have you ever seen anything so beautiful?' Cathy shouted.

'I suppose the oxygen and hydrogen levels here are slightly different to Earth's. Its biosphere must be maintained to a high level of almost spiritual perfection,' George replied.

'No winds, just a pleasant breeze and I suppose no earthquakes, storms or naturally occurring disasters either,' Jerry said.

'Everything in perfect harmony and unity with nature. Now I can understand why they kept well away from Earth and its people for all this time,' Miranda added.

'Just out of greed our Infilate parasites would have ruined such a lovely paradise like this in days, with their property developers, restaurants and other capitalistic money making ventures,' Tim said.

'Is that how God's Eden was meant to be, Darling?' Cathy asked while snugging up to George from behind. They were now almost in a trance from the intoxicating perfume fragrance evaporating from the enchanting flowers below. They could observe giant fairylike insects with the most incredibly coloured butterfly-like wings sucking and collecting the rich nectar.

'How could any place be so enchanting and smell so sweet... and how did you read that strange sign back there?' Cathy asked.

'It was written in a scripted form of Sunolingua and you know I can read that language with my eyes shut,' he replied.

'I am sorry, Darling, for asking. It must be all the excitement about,' she replied.

'Look! Just yonder, a large city and a blue sea,' Miranda shouted.

'It must be Eden City and that large structure over there must be Sarah's palace. The fourth pathway must lead to the large university on the hill to our right. But I think these pathways are just for the viewing tourists. All normal transport here must be by portal. It's the reason why we can't see any passengers for miles on-route. Or even proper roads.'

'A mobile pathway designed for the first-timer?' Miranda

thought.

Eden City also comes under Sarah's fief of the Eden Garden State,' George replied.

'We appear to be so high up here, in the air. Do you think it's absolutely as safe as houses, Darling?' Cathy inquired and they both giggled.

'If it's of alien design, it must be!' he replied.

'We must be about thirty metres above the giant ferns. But we are now moving downwards towards the palace,' he advised.

'Is there no space or ground cars here, Darling?' she inquired again.

'In such an advanced society like this one, there would be no need for any physical modes of transport. All such vehicles require air and parking spaces, not to mention the occasional accidents that are caused, as a result of faulty equipment and mad or inexperienced drivers,' he replied.

'Are you saying portals never go wrong?'

'Not during transmission, and if a receiver goes faulty during the process, which is less than one part in several thousand billion, the master computer will switch over to another local one. Anyway, all such systems run in triplicate here and each is guaranteed for a thousand years or more. Even so, they are fully serviced each year by clever androids who never make mistakes. Anyway, I think they used more advanced systems these days that repair themselves and do not require cubicles. That way they can arrive to any point on their world, given relevant coordinates. That method is more like the one used in old movies like Star Trek,' he replied.

'Beam me up Scotty!' Tim shouted from the rear and they giggled.

'Do you think we are expected?' Cathy asked.

'Yes, I am pretty sure, because I don't think we could have gotten directly to the palace from Mars, without it for security reasons. I have a special security card which the system checks on-route, so they must know of our arrival. Otherwise we would have been captured by those police androids back there at the station,' he replied.

The walkway curved downwards into one of the rear palace entrances which soon came zooming up towards them. They could see many people waiting on a large platform within what appeared to be an enclosed area that was illuminated by a bluish light.

CHAPTER 44

Within the palace

They could observe Sarah, Lumak, Meron, Jerry Senior and several of the others, with Arel waiting at the nearby platform. They came to a slow stop, their bodies were gently lowered to the surface and the rings released. Then the rings disappeared into slots in the side of the walkway.

George and Cathy were the first to leave the walkway and went directly towards Sarah.

'Thanks for coming! I trust your journey was a pleasant one?' she inquired, respectfully.

'Yes, Mam, and thanks for having us at such short notice. This must be the most beautiful planet in the whole of Osmaron,' he said. She smiled at the sincere complement. She could clearly see his features in her and felt like hugging him but kept her cool for obvious reasons.

'I know many things here will appear very strange to you at first. Just follow us for now and do exactly as we do and you will soon get the knack of it,' Sarah said.

'Then they said a personal hello to Lumak, Meron, Jerry Senior and the others. They were all dressed in ceremonious robes with jewelled swords dangling at their hips, as if in expectation of a great leader.

Meron took the lead and walked directly through the rear wall. George hesitated for a moment before taking the same route. But it was not really a wall, just a precisely projected hologram of a wall that was engineered to conceal everything behind.'

'Stranger and stranger!' Tim exclaimed.

'We have now entered the garden of dreams. This whole area is programmed to depict Earth's history during the days of the ancient Babylonian empire.'

'Beautiful hanging gardens with slaves in the distance constructing a great tower!' George observed.

'The virtual images we now see among us are almost as real as you and I. They are placed in precise positions and are activated by the palace Macron. Subliminals cause them to be as real as you wish them to be, but when you consciously try to become part of the scene you find yourself being taken back into the real world. An attachment and then a sudden detachment. That way you can never become part of the story without your full consent.'

'I see!'

'The story changes on a daily basis. Sometimes it may be a simple garden of overgrown trees and flowers, at other times, a sea with schools of beautiful fish.'

'I could use such a system for my meditations back on Earth,' he thought.

'Any concept of reality may be visualised on Eden, but we prefer the more natural ways of living,' Meron said, as they struggled along the narrow streets amidst many ancient Babylonian soldiers who appeared to be guarding an important person. Occasionally some of the local peasants and slaves would kneel and bow their heads in homage.

'In such environments one could fight realistic battles and have erotic love affairs. Even go fishing or play golf without even leaving the house,' Meron said.

'How incredible!' George replied.

It appeared as if the whole historical enactment included their group within its complex programming as players.

'In case you wonder what is going on.... You are the great king Nebuchadnezzars and Cathy is his wife. He is visiting his hanging gardens of Babylon for meditations during the fall of a most beautiful sunset. Presently, he is celebrating his conquest over a distant country and have brought back many slaves.'

'Ah... That must be from the conquest of Canaan!' George replied.

'Over there are the gardens in the distance. The setting sun is just beyond the small pyramids and temple. That new temple over there is under construction by your captive slaves,' Meron said.

'Gosh! It's almost as real as reality!' Cathy commented.

'No wonder they were all bowing to us. How delightfully incredible and what a psychological booster. Here, anyone can become a king or whatever he wishes to be. Why have wars and suffer from greed or other emotional problems when your every desire can be fulfilled in such a place?' George replied.

'We now enter the real fragrant palace garden. Both side walls are simulated waterfalls. However, the fountains and plants are real. Sounds and mist can also be added if necessary to increase the power of the scene,' Meron said.

While they travelled through the long garden, they could see the large waterfalls on either side of them, swirling, bubbling and roaring towards a lower escarpment which appeared hidden from view. The environment completely absorbed them and the experience shook them to their innermost cores.

'We now enter the Garden of Meditation. The canopy above can reflect any area of our galaxy including many different skies. The trees and other images here are also unreal, but engineered to synchronize with the human psyche, through the Macron and our brain implants during the process of meditation.'

'We have now arrived at the main palace reception area with its many young guards and helpers. They are all part of our family and are not considered outsiders. Let me call them together and you can greet them personally,' Meron said.

They were taken towards the large dining room via a broader corridor with many golden ornaments. Statues were displayed on what appeared to be a massive chess set. Then they were taken through another room. This one contained live size holograms of known rulers, past and present within Osmaron.

'This here is Bailor of Lodor III and over here is Malik of Polok II. Queen Bawaki of Tarran.... All these holograms are members of our federation,' Sarah said.

'We are all in time for lunch, so please join us while your trolleys are taken closer to your rooms on the high balcony. It's a lovely spot, with a most agreeable view of Eden City,' Sarah said, but continued.

'I hope you don't think me too presumptuous, but I have only allowed double rooms for married couples. We on Eden prefer single people to live apart and any form of cohabitation is frowned upon. This is because of long term sociological problems and the necessity for population control. Because of those and other reasons, Earth's methods of reproduction are not encouraged here,' then Sarah changed the topic.

'Arel told me that you were taking a brief holiday on Mars.'

'Yes, Mam. I wanted to visit Caefon Dome and assess their needs. They have since made me their President and might become useful in rebuilding areas of Mars for my military buildings and training camps in future. I have also to invoke some achievement goals and wealth within their almost dying society,' George said.

'Yes, My Son! I remember the original Caefon Dome, when Jeffery, Jerry, Meron and others including myself went to inaugurate her.'

'That was just before your craft disappeared in outer-space!' George replied and she smiled.

'Is there now a problem with the inhabitants?' Sarah inquired.

'Her owners went bankrupt, leaving all the inhabitants to starve on Mars, with little resources, useless equipment and virtually zero Earth status.'

'That is very disappointing news. Tell me what you want us to do and it will be arranged.'
'Thank you, Mam,' he replied, humbly.

'We brought you all some peanuts, cashew-nuts, caviar, tinned fruit and many bottles of alcoholic drinks. Including several boxes of Vodka and Tonic Water. To be honest, we did not plan for this visit and didn't know what to bring after we emptied our ship's cupboard to assist those in Caefon Dome.' Cathy said.

'Yes, George told me about their problems!'

'Anyway, I hope you don't mind, Madam Sarah, but we could only take along a few items,' Cathy continued.

'I think what you have done is very noble and for that, you have my sincerest appreciation and respect as a part of my family,' Sarah replied.

'Anyway, I love cashew nuts. You know, it also makes delicious ice-cream and we can always do with a few more bottles of whisky, vodka, gin and rum. Even the Grand Lord enjoys a few drams on occasion, for medicinal purposes or so he says,' Meron added and they all began to laugh, seeing the funny side of his type of humour.

'After you have cleaned up from your trip and have been to your rooms, why don't you join us at the main palace patio, and I shall make a special announcement,' Sarah said and snapped her fingers, as several palace children came to take them away.

'You are to call each of our visitors, uncle and aunty and you are also to remain with them until they know their way about the palace!' Sarah commanded.

'Yes, Mam!' They replied.

'Now please show them to their rooms and I shall see you all later,' Sarah said. They were then taken away by a uniformed group of young and very eager teenagers.

'Is this a real private bedroom, Darling?' Cathy asked, remembering what Ben said to her about the strange accommodation on Eden.

'I suppose the walls must be real, but the equipment about is probably interchangeable by simple voice commands, depending on requirement.'

'You mean they are made of nano-bots?'

'Could be? Suppose you wanted a single bed instead, or a smaller wardrobe and larger cupboards with more drawers. Even a different ceiling or perhaps new wall covering with a pattern of your own choosing, then you simply tell the computer and lo and behold, everything changes to your requirement,' he replied.

'Normally I would say that was impossible!'

'Not much is impossible here!'

'Darling, our planet is so much in the dark ages compared to this one. I still think I am having one of those long dreams that won't go away, and if I wake up, I'll find myself back on board Vogon in our bunk. But I am talking to you about a dream, so this must be real. Everything is so overwhelming. No wonder they are so clever. They have the correct environment for developing perfect minds,' Cathy said.

'Yes, Love. I must admit, here we are like bush people trying to find our way about a modern city. We can be compared to those not knowing what basics like toothpaste, the toilet or the shower is really all about. And the sad thing is, we might even look and smell that way to them. They even think eating meat or eggs a disgusting process akin to a type of cannibalism.'

'Really?'

'Yes! You know, many centuries ago people on Earth never

took baths and got used to each other's body odour in much the same way as we get used to our household smells and unseen bacteria laden door knobs. The average people on Earth today would keep well away from such filthy folk, even though they never think about filthy doorknobs and bacteria-laden surfaces, even those on human skin. What the eyes can't see the heart won't ache. But nature always tends to compensate in such situations of general conformity, until you find yourself in a different and more advanced society. Then, even the not so obvious may become amplified a thousand times,' George said.

'You are becoming quite a philosopher these days. Anyway, do you think the Ancients make love like we do on Earth?' Cathy asked.

'No! They think our methods to be crude and draconian to say the least.'

'What do you mean?'

'Many millennia ago they began to use artificial insemination. That way no sexual diseases could be transmitted. But they also consider pregnancy and childbirth to be an unpleasant process for Solarian women, and one only to be associated with primitive life-forms. I think they happen to be right in this case.'

'How can they be right?'

'They have since learnt to grow children in special bio-incubators, with all the necessary womb simulators. Those foetuses are assisted by different forms of visual and audible stimulation since insemination. The process pre-educates the foetus, so it is already a genius at the moment of birth. They can also control the gestation period to be longer than nine months. Even fully grown people can be produced that way!'

'You are beginning to scare me!' Cathy was not amused, but he continued with her education.

'Painful and risky childbirth should be always avoided, for both the sake of the child and its mother. Further, when using a semi transparent incubator, the mother can visit each day to reenforce the bond. Also, they are both visible to each other and senses become more acute. If anything, that method is a lot more caring, more efficient and safer than others, since all nutrients are constantly monitored for optimum foetus development. But Earth women will never accept such a technologically based method.

They still think the painful and more risky process to be the best, even when they have no intentions of trying other safer methods. I suppose those qualities are what makes us silly Earth humans.' George said.

'Our methods are not silly! We love our children and must bond more strongly with them,' she replied in disgust.

'They must get an equivalent orgasm through the use of special drugs during their meditations, but I doubt if there is any physical contact during the process. Because, to them, even kissing on the lips is frowned upon, being full of bacteria and germs. That is why you only see them kiss each other's gloves and only very occasionally on the cheek.' George continued.

'You are kidding me again!'

'No, I'm not! I never kid! When you seriously think about it, passing venereal disease and suchlike is a lot more unclean than eating poisonous or adulterated food. But we on Earth have a tendency to see truth in a biassed manner, more in favour of our emotional and self-indulgent needs. The Ancients see sex more like we do when eating a basic meal and get a lot more excitement out of beauty, science, art, recreation and their general mental development,' George replied.

'In that case, they are a very strange lot and I hope you will never become like them in sexual matters,' she replied.

'Well, my Dear, sexual pleasure is not the same as love. They are needs that can be satisfied in many different ways,' he replied.

CHAPTER 45

Grand Lord Gerra visits

George and his group were guided towards the large lower level palace balcony. The magnificent palace were in two levels with lower and upper balconies. The views from them were incredible. All solid pillars and canopies were made of solid gold and were of perfect lustre. They glistened spectacularly in the artificial lights.

'Your robes appear to fit almost perfectly. I had them specially made to your measurements. Don't you think they are more comfortably than those close-fitting suits?' Sarah asked, gently tugging at the collar of George's tunic.

'Yes, Mam, I think they are quite cute and very comfortable in this most pleasant climate,' Miranda replied.

'I would like you, George, and your friends to listen to me for a moment, because what I have to say is of great importance to all of you in the organisation.'

'Yes, Mam!'

'You all know that we are able to live forever here on Eden, within this most pleasant environment. With the aid of many different types of advanced technologies. Well, my council and I would like to offer you those very same privileges, along with your own protectorate states on Eden. They will be called by whatever name you choose and you will all be free to take up residence and commute to Earth as and when you wish. These days, such travel is no more difficult than visiting a local friend in the next street. Furthermore, we have also decided to add George's name to our list of junior councillors, which gives him the status of a Lord Protector of Eden. It's a type of knighthood, but I am sure many of you will rise to power on Eden in due course.'

'Thank you, Mam!' George said.

'George also becomes President of all of our interest within the Solar System, which includes Solarian Banking and its subs. Here again, you are at liberty to promote whoever or whatever cause you wish within the organisation, But this is if you agree. It all has to be your decision.'

'Thank you again, Mam! I accept the responsibility!' George could not be happier, while Cathy tightly held his hand.

'Now I have said my piece,' Sarah said. With that announcements there were claps and cheers among the group.

'Could I please say a few words on the Gang's behalf, if I may?' George insisted, putting his hands out to quell their excitement.

'I don't think anyone here could prevent you, even if they tried,' Cathy said, smiling.

'We are all aware of our duties in the future to the master plan. Which is to protect the Solarian Realm from all those obnoxious vermin that threaten our existence and the lives of all our primals. Well, they will have a fight on their hands and will dearly regret their notions of universal conquest. However, we must prepare ourselves and in the process transform Earth and other suitable systems within Solaria in line with technologies on beautiful Eden. Therefore, Eden is to be considered the most beautiful planet in Osmaron. From henceforth this most beautiful world will be used as our standard for all future comparisons in those regards. For that purpose, it is essential that this most perfect system be excluded from all our military activities in the future.' They were agreeable and cheered.

'We in The Gang have a most difficult task ahead of us, which also includes protecting this our most precious gem from the infidel Javols, and to those ends our minds are finely tuned and focussed. But we shall also need your assistance, by way of advanced technologies, in order to move the goal post a little closer initially to gain a more solid foothold. Once that base is firm, we can alter the game to suit our purpose, even perhaps shift them further apart during our efforts against the enemy. This will be accomplished by our own negative brand of cunning, if only to mislead the enemy with a false sense of security.'

'Nevertheless, the sooner we can solve the initial problem of weaponry and armour, the sooner we can defeat the enemy and return to a more purposeful type of existence. After those goals have been achieved, I am sure many on Eden will appreciate the occasional holiday, even permanent residence on a much cleaner

Earth.

'Therefore, I must sincerely thank you all and our Grand Lord in advance for your generous help and appreciation in pursuance of those goals and assure you of our even greater conviction and dedication in the years to come.

'Thanks again for everything my dearest Solarians,' George said, but they couldn't stop cheering and even Meron and Jon were shouting.

'Bravo! Bravo!' they cried. George had that way with his audience.

'Lord Vektron suddenly appeared, as if from nowhere in the bright sunshine and everyone immediately went silent.

'Our Lord is to visit you shortly.... I am greatly honoured to meet you George and your famous gang,' he greeted. His spherical and seemingly weightless body began bobbing up and down, while checking them out in his usual manner.

Lord Vektron, was an ancient Patriarch over ten billion years old. The gang stood frozen by the strange aberration but George walked forward.

'The feeling is quite mutual and for me it is the greatest honour!' George said. He knew that George was in control of every individual on the balcony at that moment in time; for they appeared to love and respect him to such an overwhelming extent. George also emanated an air of charisma and magnetism almost to the point of hypnotism.

The Grand Lord now in human form as a young man, walked directly towards him. He was wearing a thick robe with golden trimmings and a high collar. He stopped at George, eyeing him up and down as if sizing him physically for a fight. Then he smiled.

'You are now among your own kind, you know? Even more so than on Earth!'

'I realize that, My Lord!'

'Did you like my present?' he asked.

'Yes, thank you! Does it work?' George replied.

'As far as I know and the moon is not too distant from here. But I would like you to find that part out for yourself.'

'Would you join my gang and me for a small drink, in celebration of our first meeting?' George asked, politely.

'I would consider it a great honour and perhaps Lord Vektron could join us in human form; for I consider this to be an historical moment and turning point in our mutual futures to the greater benefit of all!'

The whole affair was unbelievable, for Lord Vektron was seldom known to transform into his most revered human form. Sarah clapped her hands and several of her young helpers entered the room pushing a large golden trolley.

Suddenly, Lord Vektron transformed into a form that was his original from aeons past and everyone began to talk freely, no holes barred, but with love, reverence and extreme respect for the Supreme Being responsible for the seventh part of our universe.

'Have you given much thought to the Javol's question?' the Grand Lord asked.

'Yes, MetraSiend! I intend to acquire some special weapons to be developed for our initial assault. The virtual systems here will be ideal for training my soldiers. When I am through, Javols will be no match for anyone!' George replied.

'Will you begin with Andromeda?' the Lord asked, as if trying to check the validity of his methods.

'No, MetraSiend, I would like to secure Triangulum and Osmaron first, including their globular clusters, but Caefon should be secured initially because of the Omegron Portal. However, some areas of Andromeda will be used as our exercise fields for playing with the enemy, in order for my warriors to gain the necessary experience and hopefully learn their weaknesses and strengths in the process. I predict Andromeda will be a very easy galaxy to conquer, with certain plans I have in mind. However, Triangulum will be the greatest threat to us and the most difficult, if they are able to gain a foothold, it being filled with more advanced life and resources.'

'Good plan!'

'I shall however require a population map of those galaxies, including Andromeda and that might take me a little while to compile without your assistance,' George said.

'Consider it done. But it is truly an enormous task you set yourself, even though they have not yet arrived in Triangulum,' the Grand Lord replied.

'Within Andromeda the plan is quite simple. I shall take over their bases and man them with my own replica drones. This process will continue until most of their main bases are under our control. We can then use them to supply the wrong information to their Master Mind. Once their foundation is sufficiently weakened from inside, we can then plan our strategic battles. But before I do, I would like to utterly confuse them and get them unsettled, much like a cat among the mice. With no single target in view. That way, their whole organisation will fragment into smaller and disoriented chunks, ready for the taking. Then our large fleets can follow to finish the job. Finally, those areas can be thoroughly swept, secured and repopulated,' George said.

'Truly fascinating. Your mind is so clear on such matters. You are truly Jull and the Son of Destiny!'

'Thank you! My Lord!'

'You and your group always have my sincerest blessings and assistance towards our common goal.'

'Are you aware of their latest mutations, being able to take the form and colour of any equivalent animal of similar mass, even trees and soil?' the Grand Lord said.

'Yes, Metrasiend, but that fact will not affect their destruction, one way or the other. It only serves to put us more on our guard and leave nothing to chance. Anyway, we are able to smell those rotting types even easier than their original forms.' George felt at ease.

'The only problem we face is their relatively long dying period. But one small consolation is that, they are able to die immediately when they try to transform after molecular disruption. Because of that weakness we can hold them in strong nets that will induce them into transforming to escape, with disastrous consequences. We are also considering a most deadly virus, but it will take a while, if not already developed,' George replied.

The Grand Lord listened and was fascinated by his methods for fighting the most hostile and deadliest alien form the universe had ever known.

They had a most pleasant social evening. One that even the

Grand Lord and Lord Vektron had wholeheartedly enjoyed. The Gang also realised that they were revered as little gods themselves, because their destinies were intertwined with George's. But then, as he grew in strength so also did they. They were very pleased with their present roles, even when there was so much risk involved.

CHAPTER 46

The ideal refuge

They spent the following two days visiting the palaces of the Andromedans and their many isolation domes amidst the giant ferns, beautiful flora and fawner, and fairylike creatures. Those little fairy-like creatures never competed for anything and as a result were never hostile or dangerous to anyone.

Those beautiful and highly intelligent life-forms were only interested in their daily supply of nectar and other wax materials required for building their homes, in return for pollination. They paid little attention to their new human masters and continued their existence in much the same way as they had since their beginnings.

Anyway, being Senots, the Solarians always considered all life to be equally important by virtue of their existence and allowed them their own space for development. They obeyed those same rules to all forms of life throughout the universe. That was what they considered to be The Greater Purpose.

There were many islands within the oceans and seas that formed isolated habitats for many of the heavier insect forms and flowers. Those places were also used for meditation, with small citadels and temples built to aid that purpose. Many included an android guardian, whose purpose was to make visitors welcome and keep an eye on life within their particular area.

Fruit and nut trees were not indigenous to Eden and neither were birds, bats nor in fact any animals other than her native fairy-like creatures. Therefore non-indigenous plants could not grow naturally without human assistance and propagation of their kind was somewhat restricted to domes and greenhouses.

Her large seas were infested with the worst types of carnivorous fish. Those highly antisocial life-forms were left to their own desires. A few isolated lakes had been cleansed and subsequently repopulated with several Earth type fish, including endangered whale species. But saline levels had to be controlled on a planet where salt was not in great abundance.

Many of Earth's endangered species and others were kept within large isolation domes. Those included several species that had since become extinct on their mother planets, Earth and Caefon. Many other life-forms had been imported from the planet Caefon in Andromeda and other areas of the Osmaron galaxy.

While on Eden they would once again be given a new lease of life while their original habitats were re-engineered and optimised for their future survival. Then when the time was right, many would be transferred back to their original home environments or within engineered habitats on worlds like Tyrrel III. That world was only a little larger then Earth with several great continents and oceans. One of it's continents called Terrania contained numerous species from Earth.

In a sense, Eden was still being run by her own insects and plants, with the human life assisting them and other galactic life in the process. No environmental decisions were ever taken without due regard for her indigenous life and there was much land; for unlike Earth with its large oceans, over two-thirds of Eden was composed of land.

Due to her mass and the lack of a real Moon like Earth's, she was a very stable world. That stability reflected in every aspect of the planet, from plate tectonics, sea floor spreading, volcanic activity and energetic atmospherics, to her surface weather conditions. But such stability also inhibited torrential rainfall and large cloud formation. Here again, a dense dewy mist occurred every morning before dawn, and a balance was met between evaporation and absorption through her thick leafy soil.

Rain or snow seldom fell on Eden. Each dawn being accompanied by a dense mist which wet the trees and collected in the water table. That mist soon dispersed as the sun rose within her bluer skies. However all artificial conditions as on Earth could always be created by their brand of technologies.

Sarah took them via portal to Eden City on a shopping spree. There was no physical currency on Eden. The method of payment was purely designed for the transfer of status by way of what they called credits. Most of the shops were run by androids while their masters followed one or more of their more creative activities.

Every individual started life at more or less the same level and moved up the ladder by his own initiative and sacrifices made to their society. Because everyone considered themselves to be part of a larger family, properties were never transferred from so-called wealthy parents to their fully grown and independent offspring. All property primarily belonged to their owners and then the state. But the state also had the powers to pass such property over to their sons and daughters if they were responsible members of society and fulfilled certain relevant criteria.

The state was also responsible to every child from birth. Who would from that moment, automatically earn a salary of credits to be invested until they became of age. Then that salary would be released to them, to aid in their future development.

Every senior member of working age was required to serve the society for three months in each year, called Benefit Time. After that period they were free to do as they pleased until the following year. But many earned extra credits by permanent employment, which could also include long holiday periods.

Many worked, not out of necessity, but to remain occupied for its own sake while doing something they enjoyed and to socialise. Therefore, there were many gymnasiums, sports arenas, colleges and workshops within the city areas where people met and mutually took turns in assisting. When they were not available, androids would take over.

Eden City was considered an extension of this process and also contained most of the required hardware for those activities.

Essential commodities like groceries and disposables could not be bought from stores. Those items were dispatched via domestic portals from the large storage depots that were dotted throughout the larger farms and warehouses. Most of those robot-controlled depositories also packed and canned such products for automatic distribution.

All forms of manufacturing were banned from Eden and sited on dead worlds throughout the federation, but linked by long-range portals. Everything was recycled at high efficiency and reused.

When they had taken in enough of the local environments, George and the others boarded Venusa's ship. She was a ginormous federation cruiser about 2 kilometres long and about three quarters of a kilometre high. They visited the most remote areas of the ship through her internal portals. Finally, they visited Melos III within the Bi-setti system. It was within their newly built city of Solaris. The second world in that system was called Melos II. Then they visited Polion II which was used mainly for manufacture.

George had heard so much about Mallory Colman and could not believe his eyes when his own reception came forward to greet them. Andy couldn't keep back his tears of joy in finding his long lost father standing close to his wife Roseanne and both embraced.

'All those years I thought you were dead. Are you happy, Dad?' he asked with tears in his eyes.

'Yes, my dear son! I am very happy taking care of this world. Here we receive many of the young from Earth. They are trained for active service within the Empire. I have also been keeping an eye on you from afar and know of most of your escapades, including the kidnapping of Jerry. I also check with your Directors Chad and Carl occasionally,' Mallory said, with his wife Roseanne, his grown children and the six specials, Ebony and others, looking on.

'I shall need your assistance in the not too distant future to fight our mutual enemy. So you are to prepare for that time, when you return to Earth,' George said and Ebony and her women warriors were once again stirred into action.

'Tell us when and where and we shall be there!' Mallory said in a firm voice. They spent several hours with Mallory and his councillors and then left.

Finally, they went to see their own Protectorate States on Eden, which was just north of Jon's fief. That area occupied tens of thousands of square kilometres with many lakes and islands, but was completely raw territory and virtually untouched by human hands. They took note of suitable places for future palaces and domes.

'Jerry's grandfather is one of the best architects these days, perhaps he can design our palaces for us!' George said.

'I can't believe it's all completely free. I feel that I owe them a lot for all that kindness!' Tim said.

'I wouldn't worry too much if I was you. Everything in the universe is free for everyone. Only us Earth humans put a price on things. If they had their way I'm sure by now we would be paying heavily for the air we breathe. From now, we must concentrate on our tasks ahead and leave the building program to the robots and androids,' George replied and Tim was satisfied with his answer. George always treated Tim as a younger brother.

CHAPTER 47

Back on Mars

After only one week on Eden George was once again thinking of his responsibilities within the master plan. They had to literally tear themselves away from beautiful Eden and its pleasant environment. George had work to do, so as far as he was concerned, it was time to return home to unpleasant planet Earth and kick some butts.

He called The Gang together and told them of his intentions and they took a deep breath with regret, but knew he was usually right in such matters. Anyway they realized it was just a temporary setback.

'Ready when you are, Boss!' Andy replied, also revving to go. He was overjoyed by the knowledge of his father's survival and the thought that he would be able to visit him in the near future via portals from Sol-Newtown or Mars. Despite that fact he couldn't get over the experience of meeting his happy and contented father, who looked even younger than he did.

Sarah had donated Venusa and Martia's ships to help the cause. They were to be permanently based on Mars under the full control of George.

Both ships were given the task of re-seeding Earth's atmosphere with the Global Antidote, which would neutralize the Terminal Disease. That important task was to be carried out before the Gang's return to Mars. Those giant twin ships were truly massive by Earth's standards. They could quite easily have contained a two hundred story building within their most central areas. They were constructed from microids and built to the most advanced technologies Osmaron had to offer.

They were originally designed to be intergalactic liners, with facilities for over a quarter of a million passengers while assisted by androids and robots. But they could equally have been converted and used for mass interstellar evacuation programs and war.

On board were every conceivable type of college, sports arenas, recreation, shopping centres and entertainment media; all manned by human-like androids. There were also the manufacturing and construction utilities for resettlement of people on new worlds. Therefore, they were complete worlds in their own right, but mostly relying on the resources of their host world.

Both ships contained portals that were used extensively throughout, thus eliminating the need for moving walkways, escalators and other mobile systems. But they also contained many mobile trucks and smaller ships, specifically designed for use on rough terrain, well away from their mother ship.

The great ships were driven by the latest inter-dimensional drives that could take them to Andromeda within a day. That incredible leap could be accomplished despite their great mass. They could also communicate through the Greater Mind, which was even more advanced than inter-dimensional means. Such were their type of technology that each ship contained tens of thousands of androids and robots, each being controlled by their powerful controlling mind.

George had decided to use both ships as his permanent bases on Mars. They were also to manufacture and test his special weapons and chemicals, to be used against the Javols. In his opinion, those military experiments and exercises were a lot safer when carried out well away from the dense populations of Earth. Mars appeared to be the most suitable for that purpose.

George now had the technology and capacity to transform large areas of the Martian surface for the training of his special soldiers and had already figured out the first phase of his Master Plan, as he called it. During that phase Mars would be equipped to accept all his special soldiers from Earth. He decided to isolate his organization well away from the turbulence of the mother planet Earth in case his efforts clashed with the insecure political systems of the day. Finally, the great ships were to be converted into military battle cruisers with the power to take hostile planets apart with their Gravitron Lasers, Plasma Beams, Nuclear Torpedoes and Missile Projectors.

The Gang arrived back on Mars via the same portal, but with two extra and larger golden trolleys. They were fully laden with presents from Eden, including several golden golf club sets.

Ulysses remained on Mars with their ship Vogon. He had finished his assignments several days earlier and was at that moment standing close to the main portal awaiting their arrival. When the door opened, he calmly walked towards them to assist and took the two trolleys away.

'Is everything in this neck of the woods, ok?' George asked him. But he knew exactly what he meant.

'Yes, master. Like clockwork. Except for the distant sounds of miners in celebration two days ago!'

'I wonder what they must be up to. I shall fax them a progress request before we leave for Earth.'

Unknowingly to them, Venusa's Ship had dispatched a large container of groceries and other items on Sarah's orders.

Sarah was one of those people who could not bear the suffering of others, even for a day and had given instructions to Arel and Jonathon, who were now back on Earth. They were to transfer as much food as they could via portals to Venusa's Ship for one of those invisible late-night drops.

Those poor miners were struck by terror when they found such a large container within their main city square, with no signs of a ship or any other means of delivery. But the real shock came when they released the catch to fine tons of foodstuffs and clothes.

With virtually no organisation for proper distribution, it soon became a free-for-all, amidst shouts of joy that could have awakened the dead from their sealed crypts miles away. Nevertheless those miners had an innate sense of justice, also revived by an honest Mayor who insisted that their Lord would have wanted his presents to be distributed equally and that there was even more to follow. After that, they decided to organise a fairer distribution system.

They had taken the following day as a public holiday, to celebrate their Lord's kindness and that celebration included an extensive fireworks display. Those were the celebrations the highly tuned senses of Ulysses saw and heard some twenty miles away through the thin Martian atmosphere.

'I must visit them again soon. But first, we must await the arrival of Venusa and Martia's ships.' George was pleased.

'I have brought you and Hercules a golf set each. Made of solid gold, you know. So I hope you like them,' George said, glancing at Ulysses.

'That is very fantastic, master!' Ulysses replied, showing symptoms of excitement in his voice; for such androids were not programmed to show those human traits. However they were very intelligent with a complex brain, so it was thought they would develop their own personalities eventually.

When they arrived on their ship, Vogon, they dressed in their original ship's clothing and suddenly realised how dead and unexciting everything on Mars had become since their incredible experiences on Eden. Even Vogon had shrunk into insignificance when compared with the beauty and technology of Eden, including its great ships.

'You see that area over there... well, within three months it will be transformed into a place of beauty and technology equal even to those on Eden, and I have ideas for changing this planet's atmosphere as well,' George said. They nodded their heads, not quite knowing how he could put such an immense plan into operation.

Both great ships arrived the following day and lay side by side south of the cluster of Solarian domes. George and the others, now carrying their immortal mind implants which they had received during a body conversion process on Eden, took the portal for Venusa and Martia's ships for their formal introductions.

The ships' namesakes, Venusa and Martia, who were human in form, were still on Eden and expected to join them within the week. Those two beautiful female humans were genetically created by the great ships to experience human feelings and emotions in like manner, and had since been made Senior Councillors by Sarah.

The ship, Venusa, continued,

'I am now permanently assigned to your organisation and consider myself part of your esteemed Gang. My namesake is still on Eden, attending one of those council meetings and will join us shortly. But you may visit Eden any time you wish through our portals.

'I must also report, that Earth's atmosphere has been seeded with the Terminal antidote. Caefon Dome has recently had a nutritional drop and I now await your further instructions, my lord!' the ship said.

'I would like you, Venusa, to build our first city to the following specifications within that area over there and you Martia, a large military training camp over here, north of the holiday camp. Each should be made in suitable sub-modules. Each module is to be linked by portal.

The city training camp and other domes are also to be interlinked by LPD trains through sealed underground tunnels and they are to be isolated from each other for security reasons.

These are some sketches and blueprints that Ron and I compiled recently. Also, see if you can research these new weapons for me as well. I would like you to construct a medium size portal at my manor on Earth. It is to be linked with all relevant Solarian Banking stations within the solar system, and I need a list from you of all such locations.

Finally, I want you to drill a sealed tunnel from the holiday camp to continue underneath Caefon Dome. The platforms should include shopping precincts, moving walkways and a comprehensive portal service between both of the main stations. But please feel free to use your creative imagination in its construction and make it your best effort yet,' George said.

'Such a challenge is refreshing. We carry several portal subassemblies that can be constructed at a moment's notice and extras can always be obtained from Eden and elsewhere or manufactured. I shall prepare one immediately and instruct its loading unto one of my boats. If you like, technicians can follow you to Earth for the final fitting and testing,' the ship said.

'Yes! That will be fine, Venusa,' George replied.

'We contain several assault ships and mining craft. Should we unload those items now? Then we can begin the drilling of the large connecting tunnel before commencing construction of the city and other installations,' the ship added.

'Yes! Please carry on and report when necessary. You have my frequency on Earth. We intend to return here on a daily basis after the portal is fitted, and expect Venusa and Martia to live with us on Earth when they return,' George replied. Then they left for Vogon.

'Guys! We start out for Earth tonight. We can contact Anne-Marie on route and find out whether she wants us to collect her and the kids. Anyway, it's time I saw the old mansion's green fields again and met a few friends, before we begin some real business on a tighter schedule. In the mean time, the construction program can continue in our absence.'

'It's the best thing you've said all day!' Jerry replied, as Cathy pulled George towards the entrance of Vogon.

'Did you enjoy your wild honeymoon, Love?' George asked, bringing her back down to Earth.

'Yes, Darling. It was truly sensational and out of this world, and I mean that in the truest sense. But I would love you to build us a beautiful palace on Eden, like Sarah's or even Jon and Lira's,' she advised, enthusiastically.

'That's already on order, my queen, and I can assure you it will be out of this world!' he replied, jokingly.

That day, they were finally on their way to Earth with Vogon. It would have taken them under ten hours through the shortest stretch of the Martian space-way.

CHAPTER 48

Action Stations

On they way back to Earth, they were happy and excited. Things couldn't have turned out better for the gang. They had been given one of the most beautiful states on Eden the size of France, along with fantastic palaces to be constructed in their absence. Nevertheless they had to come down to Earth and practise their piloting skills in order to convince Andy for their pilots license.

When they arrived on Gimbal, Anne-Marie was already waiting with five large cases and her two children.

'I'm going to take her off autopilot. Cathy, it's your turn to take her in!' Andy yelled.

'Ok, Sir!' she replied bravely, but with a nervous smile. She sat in the pilot's chair and familiarized herself with the controls. She was never a keen pilot but realized she had little choice in the matter in an emergency. Anyway, with all the technology, Vogon was an easy ride. Then she began to follow the checklist aided by Miranda.

'Guys, there is a pile of black gunge on the walkway near the kitchen!' Tim shouted. Everyone stopped what they were doing and went to see.

'Dam, it must be Ulysses. When I saw him last he appeared worried about something. Could be one of his natural processes. Let's see what happens!' George replied.

'Ulysses! That pile of gunge couldn't be our Ulysses?' Cathy shouted while observing the pungent mass. The others were equally doubtful.

'He is of microid construction and that mass is about his size and weight, so it must be him. We have no one else on board made of microids, do we?' George inquired. They could not believe it was Ulysses and soon began checking the ship for Ulysses but he was nowhere to be found.

'My God! What has happened to him?' Cathy inquired.

'I don't know, but it might be safer for us to return to the pilot's cabin and finish landing procedures before we hit atmosphere in a few minutes.' George advised. A worried crew returned to continue landing procedures. At that time they were just a few thousand miles away from Earth.

Suddenly the whole crew sensed danger and got involved with safety procedures as if their very survival depended on it. Then they set emergency procedures in case Vogon crashed.

George was worried in case his powers had caused disruption of Ulysses molecules. He soon asked Ron.

'No Master. It's nothing to do with you or I would have felt something.'

Anyway, if that was the case why hadn't it affected any of the other crew members who were equally susceptible.

George remained for a while viewing the dormant mass and before his eyes the sludge began to reform into numerous insect-like metallic creatures. They were the size of large long legged spiders.

'Oh my God! Large metallic spiders. I hate spiders! I hope they are not dangerous!' an unhappy Tim shouted. He soon disappeared towards the pilots cabin which was sealed by thick metallic doors from the rest of the ship.

'Cathy, turn the ship around. We are getting too close to the atmosphere and need time to deal with the situation here!' George shouted and she complied. The ship was set to Auto and back on her original Martian route, which was in computer memory. Ann-Marie was equally bewildered, but could do nothing except observe.

The strange metallic insects ignored the crew and continued searching every inch of the ship for something. After a short while they began to regroup at the same position on the gangway, melted back into a sludge pile and began once more to transform into Ulysses.

'Good thing I took extra Constructors along!' Ulysses shouted.

'People, Ulysses is back!' George shouted and they rushed out to observe him.

'Thank God, for that!' shouted a happy Tim. The others were equally relieved thinking the worst was over, but it was just the start of their problems.

'Are you ok, Pal?' A worried George inquired.

'Yes Master, I am! But you are all in grave danger. We have an explosive device on board!' Ulysses replied and they were stunned by that knowledge.

'What type of explosive?' George inquired.

'It's a bomb triggered by a mechanical timer. I detected it when the timer came on during our approached to Earth. It could have been designed to countdown when we approached Earth. I don't know how long we have. Any attempt to remove this magnetic device from the LPD drive module will cause premature explosion.' Ulysses replied.

'My God! The LPD module is a miniature fusion reactor. Any explosion on that part of the ship can level a large city block and more. What are we to do?' Andy said.

'Call Chad at Warland immediately. Explain our situation to him!' George ordered and Andy was on his way to communicate by H-wave.

'I was expecting some form of retaliation from our Beta 5 friends, but not like this!' George was not pleased.

Andy soon replied with a nervous but broad smile.

'They found a Beta 5 cell. They think it was their financial head office. They were all executed! Chad found documentation and retrieved information relevant to your demise. It was all planned by their head office!' Andy yelled from the cabin.

'Thank goodness for that. Now we can sleep a lot safer if we survive!' George replied.

'Any idea when it will go off... explode?' George inquired.

'Unknown. Can be a random code or triggered by a transmitted signal when we get close to Earth. The latter seems to be the most ideal, since our enemies will get the most satisfaction and know the job was done!' Ulysses replied.

'It seems to me we have few options. We can't return to Earth but must leave this ship as soon as possible. This is what we shall do. We must return to Mars as soon as possible and land about 20 kilometres from the nearest dome. Then send a small robot in to try and defuse the device. If it succeeds, well and good. Otherwise we return to Earth via portal.'

'What if the robot fails?' Andy asked.

'Then goodbye lovely Vogon and all our efforts! Good thing I insured her before the trip. But that's not the point. We'll have to get another Vogon and do it all over again. I can assure you, next time we'll do a much better job. No bloody Infilate will ever put a stop to our efforts!' George said and the others were equally defiant.

'I will go! After all its my responsibility!' Ulysses insisted.

'No you will not go! But you will program one of the simple robots near the dome. Can you do that?'

'Yes, Master! That option is available!' Ulysses replied and everyone was relieved.

The ship, Vogon, was soon on its way back at maximum velocity to an area close to Admin Dome.

'Who the hell could have planted such a bomb on our ship and when?' George yelled. No one had seen him in such a vile temper before.

'Could have been placed while in the hanger?' Miranda suggested.

'No, not possible! We had all the old LPDs ripped out before we moved ship to the new place!' Jerry replied.

'The only ones I can think of are those balloonist. I thought their landing very strange at the time. It could have been a distraction, while one of their crew planted the bomb. The elder guy did some snooping and looked suspicious to me. At that time there were lots of reporters about and many distractions,' Andy said.

'That could be the reason why the birds were making all that noise. They were warning us of danger!' Cathy interjected.

'Yea. Must have been those Beta 5 bastards. The old guy wanted to see Vogon's interior and I showed him around. Then he wanted to go to the washroom. That was when he could have sneaked away and planted the bomb.' Tim said.

'None of us are to be blamed in any of this fiasco. It's always these bloody Infilates. What have we ever done to them to deserve this?' George replied.

'Those bastards are like that. They saw an opportunity when our guard was down and took it. It's like Jerry's kidnapping all over again. Only this time, they wanted to get rid of all of us in one fell swoop for no ransom and they might yet succeed!' Miranda began to weep.

'If they think they can get rid of us that easily, they are sadly mistaken!' Andy replied.

They landed Vogon about 20 kilometres from Admin Dome and decided to take the lifeboats to the dome, leaving Ulysses behind to order the robot and do the necessary programming.

Ulysses had programmed the drone as best he could to defuse the bomb. However they knew from the start it was an impossible task. The unit was sealed in a solid block and magnetically held to the LPD Module. Any cutting into it or movement could trigger the device.

It took the robot the best part of one hour, then there was an almighty blast with a large mushroom cone. The dome shook but remained in one piece.

'My lovely Vogon is gone!' George yelled with sadness.

'After all our hard work!' Cathy yelled while Miranda kept crying.

'Luckily we had Ulysses on board to detect the device and warn us in time!' George said.

'Thank goodness we are all in one piece!' Cathy added

'Thank goodness!' George replied.

'Someone will pay dearly for this!' Andy stressed in no uncertain terms, but they knew the days of Infilates on Earth were numbered.

'This costly incident teaches us an important lesson. That is, we can never lift our guards, not even for a second. We must check everyone and everything in future. And no more balloon drops near our mansion!' George said and they agreed.

To them losing Vogon was like losing another member of their family. Vogon had been involved in many of their past efforts including memorable events and celebrations. Those included George's wedding. Nevertheless, they had no intention of mentioning their loss to anyone. Their story would be that Vogon had been left on Mars to assist the people in Caefon Dome. That was until they found a replacement called by the same name.

That day they arrived to the mansion via Sol Newtown and gave thanks for their miraculous escape from disaster. Then Clive was informed about their requirement for another identical ship.

To be continued with
Jull, The Supreme Patriarch

Epilogue

Numerous swarms of rapacious Nano-bot Javols are currently on their way to our galaxy. They will arrive within 100 years. They are so numerous that they will blacken the skies of most worlds. Their sole purpose is to dominate and rear us like cattle for their own sustenance and pleasures. On arrival they will be hungry and starving and will feed on all life until many come close to extinction.

Only George Peterson, in the form of Jull the warrior Patriarch, with his new breed of soldiers and weapons, will hopefully save the day. During that most vicious conflict many will die and he must ensure we have a fighting chance.

By the time of their arrival the human population of Earth will be reduced to just 500 million. This new situation will give Earth enough time to rebuild her forests and wild life. However during that time the whole governing structure of Earth will be AI based to be replaced by powerful Headrons, Macrons and their policing androids. They will ensure that Earth never return to the days of selfish and capitalist mankind in the form of Infilates.

Never again will mankind be given free reign to destroy a beautiful world in the name of greed. The days of Infilates are truly over.

George has quite a political fight on his hands with Earth's governments. Will he win the day?

THE PRODIGALS

Presently the two prodical sons of Earth in the form of the resurrected Dr Hal Seaton (formally the Green Chameleon) and young Dr. John Simmons (formally the elderly Professor Kane Powell), with Professor Khans assistance were creating the most deadly of all creations. It was a good thing their anti-Javol nano-bot creations only targeted Javols. Those two were only interested in saving their world and its good people and to that end all their efforts were channelled. Nevertheless to Professor

Khan's utter surprise they had also instigated the creation of ancient Dinosaurs like Tyrannosaurus Rex, Raptors and others as part of a complex food chain, leading up to the most deadly Titans. Those were also Javol killers that would harbour a thick nano-bot skin and deadly bacteria that would protect their thick fleshy body underneath. Those particular almost indestructible monsters now inhabited a large continent called Titania on the new world they called Tyrrel II.

A NEW SOCIETY ON EARTH

In the interim period, before the new Solarian empire, there was to be a new society on Earth with no financial institutions or banks.

No more manufactured money, in the form of notes and coins. Only his new credits and relevant reward cards for transactions.

All cities and towns would soon contain recycling depots for everything, from wastage to furniture and electronic equipment. All such recycling depots were to be run by Free-timers.

Every individual would be involved six months in each year on full salary. Therefore double the people would be employed.

During Free-time, every individual would give two months in each year freely to their local communities, for assisting the elderly, and the environment. During that time their communities allowed them travelling expenses and food, plus a uniform. However only credits are given as reward. After that time they would be promoted to a higher officer grade (Grade One or higher with emblazoned stripes). Grade One officers in any profession would be given a special Credit Card for 5% discount on all transactions within their community area. Grade Two Officer get 7.5% discount, etc. High grade officers are elected to run their communities.

During this two month period workers are called Free-timers. All Free-timers are compelled to wear uniforms during this time.

The last six months of each year belonged to the individual, for holidays and such like.

George's new almost moneyless society is uniquely caring, very efficient and valued by all.

The Galaxy of Osmaron Series

The Galaxy Osmaron series point a way to one of our possible futures. In this future, technology is more advanced. But our real problems come from another galaxy, where another human species have accidentally created the ideal nano-bot type soldier. They are truly unique in the sense that they are almost indestructible, can copy and replicate almost anything, can live for ever, transform into different creatures, reproduce their own kind and require living organisms like us for food. At least that was the unintended nano-bot type demon that came out of the mould after their second and final experiment.

Those nano-bot Javols went on to destroy all major animal life, including their creators, within Andromeda and are presently on their way to our Milky Way galaxy. The most advanced in our galaxy, which are non-human, decide to fight back for the survival of all naturally evolving live, but have to first inform lesser civilizations like us of the impending danger.

Before we can confront the demon Javols, we must first advance our technologies to Class 5. This is about 100,000 years more advanced than Earth's present levels. During this period Earth undergoes many changes due to Global Warming and human overpopulation, but manages to survive the onslaught.

Wars will rage, but apparently ubiquitous humans will always find ways to survive and win the day.